LIBERTY BRIGADE

A Militia Conspiracy Thriller

EVAN GRAVER

ALSO BY EVAN GRAVER

<u>Ryan Weller Thrillers</u>

Dark Water

Dark Ship

Dark Horse

Dark Shadows

Dark Paradise

Dark Fury

Dark Hunt

Dark Path

Dark Prey

Dark Fraud

Dark Drone

Dark Country

Dark Order

Dark Cover-up

Dark Angel

<u>John Phoenix Thrillers</u>

Rising Phoenix

Target Phoenix

Liberty Brigade

© 2023 Evan Graver

www.evangraver.com

ISBN-13: 979-8-9876681-5-3

Cover: Wicked Good Book Covers

Editing: Novel Approach Manuscript Services

This is a work of fiction. Any resemblance to any person, living or dead, business, companies, events, or locales is entirely coincidental.

Printed and bound in the United States of America

First Printed December 2023

Published by Third Reef Publishing, LLC

Hollywood, Florida

www.thirdreefpublishing.com

"Ultimately, government is whatever the people in power can get away with and whatever the people they govern will tolerate. This holds true for all governments whether they be republics, democracies, dictatorships, monarchies, socialist, or communist. Noncompliance is key."

– Representative Thomas Massie (R) Kentucky

CHAPTER ONE

Caribbean Sea
North of Venezuela

Kostya Dragomirov's stomach roiled at the thought of committing treason.

The seasickness didn't help, either, and to top it off, now that his journey was almost over, Dragomirov was bored. He leaned against the railing and sucked deeply on his cigarette, hoping the nicotine would help to soothe the queasiness in his stomach, but it just made him want to gag.

His stomach threatened to empty once more. Dragomirov pressed a balled fist against his abdomen and squeezed his eyes shut against the waves of nausea caused by the rolling sea and the blistering heat that radiated off the cargo containers stacked atop the steel deck of the Estonian-flagged general cargo vessel, *Alexsander Ushakov*.

As he took another drag on his cigarette, Dragomirov choked on the smoke that filled his lungs, and he flicked the butt over the rail. Straightening, he dragged an arm across his forehead, wiping the sweat from his brow, then spat a mouthful of saliva over the side. He tasted stomach bile at the back of his throat, and it burned in his nostrils.

Dragomirov couldn't wait to get off the cursed ship.

In his mid-thirties, Dragomirov was of average height and slim in build. Two of his most prominent features were his large ears, or "speed brakes," as his fellow students at university had called them. He wore his unruly black hair long, occasionally running his fingers through its thick length to corral it into place. The same applied to his mustache and goatee, his patchy beard refusing to join the two.

Pulling the last cigarette from the pack, he crumpled the package and dashed it against the stack of cargo containers. He cupped his hand to shield the flame of his lighter from the wind generated by the sixteen-knot speed of the vessel, the only saving grace from the relentless heat. He blinked back the sweat that dripped through his eyebrows as he lit the cigarette. Suddenly, he clutched his stomach again and moaned.

Dragomirov had spent the first three days holed up in his cabin, suffering from terrible bouts of seasickness. He had vomited until he had nothing left but dry heaves. Neither food nor drink had stayed in his stomach after the ship had departed from St. Petersburg and traversed the Baltic Sea in a blowing gale. From there, the going had been easier as the *Usakov* passed through the English Channel and crossed the Atlantic. Yesterday, the cargo ship had entered the Caribbean Sea via the Mona Passage between Puerto Rico and the Dominican Republic.

Once he was feeling a little better, Dragomirov realized there wasn't much for him to do on board the ship. He'd read some of the books in the ship's meager library, walked the deck, and frequently stared at a lot of steel and ocean. Every evening, he'd had dinner with the captain, Constantine Morozov, and every day, he'd scrutinized the crew, wondering who among them would help to hijack the freighter.

Three months before the ship had been due to leave St. Petersburg, a man approached Dragomirov outside his apartment in Yekaterinburg. The stranger, who'd said his name was Peter, had known about the shipment of ten SS-N-21 Sampson submarine-launched cruise missiles that NPO Novator, the manufacturer of the missiles, was sending to Venezuela. Novator had tasked Dragomirov with demonstrating the correct loading and launching sequence to the crewmen of Venezuela's newly acquired *Akula*-class nuclear submarine.

At first, Peter had presented himself as a government agent, but as time wore on, Dragomirov realized the man was working for a private contractor. And while this mysterious entity couldn't offer Dragomirov the same protections the CIA could afford against his homeland, the contractor had promised to give the engineer a new name, a new life, and a new beginning in the city of his choosing in exchange for his cooperation.

Dragomirov had dragged his feet for several months as his new handler had schooled him on a litany of cloak-and-dagger routines. The engineer never feeling sufficiently valued enough by his country or his new American friend to make a rash decision, but as the day of departure loomed, the American had helped to coerce the engineer by depositing five million dollars into a bank account under his new name at one of Grand Cayman's most prominent financial institutions.

In his youth, Dragomirov had attended the prestigious Moscow Institute for Physics and Technology, graduating with a degree in aerospace engineering and advanced mathematics. Even with all his knowledge, Dragomirov never felt he'd received the recognition or the reward for his intelligence and hard work that he felt he deserved. After executives at Novator had repeatedly passed him over for promotion, he felt bitter and slighted. The money made the decision easy enough.

But the money wouldn't pass into Dragomirov's hands until he got to the States, so he really didn't need to decide whether to defect until a team of Americans arrived to steal four Sampsons from the shipment aboard the *Ushakov*.

Between his bouts of seasickness, Dragomirov spent his days aboard the *Ushakov* in agonizing contemplation, leaving him to wonder whether he was getting an ulcer from all the stress he had put himself under.

He was walking away from the only life he'd ever known; one the Federal Security Service (FSB) would surely snatch from him if they discovered his plans. The Russian state security apparatus would either sentence him to a lifetime in prison or make his death appear to be an accident.

Tempted by the money and a fresh start in America, Dragomirov waited for the arrival of his new friends.

His handler had said he would know them by two words: Liberty Brigade.

<hr>

CHAPTER TWO

<hr>

Oleg Brega, first mate aboard the Estonian freighter, climbed the ladder toward the bridge, knowing it would forever change his life once he pulled the Grach pistol from his pocket. From that moment on, he would be unable to return to the sea, for every shipping company on the planet would blackball him for his actions.

Still, the anticipation boiled inside him, and Brega had repeatedly checked the satellite phone the young American agent had given him before he'd left port. It had finally pinged with a message just moments ago, marking the coordinates where Brega was to bring the ship to a stop and allow the team of mercenaries from Liberty Brigade to board.

Unbeknownst to the bald, stocky Brega, the American who'd bribed him and issued orders on the other end of the phone was the same person who had spent months stalking Kostya Dragomirov. While Dragomirov had needed someone to stroke his ego, Brega had only required cash in hand—and they had paid him handsomely for the act of piracy he was about to commit.

Brega stepped through the bridge hatch and closed it

behind him, ensuring he dogged the latches tight. Captain Mozorov greeted his first mate with a grunt and continued to sip his coffee as he stood beside the automatic helm.

Brega crossed to the chartplotter and examined their course. The cargo ship was nearing the specified coordinates for Brega to seize control of the *Usakov*.

Oleg Brega glanced at the second mate, Stephan Tverdovsky, who was standing watch. Tverdovsky gave Brega a slight nod. The first mate took two strides toward the captain, pulled a MP-443 Grach from his pocket, and pressed the semi-automatic pistol against Mozorov's back.

"Do as I say, Captain," Brega said calmly in their native Russian, "and everyone will live to see another day."

Captain Constantine Mozorov reddened with anger. He whirled around, intending to snatch the gun from his first mate's hand. Mozorov knew the importance of the cargo the *Usakov* carried and had accepted the risks that someone might attempt to hijack it. Yet, he'd never suspected it would be at the hands of his own men.

Mozorov's crew had been with him for almost a decade, hauling cargo and freight around the globe. This trip wasn't the first time the *Usakov* had carried deadly munitions to foreign ports. The captain had always kept the cargo manifest a secret so the crew wouldn't be tempted to pick the low-hanging fruit and sell it to the highest bidder.

Brega had always known better. And the opportunity to capitalize on that secret was finally at hand.

The captain clamped his fingers around the first mate's thick wrist, catching the man by surprise. Anticipating the captain's move, Morozov recovered quickly and reared his fist to smash it into his attacker's face. Before Brega could deliver the blow, Tverdovsky slammed a fire extinguisher into the base of the captain's skull, and Mozorov crumpled to the deck.

Brega checked the captain's pulse: he was dead. They had known all along that someone might get hurt during the mutiny. Still, Brega hadn't wanted to kill anyone.

"We must dispose of the body," Tverdovsky urged, discarding the dented extinguisher. "I'll handle it while you steer the ship onto the new course."

Brega stepped to the automatic helm and punched the new coordinates into the system. Slowly, the giant cargo vessel turned to the south, away from the shipping lanes into the deserted waters of the Caribbean Sea along Venezuela's maritime border.

In the bowels of the ship, an engineer and one of the hijackers' co-conspirators would ensure no one tampered with the engines as they changed course.

With the destination on the horizon, Brega lifted the microphone for the ship's intercom to his lips and hailed the crew, telling them to gather in the galley. After he did so, he pulled a red baseball cap from his back pocket and fitted it to his head.

———

FIVE MINUTES after issuing his call to muster, Brega arrived in the galley. Of the twenty men gathered there, only five others wore red baseball caps that matched his own.

Still clutching the Grach, Brega gestured to the room. "Everyone, sit down, please."

The crewmen mumbled and complained, but those still standing took seats at the tables.

Brega glanced around at the expectant faces. "There has been a change in command. I am now captain of the *Ushakov*. Please be patient, and no one will get hurt. Those with red caps step outside. Dog the portside galley hatch and jam it shut."

Angrily, the other crewmen rose from their seats, voicing their concerns as they approached Brega. He swept the Grach across the crowd. The seething crew stepped back as one at the threat of Brega using the gun. Holding them at bay, Brega pulled another red hat from his back pocket and handed it to Dragomirov.

"Comrade, you are to come with me," Brega said to the engineer. "The rest of you move!"

The Red Hats headed off to follow his instructions. Brega backed Dragomirov into the passageway. He stood in the hatch with his gun trained on the crew, ready to fire if one of them made a move. The disgruntled crewmen could hear the Red Hats working beyond the steel bulkhead, jamming the wheel to prevent the door from opening.

A few minutes later, Tverdovsky reported that they had dogged the portside hatch.

Brega stepped back, and Tverdovsky immediately dogged and jammed the open hatch they'd been standing in to prevent the crew from escaping.

"Get to your stations," Brega ordered the assembled Red Hats. "Dragomirov, stop fiddling with your hat and follow me."

Dragomirov adjusted the red cap on his head before following the new captain to the bridge.

Once they reached the helm, Captain Brega checked the chartplotter and then picked up a pair of binoculars to scan the water ahead. As they waited for the American vessel to appear, Brega passed the time by telling Dragomirov about his plans for the future.

"I will have our benefactors put me off on the closest island so I can buy a sailboat. I'll spend the rest of my days leisurely sailing around the world." Brega spoke his next words emphatically while thrusting a thumb at his chest. "I will be my own boss." He grinned at Dragomirov. "I will find a beautiful woman who looks great in a bikini and keep her on the bow of my boat after I divorce that hag of a wife I have now."

The beeping of the radar interrupted his reverie, announcing another ship was approaching the *Ushakov's* position. Brega glanced down at the chartplotter, checked the coordinates on the global positioning system, then pulled back the throttle of the freighter's massive diesel engine, slowly bringing the *Ushakov* to a stop.

As Brega worked, Tverdovsky returned to the bridge and took over the ship's controls.

Kostya Dragomirov pointed to the blip on the radar. "Are those our friends?"

Brega smiled grimly. "Heaven help us if it's not."

The implied warning of his words echoed in Dragomirov's ears. If the Russian security apparatus had somehow gotten wind of the plot to hijack the *Ushakov*, they were all dead men, including the crewmen locked in the galley.

The newly minted captain and the defecting engineer stepped out onto the bridge wing to watch the approach of a smaller break bulk freighter through binoculars.

With a broad smile, Brega said, "Comrades, our ship has finally come in."

CHAPTER THREE

Dragomirov watched with a pounding heart as the engine in the rusty *Yucatan Star* hummed and labored to bring the smaller vessel alongside the *Ushakov*.

Once the two ships lay side by side, separated by a mere fifty yards of frothing ocean, crewmen from the *Yucatan Star* lowered a black inflatable boat over the side. A group of armed men climbed down into the inflatable and drove across the water to the Estonian freighter.

Each man in the boarding party wore identical black combat fatigues. They carried pistols on their hips and short-barreled M4 rifles on slings across their chests. The men leaped adeptly from the inflatable as the small craft idled alongside the freighter. They climbed aboard the *Ushakov* via the steel rungs welded to the side of the vessel.

As soon as the American team was aboard, they immediately spread out, ensuring the *Alexsander Ushakov's* crew was secure and that only the Red Caps roamed free.

While the rest of the heavily armed team searched the ship, the boarding party leader climbed up to the bridge. Dragomirov was immediately impressed by the man's neatly pressed uniform, shined boots, and dust-free weapons. The leader looked like a poster boy for U.S. Special Forces with broad shoulders, narrow waist, and close-cropped hair.

"I'm Kenny Orlando," the man announced as he shook hands with the three men on the bridge. So confident and assured was the newcomer's grip that Dragomirov's hand ached the moment Orlando let go. Dragomirov flexed his fingers, trying not to look weak, as Orlando said, "I'm from Liberty Brigade. We're here to take you to America."

Beyond the bridge, the boarding party had finished securing the *Ushakov*. They were now retrieving leader lines fired from specially designed rifles on the *Yucatan Star*. The boarding crew used the leader lines to pull heavier ropes across to the *Ushakov*. Once they had plenty of line aboard, they wrapped them around the bollards studded into the freighter's deck. Crewmen on the *Yucatan Star* used massive winches to pull the two vessels abreast of one another, then deployed pneumatic fenders—cylindrical airbags covered in a protective net of heavy chains and old car tires—to prevent the shearing of metal on metal as the waves passed beneath the hulls of the two freighters.

With the two ships rafted off, Dragomirov led Orlando and his team to the cargo containers that held the Sampson missiles. The Russian engineer stood back and watched as the Americans rigged a portable hoist to remove the missiles from their containers.

It took several hours to maneuver the first 3,750-pound missile from its plastic casing in the shipping container out onto the deck of the *Ushakov* and then across to the *Yucatan Star*, using the crane aboard the smaller break bulk freighter.

Each Sampson was twenty-six feet seven inches long with a 20.1-inch diameter. Conceived initially as a nuclear-tipped first-strike deterrent weapon, the Russians had fitted these Sampsons with conventional explosive warheads. But no matter which payload the Sampsons carried, Dragomirov knew they were deadly in the hands of the American mercenaries.

By the time Orlando's crew had loaded the fourth missile aboard the *Yucatan Star*, they had gotten into a rhythm, cutting down the completed transfer time to an hour and a half. The mercenaries knew time was of the essence and every action needed to be precise, with no wasted effort. Once the Venezuelan Navy realized their shipment of missiles was overdue, they would dispatch an offshore patrol boat to search for their missing military hardware. None of the pirates wanted to be around when the Venezuelans arrived.

After the hijackers had loaded the final missile aboard the *Yucatan Star*, the American commandos herded all the Red Hats into an empty cargo container except for Brega and Dragomirov.

The engineer ducked involuntarily at the sound of gunfire, diving for the deck and covering his head with his hands. As the echoes of the gunshots died away, one of the Americans hauled Dragomirov to his feet.

"Relax," the hijacker appeased with a cocksure grin. "No one is going to shoot you. You're our golden goose."

Dragomirov glanced into the container and then ran for the rail to vomit over the side at the gruesome sight of the gun-downed Red Hats. The image of their bloodied and unnaturally twisted bodies stayed fresh in his mind as he emptied his stomach.

One of the mercenaries gripped Dragomirov by the arm and helped him clamber over the flexing gap between the two freighters. Dragomirov turned to see Orlando cross over to the *Yucatan Star*. Then, the big American poster boy turned to help Brega. Dragomirov assumed he was dreaming of sailboats and bikini-clad women serving him brightly colored drinks with little umbrellas. As Brega started to cross the breach, Orlando shot him in the forehead. The Russian seaman fell between the widening gap of the two ships created by the *Yucatan Star* pulling away from the Estonian freighter.

As the dead man's corpse slipped beneath the waves, Dragomirov accepted he was just as expendable as Brega and steeled himself for what lay ahead.

CHAPTER FOUR

United States Coast Guard Cutter *Valiant*
Caribbean Sea, North of Venezuela

Captain Jim Booth sipped coffee from his chipped mug. He listened to the chatter on the bridge of the *Valiant* as his crew maintained a careful vigil over their position. Their primary missions on this thirty-nine-day cruise were counter-drug operations, migrant interdiction, enforcement of federal fishery laws, and search and rescue efforts to support other U.S. Coast Guard operations.

Thus far, the ship had rescued fourteen Haitians from an unseaworthy vessel and detained a drug-smuggling submersible with five tons of cocaine aboard. Booth felt his best chance for increasing the success of his interdiction operation was to stay as close to Venezuela as possible. The country was a primary shipment point for Colombian cartels and other narco-terrorists, and Booth hoped to put just a tiny dent into their operations.

As he sipped from his mug again, Booth was unaware of the important role his ship was about to play in history because of that decision.

Below the bridge in the Combat Information Center (CIC), Petty Officer Second Class Markus Ford turned in his seat at the sonar control panel. He pulled the headset off his right ear and said, "Chief, I've picked up an SOS signal."

Chief Stanley Kirk walked across the CIC to Ford's console. "Put it on speaker."

Ford turned back to the control panel and pressed a button. Instantly, the room filled with the sound of water rushing over the *Valiant*'s hull. And, in the background, they could hear the faint tapping of an SOS in Morse Code.

"Do we have anything on the radar?" Lieutenant Gary Preston asked. He stood nearby with his arms crossed and head cocked as he listened to the tapping of the distress call.

"Sir, we have a radar contact thirty miles south-southwest. It appears to be stationary, or at least it has been for the last five minutes that I've been watching it," Petty Officer First Class Karen Troy responded.

"What direction is that SOS coming from?" Preston asked.

"Triangulating now, sir," Troy said.

A minute passed before Ford confirmed, "South-southwest."

Lieutenant Preston picked up the phone that connected him to the bridge.

"Bridge here," Captain Jim Booth answered.

"Bridge, CIC. We have a stationary ship thirty miles south-southwest on radar with an SOS coming from the same vicinity."

"Which frequency?" the captain asked.

"Sonar picked it up, sir," Preston replied.

Captain Booth stepped over to the radar display on the

bridge and looked at the stationary blip. "How close are they to Venezuelan waters?" he asked Preston.

"The ship is about two miles outside their twenty-four nautical mile exclusion zone, sir."

"Hail the Venezuelan Navy, and let's go investigate. Tell the sonarman excellent work." Booth hung up the phone. "Helm, steer south-southwest and make for the stopped ship at full speed."

"Aye, Captain," the helmsman reported as he made the necessary course adjustments.

———

AN HOUR LATER, the USCGC *Valiant* was hove to alongside the *Alexsander Ushakov*. The Visit Board Search and Seizure (VBSS) team immediately launched in a small boat. They motored across the open water to the cargo vessel before climbing up the steel ladder built into the hull.

Once on deck, the six-man team broke into groups of two. One team headed for the bridge, one for the crew quarters, and the third moved forward to secure the cargo deck.

The duo searching the crew quarters heard pounding in the crews' mess on approach. They quickly removed the chains securing the hatch and pulled it open. Weary crewmen staggered into the passageway, covered by the two heavily armed Coast Guardsmen.

"We've located fifteen crewmen locked in the galley," Petty Officer Ralph Peters reported over comms to his team leader, Chief Carl Hadden. "They claim the first mate locked them inside the galley two days ago when he hijacked the ship."

Captain Booth listened to the report over the loudspeaker. Beside him, the phone rang, and he snatched it from the cradle. "Bridge."

"Bridge, CIC. Someone is still broadcasting an SOS from the ship. It appears to be coming from below the waterline, which is why we picked it up so easily."

Lieutenant Preston didn't need to tell his captain that sound traveled twenty-five times faster underwater than through the air, allowing them to hear the SOS from many miles away.

Captain Booth ordered the VBSS team to investigate the engine room for survivors. In short order, the Coast Guardsmen found another *Ushakov* crewman in the engine room and reunited him with his comrades on the ship's deck.

With all the living crew accounted for, the VBSS team began to search the ship for the others. It didn't take long to find them.

Chief Hadden radioed Captain Booth with a report. "We have five dead bodies inside a cargo container. They appear to have been executed at close range."

Based on all the evidence, Booth concluded the *Ushakov* crews' tale of being hijacked was accurate, so he asked his team leader, "Chief, can you determine what's missing?"

"I hope to have an answer for you soon, sir," Hadden replied. "We're trying to locate the cargo manifest as we speak."

———

After completing their analysis of the cargo manifest, Chief Hadden could not determine the supposed contents of the containers. The manifest incorrectly listed them as being loaded with humanitarian relief supplies.

According to the crewmen of the Estonian-flagged vessel, the missing men included Captain Morozov, first mate Oleg Brega, and a civilian passenger. The rumor circulating amongst the crew was that the civilian was an engineer for

NPO Novator, catching a ride to Venezuela so he could work with the military there. One of the *Ushakov*'s crewmen claimed he had overheard the first mate and the engineer discussing a shipment of Russian cruise missiles they had aboard.

Before the VBSS team could investigate further, an offshore patrol boat from the Venezuelan Navy arrived to take charge of the stranded *Ushokov* as it had drifted into their territorial waters. Booth had no recourse but to let them take command, so he recalled his VBSS team to the *Valiant*.

Back aboard the Coast Guard cutter, Chief Hadden briefed Captain Booth on what they had discovered, including the five dead and three missing crewmen and their suspicion that the *Alexsander Ushakov* carried Russian-made weapons.

This wasn't the first time Booth had heard of the Russians using civilian freighters to disguise shipments of military hardware. As the *Valiant* steamed away from the hijacked freighter, Booth flashed a message up his chain of command detailing the potential theft of cruise missiles from an Estonian-flagged cargo ship and the disappearance of a Russian engineer.

CHAPTER FIVE

Port Arthur, Texas

Kenny Orlando stood at the side rail of *Golden Rod*. The aging longliner fishing vessel had seen better days as it pulled alongside the decrepit docks jutting off Mesquite Point, just inside the Port Arthur Shipping Channel. Even the dock seemed to match the age of the longliner. Some of the dock boards were half rotten, while others were missing. The concrete supports jutting out from the water had been chipped and gouged by the passing of many vessels. Shrimp boats moored at the piers creaked and moaned in the longliner's wake.

Sandwiched between the road and the shipping channel, old warehouses, discarded semi-trailers, and rusting machinery crowded the rickety dockyard, all of it overgrown with weeds and shrubs. The place looked more like a junkyard than a marina in the dull glow of the sodium-vapor lamps.

The smell emanating from the place was a physical blow to Orlando's senses, creeping up his nostrils and lodging there. He breathed through his mouth, trying not to inhale the stench of rotten fish, motor oil, and diesel fuel.

Orlando clambered off the boat once the crew had secured the *Golden Rod* to the pier. He carefully avoided the missing planks as he stretched his back. His legs wobbled under him for the first few steps as he made his way toward a highly polished Kenworth T2000 semi-truck in the gravel parking lot.

Wayne Patterson opened the door and swung down from the truck's cab. He wore jeans, cowboy boots, a faded trucker cap, and a flannel shirt with sleeves rolled up to the elbows. Patterson pulled off a leather glove to shake hands with Orlando. The older trucker had spent too many hours behind the wheel and had developed a bit of a paunch above his belt buckle. But like Orlando, he was a trusted confidant of Paul Moran, the head of Liberty Brigade.

"You guys are runnin' a little late," Patterson commented as he checked the airlines and hydraulic hoses that connected the Kenworth to a polished aluminum end dump trailer.

"We ran into some nasty weather in the Gulf of Mexico. We had to ride it out because the high waves made it too rough to transfer the missiles to the longliners. I'm glad I was on the bigger freighter because those fishing boats sure took a beating."

After leaving the *Alexsander Ushakov* to drift in the Caribbean, the *Yucatan Star* had headed north, steaming around the clock for the vastness of the Gulf of Mexico. The plan had been to transfer the missiles onto four purposely modified longliner fishing vessels that would carry the cruise missiles in their holds. Flagged as U.S. vessels, these smaller boats ported all along the Gulf Coast from Florida to Texas. They could easily come and go without suspicion from

Customs, the Border Patrol, or the Coast Guard. In contrast, the much larger *Yucatan Star* was subject to more scrutiny from all the alphabet agencies. The *Star* also needed to berth in a much larger port, where more prying eyes might notice her dangerous cargo.

Unfortunately, as the *Yucatan Star* had approached the rendezvous with the longliners, a storm swept into the area, raising the seas into a confused state. The large waves had made transferring the missiles hazardous to all involved, so the longliners had scattered and returned to the *Star* once the weather calmed. While the waves had still made working conditions treacherous, the crews completed the transfers without incident, and the longliners again dispersed to carry their deadly cargo to out-of-the-way ports.

"You're the last to come in," Patterson said. "All the other boats made it safely to port, and their cargo is already on its way to Ohio."

"That's good news," Orlando replied, following the older man around the semi as he kicked the tires on the truck and trailer.

Patterson finished his inspection of the T2000 and used the hydraulic controls to raise the trailer's dump bed. As the two men watched corn spill out the back, the truck driver asked, "Where's our friend?"

Orlando laughed. "He's still on the boat. Poor boy's been seasick since we left the *Ushakov*. I've never seen someone have such a nasty case of it."

Patterson chuckled. "Sure hope he don't get carsick."

"You and me both. I'm tired of cleaning up puke. Those lousy mates on the boat wouldn't do a thing to help. Said the engineer was my problem."

The corn formed a small hill behind the trailer. When the trailer was empty, Patterson lowered the trailer back to level and closed the rear gate before saying to Orlando, "Your turn, hoss."

Orlando went to the ancient crane kept near the docks to repair various boats that visited the marina and climbed into the cab. The diesel engine belched a cloud of black smoke when it caught, and he choked on the fumes and the smell of rotting fish, forgetting to breathe through his mouth. Orlando ran his tongue over his teeth, trying to scrape away the foul taste as he swung the cab ninety degrees and dropped the crane hook toward *Golden Rod*. A crewman on the dock directed him with hand signals to continue to lower the hook through the open cargo hatch right over the top of the missile.

The mercenary leader watched as the crewman attached the crane hook to four chains stretched from each corner of the specifically designed missile cradle. Once the chains were secure, the crewman stood back, raised his arm straight up, and began rotating his hand in a circle. Orlando pulled back a lever to retract the hook.

As the missile cleared *Golden Rod's* gunwales, Orlando's guide motioned for him to stop while another crewman attached two ropes at opposite corners of the cradle to keep it from spinning in circles while airborne.

Swinging the crane cab through a slight arc so the missile was over dry ground, Orlando lifted the cradle high enough for Patterson to back the semi-trailer under it. The crewmen used the control ropes to center the cradle over the trailer. Following the guide's hand signals, Orlando lowered the cradle into place. Out of the corner of his eye, he saw the engineer, Dragomirov, stagger off the boat and fall to his hands and knees on the dock.

Orlando shut down the crane and went to help Patterson, who had climbed into the trailer and was using chains to fasten the cradle to the trailer's floor. Next, they spread heavy canvas tarps over the missile and cradle before securing them in place with bungee cords.

"I just saw our friend get off the boat," Orlando said as Patterson climbed out of the trailer. "I'm going to check on him while you put the corn back."

Patterson gave him a thumbs-up and headed for a nearby skid loader, ready to cover the missile with the corn he'd dumped out earlier.

Orlando boarded the *Golden Rod* and retrieved their bags, stopping by Dragomirov on the way to the semi. When he returned, he found the engineer sitting on the dock with his back to a post.

"You okay?" Orlando asked.

"I am now that I am on dry land," Dragomirov replied weakly. The man looked pale even in the weak light cast by the dock lamps.

Orlando handed a bottle of water to the engineer. "I hope you don't get carsick."

"*Nyet*." The Russian clutched his stomach between sips of water. "Just on boats."

Orlando thought the man might puke just thinking about riding on another boat. "Come on, big boy," he said. "Let's get you in the truck."

He helped Dragomirov to his feet. Seeing the engineer was still unsteady, Orlando put the man's arm around his neck and clutched the back of the shorter man's pants. Together, they walked to the truck.

"Do you want to lie down?" Orlando asked once they were inside the Kenworth.

"No, I will sit up," Dragomirov responded. "It might help if I ride in the passenger seat."

For a moment, Orlando considered hiding the Russian in the sleeper cab. He decided Dragomirov might benefit from seeing the American countryside if it meant he didn't have to clean up puke. Orlando climbed into the sleeper cab and stretched out on the bunk.

Once Patterson had finished loading the corn back into the trailer, he climbed into the truck cab, pulled a packet of papers from behind the driver's seat, and handed them to Dragomirov. "I'm supposed to give you this."

"What is this?" Dragomirov asked tentatively.

"Your travelin' papers. There's a passport, international driver's license, green card, and a cell phone in there, plus your paycheck. Your new name is Roger Kozak. You're an engineer from Belarus."

As Patterson threw the transmission into gear, he glanced in the mirror to see the longliner pulling away from the dock. His eyes shifted to the road ahead as he drove the Kenworth out of the parking lot.

They had just completed one giant step in the plan to retake America from the grip of the global elite.

CHAPTER SIX

Allen Montgomery had been ambitious tonight. He'd ridden his old Schwinn bicycle twelve miles along Highway 82 to Mesquite Point. Going out to Walter Humphrey Park on the end of the man-made peninsula had been the easy half of the journey. Now, bags of crushed soda and beer cans weighed down Allen Montgomery's rusty bicycle as he headed back to Port Arthur. He'd gleaned the aluminum cans from the trash bins at the boat launches that straddled the concrete bridge leading over Sabine Pass to Louisiana.

Montgomery had made it a routine to check the trash cans on Sunday evenings after all the recreational boaters and fishermen had gone home and before the sanitation department picked up the refuse on Monday morning. The load usually netted him twenty dollars to pad his whiskey fund.

On his way back to Port Arthur, the lanky Montgomery decided to poke around the rusty junk at the cluttered shrimp docks and adjoining construction yard. No one was there to stop him as he loaded his bike with more trinkets and tried to figure out how to carry some of the larger pieces of metal. Every pound of scrap was money in his pocket and whiskey in his belly. Drinking had left him homeless but not industrious.

As he pushed the bike through the shadows along the docks, a longliner fishing vessel glided out of the darkness and tied up at the pier.

Montgomery laid his bicycle in the weeds and sat down to watch the men work. He scrambled backward behind some old concrete barricades when the heavy equipment started, and the overhead lights flashed on. He cursed to himself when he tore another hole in his already tattered jeans, and he brushed blood onto them from his palm where a sharp rock had penetrated the skin.

When he looked up, Montgomery found he had an unobstructed view of the semi-driver and the man accompanying him as they walked around the big rig and then dumped the trailer's load of grain on the ground. The second man climbed into a crane and used it to hoist some cargo from the longliner's hold. Montgomery could clearly see a metal cradle but not what it held.

Curious about what the fishermen were loading into the semi, Montgomery scurried through the weeds on his hands and knees to get a better look. He stopped as the cradle turned, and suddenly, he could see what was inside. Montgomery blinked hard and looked again. Even though the cradle was slowly turning, he knew with certainty that it held a cruise missile.

Before the U.S. Navy had kicked Montgomery out of the service for punching his captain in a drunken haze, he'd spent seven and a half years working with cruise missiles. He knew a cruise missile when he saw one.

And the homeless man was more than confident that the missile he'd just seen was not an American-made Tomahawk but a foreign design.

He backpedaled into the deeper shadows between the buildings, hoping the smugglers wouldn't discover him.

"I ain't gettin' myself killed, no siree. I ain't gettin' killed," Montgomery muttered to himself. His hands shook as he pulled a pint bottle of Jack Daniels from his pocket.

A long swig comforted his nerves.

———

THE HOMELESS MAN waited until the fishing boat and the semi-truck were long gone before he crept from his hiding place. Moving cautiously through the still night to where the semi had disgorged its load, Allen Montgomery ran his fingers through a small pile of field corn left behind by the trucker after he'd covered the missile with it.

Taking one last look around, he reclaimed his bicycle from where he'd dropped it and fled the scene. Something told him that if he got caught poking around the old docks, he would be a dead man.

"It ain't right. It ain't *right!*" Montgomery argued with himself as he peddled. "Ain't right sneakin' no cruise missile into the U.S. Oh, trust me, I know. I used to work on 'em, and those things are dangerous. Ain't right."

After a long and exhausting ride, Montgomery parked his bicycle outside the Port Arthur police station. Inside, he asked to see Detective Bryce Nixon. He and Nixon had mixed it up a few times on the streets, but he was one of the few cops Montgomery trusted to listen to him and to take him seriously.

Once Nixon finally made time to see Montgomery, he welcomed the man with a hot cup of coffee and a sympathetic ear. The short detective with thick brown hair and questioning brown eyes listened intently as Montgomery told his story.

"Allen," Nixon started in his Southern drawl, "how much have you had to drink tonight?"

"Just a little to calm my nerves—honest, Nixon. Ya gotta believe me. I know what I saw."

"I know you served in the Navy, Allen, but come on—a *cruise missile?*" Nixon asked in disbelief.

"Ya gotta believe me, Detective. I worked on 'em things, and it ain't right smugglin' one of 'em into this country. It just ain't right."

"I hear you, Allen. I guess you haven't steered me wrong—*yet*."

While Montgomery downed three cups of coffee, Nixon typed up the report and took it to his boss.

Chief Todd Beckley read the report and tossed it brusquely back to Nixon. "Why did you bother to write that piece of trash?"

"It comes from a credible source ..."

Beckley sneered. "A drunken homeless man is *not* a credible source, even if he is your snitch."

Nixon cleared his throat. The homeless were just as credible as any other source, and they'd proven valuable to Nixon in the past, helping to solve more than a few crimes. "Let's not be too hasty here, Chief. I think this has legs. The man worked with cruise missiles for seven years. He knows one when he sees it."

Beckley waved his hand, dismissing the young detective.

Unfazed, Nixon picked up the report. He believed Montgomery, even if the chief didn't. Leaving the chief's office, Nixon returned to the bullpen and emailed a copy of the report to the FBI's field office in Houston.

Regardless of the chief's ignorance, at least Nixon could say he'd passed the details along.

CHAPTER SEVEN

Liberty Brigade compound
Kenton, Ohio

Wayne Patterson pulled the dark blue Kenworth T2000 onto the quarry road, thankful to be back on his home turf after the long journey to and from Port Arthur, Texas.

Moments later, he made a U-turn in a wide gravel parking lot and backed his dump trailer into the row of three others already parked there. He was the last to arrive, just as the *Golden Rod* had been the last of the longliners to arrive in port.

With a weary sigh, Patterson climbed down from the cab and slipped on his leather gloves. While the T2000—or "Terminator," as he called it, due to the implied reference to the Schwarzenegger sci-fi film—was his favorite rig, he was tired of driving. It seemed the older he got, the harder it was to make the long-distance trips. The longer Patterson drove, the more his back and legs ached, and he needed to stop frequently to stretch and urinate.

As Patterson disconnected the trailer, Orlando and the Russian engineer exited the cab. Both men stretched their backs and legs as they stood in the chilly darkness of the late April evening.

Hearing gravel crunching on the other side of the trailer, Patterson looked between the tractor and the trailer to see two men approaching, backlit by the dazzling lights affixed to the enormous barn in the distance. The lights on the other buildings in the compound had been extinguished, leaving the two-story headquarters building and two barrack-style buildings in darkness. They were miles from the nearest town, and only the lights from private homes glowed against the night sky. Next, Patterson glanced up at the guard tower that also doubled to train militia members in climbing and repelling. He knew someone was up there watching them now, ready to shoot any trespassers.

The two men walking from the barn were there to greet Dragomirov, or, as his new green card called him, Roger Kozak. Patterson knew the first man would be Paul Moran, the charismatic leader of the national militia movement Liberty Brigade. Moran had thinning salt-and-pepper hair, a strong chin, and piercing blue eyes. He was of medium height and physically fit. While still handsome in his late forties, he preferred to lean on his charismatic personality to sway people's beliefs.

The second man was one of Moran's financiers and Patterson's business partner in their trucking firm, JP Transit.

Steven Jackson wore his usual blue jeans, button-down shirt, round-toe cowboy boots, and his ever-present Ohio State Buckeyes fitted ball cap. As Jackson came around the truck to shake hands with his business partner, the light glinted off his steel-framed glasses and deepened the blue of his eyes. With a wide grin, the fifty-five-year-old entrepreneur said, "Welcome home, Wayne."

"Glad to be back, sir," Patterson replied, even though he knew Jackson preferred Patterson call him by his first name. It was something Patterson would never do while Jackson called the shots.

If daylight were upon the land, Patterson knew that no matter which direction he turned, Jackson owned most the land for as far as the eye could see. He was a mega farmer, owning nearly ten thousand acres of land and renting another two thousand acres to farm. Jackson raised and harvested everything from corn to soybeans to winter wheat. He owned stands of hardwoods that he stewarded to maturity before selling. He also kept several thousand heads of beef-producing cattle and held a dozen hog barns in his inventory.

Over the years, Jackson had made more money than he'd known what to do with, so he'd branched out into buying and renting commercial and residential real estate and became part owner of several local businesses.

After Wayne Patterson had gotten out of the Army twenty-plus years ago, following his stint in the 101st Airborne, Jackson had partnered with Patterson to form JP Transit. The joint venture allowed Patterson to operate an independent fleet of semi-trucks, hauling cargo up and down the East Coast while supplying Jackson's farming operations with much-needed capacity to transport the corn, beans, and grain from the field to the market.

When Jackson had come looking for a way to transport the stolen Sampson missiles from various ports to the militia compound, Patterson had struck on the idea of hauling them across the country in grain trailers, as these trailers were so numerous on the roads. If law enforcement did get wind of the missile theft, searching every grain trailer would become a logistical nightmare, and concealing the missiles under corn would require a closer, more comprehensive inspection to uncover the ruse.

While Patterson began cranking down the legs on the trailer to disconnect it from the truck, Jackson and Moran congratulated Kenny Orlando on a successful mission. Patterson had brought the last missile home to the Liberty Brigade compound, a property also owned by Steven Jackson. After decades of providing limestone, rock, and sand to support the local economy and the building trades, the owners of Tri-County Stone Quarry deemed the operation no longer profitable, leading to its closure. When they'd shut off the water pumps, natural springs bursting forth from the aquifer below had filled the quarry to three-quarters full. White limestone cliffs overhung with green trees and shrubs backed the quarry's shimmering blue surface.

Jackson had purchased the property with the intention of building houses or condos around the old quarry, but that plan had never come to fruition. Instead, he'd donated it to Moran when the militia leader needed a site to establish Liberty Brigade's headquarters. Jackson had quickly volunteered his quarry facility, believing in Moran's vision of a unified militia front to retake the corrupt and inept national government.

As the semi-trailer legs settled into the gravel, Patterson heard Moran greet the Russian in the engineer's native tongue and then add in English, "Welcome to Liberty Brigade."

CHAPTER EIGHT

Kostya Dragomirov said nothing as he shook hands with the militia leader. Looking into Moran's eyes, he couldn't help but feel he had traded one devil for another—Mother Russia for Father Fanatic.

He tightly clutched the packet of papers that the old truck driver had given him, especially the bank book that said he was now worth five million dollars. It was the only piece of paper that Dragomirov treasured. It meant that he had hope—hope to escape, hope to live, and hope to never be a slave to a master ever again.

Dragomirov put on his best smile and, in English, said, "It is pleasure to work with you."

"Come, we have everything ready for you." Moran released his grip and turned toward the enormous barn that covered ten thousand square feet on the compound's ample acreage.

"Show me control station, please," Dragomirov said in faltering English as he followed Moran into the barn.

"We'll get a fresh start tomorrow," Moran suggested good-naturedly. "I want you to get a good night's rest."

Dragomirov realized this was the first time since leaving Russia that he wasn't on the move. His stomach felt suddenly queasy—not from seasickness, but from remembering that he, like Oleg Brega, was an expendable asset. He knew Moran had recruited him to Liberty Brigade for one simple reason: to reconstruct one of Novator's launch control panels for the Sampson missiles. He was one of the few men in the world who knew the controls inside and out, hence his trip to Venezuela.

As Moran steered his guest across the barn's clean concrete floor to an enclosed section of the building, Jackson and Patterson continued to chat beside the Kenworth, and Orlando headed for home in his pickup truck. They had a big day ahead of them, and they all needed rest.

Moran opened the door to an apartment inside the barn and gestured for Dragomirov to go inside.

The Russian stepped into a narrow kitchen with a long row of cabinets over a sink, a stove, and a modest refrigerator. A small table stood in the corner to his left, and at the far end of the room was a bathroom with a tiled shower. After the engineer took in the lower level, Moran pointed toward the stairs, and together, they headed up. At the top was a bedroom with a closet and a dresser full of clothes sized to fit the newly arrived collaborator.

"This is your apartment," Moran said. "Feel free to come and go as you please. I know you're tired from your long trip, so I'll leave you alone. Use the cell phone from the packet Wayne gave you if you need anything. I've already programmed my number into it. Don't hesitate to call me."

Dragomirov merely nodded as he looked around the apartment. It was nicer than anything he had rented in Russia, and this place was inside a *barn*.

"Where is workshop?" Dragomirov asked.

"It's downstairs," Moran replied. "Like I said, I'll give you a tour tomorrow." He led the way back down to the kitchen. "There's a fridge full of food and drink. Help yourself to whatever you want. It's all yours."

Dragomirov nodded again. The devil he was getting to know did not seem so much like a devil after all.

Once Moran was gone, Dragomirov opened all the cabinets in the kitchen and examined their contents. He did the same upstairs with the nightstand, dresser, and closet. After years of living under the constant threat of prosecution from the FSB or one of the other Russian security apparatuses, the engineer was instinctively wary of his surroundings. When he found no obvious listening devices or secret cameras, Dragomirov returned to the kitchen and made himself a sandwich.

Sitting at the table with his half-eaten sandwich and a cold beer, Dragomirov turned on the smartphone from his packet. He logged into the bank account in the Cayman Islands using the account and routing number on the paperwork Orlando had given him. After verifying the money was in his account, he created two accounts in the name of his new alias, Roger Kozak. After establishing those accounts, he transferred his money, dividing it between the new accounts.

With a smile, Dragomirov contemplated the miracles of the Internet and the feeling that he had pulled a fast one on Moran. By moving the money, even if Moran killed him, the militia leader could never reclaim the cash from the bank.

Satisfied with his duplicity and buoyed by the knowledge that his newfound wealth was safe, Dragomirov finished his sandwich, took a hot shower, and went to bed.

———

THE MORNING SUN was barely shining through the Venetian blinds when Dragomirov awoke to the sound of a diesel engine idling inside the barn. He hurriedly pulled on his clothes and exited the apartment.

A gang of workers had surrounded the semi-truck and trailer that Dragomirov had ridden in last night. Two workers climbed into the back of the trailer and secured chains from the missile cradle a hook connected to an overhead hoist built into the roof of the barn.

As Dragomirov watched, the hoist lifted the Sampson from the trailer. Once the missile was suspended in the air, Wayne Patterson pulled the rig out of the barn. Hurrying over to where Moran stood, watching the workers slowly lower the missile to the floor, Dragomirov asked what they were doing.

"We're building the launch tubes for the Sampsons," Moran replied, motioning for his men to continue their work.

As the cradled Sampson came to rest on the ground, the men unhooked it from the hoist, and the Russian engineer moved forward to check on the subsonic cruise missile. While the truckers had covered the missiles with tarps before dumping grain over them, Dragomirov wanted to ensure the turbofan engines and the swing wings that stabilized the cruise missile in flight were free of restrictions.

"I need tools," the Russian ordered. "I need to take the covers off."

"They're fine," Moran replied.

Dragomirov looked up sharply. "You pay me to make launch ready. I do my job."

Moran ordered someone to roll a toolbox over to where Dragomirov hunched over the missile. The sheer size of the box shocked the Russian. He had never seen an eight-foot-long rolling toolbox before. When Dragomirov asked for a five-millimeter hex key, the man who'd wheeled the box over produced two types of hand-operated keys: a socket version to use on a ratchet and one on the end of a battery-powered impact driver. Dragomirov felt like a kid in a candy store, and he had to remind himself that instead of browsing through the toolbox, he was there to ensure the quality of his product.

Using two nearby cargo straps, Dragomirov fashioned a sling to lift the missile from the cradle and used the overhead hoist to bring it to working height. Then, he removed the cover of the swing wings with the impact driver and hex key. Once satisfied there was nothing amiss with the system, he replaced the cover panel and moved on to the turbofan engine and, finally, the warhead bay.

The examination took the better part of two hours, even with Moran breathing down Dragomirov's neck. The engineer refused to work faster, explaining that if grain had gotten into any part of the system, it could cause the missile to malfunction and, therefore, fail to hit Moran's desired targets. Still, Moran grew impatient, and they had three more missiles to inspect.

Once Dragomirov had the Sampson buttoned back up, the workmen lowered it back into the cradle they had swept clean with pressurized air to remove any offending particles of dust. The workmen hoisted an identical cradle over the existing one and bolted the two halves together, creating, Dragomirov realized, a perfect imitation of a submarine launch tube.

All Dragomirov had left to do was to construct the launch controller, and Moran could unleash his private terror on the world.

CHAPTER NINE

Three more times over the next six hours, Dragomirov thoroughly inspected the missiles before the militiamen bolted them securely into their steel housings.

With all four missiles securely in their tubes and still lying on the concrete, the militia workers removed several steel panels from the side of the barn to expose a narrow gap between the barn and a series of three squat metal grain silos, each forty feet high and twenty-five feet around.

Dragomirov stood transfixed, watching the workers remove a section of the middle silo in line with the missing barn panels. With the silo open, he saw it was devoid of grain, but in the center sat a dolly on railroad wheels. The workers laid bunker wood between the barn and the silo to fill the four-inch gap between the silo's concrete pad and the ground below. Then, they wheeled in a cart bearing steel rails for the dolly cart to roll across. They laid these quickly, using specially built clamps to hold the ends of the rails in place.

Moran took great pride in pushing the cart out of the silo to the center of the barn. Once there, the crew raised the missile tubes into their vertical position and, using the steel tubes that had held the cradles in place inside the semi-trailers, bolted the launch tubes into a square, with a missile at each corner. After the crew had the main braces in position, they bolted on cross braces, fixing the entire assembly to the rolling cart.

"The specifications you provided us from Novator allowed us to build these launch tubes," Moran explained to the Russian engineer with a grin. "We purposely designed them to fit inside the semi-trailers and to be bolted together when they arrived. Now, we'll move them to their final destination, and you can begin your work building and programming the launch controls."

Dragomirov nodded as the workers rolled the entire assembly into the grain silo. Once centered, some of the men began securing braces from the launch tubes to the interior of the silo. At the same time, another crewman welded the railroad wheels to the steel tracks bolted to the concrete pad below. The intricate web of steel would hold the structure in place against the violent forces of the cruise missile launch.

Stepping into the makeshift missile silo, Dragomirov looked up at the conical roof of the grain silo and wondered how the missiles would get through. As if reading his thoughts, Moran pressed a red button mounted at waist height just inside the opening. High above them, hydraulic cylinders drew back hatches at the top of the silo, giving the missiles unfettered access to the sky.

Moran hit the button again and the hatches retracted into place. Dragomirov realized the silos were the perfect hiding place for the missiles. On the ride from Texas, he had seen thousands of grain silos, much like the one he stood in now. No one would ever suspect what death and destruction hid in plain sight.

"Come on, Dragon, let's leave these guys to repair the silo and the barn. I want to show you the control room."

"Finally," Dragomirov muttered under his breath, impressed by all the work Moran had already done. The Russians had expected to engineer everything to prepare the missiles for launch. His only concern now was to build the launch and guidance control panel.

The two men left the workers to replace the side panels on the silo and the barn, crossing the barn floor back to Dragomirov's apartment. The building was a wide-open space with only Dragomirov's apartment and a second bathroom for the workers to use intruding into the space. Like the outside of the apartment, the builders had clad the bathroom with plywood.

Moran motioned for the Russian to enter the workers' bathroom with him. Once inside, the militia leader pressed a hidden button next to an instant hot water heater that Dragomirov wouldn't have paid any attention to if Moran had not shown it to him. A section of plywood popped out from the wall at the press of the button. Moran swung it all the way open to reveal a set of stairs leading underground. He motioned for the engineer to go down.

Dragomirov glanced nervously over his shoulder as he descended the concrete stairs.

Behind him, Moran pulled the plywood back into place, leaving them in near darkness with only a dim bulb glowing above them and the shine of a keypad on the wall below. Moran brushed past the engineer and punched in the code, repeating the numbers to Dragomirov as he did so. The keypad unlocked a steel door, opening into a long concrete tunnel.

Without hesitation, Moran set off along the corridor. The concrete puckered outward every four feet where the forms hadn't contained it. The ceiling appeared to be made of precast slabs of concrete laid over the walls. Wherever a tiny gap appeared between the walls and ceiling, small trickles of dirt and stone had left piles on the tunnel floor or clung to the damp walls. Bright LED lights lit the length of the tunnel.

As they walked, Moran explained the tunnel system. "This is the main tunnel that connects the barn to our training facilities. It continues through two supply bunkers before ending at the barracks on the far side of the compound."

Dragomirov would discover later that one bunker contained a massive cache of weapons and ammunition, while the second housed gear and supplies for a dozen men for two years. Off the main tunnel were small bunk rooms for those dozen men to live in during an invasion or an apocalypse.

Moran continued to explain the network. "There's a tunnel up ahead that branches off to the right and runs south to a garage, and this door right here is the control room." He opened another steel door using a keypad before stepping inside. The room was approximately ten feet by ten feet, with an eight-foot ceiling to match the rest of the tunnels. "We're directly beneath the missile silo," Moran added. "You can gain entry to them through there." He pointed to a hatch in the ceiling accessed by a steel ladder.

Laying a hand on one of several large crates scattered about the room, Moran gave a conspiratorial grin. "These, my friend, are the controllers for your launch system. All you have to do is put them together."

Dragomirov opened his mouth to speak, but he was too bewildered by the effort Moran had already made.

"You see," Moran began, "your countrymen don't seem to care who they sell military hardware to as long as they can make a buck. It wasn't hard to bribe our way onto the submarine base in Murmansk, where they were busy decommissioning the old nuclear fleet. We paid a group of men to strip the missile launch gear from an *Akula*-class submarine that was taking on water."

Packed in crates labeled "URAL MOTORCYCLE PARTS," it had taken five million dollars to transport the equipment out of Russia. Moran had spent most of the money bribing the admiral overseeing the decommissioning. He'd spent the rest on shipping expenses and paying off dockworkers and customs inspectors.

The sensitive electronics now sat wrapped in bubble wrap and foam in packing crates all around the two men. Someone had removed the lids of the crates to check for damage, but Moran's men did not know what they were looking at. The suggestion to bring Dragomirov onto the project had come from the Russian admiral, causing Moran's out-of-pocket expenses to reach ten million without even firing a missile.

Dragomirov stepped over to the closest crate and pushed aside the lid to inspect the electronics. He smiled in satisfaction. He had worked on these very same systems for Novator.

Glancing over at Moran, Dragomirov asked a question weighing heavily on his mind. "Which targets do you plan to destroy? We are in middle of America. The Sampsons only have a range of three thousand kilometers."

"I plan to hit strategic targets here in the U.S.," Moran explained. "In order to restore our country back to the republic it once was, we must destroy the bastions of the Deep State."

Dragomirov kept his mouth shut. He'd heard lunatics speak before and recalled his first impression of the militia leader from the night before—Father Fanatic.

"What do you need to finish the controller?" Moran asked.

"I'll need to inspect all electronics and make list. I will let you know when I finish." Dragomirov picked up a nearby hammer and crowbar and began disassembling the crates to remove the gear. "Send someone to collect wood. I need all the space I can get."

Moran watched for a few minutes as the engineer tore into the crates as excited as a schoolboy at Christmas. He smiled to himself as he left the room.

Reverently, Dragomirov removed each piece of equipment from the crate. The disassembled pieces of the launch controller were rectangular black metal boxes containing sensitive electronic components. He arranged them against the wall next to the ladder in the order of which components he thought he might need first.

Several militiamen appeared in the bunker to remove the crates and clean up the packing material as Dragomirov continued to inventory the electronics. He methodically wrote out a long list of supplies he would need to make Moran's dreams of launching cruise missiles against strategic American targets a reality.

CHAPTER TEN

FBI Resident Agency Office
Lima, Ohio

R alph Pratt looked up from the file folder on his desk and glanced at his partner, Parker Rybeck. "This is some great assignment you pulled for us, Parker."

Rybeck held up his hands. "I didn't draw it, Ralph. The SAC handed it to us."

The SAC was Roger Talbot, the Special Agent in Charge of the Cleveland Field Office. Under his jurisdiction were thirty-nine of Ohio's eighty-eight counties, while the Cincinnati district handled the remainder. The FBI considered the Lima location a resident agency office, with several others spread across the state to allow an even distribution of agents to work alongside local law enforcement.

Pratt, a burly, six-five Black man who had played college football at the University of Maryland before joining the FBI ten years ago, sighed and put his feet on the desk before picking up the folder again. "I don't know what's worse: the people who believe these conspiracy theories or that I'm starting to believe in a few of them myself."

"Don't go off the deep end," Rybeck warned. "But I know what you mean. Some of these theories make a lot of sense—and if you believe one, you might as well believe them all."

The FBI had assigned the two special agents to look into the operations of Paul Moran, his burgeoning Liberty Brigade, and his local militia chapter, the 19th Ohio Militia Infantry. According to the file, the name paid homage to the 19th Ohio Infantry regiment that had served during the Civil War, seeing action at Chickamauga, Chattanooga, and Missionary Ridge, among other great battles, before being disbanded in San Antonio, Texas, in October 1865.

Rybeck wondered what the veterans of that outfit felt about Moran picking up the mantle.

"So, explain this to me, Rybeck," Pratt said. "Why two militias? The 19th Ohio and Liberty Brigade?"

"From what I understand, Liberty Brigade is just the umbrella organization Moran is using to unite all the other militias under. The 19th Ohio Infantry is a localized unit started by Steven Jackson."

Pratt nodded, continuing to skim through the information contained within the file. The few pages the Cleveland Field Office had sent over made for quick reading, but Rybeck knew more about the Liberty Brigade than he let on. He'd been sending reports about the militia organization to SAC Talbot for over a year. Since being approached by two members of the Kenton Police Department about joining Liberty Brigade's ranks, Rybeck had been diligently monitoring the militia as a pet project.

"I can't imagine these guys running around playing war games and stocking up for the end times," Pratt said, swinging his feet off the desk and tossing the file into his "In" tray. "How many times has some nut job predicted the end of the world, and yet here we are?"

"Probably more times than we realize," Rybeck replied. "But if Moran can unite all the militias like he's planning, the government could have a major coup on its hands."

"Would that be so bad?" Pratt mused sarcastically.

"Maybe they'll give us a pay raise," Rybeck joked. He wasn't opposed to some of the ideology Moran spouted during his unification speeches, but he also believed in the rule of law and the republic set up by the Founding Fathers.

"Or maybe they'll just give us a bullet in the back of the head for working for the Bureau," Pratt suggested as he stood. "I'm gonna take an early lunch. I have to be in court by one thirty. What's your plan for the afternoon?"

"I might ride over to Kenton and look at Moran's operation again."

Pratt shrugged into his suit jacket and headed for the door. Before opening it, he turned and said, "Be careful, Parker. Don't do anything rash. We're dealing with fanatics, and you never can tell what their twisted minds are capable of."

Returning to the file, Rybeck perused the information collected on Paul Moran. After spending a quarter of a century as an Airborne Ranger and Special Operations chief, the man had mustered out of the U.S. Army on a colonel's retirement package. For the last five years of his career, Moran had worked for the Joint Special Forces Operations Command (JSOC) in Tampa, Florida.

After retirement, Moran had taken a job at a small Washington think tank and began the talk show circuit, appearing regularly on CNN and Fox News as a military expert. As he got farther from his military career, his ideals became more radical. Eventually, Moran had dropped out of the limelight.

A couple of years later, he turned up in Ohio, recruiting for a new militia movement called Liberty Brigade, trying to unite the fledgling militia units scattered across the country.

The media consistently portrayed Moran as a right-wing nutcase, but, in reality, he was just tired of watching his country fall deeper and deeper into the clutches of socialism. He felt the rights of U.S. citizens were being eroded daily by a government that no longer represented the people, instead favoring lobbyists, wealthy donors, or anyone else with enough dollars to buy the vote of a congressman or senator.

While monitoring the Liberty Brigade, Rybeck had also spent some time learning about militias. The basis for the civilian units had it's roots in the Second Amendment of the Constitution, which reads, "A well-regulated militia, being necessary to the security of a free State, the right of the people to keep and bear Arms, shall not be infringed."

While militia organizations centered on varied objectives and convictions, many espoused common themes of anti-tax, anti-immigration, survivalism, sovereign citizenship, libertarianism, and the view that they must confront a despotic government through armed action.

Another popular theme among these militia conspiracy theorists was that a New World Order, headed by a secret cabal of global elites, was conspiring to rule the world through an authoritarian one-world government, replacing the sovereign state.

The government liked to keep a close watch on militias and their activities across the country, comparing them to domestic terrorism groups in light of their anti-government views. Militias were often well-armed, working to obtain or traffic illegal weapons and ammunition, including fully automatic firearms and improvised explosives. In more extreme cases, their usual targets were politicians, law enforcement officials, the courts, and government buildings.

The FBI had divided the militias into four distinct categories, the first being the "civil defense organization," which concerned itself with providing relief for natural disasters or emergency incidents. Second, were the revolutionary groups that looked to spark an uprising in the general population by peacefully persuading people to change political policies or social norms by holding rallies and demonstrations, printing newsletters, and engaging the populace through social media. The third followed the structure of a neighborhood watch, working with law enforcement to curtail crime in their community. The fourth class, and the one that concerned the FBI was most, was the armed militia that trained for waging war. Those radicals had developed a battle plan to ensure their proper response if their country, town, or homes came under attack.

Paul Moran's Liberty Brigade combined the civil defense force and the armed militia to create a hybrid. The people within its ranks were well-trained in skills such as firearms safety and marksmanship, wilderness survival, disaster preparedness, basic medical treatment and wound care, rescue and recovery, firefighting, and escape and evasion. Moran had brought in former Rangers and Special Forces veterans to train his civilian force in close-quarters combat, hand signals, house-clearing techniques, and combat shooting skills. Moran was a master of these training drills, as he had worked with the military to develop and implement much of the training doctrine currently employed by JSOC and the U.S. Army.

For Moran's militia operations, his associate Steven Jackson had donated the use of a defunct stone quarry eleven miles east of Kenton. The militia members used the surrounding woods, rivers, ravines, and farmland to practice maneuvers and hone their outdoor and military skills, incorporating SCUBA training and other combat operations.

Moran and his core cadre had torn down the old rock-crushing equipment, sold the metal for scrap, and built a large building that housed Liberty Brigade's headquarters, mess kitchen, and meeting and training rooms. Once Moran had established Liberty Brigade's base of operations, they'd continued to remove the old quarry equipment, improving the compound with two barracks buildings and a rappelling tower.

The satellite photo included in the file handed down from SAC Talbot revealed that Moran had constructed two large underground bunkers covered with thick concrete caps between the headquarters building and the two barracks. The Cleveland analysts had also marked what they thought was a system of underground tunnels based on depressions left in the dirt.

Liberty Brigade's establishment and the rapid buildup of men, matériel, and supplies had caught the attention of the Federal Bureau of Investigation.

The FBI didn't usually intervene until the militias began threatening to advance their ideology through force or violence—but the Liberty Brigade, through Moran's actions, was starting to fit the bill. Rybeck's investigation, he knew, could lift the lid off a volatile can of worms. Given what he knew of Moran and his ideologies, the FBI agent suspected he would soon be hard at work, placing himself directly in Liberty Brigade's path.

———

AN HOUR and a half after leaving his office, Rybeck stood on a high berm between the road and the fifty-foot drop into the quarry below. He had dressed himself in jeans, a T-shirt, work boots, and a ball cap, looking much like the farmers in the area. Rybeck pressed a pair of binoculars to his eyes and scanned the grounds of the Liberty Brigade compound across the quarry.

Methodically, he examined the structures in as close detail as his vantage point would allow. As he worked his way up a tower used for rock climbing and rappelling, he found himself staring at a man who was staring right back at him through his own binoculars. Rybeck's first instinct was to drop his field glasses and crouch in the weeds to hide, but he knew it wouldn't do any good as the sentry had already seen him. Casually, he resumed his scan of the grounds.

The sound of a vehicle approaching disrupted Rybeck's focus. Out of the corner of his eye, he saw a cruiser from the Hardin County Sheriff's Office stop nose-to-nose with his truck, parked just off the road. He turned to see a female deputy climbing out of the Ford Explorer. The uniformed brunette came around to the passenger side of the vehicle and leaned against it.

Hooking her thumbs in her duty belt, the deputy asked, "Do you know you're trespassing, sir?"

Rybeck glanced over his shoulder at the Liberty Brigade compound, wondering if the guy in the tower was still watching him. To the deputy, he said, "I'm standing in the right of way. How can I be trespassing?"

The deputy shrugged as if it didn't really affect her. "The owner called the station and asked us to tell you to move along."

Rybeck calculated how long he'd been standing on the side of the road versus how long it had taken the deputy to drive from the sheriff's station in Kenton, a place he'd been several times on business. "You responded pretty quickly to a guy standing on the side of the road on the very edge of the county."

Again, she shrugged. "The guy who owns the place kisses

enough backsides that he gets pretty much whatever he wants when he calls."

"Moran couldn't come to tell me himself?" Rybeck asked.

The deputy pushed off the vehicle, and her voice carried more force when she spoke. "I need you to get in your vehicle and leave, sir."

Rybeck glanced back across the quarry and saw the glint of sun reflecting off glass. The man in the tower was still watching. Rybeck put his binoculars back to his eyes and peered at the sentry again, except this time, Rybeck waved to him.

The deputy shifted again, drawing her right foot back and finding her balance on the uneven ground as her right hand reached for her sidearm. "Let's go, sir. Put the binoculars away and get in your vehicle."

"You don't need to do that," Rybeck said, spreading his arms so the deputy could see he wasn't making a move for a weapon. "I'm moving to my vehicle now."

He walked down the embankment and around to the driver's side of his truck, which blocked the view of the tower watchman. The deputy moved with him, staying well out of his reach.

Rybeck took a moment to assess the young woman. She stood about five-seven in her combat boots, had pulled her dark hair into a ponytail, and sunglasses shielded her eyes. The deputy had a set look to her mouth as her hand stayed on the butt of her pistol. He noticed she had knocked aside the retention snap at her thumb.

"I'm reaching for my ID. Are we cool?" Rybeck asked.

The woman nodded, her hand not wavering from her gun.

Pulling his credential pack from his pocket, Rybeck flipped it open, carefully keeping it out of sight of the watcher. "I'm Special Agent Parker Rybeck."

The deputy's hand slowly moved away from her gun, and

her whole body visibly relaxed. Rybeck extended his hand, and she shook it, introducing herself as Deputy Caroline Thurmond.

"Can I see that?" She motioned to his ID, and the FBI agent handed it over so she could inspect it. She glanced from the picture to Rybeck's face and back. He was handsome, in a rugged way, with neatly styled brown hair, light blue eyes, and an easy smile. She guessed he stood just north of six feet, and with his broad shoulders, thick arms, and muscular legs, he looked like he spent plenty of time in the gym.

"Can I buy you a cup of coffee, Deputy?" he asked, hoping to use the time to gather more information about the Liberty Brigade.

"I'm working right now."

"After you're done, then?" he asked.

Caroline shrugged noncommittally. "I need you to move along so I can do my job."

"Are you going to arrest me if I don't?" Rybeck asked.

"I don't want to arrest you. Unless this is part of an official investigation, I need you to move along. I'm just trying to do my job and keep the peace."

"How about we have dinner after your shift?" Rybeck grinned. "Just tell me where to move along to and I'll meet you there."

With an exasperated sigh, Caroline relented. "Fine. Meet me at Skinny's Tavern at six."

"Where is that?" Rybeck asked.

Grinning, Caroline said, "I guess if you want to buy me dinner, you'll have to figure that out for yourself. You being a *special* agent and all."

CHAPTER ELEVEN

Washington D.C.

Nursing his third beer of the evening, Phillip Upton stared at the television in his townhouse. A half-eaten pizza sat in a box atop a stack of three other empty pizza boxes on his coffee table. An ashtray on the table overflowed with discarded cigarette butts, as did the one on the end table beside the sofa.

Upton lit another cigarette and pulled deeply on the tobacco. The Washington Nationals were in the middle of a three-game series against The Colorado Rockies. Both teams were vying for the basement of their leagues, and while Upton was a fan of the Nationals, he had no strong feelings about which team won. Frankly, they were so far behind that it would be a miracle if they ever made the pennant race.

Since his divorce, the *Washington Post* reporter had let his blond hair go shaggy and favored a perpetual three-day stubble. He was of medium height and often used his bland appearance to blend into the crowd and get the story where others had failed.

Upton's editor at the *Post*, George Parsons, an overweight grandfather figure with a head of gray hair had assigned him to cover one the hottest current affairs stories in the country. A former Army colonel in Ohio was beating the drums of war, trying to unite the unorganized militias across the United States into one cohesive unit. Upton didn't feel impressed, but his editor had managed to secure an interview with the militia leader. Upton couldn't refuse when Paul Moran personally had asked for him.

The reporter leaned back in his chair and stared at the TV. The count was two to three, with runners at first and second. Over his shoulder, the pitcher checked the second-base runner, who was leading off by two steps. The pitcher fired the ball to second, keeping the runner honest.

Upton shuffled through the paper research on the arm of his chair. Much like the pitcher, it was *his* job as a reporter to keep the subjects of his story honest, checking them up and preventing them from stealing a run. Yet, many of his fellow journalists didn't feel the same way. Instead, they just filed stories along the party lines. If Upton changed the channel to any televised news program, be it local or national, the talking heads would say the same thing verbatim. Many of the old wire services, like Reuters, were the same way. Upton, however, liked to mix things up.

He wanted to give Paul Moran a fair interview when he sat down with him in just a few days. The paper research lacked depth, so Upton picked up his phone and scrolled through endless Internet sites, looking for background and contextual information he could use when interviewing the former colonel. He picked up his beer and took a long swig. Digging into this conspiracy stuff was not his forte, and, quite frankly, he found some of it strange, like the theorists were grasping at shadows in the dark.

The most renowned militias, Upton had learned, were the paramilitary type. Over the years, he'd covered his fair share of them for the *Post*, from the Proud Boys to the Three Percenters. Law enforcement considered these groups to be far-right extremists and the news media always painted them in the harshest light possible.

After reading a few more stories on the Internet, it was easy to see why people had so severely convicted them in the court of opinion—like when they sentenced members of the Wolverine Watchmen for trying to kidnap Michigan governor Gretchen Whitmer in 2020 or the Oklahoma City Bombing in April 1995—the largest terrorist attack on U.S. soil before 9/11. Timothy McVeigh and Terry Nicols had attended early meetings of the Michigan Militia before loading a U-Haul truck with ammonium nitrate, liquid nitro-methane, and the explosive Tovex and then detonating it under the Oklahoma City Federal Building.

Upton paused his reading and wondered where Paul Moran stood on using such extreme measures to defend his country against what he'd called "an increasingly tyrannical government."

Diving back into the Internet articles, Upton learned that after the Oklahoma City bombing, Norman Olson, the leader of the Michigan Militia, had testified in front of the United States Senate Subcommittee on Terrorism. His opening state-ment included his opinion on the right to form a militia, saying: "Not only does the Constitution specifically allow the forma-tion of a federal army, it also recognizes the inherent right of the people to form a militia ... While the Second Amendment to the U.S. Constitution acknowledges the existence of state militia and recognizes their necessity for the security of a free state; and, while it also recognizes that the right of the people to keep and bear arms shall not be infringed, the Second Amendment is not the source of the right to form a militia, nor to keep and bear arms. Those rights existed in the States prior to the formation of the federal union. In fact, the right to form a militia and to keep and bear arms existed from antiquity. The enumeration of those rights in the Constitution only underscores their natural occurrence and importance."

A subsequent article included a segment of Paul Moran's stump speech delivered to a militia in Tennessee. "The militia is needed to keep the government in check. The Founding Fathers dealt with a tyrannical government under the British crown. King George imposed unfair taxes on Americans, attempted to seize their firearms, and allowed British soldiers to be quartered in their homes and towns without compensating the landowner. After Americans rebelled at the Boston Tea Party, the king passed the Intolerable Acts, which closed the port of Boston and revoked Massachusetts' colonial charter. The Founding Fathers knew what it was like to live under tyranny—and now we live under tyranny again. Our liberty is under constant assault from the left and from the Deep State. We, the citizens of the United States, are being subjugated to produce a New World Order, one that will force us to bend to the will of the global elite and strip away the God-given rights endowed by our Creator. It is under such oppression that we must unite and defend ourselves. It is up to *us*, the citizen soldiers, to protect our great republic from a government that is becoming more tyrannical with every passing day."

Upton continued to read, finding an article in the *USA Today* that asserted all fifty states had passed some version of a law that prohibited paramilitary activity by civilian groups. Many left-leaning analysts claimed the phrase "well-regulated militia" referred to one that was sanctioned and regulated by the government, such as the National Guard, and that the

Supreme Court had also clearly stated that the Second Amendment did not protect paramilitary activities.

Left-leaning pundits frequently cited *Dennis v. United States,* in which the Supreme Court rejected the insurrection theory, stating that as long as the government provided free and open elections and trials by jury, the militias had no right to rebel.

The militias countered by referencing *District of Columbia v. Heller.* The highest court in the land had stated that gun ownership and being a part of a militia were mutually exclusive. The court also emphasized that the term "militia" should not be limited to those serving in a government-sponsored military but should include able-bodied men capable of being called to such service. Restricting the right to bear arms to personnel in a controlled military force would create the type of state-sponsored power the Second Amendment was intended to protect the American people from.

To Upton, the entire concept was like looking at the online meme where the woman yells at the cat. The woman screams, "You don't have the right to bear arms," while the cat calmly responds, "Suck it! Heller, baby."

When Upton sat down with Moran, he would have a lot of questions. Moran would need to justify the existence of the Liberty Brigade against the backdrop of American society.

As Upton jotted down a list of the questions he wanted to fire at Moran, he didn't realize that he'd become a pawn in a much broader game.

CHAPTER TWELVE

Liberty Brigade compound
Kenton, Ohio

Paul Moran climbed from the secret tunnels connecting the buildings and bunkers of his private fiefdom, leaving Kostya Dragomirov to work alone in the launch control bunker. He walked across the sprawling compound to the building the men of Liberty Brigade referred to as The Hall.

In the kitchen, he filled a large cup of coffee from an urn and then ascended the stairs to his office. He sat in the leather swivel chair behind a large wooden desk. Moran didn't miss the sterile Army-issue steel desks that every officer coming up the ranks had used. His desk was a sizable chunk of oak handcrafted by someone a century ago, and he loved the rich dark wood. He ran a hand over the smooth top and tried not to look at the speech he'd been preparing for the upcoming rally.

Moran was engaged in a grassroots speaking campaign at

local militia units across the country, intending to light the fire in their bellies to prepare to take back the government. He wanted these men and women to take the fight from the training grounds to the streets. If he failed to retake the government through political means first, he wanted to deliver a fatal punch via insurrection. The former colonel encouraged the militia members to run for city council, mayor, governor, and every job in between so true patriots could occupy the halls of government.

But Moran knew that putting people into government would take too much time, especially if he had to fight a rigged election system. In all good conscience, he didn't believe the country could wait that long. He wanted to hasten the downfall by striking critical components of the government and by destroying the United Nations buildings in New York City.

In essence, Moran wanted to hit the reset button on Washington and bring in some sensible, level-headed leadership to eliminate the waste, the inefficiencies, and the unauthorized departments that bogged down the system with excessive regulation and intruded on the daily lives of individual citizens and corporate businesses. Moran wanted to free the reins of the capitalistic society and restore the sovereign citizenship of every individual.

But first, they had to ax the dead weight of the senators and the congressman who did nothing but protect their own slice of turf. Moran knew there were some good people among them. But for the most part, the politicians seemed to forget about anything but bellying up to the special interest pig trough and gorging their bank accounts once they got into office. And since the politicians had to declare their financial records every year, it wasn't hard to tell who had been rooting in the slop the most.

Even the most tenacious of investigators couldn't always

tell where the money came from. Yet, something was definitely off when a U.S. senator left office after six years and was a multi-millionaire despite their $175,000 annual salary. Moran didn't believe these guys would ever vote for term limits since they had built-in pay raises that they had to vote *not* to take, and who in their right mind was going to vote against a pay raise?

In Moran's mind, the only way to deal with these tyrant bullies was to fire them wholesale. While the best way to rid the earth of their scum was to kill them, Moran figured it would be better for all concerned if every politician was sent home and banned from ever running for *any* political office again. Too many politicians left their national posts to return to state and local-level government positions, all because they enjoyed having someone stroke their ego.

Moran had a plan to deal with their belligerence. It was unconventional, but he knew it would work. Until new elections could be held, Moran planned to install a benevolent dictator in office.

The militia leader had a long list of plans and objectives for retaking the country, and establishing a well-armed, well-equipped group of like-minded supporters was his first goal. To Moran's credit, he was succeeding beyond his wildest imagination.

When he first began establishing Liberty Brigade, several other militias were already active across Ohio. Moran's dramatic leadership, knowledge of the military and Special Forces, and access to copious amounts of cash from his benefactors helped establish his militia as the best. Several smaller groups had later joined with Liberty Brigade, while some of the older, more obstinate factions did not share his vision of a large collective force.

Their refusal to collaborate was acceptable to Moran. Many other patriots were willing to take their place. His nationwide speaking engagements and lecture tours had enlarged the fold, and he believed that, in time, all would eventually join. Moran always received a warm welcome as he spoke about issues that resonated with many militia recruits: individual and States' rights, the dysfunction in government, the threat the United Nations posed to the sovereignty of the United States, and how to effectively prepare for the coming insurrection.

Moran recognized the fundamental importance of establishing consistent training across all militias so that the units would easily mesh when the need arose for them to work together. Much of the training delivered by the militias varied widely from group to group. Some militia members had no military training at all, and if they did, it was customarily not in small unit tactics or infantry maneuvers. Those with a military background often received training in roles such as mechanics or administrators, which did not adequately prepare them for combat.

To that end, Moran had written training regimens and doctrines, taken mainly from the Army Ranger and Special Forces manuals. In Moran's view, most militias, being small in number, worked to their benefit, as many wars had been won through small-group tactics, as seen from the Roman legionaries to the participants on the other side of the U.S.'s Global War on Terrorism.

Also, Moran saw the need to arm the militias just as the military armed themselves, so armaments in the field would be consistent across the board to provide ease of acquiring parts and ammunition. Militia members supplied their personal firearms and ammunition for training, with the most common being AR-style rifles chambered in .223 or .308 and handguns in nine-millimeter and .45.

Part of Moran's recruitment pitch was to provide arms and munitions to militia members at reduced prices by buying in bulk. Unfortunately, the government took a dim view of citizens buying that many weapons and munitions at one time, so he had turned to acquiring firearms through illegal means. It was not his first choice, but Moran felt the end justified the means.

Establishing a pipeline of arms and training had taken time. Many years of arduous work had gone into connecting the militias across the United States with his STAMP program—Standard Training and Militia Procurement. Each militia had been armed and trained to assist with civil defense, aid the government during natural disasters, and guard the national borders to prevent illegal immigration. Podcasts, webcasts, shortwave radio broadcasts, television appearances, and technical demonstrations had supported Moran's training videos—until the FBI had coordinated with social media companies to shut down accounts they deemed harmful to the globalists' narrative.

Moran thrust aside the papers that littered the desktop and leaned back in his chair. Anyone who had been involved with a militia at even the most basic level would know all of this information already. What he needed to present to the public was something new—a stirring speech that would galvanize the American people into action. But so far, the words had yet to find their way onto the page.

Since he was having trouble concentrating on his work, Moran distracted himself by turning on a cable news program. It didn't matter which one he chose; the talking heads repeated the same monotonous sound bites. Even Fox News had turned liberal, leaving its conservative base behind.

The news program cut from the four-person panel at the desk to a live feed from the interior of the U.N.'s General Assembly Hall. Members of the assembly were taking turns denouncing gun violence and decrying the U.S. for once again rejecting the proposed Arms Trade Treaty.

Moran scoffed. Over the years, he frequently criticized the United Nations, viewing the U.N. assembly as corrupt due to the absence of references to God and unalienable rights in the Universal Declaration of Human Rights. Instead, the U.N. asserted that man granted these rights through written laws, conflicting directly with the Constitution and the Declaration of Independence.

His disdain for the U.N. extended to its headquarters in New York City. Moran frequently expressed his desire for the foreign interlopers to be ousted and proposed repurposing the buildings to shelter the homeless. His current plan, however, involved reducing the buildings to rubble, envisioning one of the Sampson cruise missiles launching from the grain silo to wing its way across the American Heartland and smash straight down into the middle of the Secretariat Building, where the resultant blast would decimate the General Assembly and the surrounding buildings.

Not that the homeless couldn't use a new shelter, but targeting the U.N. headquarters in Turtle Bay, Manhattan, would be a show of force to the world, proving beyond a shadow of a doubt that Moran wasn't playing around. The United Nations would come to an inglorious end, and the U.S. would stop shelling out billions of taxpayer dollars to an inept organization.

Another target of Moran's criticism was the Federal Emergency Management Agency (FEMA), which he saw as a sinister force embedded within the U.S. government. If the U.N. wanted America to fall to her knees, then FEMA was the key the supposed peacekeeping organization would use to wreck her.

Established by executive order in 1979, FEMA's stated dual purpose was emergency management and civil defense. According to its own drafted legislation, if the president were to declare martial law it would trigger a FEMA takeover of the U.S. government, effectively suspending the Constitution, eliminate private property, and abolish free enterprise. Once FEMA had complete control, they could appoint a non-elected national government, imposing a totalitarian regime from atop its mountain lair on Mount Weather in West Virginia.

But Paul Moran believed the organization's true purpose was to control the populace.

The first step to gaining that control was to remove the right to bear arms, hence the U.N. Arms Trade Treaty. While there was no specific language in the treaty that said U.S. citizens would forfeit their right to own firearms, there wasn't anything in it that said the opposite. Like most U.N. treaties, this one was full of legalese and mumbo jumbo.

Moran warned politicians against signing the treaty, drawing parallels to countries like Australia, Canada, England, and New Zealand, where citizens had relinquished their firearms, rendering themselves defenseless against tyranny. History showed that disarming was a tried-and-true tactic from Hitler to Mao Tse-tung and, more recently, Hugo Chavez in Venezuela.

Whether or not American citizens retained gun rights, the treaty was still about control—and specifically, how much control the U.S. government was prepared to surrender. To that end, FEMA had collaborated with past U.S. presidents to enact executive orders that would grant the organization control over transportation, media, agriculture, natural resources, power generation, military activities, and the establishment of prison camps in times of crisis.

Moran asserted foreign troops were being housed on U.S. soil to enforce martial law. These troops were from Australia, Canada, Mexico, and the United Kingdom and trained at various bases across the country to coordinate the warrantless arrests of those on FEMA's watch lists since the fear many

FEMA executives postulated was that U.S. military personnel, law enforcement, and other public servants, who have sworn an oath to support and defend the Constitution of the United States of America against all enemies, both foreign and domestic, would not cooperate in the arrest of private citizens. Foreign troops with no sworn allegiance to the U.S. would have no conflict when they rounded up "enemy combatants" on American soil.

Under the pretext of the Patriot Act, the Department of Homeland Security (DHS) had allegedly begun amassing arms and military equipment to coordinate with foreign troops to put down "insurrections" by armed citizens, military, or police who upheld in their oath of duty.

Moran believed he was one such combatant against the tyrannical government.

The leader of Liberty Brigade stared off into the distance, ignoring the chest-pounding ingrates on the television. Despite struggling to articulate a compelling speech, he felt a profound fear for his country and fellow citizens in the face of unprecedented covert subversion. While evidence of U.N., FEMA, and government misconduct existed, the lamestream media preferred to focus on distractions such as celebrities and sports—precisely as planned by CIA's Operation Mockingbird, a deliberate and systematic program of widespread manipulation of U.S. citizens by the news media.

The evidence was clear, but people had turned a blind eye to it. It was Moran's job to awaken the public and stoke the fires of liberty.

Frustrated, Moran wadded up his meager attempts at writing a resounding speech and threw it hard against the wall, watching the paper bounce and fall.

In the end, Moran would need only one speech—the one he would make from the Resolute Desk in the Oval Office after he'd taken over the government.

CHAPTER THIRTEEN

Skinny's Tavern
Kenton, Ohio

At six p.m., Rybeck pulled his Chevy pickup truck into the parking lot of the tired-looking Skinny's Tavern and climbed out. He'd figured the place would have been in a more commercial area of town. The tavern, however, was on a residential side street. If one didn't know it was there, one would drive right past, which made it a perfect watering hole for locals.

Skinny's appeared to be an old house with a two-story center section and single-story sloping roofs off each side. The owner had recently painted it a dark shade of blue and roofed it with tan shingles.

Out front, a low picket fence closed in an outdoor seating area, and the June weather had finally warmed enough for several patrons to hoist frosty tallboys at the patio tables.

Usually, after Memorial Day, Mother Nature turned up the heat in the Midwest, but tonight, the evening was still chilly.

Stepping through a red door, Rybeck entered the bar and quickly glanced around for both entrance and exits, but also at the décor and for his date. The scent of cooking meat and cold beer made Rybeck's mouth water. It smelled good, that was for sure.

The place was bar chic, sporting a mixture of wooden slat walls painted tan and old wood veneer paneling that had been all the rage in the seventies. Hanging from every wall were neon beer signs, mirrors, old metal signs representing bygone businesses or factories, pictures of old buildings, and Little League teams that Skinny's had supported over the years. It appeared to be a place where a good bar fight could occur without much getting broken. Even the chairs were steel and wood, like they'd come from an old school cafeteria.

Caroline Thurmond waved to him from a corner booth. Rybeck didn't recognized her at first since she'd changed out of her uniform into jeans, a T-shirt, and a blue windbreaker. Her chestnut hair was now loose instead of bunched in a ponytail, and it fell down her shoulders in waves.

As Rybeck walked over, Caroline motioned for him to sit opposite her. With a conspiratorial grin, she said, "I'm glad you found the place."

"Can't go wrong with Google Maps," Rybeck replied, sliding into the booth.

"How was your afternoon?" Caroline asked.

"Uneventful," he replied, picking up the single laminated menu sheet. Rybeck had spent the afternoon driving the tangle of back roads around the Liberty Brigade compound and Steven Jackson's home.

The waitress sauntered over, and Rybeck ordered a Coke and a hamburger while Caroline ordered a Sprite and a salad.

With the food formalities out of the way, the deputy asked, "First question, Agent Rybeck: business or pleasure?"

Part of Rybeck wished that he'd taken the invitation to join Liberty Brigade. He might have been the inside man, perhaps privy to Moran's plans. But he also believed he'd done the right thing both personally and professionally by not joining Moran's militia. He mentally smiled. If he had joined, he wouldn't be sitting in a tavern about to grill a beautiful young woman about Liberty Brigade right then. Sometimes, the stars aligned, and poor Rybeck was smitten.

And while the agent in him wanted to get right down to brass tacks, Rybeck could also sense Caroline's reluctance to discuss work, so he pitched her a softball. He hoped that by getting her to talk about a familiar subject, she would remain open when he started digging for information about the Liberty Brigade. Leaning closer, he asked, "So, what's a pretty girl like you doing in a bar like this?"

Caroline rolled her eyes but couldn't stifle her laughter at his cheesy line. "What's next? Are you going to ask me if I come here often?"

It was Rybeck's turn to laugh as he leaned back in his seat and tried to formulate a better question about how long she had lived in the area or how she enjoyed being a deputy. All he could muster, however, was, "Well, do you come here often?"

"Yes, since you asked," Caroline replied. "I've been coming to Skinny's Tavern all my life. My dad was a deputy, too, before he died of lung cancer. He brought me in here a lot when I was young. Our waitress, Marge, used to babysit me in this very booth."

"What about your mom?"

Marge brought over the drinks and affectionately touched Caroline's shoulder. "You be good to my girl here. She deserves a good man."

Caught off guard, Rybeck's eyes widened, and for a moment, he was unsure what to do. Caroline rescued him by saying, "It's not like that, Marge. Parker works for the FBI. He just wants to pick my brain."

"Uh-huh. All that laughter doesn't sound very professional." Marge looked pointedly at Rybeck. "Make sure her brain is the only thing you be picking, mister. I'm too old to be a babysitter again."

"Yes, ma'am," Rybeck replied, then sipped his Coke with his eyes downcast as if the older woman could read lustful intentions in them.

"Sorry about that," Caroline apologized after Marge had moved away to serve another table. "She's overprotective."

"As she should be," Rybeck said. He sipped his Coke and asked, "What about your mom?"

"She died when I was five," Caroline said quickly. "If you haven't noticed, there are a lot of Amish around the county. They're Old Order and use candles on their buggies for lighting. Anyway, Mom misjudged a turn at night in the rain and hit a buggy. The horse flew up on top of the car and flattened the roof, killing her instantly—or so I'm told. I don't remember much about it except that the collision killed the lady driving the buggy, too."

"I'm sorry," Rybeck offered considerately.

"It was a long time ago." Caroline cleared her throat and pushed her hair off her forehead. "So, I grew up here. Marge was my surrogate grandmother. After high school, I did four years in the Army, went to college at The Ohio State University for criminal justice, and ended up right back here. I was lucky enough to work with Dad for a few years. It was kinda nice riding the roads with him."

Rybeck had not expected her to share such a personal story during their first meeting. He mustered a weak, "I'm glad it worked out for you."

"I guess," Caroline said with a shrug. "Pretty crappy childhood, though, if you ask me." She sipped her Sprite to center herself, then asked brightly, "How'd you become a special agent?"

"I joined the Coast Guard after high school and worked as a maritime enforcement specialist. I used my G.I. Bill to get a criminal justice degree, then applied to the FBI … and here I am."

"Where are you from, originally?" Caroline asked.

"North Dakota." She made a face, and he laughed. "That's how I felt, too. I couldn't wait to leave."

Their food came, and Marge gave Rybeck a look of disapproval as she set his plate down, jostling some fries onto the tabletop, giving him a mock, "Oops."

Rybeck smiled up at her, then turned to Caroline. "Does she do this with all your dates?"

"Oh, this is a *date* now?" Marge shot back, her blue hair bobbing and her voice sounding like she'd smoked too many cigarettes.

"No, Marge," Caroline replied flatly. "We're fine. This is business. Parker wants to know about the Liberty Brigade."

Marge snorted. "Bunch of wannabe pussies, if you ask me. They should go join the Army like real men." She turned and stalked off.

"Is she always that opinionated?" Rybeck asked.

Caroline smiled. "About everything."

They tucked into their food to ease the conversation. Despite Marge's surly disposition, Rybeck found the hamburger was excellent and made a mental note to bring Ralph Pratt to Skinny's. His partner would love the place, with its old beer signs, delaminating tables, the faded green felt on the pool table, and framed articles cut from newspapers of yesteryear about Kenton's history.

After Caroline had picked at her salad for a bit and grown

bored of watching Rybeck mow through his burger, she put down her fork and rested her crossed arms on the table. "Let's get it over with. Let's talk about the Liberty Brigade."

Rybeck looked up from dunking a fry in ketchup. The question was on his lips without thought. "Let's start with why you came so quickly to ask me to move along."

"You were trespassing," she replied simply. "I was in the area when I got the call, so I responded."

"I was standing on the edge of a public road—technically the right of way owned by the county," he countered.

Caroline shrugged. "I got a call from Dispatch about a guy trespassing, so I went to investigate. According to standard operating procedure, I had to ask you to move along, which you did."

"What makes Moran so powerful that he has the local sheriff in his pocket?"

The sheriff's deputy chuckled. "Well, Moran and Steven Jackson. Jackson actually owns the property. Together, they bring a lot of dollars to this community, which is why the powers that be—aka the city council and county commissioners—look the other way and help them out where they can. The police and sheriff departments are part of that help if need be. I don't understand, but the system seems to work for them. Some of the guys in the police department and a few of the deputies even go out there on training weekends."

"What do they do there?" Rybeck pressed.

"From what I hear, they either teach courses or provide security."

"What about you?" Rybeck asked. "Do you participate?"

Caroline laughed. She unfolded her arms and sat back in her seat. "I think most of those guys have a few screws loose."

"Why do you think that?"

"Have you heard the conspiracies they've come up with? FEMA is going to ride in on black helicopters and round them all up before taking them to prison camps. The U.N. is trying to take over the country. 9/11 was an inside job orchestrated by Bush and his Department of Defense cronies. The list goes on. I just don't buy it."

"Good for you," Rybeck replied.

Caroline looked at him curiously. "Are you suggesting you buy the crap Moran's selling?"

"Not exactly, but I can see where some in the government are pushing for a socialist agenda. They just disguise it by calling it the 'Green New Deal.'"

Caroline crossed her arms, asking petulantly, "So, you're one of them?"

"I didn't say that," Rybeck replied. "My job is to investigate Moran and the Liberty Brigade and see if they pose a material threat to the government or if Moran's posturing is all bluff and bluster."

"Believe me," Caroline stated, "Moran isn't bluffing. If he could cause an insurrection like J6, where they stormed the U.S. Capitol, I think he would."

Wanting to remain focused on the facts, Rybeck moved on. "Have you had contact with Moran or Jackson?"

Caroline shook her head. "Not Moran, but I've known Mr. Jackson for a long time. I went to school with his kids, Kim and Brett. Kim and I were pretty close in high school, but I haven't seen her in years. I think Brett works on his dad's farm."

She seemed to relax as she reached for her soda to take a drink.

"What's Jackson like?" Rybeck asked/

Caroline shrugged. "He was always nice to me. He's a local church member and used to be a township trustee and a county commissioner. As far as I know, he pays his taxes on time and has never been arrested. But I'm sure you know all this—you probably have a file on everyone related to the Liberty Brigade."

Rybeck shook his head. "Not everyone."

Marge wandered over to refill Rybeck's Coke.

"You got a file on me?" Caroline asked once Marge had retreated behind the bar.

The FBI agent grinned sheepishly. "I'm working on that right now."

Caroline coyly asked, "What have you got so far?"

Rybeck didn't want to sound trite by telling her she was pretty or intelligent or that he empathized with her over personal tragedy, but all those things were true. Instead of admitting his feelings and saying he would like to spend more time with her, Rybeck changed the subject in true guy fashion. "You said the militia brings business into the area?"

Caroline didn't show it if she was disappointed that he hadn't picked up on her romantic hint. Rybeck had pried open a subject that annoyed her. "You bet they bring in business. People come from all over. They cram into the motels and spend money at the restaurants and the other shops—especially the gun store."

Rybeck perked up at the mention of the gun store. While he had been in Roy's Guns and Ammo several times, he had never connected it Liberty Brigade.

Picking up on his nonverbal cue, the deputy said, "I would have thought that you guys knew all about that."

Rybeck shook his head. "We're just getting up to speed on Moran's operation. Is the gun store affiliated with the militia?"

"Not that I know of. Roy Dombek's gun store has been around longer than the Liberty Brigade. It's in the shopping center as you come into town from the east on State Route 67, and he practically sells out of ammo on training weekends.

If it were up to me, I'd be investigating the guy—for tax evasion, if nothing else."

Rybeck raised his eyebrows. "Has anyone investigated him?"

"I can't say for sure. If the police department is doing something, I wouldn't know about it. I highly doubt anyone is looking at Dombek's books but him. All the LEOs buy ammo from the guy. Unless you want to drive forty-five minutes to another store, he's the only supplier in town."

Rybeck nodded and made a mental note to have the man's professional and personal finances checked out. Still, he was curious about Caroline's reasoning. "Why tax evasion?"

Caroline leaned forward, glancing around conspiratorially, and, for the first time, Rybeck noticed how her brown eyes had flecks of gold in them. When her gaze met his, her eyes sparkled. Whatever annoyance she felt about being questioned about the Liberty Brigade had shifted to excitement.

"I can't explain it," Caroline said. "Dombek just has a slimy feel about him."

"Do you want to investigate him?" Rybeck asked, leaning forward, too.

"I think *someone* should. Dombek also owns a used car lot on the west side of town. You probably passed it when you drove through. Anyway, he deals in a lot of heavy equipment, tractors, combines, semi-trucks, and trailers—that sort of stuff. There are always vehicles coming and going, and sometimes at odd hours of the night."

"Could be anything," Rybeck replied.

She lowered her voice to a whisper. "Or he could be running guns or drugs or trafficking people."

"*Now* who's the conspiracy theorist?"

Caroline laid a hand on his to emphasize her point, and Rybeck tingled with excitement. "I think you need to check him out. I'm not saying he's guilty. I'm just saying there's something hinky going on."

Rybeck glanced down at her hand, resting gently on his, and made no move to draw his hand back. He looked her in the eyes again, where the gold flecks seemed to catch the low light and sparkle with intensity.

"All right," he said. "I'll check him out, but stay away from Dombek's operation if you can. We don't want to taint the process."

Caroline smiled as she gripped his hand a little tighter. "So, are you going to ask me out again, Agent Rybeck? I see the way you keep looking at me."

"Caroline, I think you're smart and pretty and—"

She cut him off by removing her hand from his and held it up in frustration. "Don't give me the old 'we're *just two professionals*' routine."

"I wasn't. I was about to say that I wanted to see you again and ask you for your phone number."

Blushing, she said, "I guess I jumped the gun. Most guys don't like to date a woman in law enforcement."

"I have no problems dating a fellow officer," Rybeck replied. "In fact, we should do this again soon." He created a new contact in his phone and typed in her name, then handed the phone to Caroline for her to put in her digits. Once she had done so, he texted her a winking face.

Caroline glanced down at her phone. "*Agent* Rybeck, that's quite forward of you."

He shrugged. "I'm not hip on my emojis."

"I think you knew exactly what you meant," Caroline said, texting back a smirking face.

Rybeck paid the tab, and together, they walked outside. Despite the house lights and the bright glow of the security lamps around the nearby factory, they could still see some stars in the cloudless sky.

Caroline pointed up at a particular constellation on the southern horizon. "That's Leo. You can see what looks like a backward question mark. That's the 'sickle' and part of his mane."

Rybeck pivoted and pointed at the Big Dipper. Moving his finger along an imaginary line, he stopped at a bright star and said, "And the North Star."

Slipping her hand in his, Caroline stared up. "Kinda makes you feel insignificant, doesn't it? Like nothing matters down here."

Rybeck turned to her, pushing a loose strand of hair off her cheek. They were already discussing a second date and had sent suggestive emojis, so he felt brave enough to kiss her. Her arms slipped around him, and he held her close, enjoying the moment.

"Keep it in your pants!" Marge yelled from the open bar door.

Rybeck and Caroline laughed. Marge's interruption had broken the magical spell they'd been under. He didn't want their evening to end, but it was late, and he had to work the following day.

He promised to call her tomorrow, then climbed into his truck and waved goodbye.

———

As he drove home, Rybeck thought about his past. He'd given Caroline a taste of it, just as she had, and he figured she carried her own secrets and scars the same as he did. She, too, had seen heartbreak and tragedy in her personal life, and they both saw it every day in their professional careers.

Rybeck had grown up on a farm in North Dakota, the youngest in a band of foster children taken in by Dave and Sharon Rybeck. He had been an infant when his mother had dropped him off at a fire station in Bismarck. Child Protective Services had cared for him until the Rybecks had learned about Parker and swiftly brought him into their family.

The Rybeck children had worked hard, milking cows, bailing hay, plowing, planting, and harvesting corn, green peas, and lentils. Much of the food they'd eaten had come right from the garden or from the animals they'd raised. Rybeck was proud of his childhood and loved his foster parents but never intended to become a farmer.

Young Rybeck loved spending time on the water, and his favorite pastime had been sailing Lake Sakakawea. The man who taught Rybeck how to sail was also a scuba diver, and the two had explored the lake above and below the waves.

During Rybeck's junior year of high school, he'd convinced his parents to allow him to take a sailing course on Lake Superior with five other young people. Rybeck had hit it off with a girl named Amanda, and the two of them had become close friends within a few days.

The sailing center had scheduled the course to last a week, but a storm ravaged the boat on their fourth day out. A microburst snapped the mast and toppled the sails overboard. As the sailboat began to capsize, dragged under by the weight of the water-filled sails, Rybeck had sprung into action, digging for the bolt cutters in a cockpit locker to cut loose the steel rigging and stop the boat from rolling completely over. Picking up the cutters, he'd heard the captain on the radio, calling out an S.O.S. to the Coast Guard.

It had taken all of Rybeck's strength to cut the first cable. When it had finally snapped loose, the boat had rocked violently but settled at an even steeper angle as the water rushed into the cockpit and swirled at their feet on the cabin roof. Another of the sailors had finally come to Rybeck's aid, and as they sliced through the last rigging cable, the hull broke free and rocked violent back and forth.

Out of the corner of his eye, Rybeck had seen Amanda lose her balance and fall into the sea. Without thinking, he dove overboard, swimming hard to reach his friend's side. Having donned life vests before the storm had hit, Amanda and Rybeck clung together as the sailboat slowly drifted away in the pitched battle of the storm.

Suddenly, a light snapped on above them, and an angel of mercy had dropped from the skies in a bright orange survival suit. Their rescuer had loaded Amanda into the basket and sent her skyward, waiting with Rybeck in the churning waters beneath the helicopter. It was at that moment that Rybeck had found direction in his life, and he'd joined the Coast Guard to save lives.

But instead of training as a rescue swimmer, Rybeck became a maritime enforcement specialist.

After graduating high school, he'd gone to boot camp in Cape May, New Jersey, and then to the Maritime Law Enforcement Academy. Over the next eight years of his life, Rybeck spent his days working up the ranks and becoming a competent law enforcement officer. He'd also taken college courses in criminal justice to prepare for a career after the Coast Guard.

As part of the Global War on Terrorism, Rybeck had spent a year in the Persian Gulf working with the Navy, doing Visit Board Search and Seizures on commercial vessels, looking for weapons, drugs, and terrorists. His last assignment had been with the Coast Guard Investigative Service, working cases with civilians as the investigated the criminal activities of Coast Guard personnel.

The FBI that had recruited him away from the Coast Guard. Rybeck left the service, went through the academy at Quantico, and spent his first few years in Georgia before being transferred to Lima, Ohio, to fill the post of a retiring agent.

At the angry honking of an SUV's horn behind him, Rybeck shook himself from his thoughts and realized the light he'd stopped at had turned green. He sped through the intersection, thinking about the last time he had been to North Dakota. A wildcatter had discovered oil on the old homestead, and between the oil royalties and the high crop prices, the Rybeck family was in great shape. They were proud of Parker and his service to his country and never questioned why he didn't come home more often. He'd always been the wanderer, the dreamer, and the explorer. They just figured he was doing what he needed to do.

And what he needed to do now was focus on Liberty Brigade. Rybeck sensed Moran wasn't like other militia leaders who were content to wait for the government to collapse. If Moran was as dedicated to his cause as Rybeck believed him to be, then Rybeck needed to step up his game and thwart Moran's plans before they unfolded.

CHAPTER FOURTEEN

California Vintage Estates
Sebastopol, CA

Paul Moran glanced around at the gathering of prominent individuals in the intimate study of the Spanish-style ranch home. As an old Army Colonel, he was more used to roughing it in the field than indulging in the luxury trappings of command, so he felt slightly out of place in a home that cost more than he could probably save in his lifetime. But being at the gathering was what he needed to do to advance Liberty Brigade's agenda.

Joining Moran in the study were Steven Jackson; Chet Gravely, the reclusive Internet billionaire and owner of California Vintage Estates; General Kevin Killian, commander of the Joint Chiefs of Staff; and Ian Shipley, renowned talk radio host, author, and conspiracy theorist.

Gravely's house sat on one hundred acres of rolling California vineyards that had provided fermented grapes to the masses for almost a century. Gravely had built it as a private getaway from his other business interests and to keep outsiders at arm's length. With built-in soundproofing and bulletproof glass, the study now served as a secret meeting place for the five men intent on revolution. In this isolated house, they could each talk freely about their ambitions.

The men sat in leather tufted nailhead chairs and couches that faced each other in a rectangle, with the chairs at the short ends separated by a glass-and-steel coffee table. Underfoot, a woven rug defined the seating space on the polished hardwood that matched the rest of the flooring in the house.

A large wooden desk sat at the far end of the room before a panoramic window. Along two sides of the room were floor-to-ceiling bookshelves containing many rare or first-edition books in a wide variety of subjects. Gravely was an obsessive bibliophile, reading at least twenty books per month along with multiple trade journals, newspapers, and magazines.

Gravely was the principal financier of Moran's revolutionary enterprise. Killian represented the military, while Shipley's job was to stir the pot and keep his listeners ready to revolt. As the number three radio talk show host in the nation, he reached millions of people daily. Once his three-hour radio show ended, Shipley continued his programming via his cable news channel, broadcasting twenty-four hours a day. Across his media platforms, Shipley kept his followers informed of the tyranny of the government against the peaceful citizens they were supposed to serve. If the Democratic Party could control the information being passed by the media, as they were, then the Liberty Brigade would need to do so once they secured the country. And Shipley was an intricate part of that plan.

"How is Halberd Security doing?" Gravely asked, his bald head glistening in the sunlight streaming through the broad windows. He was a portly man dressed in baggy khaki shorts, a red camp shirt, and sandals.

Moran sat forward, resting his forearms on his knees, his broad shoulders pulling taut the suit jacket he wore. He maintained his powerful build with a stiff exercise regimen, a discipline he'd learned early in the Army. "Halberd is doing extremely well, thanks to our many contacts in the government and private sectors. They've turned a profit from the beginning, financing the Woodlot operation and purchasing a farm outside Bluemont, Virginia. Orlando has the men on track for our Mount Weather operation date."

Gravely nodded. "I've been reading their financial reports. You and Orlando are doing very well."

Moran nodded his thanks. He poured whatever profits their private security company made back into preparations for the future Liberty Brigade uprising.

"Are we still planning to go forward after the rally?" Killian asked.

Moran swiveled to face the general, who had forgone his dress uniform for casual business attire. At nearly fifty years of age, he still had a full head of dark brown hair, cut short on the sides, but his six-foot frame was going soft in the middle from the endless hours he spent behind a desk.

"Yes, preparations for the rally are almost complete," Moran said. "We have over two thousand people coming, maybe more. Some are coming for the entertainment aspect of the rally, but once they are there, I'm confident we can convince them of our worthy cause. We're still on track for the Sampsons to be launched after the rally when we feel sentiments will be at their strongest. The rest of the country will become active in our plan when the militias engage. It's that first step that most people are unwilling to take, but once we've made it, they should all fall in line like dominos."

"How are the Sampsons coming?" Shipley asked. "Do you think they'll be ready by then?"

Jackson leaned back in his chair, a snifter of whiskey in his hand. "Our Russian friend is working as fast as he can to get them online. We expect them to be launch-ready ahead of the rally and on schedule for our plans."

"Good," Gravely purred as he walked over to the sideboard to pour himself another drink. "Then we're on track."

He filled a glass with red wine pressed from grapes grown in his own vineyards.

The rest of the men remained silent as their benefactor sipped his wine, but Moran pressed on. His most burning question centered on whether he would become president in the days after the attack. However, he decided the topic called for a subtle approach and simply said, "We need to discuss what happens after we take control of the government."

"We have that all worked out, Paul," the billionaire chided as he returned to his seat. "You'll take care of marshaling the forces, and we'll take care of the politics. If you need Mr. Killian's help, I'm sure he'll be on hand to provide it."

Moran hated being spoken to like a child, especially by a short, overweight, bald man who had never put his life on the line for his country. Not to mention that the insurrection was Moran's plan. Gravely was used to bossing people around and getting his way, but he wasn't the brains behind their proposals. He came from money and had grown his fortune by making savvy investments in the stock market, seeding businesses as an angel investor, and building companies that filled niche markets in the tech sector.

Though they seemed to have forgotten it, Gravely and Shipley had come to Moran for help, not the other way around.

"I must have missed a meeting …" the retired colonel growled, immediately feeling defensive.

"Indeed, you did," Gravely replied. "I met with Steven and Ian a month ago, and we agreed upon who our benevolent dictator should be. We know *we* can't do the job; the people, fickle though they may be, would not stand for that." He stabbed a finger at Moran. "You're the leader of their resistance movement—the sacrificial lamb as it may be." Gravely waved his hand dismissively. "We've been over all this before."

They had been over it before. Paul Moran, retired Army colonel and leader of the Liberty Brigade, was the face of the movement and the hero of the people. If their coup failed, they expected him to take the fall. He would end up in prison as the scapegoat, protecting Gravely, Shipley, Killian, and Jackson, along with the members of the existing government who were helping to facilitate Liberty Brigade's plan.

"Steven," Gravely purred again. "Can you bring in our guest of honor, please?"

Jackson went to the office door and stepped outside. A moment later, Jackson returned with a woman. Moran felt his jaw unhinge, but he was professional enough not to let it sag all the way to the floor. He had not expected to see Diane Warrick, the former Republican governor of Arizona now serving as the president pro tempore of the United States Senate, anywhere near their secret cabal. Yet, there she was, making Moran's heart beat just as fast as she'd ever made it.

"I believe you all know Diane Warrick, the next President of the United States," Gravely said proudly as he greeted her with a gentle hug and a kiss on the cheek. The rest of the men stood to greet her with either hugs or handshakes.

Moran was the only one who hadn't risen from his seat. Instead, he stared in awe as Warrick walked in. She wore a dark blue business suit with a skirt, a light blue blouse, and matching high heels that clicked on the hardwood floor. Over her left shoulder was the strap of her leather satchel. Her jet-black hair hung straight and loose, and her brown eyes sparkled as she smiled at him.

Moran gulped.

Warrick held the distinction of being the very first senator to be declared president pro tempore and not be the oldest sitting member of the Senate. Her election into the position had shocked many in Washington. It wasn't because she was skilled and educated at Senate procedure but because so many other senators had secrets they wished to keep out of the public eye. Blackmail and bribery had leveraged those secrets into votes, putting Warrick in succession for the presidency.

"Paul, it's so nice to see you again," Warrick said, taking his hand once Moran finally rose from his seat.

He could do nothing but smile and nod. In fact, he blushed—and he couldn't remember the last time a woman had made him blush. As their hands interlocked, Moran couldn't help feeling like his old drill sergeant was thumping him in the chest once more and calling him "*Moron!*"

Warrick smiled, sensing his discomfort. "You don't look half as scary as the reporters make you out to be."

"It's a pleasure to see you too, Diane," Moran finally murmured. He glanced around the room, hoping none of the others had caught him fanboying over the dazzling senator.

Gravely looked puzzled at the interaction. "I didn't know you two knew each other."

"I met Paul at a charity event in Washington when he was with The Heritage Foundation," Warrick responded with an amused half smile.

Again, Moran felt the blood rise in his cheeks. They *had* met at a fundraiser in D.C. But before that, they'd been college students together at Arizona State, where they'd briefly dated. Moran refrained from elaborating on their past relationship when Warrick did not. Some things were better left unsaid.

"Can I get you a drink, Senator?" Steven Jackson asked as he headed for the sideboard.

"Certainly, tequila on the rocks would be perfect. And please, call me Diane. We're all friends here."

"Certainly. Is Don Julio Real okay, Diane?" Jackson asked as if trying out her name for the first time.

"Yes." Warrick shed her suit jacket and laid it on the back of a sofa. "You boys don't mind if I dress down, do you?"

The men all shook their heads.

"Good. I wouldn't mind dressing like you, Chet," she said wistfully as Jackson handed her the tequila in an old-fashioned glass. "I'm more of a shorts and T-shirt girl myself. I've always found these business suits to be quite stuffy.

"You're welcome to change," Gravely replied, watching her sip the tequila.

"I'll be fine, gentlemen." She looked around at each man. Only Paul Moran seemed affected by her presence, and she looked him in the eye, locking her brown eyes on his steel blues.

"Do you agree with the council's choice, Colonel?" Warrick asked a in playful tone.

"You'll be a capable leader, ma'am," Moran replied, feeling his answer was stilted and robotic. He wondered whether he was indifferent or upset that they had picked her to be the next president over him. He certainly wasn't happy about being left out of the decision-making process. Unlike the stern-faced Moran, Diane Warrick could provide the sweet, trusting countenance the American people would need to turn to in a time of crisis.

Gravely pulled the conversation back to center on the group. "Now, with that announcement made, we can move forward and discuss the changes we'll make after we take command."

Diane Warrick placed her Italian leather briefcase on the coffee table and unbuckled the clasp. She pulled out several sheets of paper and passed them to the men. Moran skimmed over the first page of the six-page document and read a few of the bullet points, under which Warrick had included detailed summaries.

"As you know," Warrick said, "I've tried to cut government waste throughout my entire political career. My first act will be to remove all funding from FEMA and the United Nations. We all agree that it is a uselessly corrupt organization that needs to be shut down. If they want to continue their operations, it won't be on U.S. soil."

"I'd like to say something before you get too far into this," Moran said, holding up the stack of papers. "Your first act should be to assure he American people that we're not going to jeopardize their way of life—that they'll still be able to get up in the morning and go to work, that the lights will still turn on, and the grocery stores will still be fully stocked. We need to let them know this is a fundamental shift in government, a realignment of policies and statutes, not a referendum on their way of life. And the rest of the world needs to know that just because there was a government coup in America, it doesn't mean we're weak and ripe for the taking. Let's make sure we don't give terrorists, crazies, and our foreign enemies the chance to cause chaos while we're not paying attention."

"I couldn't agree with you more," Warrick replied. "That's why I plan to address the nation from the White House as soon as we have control of the government."

"Glad you have it all planned out," a disgruntled Moran growled.

He sat back in his chair and stared at Warrick, who

shifted her gaze to her paper agenda. Moran lifted his drink to his lips and thought back to when they were freshman college students. Warrick had been pursuing a degree in political science, and he had been going through ROTC to get an economics degree. They had dated frequently during their first easy year of school, but their schedules and studies had drawn them apart as time passed. Moran had always wondered what might have happened had he done a better job of keeping up with her.

Instead of letting Warrick continue to discuss her agenda, Moran, still feeling testy, put down his drink and addressed her again. "Just so we're clear on the content of that address, I think the people would like to know their country isn't going to devolve into *The Lord of the Flies*. I think they'll want to know their government is still going to protect them and will build straight roads and big guns. They'll want to know their 401(k)s will be safe and that the value of their house won't go down. No matter how much tweaking of the government we do, if we don't take care of the people, then we'll have failed at our attempt at change. We can't let society devolve into chaos, so we have to instill martial law. My goal has always been to restore order and balance. We must maintain our status as a First World nation and allow our citizens to continue pursuing the American dream."

"Hear, hear!" Killian held up his glass in a toast. "Well said, Colonel. We all want the same thing here. None of us wants chaos."

"Order and balance must come from the chaos *we* create," Gravely interjected. "Changing the government is our chief goal, and it may take some time for those changes to take effect across the board, but in the meantime, we expect a decline in housing and stocks. That's why we agreed to shut down the exchanges. But we're digressing. For now, let's discuss what Senator Warrick has for us."

Moran's team of hackers had broken the firewalls of the servers running the New York Stock Exchange (NYSE), NASDAQ, the American Exchange (AMEX), the Chicago Mercantile Exchange (CME), and the Chicago Board of Exchange (CBOE). The first three represented the largest stock exchanges in the United States and some of the most heavily traded exchanges in the world. In terms of option exchanges, the CME and CBOE were the largest in the country. Moreover, the CME was responsible for trading futures in agricultural and commodity products like coffee, corn, sugar, gold, and silver.

The hackers were poised to shut down the exchanges simultaneously with the launch of the cruise missiles. In the moments after the attack, people would flock to their computers and brokers to sell their holdings, and billions of dollars would flee the markets, as they always did in a time of panic. Shutting down the exchanges would prevent the outflow of money and potentially prevent a major crash from happening. Without access to the markets, the situation would compel people to sit on their fear and refrain from moving their money.

The plan was to secure the country, prove there was no need for panic, and then gradually turn the markets back on. The rest of the world was welcome to panic and sell to their heart's content. Still, Moran, Gravely, and Jackson wanted to ensure that the billions of dollars Americans had invested in the markets through IRAs, 401(k)s, and other investment vehicles held their value.

Warrick pressed past Moran's animosity to continue discussing what needed to be done once they'd seized control of the government.

"We will shut down the Internal Revenue Service as we move to add more tariffs and implement a sales tax revenue system.

"The Environmental Protection Agency will be revamped and downsized. We need to protect our environment, but not at the cost of harming our economy, citizens, and international standing. Removing ineffectual regulations that needlessly bind or restrict businesses from operating at their full potential will be a key component of all our revamping efforts, not just in the EPA. For our second experiment at capitalism, we need to remove the throttles from the system and allow the people and the marketplace to find equilibrium.

"This brings me to my next point: eliminating the Federal Reserve. Any organization that prohibits government oversight or auditing should be disbanded as it does not have the best interest of the people at heart. As the Constitution states, the government will take over printing money, and we will work to re-establish a gold and silver standard and allow the market to dictate interest rates.

"We'll also need to restore the greatness of this country in the hearts and minds of the people, and that means doing away with the Department of Education and Common Core. We plan to empower the States to take charge of education and decide the curriculum, prioritizing vocational studies. What we really need are tradespeople, not bureaucrats and politicians. And, since many teachers on tenure are staunch liberals, we'll remove tenure and allow teachers to be hired and fired based on performance. I'm hoping this will remove much of the liberal indoctrination that happens in our education system from preschool to university."

Warrick looked up from her dissertation and glanced around the room. Much of what she was saying wasn't new, and she'd had similar conversations with men and women all over the country. "Can I get a glass of water, Steven?"

"Of course," Jackson said, rising from his seat and going to the bar. He returned with ice water in a highball glass.

She took a long drink and set it down on the table on a coaster beside the tequila, which was slowly becoming watered down as the ice melted, just the way she liked it. Warrick raised the tequila to her lips and took a sip, letting the liquor burn down her throat and spread across her abdomen. She chased it with ice water and then looked back at her paper. She flipped a page and cleared her throat.

"With record crop prices, we plan to eliminate specific parts of the Department of Agriculture, such as subsidies. Many of you farmers make as much on subsidies as you do on actual crops." She looked pointedly at Steven Jackson, who shrugged. "You're only working the current system, so you're not to blame, but we will eliminate it."

"As it should be," Gravely countered. "Steven and I enjoy our perks as farmers, but we don't need them. Why not eliminate the department altogether?"

"Because we need to teach farmers new methods of farming that do not involve the heavy use of chemicals, herbicides, and pesticides. Only in the U.S. do we allow these large corporations to dictate what goes into our food and how we can label it. GMOs are destroying the health of our citizens and contributing to the rising cost of health care."

Warrick took another drink of water and watched Gravely nod in agreement.

"Next on the list are spy agencies. The NSA will definitely experience a setback from our Sampson strike, and the Defense Intelligence Agency will integrate the CIA into its operations. Many of our security agencies are redundant—nothing more than budgetary black holes. I have a lot of other ideas on how to consolidate our clandestine services, but now isn't the time for that.

"Homeland will be disbanded. It's a massive bureaucratic wasteland of ineptness. Also, we'll revoke the military and police charter capabilities from all government agencies that do not need them. The Post Office, EPA, and many others do not need SWAT teams to carry out their dirty work. That is what we have the U.S. Marshals for."

"This is a great start, Diane, but we have other issues to work through," Shipley said. "What will we do with all the people who are out of work from the government shutdown? There're a lot of things to fix besides axing government dead weight." The radio host heard from his listeners daily about what needed to be addressed outside the Washington Beltway.

Gravely held up a hand to calm his contemporaries. "That's why we are here, Ian—we'll work through all these things and more. But right now, let's take a break."

Moran was thankful to escape the room. He wanted a few moments alone to digest the most recent developments in his planned insurrection.

As the others stood talking in the study, Moran walked outside and stood in the warm sunshine, gazing out over the rows and rows of grapevines stretching to the horizon in every direction. Gravely's house was an island of grass amongst the vines.

A stamped concrete patio surrounded a swimming pool of cool blue water at Moran's feet, and manicured grass extended from the patio to a low concrete wall that enclosed the entire housing compound. There were two ways to reach Gravely's retreat. The first was via a long driveway guarded by a heavy iron gate at the road a half mile away, and the second was by helicopter. And from Moran's vantage point, he could see a sleek black MD 500 Defender glistening in the sunshine on the landing pad.

After Gravely had come on board as an investor, Halberd Security suddenly came into possession of four Defenders matching the one sitting on the pad, except Halberd's

Defenders sported FN HMP400 machine gun pods on the hardpoints.

Moran walked to a small iron gate set into the wall, swung it open, and stepped out into the manicured vineyard.

As an Army officer, Moran had served his country as best he could. After he'd retired, he'd looked at the work he had done from a fresh perspective and saw that much of it had been a waste of time. He'd fought wars on three continents, perpetuating the American petrodollar system and propping up dictatorial regimes friendly to U.S. policies. And when public opinion had swayed one way or the other, he and his fellow soldiers had been the ones caught flapping in the breeze. In time, his civilian views had become more militant, identifying with the radical right that believed it was time to shed patriotic blood to refresh the tree of liberty.

But it was his time on the talk show circuit as a consultant for Fox News and CNN that prompted Moran to examine the real crisis in the world—the decline of strong, effective leadership from the United States. Since World War II, the U.S. had acted as a de facto international policeman. It dictated policy to weaker nations, effectively keeping the peace for millions of people around the world. Through this policy of strength, others saw that democracy was for the people and adopted it for their nations. With America's decline and the current president's worldwide apology tour for any mistakes or wrongdoing that America might have committed along the way, the world was losing faith in the United States to continue to act in the role that many had come to expect.

At the same time, Moran saw opportunities to profit from the doom and gloom, particularly as the U.S. military scaled back operations in the Middle East and began relying on private contractors to provide physical site security, protection details for dignitaries, and to perform combat operations. Moran and Kenny Orlando had started Halberd Security, recruiting men Moran had worked with during his Army days. The company had quickly grown from escorting dignitaries to performing armed combat operations in Africa. As a result of the company's growth, Moran relocated some operations to a former lumber mill in West Virginia and began building a strike force intended to take out FEMA's headquarters at Mount Weather.

While many pundits pointed to the peaceful transition of power in the United States every four years, Moran saw it as just a back-and-forth between the two ruling parties. And the only people winning were the politicians, not the American people.

Moran had come to realize that forcibly removing the offenders from office was the only way to bring about the sorely needed change. To accomplish this goal, he knew a coup from within the U.S. military was out of the question, so he'd begun studying the militia movement and believed the men and women who constituted it were the people he sought to lead a revolt. The birth of Liberty Brigade had been the result of Moran's desire to unite the militias under a common umbrella with standard tactics, operations, and governance. Even before reaching out to various militia groups, he'd developed manuals to help standardize their training. Once he'd had them in hand, he'd set out to bring his vision to as many militias as possible.

During a stop in Northwest Ohio, Steven Jackson had invited Moran to his home and listened patiently as Moran laid out his vision of a united militia and the strength they would have to overthrow the government and change the country's direction. When he'd finished speaking, Jackson had embraced him. He told Moran he would do whatever Moran needed to help achieve the dream.

Moran had explained that he was running his campaign

from a townhouse in Washington, D.C., and that he needed a place to train militia members from around the country. Jackson had shown him his quarry property, offering the site to act as Liberty Brigade's headquarters. The compound had quickly taken shape, and it hadn't been long before militia members from all over the country came calling.

Their activities had also brought the attention of the federal authorities and, in turn, the national media. With the spotlight on him, Moran had soon found himself in Ian Shipley's orbit.

The prominent radio personality had asked Moran to be a guest on his radio show. After a lengthy interview, Shipley had asked him to stay over to have dinner with him. In private, Shipley revealed that he, too, felt the militia movement was the best way forward.

When Moran had left that evening, he'd known he had a new ally in the fight.

CHAPTER FIFTEEN

Two years ago

Several weeks after Moran had met privately with Ian Shipley, the radio talk show host's assistant called to inform Moran that Shipley wanted to meet with him again, but in Puerto Rico this time. She also told him that a private jet would be waiting for him at the general aviation terminal at Allen County Regional Airport in Lima, Ohio, later that evening.

Since it was snowing and Moran had no pressing plans, he gladly accepted the invitation to meet in a much warmer climate, especially since he'd spent the later years of his military career in Tampa, enjoying the year-round sunshine.

Stepping out of his house on the Liberty Brigade compound, Moran found a black SUV waiting for him. Inside was Steven Jackson, who, as Liberty Brigade's first financier and ardent supporter, had also received an invitation, and he'd come to give Moran a lift to the airport.

Once they arrived at the terminal, the two men disembarked the SUV to find a pretty blonde stewardess in a very short, very tight uniform. She led them across the tarmac to the waiting Bombardier Challenger 3500 business jet, which Jackson salivated over as it put his own twin-engine Cessna to shame. While the pilots spooled up the engines, the stewardess offered them a drink and got them situated in the cabin for takeoff.

Several hours later, the jet set down at Antonia Rivera Rodríguez Airport on Vieques Island, Puerto Rico. A car met them at the hangar, and a driver took the two men to a boutique resort several miles away. Inside the resort, a porter showed the men to their rooms and told them to be at the pool bar by five p.m.

Moran tossed his bag on the bed and left the room to find the bar. He needed a stiff drink and to stretch his legs after the long flight. Moran located the bar, ordered a beer, and then made his way to the beach, where the soft crashing of the surf greeted him. As he watched the water rolling in from the Caribbean Sea, he reflected on why he hadn't retired to a place like this instead of Washington, D.C. The reality was that he was never destined for retirement on a tropical beach but to lead Liberty Brigade to a bright new future.

Ian Shipley, Steven Jackson, and a third man Moran didn't immediately recognize were waiting for him when he arrived at the meeting. After getting a fresh beer from the bar, having to help himself as the bartender had ghosted them, Moran sat under the large red umbrella with the other men.

Shipley made the introductions. "Paul, I want to introduce you to Chet Gravely."

Moran shook the entrepreneur's hand, feeling a firm handshake that belied his ample bulk. Sweat glistened on the bald man's head and ran down his face, prompting Gravely to dab at it with a handkerchief. "I'm happy to finally meet you,

Paul. These men tell me good things about you and your operations."

The leader of Liberty Brigade glanced quizzically at Jackson and Shipley, wondering what exactly they'd said.

"Don't worry, Paul. No one is telling secrets out of school," Gravely said reassuringly. "We're all on the same page with what you want to do for our country."

Moran glanced around and, for the first time, realized the resort was devoid of other patrons.

Gravely answered the unspoken question. "I own this little slice of paradise. We're the only guests for the weekend."

"Must be costing you a small fortune to shut it down," Moran remarked.

"I close the place down every year for routine maintenance, but I'd gladly shutter it just to have this meeting. Nothing is more valuable than securing the direction of our country." Gravely stated. "But we're not here for a vacation, are we, gentlemen? We're here because I'm interested in backing your venture, Paul. Ian and I have talked extensively about the direction the country is headed and the radical changes that need to be made to correct the course. We felt it was best to bring you into the conversation since you seem to be the only one doing the work."

Moran had heard of Gravely, his conglomeration of companies, and his billions of dollars in assets. However, he knew little about the man because he was a bit of a recluse. Moran had known right then that he had to either trust Gravely or walk away from the meeting. He had shared part of his vision with Jackson and Shipley, but he hadn't spelled out the entirety of his plan to retake the government to anyone. But he needed help, and if these men were to provide financing and political clout to bring about a revolution, then Moran accepted that he had to trust them fully.

"If you've already spoken with Steven and Ian, then you know about my unification efforts, but unification doesn't mean anything without a catalyst."

"And what might that be?" Gravely asked.

Moran leaned forward, placing his arms on the table, as he outlined his plan, from stealing the missiles and buying the guidance and launch systems from the Russians to uniting the militias into one cohesive unit. Moran took several hours to reveal his master plan. When he finished, the other three men sat back, stunned and breathless at the scope of his plan to overthrow the government.

The next morning, the men gathered at the same table. Chet Gravely looked Paul Moran square in the eye. "I've spent the night thinking about your proposal. As audacious as it is, I think we should proceed."

After the Puerto Rico Summit—as Moran thought of it—Gravely established a shell company and funded it with fifty million dollars with the explicit aim of enabling Moran to dismantle the incumbent U.S. government.

CHAPTER SIXTEEN

Present Day
California Vintage Estates

The Puerto Rico Summit seemed so long ago, yet to an old man like Moran, it had happened in just a blink of an eye. He shook his head in amazement at all they had accomplished, from establishing the Liberty Brigade compound to stealing the missiles and now holding this meeting, where they were solidifying plans for overthrowing the government and deciding who would be the country's next leader.

Moran had always thought a benevolent dictator would be necessary to right the ship before handing it back to the American people, and he had hoped to be at the helm. But his associates planned to make Diane Warrick the new face of the nation—a de facto president until they held new elections.

"Paul?" Warrick said softly.

He turned to find the Senator standing about ten feet away from him. She had changed into blue shorts and a white, collared shirt that flattered her shapely figure. He tossed down the grape leaves that he'd been twisting in his hands during his trip down memory lane.

She's still a beautiful woman, he thought. Warrick had held up well, raising two children and losing her husband to cancer, all in the public spotlight.

To Moran, Warrick looked radiant in the warm California sun—tanned, fit, and relaxed despite planning to commit treason.

"We'd like to get started again," she ventured.

He nodded and began to follow her toward the house. Walking single file through the vines, Moran reached out and took Warrick's elbow, and she turned to face him. Still holding her elbow and standing close, Moran felt breathless and reckless. They'd crossed paths multiple times in Washington, but he'd always refrained from becoming involved with her. At the time, he'd still been married to his wife of twenty years, but she had left him as his fanaticism had grown, taking their two children with her.

"Are you sure about this, Di?" Moran asked. "I mean, if this fails ..."

"It can't fail, Paul. We're doing the right thing." She put her hand on his cheek. "And I'm glad we're working together again."

Moran closed his eyes for a moment, savoring her touch as he visualized the Sampson missiles racing from their launch tubes. Opening his eyes again, he smiled down at the shorter woman. "I'm glad you're on the team."

"Me, too," she replied, pulling back her hand. "I'm counting on your support when this comes to fruition."

"You don't have to worry about—"

Warrick held up a hand to cut him off. "I want you to be

my chief of staff, Paul. If we pull this off, we need to put out a strong front to the world and let them know that even though we've had some internal changes, we are not weak and are not to be trifled with. For that, we need good leaders, both civilian and military. Men such as yourself."

Moran nodded. "Thank you, ma'am." He knew she was stroking his ego—and he didn't mind one bit.

Back inside the house, the servants had laid out a large spread of food for supper. The group filled plates and found seats at the dining table.

Once they'd finished eating, they retired to Gravely's study for another conference that lasted late into the night.

———

MORAN AND GENERAL Killian were up early and ran five miles together before using the weight room. They discussed their issues with the militia plans and the changes they would address within the military. What they didn't talk about, and what Moran could feel the underlying tension from, was what would happen if they failed in their endeavor. As the scape-goat, Moran knew all the players and could bring them all down with him, but he had no plans to do that. He had known Killian for many years and did not want to see any harm come to him.

While everyone else was dressed and ready for the day, Chet Gravely arrived at the breakfast table in his pajamas and robe. He buttered his toast and sipped coffee and orange juice while reading a newspaper, then shuffled off to get dressed, leaving the rest of the group to their own devices until he was ready to begin the day's meeting. To Moran, it seemed quite absurd that the fate of the nation rested on the pudgy billionaire. Regardless of the personalities and posi-tions the rest of the conspirators held, they all had to appease him. When it came down to it, all revolutions required money, and Chet Gravely provided them with boatloads of it.

With everyone seated in the office an hour later, Shipley led the conversation. "One of the biggest complaints I have been hearing is about border security and illegal immigration. How are we going to address that?"

"Easy. We round them up and send them home," Killian retorted. "We already give them cell phones, so they should be easy enough to track. Once they're on their way home, we finish the border wall."

"Or we could just orchestrate another incursion into Mexico and make them part of the United States," Shipley joked.

"We're trying to avoid international incidents," Gravely said condescendingly.

"The border wall has been controversial from the start," Moran interjected. "Trump did a good thing by pushing it through, but I think it will serve us better if we position the military on the border and then implement the laws we already have in place to restrict the hiring and housing of illegals."

"So, what do we do with the immigrants who are already here?" Shipley said, steering the conversation back on topic.

"Like the general said," Moran replied, "we round them up and ship them out. There are lots of buses and trains that we drive into Mexico, unload, and then drive back. Let Mexico sort them out."

"Does that include everyone here illegally? What about the prison population? Muslims? Canadians? Asians?" Warrick wanted to know.

"We would have to sort them out somehow," Shipley said. "We could use the old FEMA camps for that. They're already set up. And once we have the people sorted, we send them back to their home countries."

Everyone nodded in agreement.

"That just leaves all the unemployed workers after we shut down three-quarters of the federal government," Killian said. "What are we doing about them?"

Warrick picked up the ball. "We all know the States can do things better for themselves than the federal government ever can, and the private sector is even more efficient. They'll provide jobs for those who need them as we bring back jobs from overseas and revive industry. In addition, there will be lots of jobs to be filled when we've deported all the illegals. Plus, our infrastructure is falling apart, and I want to establish a program similar to the Civilian Conservation Corps of the early 1930s."

"Great for untrained labor and those with vocations, but what about skilled labor? We know there's a huge shortage of engineers, chemists, mathematicians, and other scientists in our country," Shipley said.

"You're right, Ian," Warrick continued. "We'll still grant entry for candidates with college degrees in certain fields, as we do now with our current visa program. In particular, we'll focus on the STEM vocations—Science, Technology, Engineering, and Math. We'll work to rebuild those programs in our universities and encourage kids to obtain those degrees. In the meantime, we encourage highly skilled foreigners to come to our country legally. Hopefully, we'll have to beat them off with a stick as our economy jump-starts under our decreased regulations and changes."

"If illegals want a path to citizenship, we should provide one," Moran said.

"What's your proposal?" Warrick asked, intrigued.

"We have record low recruitment across the board for our military," Moran said. "I propose they join any branch of service. After their four-year hitch, they're eligible for citizenship."

The group spent the rest of the day deep in discussions about the future changes they had planned for the country. Moran often sat in silence, listening to Gravely, Shipley, and Warrick lay out their ideas, dueling over them and shaping them into the building blocks of the new society they envisioned—a society of doers, thinkers, and performers who desired to better themselves and the world around them.

But Moran knew that in any society, there would be an element of underachievers who lived on the fringes, who allowed others to do the work for them. Completely eliminating them was impossible. Moran accepted them as a necessary element in society because there was no way to change them. He had seen them in the military, which functioned as a microcosm of the real world, taking people from all walks of life and mashing them together to work as a cohesive unit. There were those who outperformed, those who survived, and those who did only what needed to be done to get by. It was the same in any society, be it capitalism or socialism.

Moran also realized he had a limited view of the scope of work that lay before them if they accomplished their coup. He was only a cog in the machine. Though he was the face of a movement intent on reining in tyranny, his job was to lead men of a certain type, not lead nations, and he had could except that.

Coming to terms with his new position in the hierarchy had been a struggle. He wanted to be the leader, the face of the nation. If this conference had taught him anything, it was that he had a single job to do, and it was time to focus exclusively on it. There was precious little time to get bogged down in petty politics with his associates when the coup attempt was just months away.

CHAPTER SEVENTEEN

Liberty Brigade compound
Kenton, Ohio

Kostya Dragomirov glanced again at the balances of his Cayman Islands' bank accounts with a wide smile.

He logged off the banking website, deleted his Internet browsing history, and left the cramped underground bunker where he seemed to spend every waking moment. The underground bunker was small, damp, and cold despite being environmentally controlled to protect the precious electronics.

Stepping out of the barn into the brilliant sunshine, Dragomirov stretched his long, thin limbs before plucking a pack of Sobranie Black Russian cigarettes from his pocket. He lit a cigarette with a plastic lighter and took a deep drag of the heavy smoke, blaming the English for wrecking on the Russian coast in 1553 and bringing tobacco to the masses there. Although the Russian government had outlawed smoking in many public areas, many Russians still smoked like chimneys, and Dragomirov was one of them. He'd smoked since he was thirteen when he'd found a pack of Belomorkanal outside the apartment block where he lived. Dragomirov and a friend had tried them, and he'd been hooked ever since.

Sliding into the driver's seat of one of the many golf carts found around the Liberty Brigade compound, Dragomirov pressed the pedal, and the electric cart sped quickly along the drive that led north from the barn toward the quarry. When the road made a ninety-degree bend to the left, he stopped the cart and got out, walking to the edge of the quarry. Dragomirov often came here to be alone and have a few moments of peace. He smoked his cigarette and lit another one, thanking his lucky stars for the websites that allowed him to purchase his favorite cigarettes and have them shipped directly to the mailbox at the end of the compound's driveway.

It was good to be out of the bunker, away from the struggle to assemble the old equipment that Moran had smuggled in. Dragomirov had to fabricate the missing or damaged parts from scratch based on the schematics, which frustrated Dragomirov due to the pressure Moran and Jackson were putting on him to finish the job quickly.

Dragomirov spent twenty minutes sitting on a ledge above the water, enjoying the warm sunshine before returning to work. He didn't want to go back underground, but Moran had paid him extremely well to do the job. Once he finished, he would jump on a plane to the Caribbean, where he'd never have to be cold again.

As he parked the golf cart beside the barn, Dragomirov found Steve Jackson waiting for him. When Jackson saw Dragomirov slacking off, he demanded, "How much longer?"

Dragomirov shrugged. "It is difficult job putting together the junk you buy."

Jackson glanced away, pursing his lips and placing his hands on his hips. Looking back, he said, "You need to speed it up. We're running out of time."

Dragomirov shrugged again. "I will do my best."

He turned and walked toward the door to the bunker with Jackson right behind him.

Inside the would-be launch control bunker, Jackson took in the electronics scattered around the room. Dragomirov had disassembled the components, spread parts across workbenches, and stretched wiring looms from one side of the bunker to the other, with the assembly racks stacked in one corner.

"Have you done anything in here?" Jackson asked dubiously.

With this American bothering him, Dragomirov immediately yearned for another cigarette. Trying to explain what he was doing to this simple farmer was no use. Jackson and his associates paid Dragomirov to do the work because they couldn't understand the complicated electronics. "I am putting together. I disassemble, clean, repair, and make new. This junk came from twenty-year-old submarine. If equipment was good, different story, but you are asking me to be miracle worker."

CHAPTER EIGHTEEN

Kenton Truck and Machine
Kenton, Ohio

Roy Dombek was like a lot of people. He wanted to be comfortable. His comfort level meant several million dollars in the bank and retirement to his beachfront home in Fort Myers Beach, Florida.

Since he couldn't afford to quit work today, Dombek took comfort in a mason jar partially filled with whiskey and a fine cigar.

His office above the car lot showroom was as comfortable as he could make it, with a heavy oak desk, a leather swivel chair, and an overstuffed leather loveseat. On the wall, Dombek had mounted several televisions that played sports day and night, another for Fox News and one for CNBC. The worst part about his little slice of personally decorated paradise was the sun blazing through the big south and west-facing windows. No matter the season, the sun always seemed to warm the room to a boiling temperature despite two layers of drapes and blinds, and the air conditioner worked overtime during the hot, humid Midwestern summers.

His Alec Bradley Black Market Churchill cigar burned down as Dombek scrolled through the Grosvenor Limited online banking portal, a boutique bank in Freeport, The Bahamas. Shortly after establishing Roy's Guns and Ammo, he had hired a lawyer to set up an offshore bank account under a dummy corporation, Tahoe Unlimited.

Roy's Guns and Ammo, LLC, paid Ammunition USA to purchase ammunition and accessories for the gun shop's brick-and-mortar premise. They, in turn, paid "consulting fees" to Tahoe Unlimited in The Bahamas. It was a complicated system that seemed perfectly legitimate to Dombek, even if he was dodging the IRS by using so many legal entities. This wasn't the first time his attorneys had set up accounts for him, either. He had money stashed in several places, to the tune of two million dollars.

Tahoe Unlimited had grown to just over a million dollars since Paul Moran had moved into town, and Dombek hoped the militia leader would continue to fill his coffers with cash. Despite the legitimate sales at the gun store, he couldn't keep up with Moran's demand for firearms. The former colonel had turned to Dombek to smuggle in weapons as Liberty Brigade's primary supplier, and he paid Dombek handsomely to do so.

The used car dealer leaned back in his chair, took a long pull on the cigar, and blew the smoke toward the vent fan. He logged out of the banking website and settled his bulk before hauling his feet up on the polished wood of the first drawer of the desk.

At fifty-three, Dombek was a fixture around town. His first business venture had been a small auto parts store, which he'd sold to a nationwide chain. Then, he'd established his used car lot that handled farm implements, semi-trucks, and trailers. His comb-over was a source for jokes, but his ability to make money was not—and he had done well over the years. He'd opened the gun store for kicks about five years ago, mainly because he liked to shoot automatic weapons. Now, Paul Moran was in the picture, paying him good money to maintain contact between himself and the underworld and to facilitate the transfer of firearms between the two.

If the Feds were watching him, Dombek didn't know about it, and he'd been extremely careful over the years to mask his dealings with the gun traffickers he favored.

Now, Moran wanted another shipment and was willing to pay top dollar for it. The cost of business had gone up for Dombek's criminal contacts, and he happily passed on the inflated costs to his client. This shipment alone—a consignment of five hundred U.S. Army Colt M4 rifles pilfered from the docks in New York—would net him one hundred thousand dollars for his troubles.

The guns had arrived at the port from the weapons manufacturer, but instead of being loaded onto a ship bound for Ukraine, they had found their way into two van trailers Dombek had purchased explicitly for transporting the firearms. He then hired a trucking company to pick up the trailers and haul them across the country to his car lot. Once the trailers arrived, Dombek would call Wayne Patterson and have him pick them up. Patterson would offload the weapons at Moran's compound and return the trailers to Dombek, who would then resell them and make money on both ends of the deal. The sly salesman always tried to make the shipments look legitimate and make an extra dollar off them while doing it.

Dombek shut down his computer and stubbed out his cigar before swallowing the last snort of his whiskey. He ambled down the stairs to his SUV and headed for home, whistling a cheerful tune. Soon, he could run off to the equatorial sun and forget all about his problems, but that day was far off.

Unbeknownst to Dombek, he was on the brink of being squeezed out of his comfort zone.

CHAPTER NINETEEN

Liberty Brigade compound
Kenton, Ohio

Following a tour of the Liberty Brigade compound, Phillip Upton sat down in Paul Moran's office.

He'd arrived early that morning for his prearranged interview. While Moran hadn't shown him the underground bunkers or the missile control room, the reporter seemed satisfied to take Moran at his word that the militia leader had nothing to hide.

"Beer?" Moran asked good-naturedly. "I know you like your Coors Light."

"Not right now," Upton replied. "I'm on the clock."

"Suit yourself," Moran said. "Coffee?" He held up the pot in his hand.

"Water," Upton said. "If you've got it."

Moran retrieved a bottle of water from a mini fridge and handed it to the reporter. After sipping his black coffee, the militia leader sat behind his desk and asked, "So, what do you want to talk about?"

"The floor is yours," Upton replied, switching on a recording app on his smartphone and reaching for a pad and pencil to jot down the more pertinent parts. "We can discuss the U.N., liberalism—whatever you want."

"How about the plot to destroy the United States since its inception?"

Upton raised his eyebrows.

"No sooner did the signers of the Declaration of Independence declare themselves free of King George III than someone was conspiring to destroy America. At first, it was King George who sent more troops to fight the Revolutionary War and then the subsequent War of 1812. Once the British determined that military might couldn't defeat our young country, others began plotting to bring us down from within."

"Who?" Upton inquired.

"Nowadays, we call them the Deep State, but back then, it was people like the Rothschilds and their banking puppets. These sick people have a fundamental belief that *they* should be considered the elite and everyone else should be enslaved by them. In their twisted minds, it is not for us to decide our fate but for them."

"How are the elite and the plot you mentioned connected? I don't understand."

"In 1922, Alice Bailey established the Lucis Trust, which prints and distributes materials on behalf of the U.N. In tandem, it also publishes Bailey's pagan books. One of her books outlines how spiritual master entities run the world from behind the scenes—which is exactly how the U.N. approaches all of its decision-making. Bailey also developed a ten-point plan to usher in the new world order, and the U.N. has also adopted those goals. The problem with Americans is that we're too trusting. The elite tell us precisely what their plans are, but we're just too dumb and blind to believe what they're telling us.

"In 1958, Cleon Skousen published a book called *The Naked Communist*. In it, he spelled out forty-five goals the Communists had established to take down America.

"Saul Alinsky published *Rules for Radicals* in 1971, and Hillary Clinton studied at his feet, but like everyone else with a set of rules, all they wanted was power. Obama used Alinsky's community organization approach and got elected president. But Clinton and Obama are just two examples. Many in our government still follow Alinsky's teaching and consider his *Rules* as a playbook to end capitalism and destroy America."

"You gotta help me out here, Paul, because I'm still lost," Upton confessed.

"I guess what I'm saying is that all these rules have things in common. They all seek to destroy the family unit, remove religion and God from our lives, and indoctrinate our children to believe in social justice. Do you think those things are happening in our country as we speak?"

Upton seemed unsure but nodded his head as if he concurred.

"Do you know what the difference between socialism and communism is, Phillip?"

"Tell me your version," Upton replied, unsure of what Moran would say but positive it would make an excellent sound bite.

"Truthfully, there is no difference. It's just how they get there. Socialists—or *collectivists*, as I like to call them—believe they can take peaceful control of the individual, their land, and industry by slowly changing government legislation. The communists will just shoot everyone until the rest fall into line. Ultimately, they both want the same thing: a stateless and classless society. Except it's not. There are two classes—the haves and the have-nots. They want to eat prime beef and force you to eat crickets. They want to fly in private jets and ride in limos while you ride a bicycle or walk. They want to live like rock stars in mansions and tell you to be happy that you have nothing.

"The point is that all throughout history, America has been a target for every one of these liberal idiots to direct their anger at, but it's all about power and control for them—which I get. I think some skeptics look at what I'm doing by trying to unite the militias as me building a power base, but that's just media spin. What I'm *trying* to do is give these patriots the best chance to survive when our tyrannical government decides it no longer wants to abide by the rule of law."

"You really think the government is out to get you?"

"Absolutely, it is," Moran retorted. "The ATF keeps a gun registry. The NSA is spying on American citizens through its listening posts in Australia, Canada, New Zealand, and the UK, as well as here at home. Someone intentionally released COVID-19 from the Wuhan laboratory. Bill Gates and Doctor Fauci are telling us another even stronger pandemic is on the horizon. Each of these elements is all about fear and control, just like when the CIA used Project Mockingbird to *control* the U.S. news media. Have you seen the videos where dozens of anchors are all reading from the same script?" Upton nodded as Moran continued. "The FBI colludes with social media platforms to subvert conservative views and censor anyone they deem to be spreading disinformation. So, yeah—I think the government is out to get us."

"I appreciate your knowledge of obscure history, but you haven't given me anything substantial, Paul. I mean, some of it *is* true, but still, everything you've said makes you look like a whack-a-doo."

"You're sitting across from me, Phillip. Do I look like a crazy person to you?"

Upton shook his head as Moran continued. "What I believe is what I believe. But we both know that your censors will chop up whatever you write and edit it to make me look like an even bigger monster, so what do you want me to say?

The reporter pondered Moran's response for a moment, then said, "I want you to give me a frank answer. Why Liberty Brigade? And why now?"

"The United States is at a crossroads, brought upon us by the infiltration of our government by Deep State actors. We can either return to the constitutional republic we were created to be, with a constitution that limits the power of the government, or we can let tyranny reign. The Deep State worships at the altar built by Stalin and expounded upon by Mao Tse-tung, who killed over 86 million people—more than Hitler and Stalin combined.

"What we're facing is a war for the hearts and minds of the American people. The question we need to ask ourselves is, will we be individualists or collectivists?"

"What's the difference?" Upton asked.

"An individual believes their rights must not be subverted by the group, whereas a collectivist believes the rights of the individual must be sacrificed for the greater good. In other words, the group is greater than the individual. An individual provides for himself first, his family second, and then others. A collectivist believes the government is charged with caring for all and will prostrate themselves for the crumbs the group doles out."

"Interesting analogy," Upton observed.

"Our young people are being trained to see capitalism as the enemy and the government as its superior alternative. When Mao rose to power, he instituted a cultural revolution to wipe out all the old ways of life. His Red Guard toppled statues, burned buildings, demonized all religions, and pursued dissident voices. They turned neighbor against neighbor, family against family, and brother against brother. And once Mao had the populace under control, he went even further by shaving women's heads and dressing everyone in the same clothing, basically asexualizing the population to be automatons, so they had no identity. When the Chinese could no longer look to themselves for what they believed, they turned to communism, with Mao as their new god.

"If we look around the globe now," Moran continued, "we'll find our 'leaders' believe China to be a shining example of what our world should look like. Justin Trudeau, the Canadian prime minister; Klaus Schwab, head of the World Economic Forum; and even our president openly admire China and their approach to global governance and population control.

"These men look to Chairman Mao and his revolution as an example of what needs to be done in the U.S. to topple us from the inside. We can compare some of what took place after the death of George Floyd and the resultant Black Lives Matter movement to Mao's revolution. There were riots in the streets, buildings burned, statues toppled, and then, during COVID, everyone from celebrities to politicians told us to screw our rights and mask up. If we didn't, they demonize, ostracized, denigrated, and called us names for not trusting their made-up science.

"Once people live in fear, they demand that someone lead them to safety. And who do the people look to for leadership? *The government.* Obama liked to say, 'Never let a good crisis go to waste.' What he meant was that a crisis is an opportunity for the government to seize power. They will create a bill applauded by the populace as a solution, but in reality, the government is consolidating its power. Over time, if we don't stop their power play, our beloved country will be like China: a nation controlled solely by the government. We'll have a social credit score that forces compliance with government mandates. Suppose one chooses to go against those policies. In that case, the government will shut down their bank accounts, strip them of their property, establish a blacklist to serve as a whip to reestablish moral values, and incentivize the dissidents friends and family to report on their activities. For those that don't comply, they'll put them in a prison camp to 'reeducate' them—another code word for torture, by the way.

"But I want to circle back to Carl Marx and his little manifesto because we can see how his theories are playing out right here in America. One of Marx's central ideologies was to destroy the nuclear family. Children with a mother and father have a central system of support and loyalty that is higher than the state. What we see in our education system is indoctrination that teaches children to fear their parents and that parents do not have the right to choose what is best for their offspring. This forces young minds to look elsewhere for the support they need, be it from teachers, coaches, peer groups ... And when all else fails, as in China, they will turn to the state for guidance."

"Seriously?" Upton broke into Moran's tirade. "You're suggesting that our demand for equal justice after the death of George Floyd equates to Mao's Red Guard? Mao imposed a cultural cleansing, launched under an authoritarian system. While the BLM protests were mostly peaceful, they were intended to raise awareness of racial discrimination in the United States. BLM didn't want to destroy the entire history and traditional culture of our country."

Moran laughed. "Alicia Garza, Patrisse Cullors, and Opal Tometi—the founders of Black Lives Matter—all claim to be trained Marxists and, as such, follow his playbook. Intense financial background checks against BLM and other movements organized by these three women proved they were funded directly by the Chinese and by guys like George Soros, who openly state they want a centralized world government."

"What is the point of this history lesson?" Upton asked irritably.

"You wanted to know what was on my mind," Moran stated. "I think we're at the crossroads of civil war."

"Is that why you founded Liberty Brigade?"

"Liberty Brigade is nothing more than an umbrella organization. I'm not asking anyone to give up the work they're doing with their home militia to join me. My goal is, and has always been, nationalizing what I call the STAMP program—Standard Training and Militia Procurement. When the Founding Fathers wrote the 2A, they wrote 'a well-regulated militia.' That doesn't mean controlled by the government. It means well-trained, well-armed individual citizens who are prepared to defend the country. So, my partners and I have developed standardized training manuals to ensure U.S. militias can operate as cohesive units should the need arise. Much like the training systems we use in the military, these allow for seamless integration of units and practices.

"The procurement portion is to help militia units acquire the gear, tools, vehicles, or whatever else they may need via simple supply chains. There are a lot of companies out there that build military-style gear, and I've made deals with them to sell equipment to my people at reduced rates. The same goes for survival companies, firearms and ammunition manufacturers, and outdoor supply corporations."

"I'm glad you brought that up," Upton stated. "There have been rumors floating around that you're selling black-market firearms stolen from the U.S. Army. What do you say about those allegations?"

Moran's face turned deadly serious as he leaned forward and placed his forearms on the desk. "Phillip, I can assure you that neither myself nor any of my people are selling weapons stolen from the U.S. Army." It was a true statement because Moran had safely cached the guns in his bunker. Everything from SIG Sauer pistols to Stinger missiles resided beneath their feet. "Anytime a guy like me surfaces, the media likes to paint us with the same brush. They think we're all Bible-thumping, gunrunning, white supremacists. Sure, some are, but not me. I love God and want you to know Him personally, but I'm not going to take away your free will to choose what to believe. During my military service, I had the privilege of working alongside people of every race and religion. I never had a problem with any of them unless they didn't do their job."

Moran, wanting to get off the topic of gunrunning quickly, switched to talking about one of his favorite topics, Liberty Brigade.

"Standardizing militia training also saves lives by preventing mistakes. If all personnel receive the same training, working together will be easier. And we need to be as strong as possible. Some of the more liberal states are cracking down on militia movements, branding us domestic terrorists."

"All fifty states have rules prohibiting private militias," Upton said. "And the FBI would brand you as an extremist for your views."

Again, Moran laughed. "Can you believe *anything* the FBI has to say these days? They take orders from the highest bidder."

"Not every agent is on the take, Paul," Upton replied cynically.

"True. There are some excellent agents out there—and we need them. We need effective law enforcement, from the U.S.

Attorney General down to the lowest recruit in the local police department."

"But you don't believe you're extreme?"

"If I'm extreme, it's because my critics have labeled me as such. Obama called us 'bitter clingers' for holding onto our guns and religion to explain our frustrations. Hillary Clinton called half of America a 'basket of deplorables' because she thinks we're racist, sexist, homophobic, xenophobic, Islamophobic, or whatever label she wants to throw at us, which is another Marxist tactic. And that's what left-leaning politicians are good at. They call us names. They put us in boxes. They can't stand the fact we have independent thoughts and views that counter their liberal lies.

"I don't think my ideas are any different from what our Founding Fathers had or those of my father and grandfather. No one wants to pay taxes, and no one wants to live under the thumb of an oppressive government. I want the government to stop growing and demanding changes to the Constitution. I think it's time for the government to listen to the people again. After all, we are not a democracy but a constitutional republic. We elect *representatives*, not leaders.

"And that's another progressive ideal: shift the language so we think differently. Representatives become leaders, and electors become slaves. Our culture is being assaulted, and we're being told to bend over and take it. Who will stand up for the people when the elections are rigged, Phillip?"

Upton raised his eyebrows.

Moran smiled as he said, "Liberty Brigade."

CHAPTER TWENTY

Kenton Truck and Machine
Kenton, Ohio

Caroline Thurmond sat in an old Honda Civic she'd borrowed from a friend. The lights above the bowling alley parking lot cast a dull glow across the stone and asphalt as she checked her watch for the third time in the last ten minutes.

It was five minutes past one in the morning.

While the sheriff's department had not authorized her stakeout of Kenton Truck and Machine, Caroline couldn't let the rumors she'd told Parker Rybeck about pass as just that. She was certain Roy Dombek was doing something illegal. To her, he always seemed too slick, his money too easy, his companies too busy for the small town they operated in.

Last night, two tractor rigs had pulled into Dombek's overflow lot across the street from his dealership and had unhooked twin van body trailers. Caroline just happened to have been sitting in her cruiser just down the street, doing end-of-shift paperwork. Out of curiosity, she'd watched the two drivers park, unhook, and then remove the temporary dealer plates from the trailers before they climbed back into their tractors and headed off into the night.

It had seemed ultra suspicious to the trained investigator.

The following day, she'd made a slow pass through the lot in her private vehicle, discreetly photographing the trailers, before she'd been interrupted by a salesman she knew socially. She'd let him talk her into test-driving a newer model SUV to maintain her cover. When Caroline had asked him about the trailers, his only advice was to "leave it alone," which made her even more interested in what they contained.

Now, in the Honda, Caroline was wide awake despite the late hour. Dispatch had recently moved her to the night shift, so she was used to being awake when everyone else was asleep.

If someone caught her breaking into the trailers, Caroline would find herself out of a job and unable to work in law enforcement ever again.

It was a risk she was willing to take.

Climbing from the compact car, Caroline crept through the shadows, careful to keep out of view of the security cameras mounted on the roof of the car dealership. Staying low and dodging from one large farm implement to another, she quickly covered the ground to the semi-trailers.

When she'd done her earlier recon, Caroline had seen that the shipper had sealed the locked doors with small metal tags. After her hurried test drive, she'd stopped by a local trucking company to ask if they had any tags to match, showing them a picture of the tags she'd taken with her cell phone. Since Caroline was an officer of the law, they had kindly given her two tags and the special pliers used to attach them. She promised to return the pliers as soon as possible.

Slipping the pliers from the back pocket of her jeans, Caroline used them to break the seal on the trailer and then swung the door open just enough for her to climb inside. She pulled it gently shut behind her, careful not to close it completely lest she get locked inside.

Clicking on the flashlight app on her phone, Carolina saw several pallets with multiple green metal boxes strapped to the trailer's deck. She counted twelve boxes in total as she photographed them. Unfastening one of the ratchet straps that held the boxes fast, Caroline opened the lid on the top box and drew in a sharp breath when she saw the Colt M4 rifles inside.

She'd figured there were rifles in the crates since she had seen plenty of rifle shipping containers while serving in the Army, but seeing brand-new rifles was a shock. Caroline knew from handling an M16 and an M4, as both an Army private and a sheriff's deputy, that the manufacturer stamped serial numbers on the left side of the magazine well.

Quickly, she unscrewed the two wing nuts for the metal bar that held the guns in place. Once she detached the bar, Caroline removed a rifle and photographed the serial number. Replacing it, she reached for a second rifle and snapped a photo of it, too.

Handling the rifle felt good. It brought back old memories, but Caroline wasn't there to relive her glory days on the battlefield. Caroline shoved the rifle back into the crate, refastened the bar into place, closed the lid, and tightened the cargo strap.

Back outside, Caroline found she was sweating heavily. Not only had the heat in the trailers been stifling, but she was also scared. Now that she knew what Dombek was into, she also figured the smugglers probably had no qualms about killing her to keep it a secret.

With shaky hands, Caroline fumbled for the new metal

tag, dropping it once before getting it fastened in place on the trailer. She was breathing too fast. Her heartbeat sounded like thunder in her ears.

Moving to the second trailer, Caroline paused to take a deep breath. She had to get the photos she'd taken of the M4s to Rybeck so he could figure out the source of the weapons, but Caroline wished she had brought a tracking device to find out where the guns were going.

Before she could break the tag on the second trailer, Caroline heard a diesel engine and the crunch of tires on gravel. Glancing around the corner of the trailer, she saw two semi-tractors backing into the lot, preparing to align with the trailers she was hiding behind.

Moving backward, Caroline kept the trailer between herself and the nearest truck. When she reached a large bucket truck, she rolled underneath it. From her vantage point, she could see the tractor's license plate. Fishing her phone from her pocket again, Caroline pointed it at the semi and took several pictures.

A large piece of gravel was digging into her knee, and Caroline had to bite her lip to keep quiet. She dared not move as Wayne Patterson helped another man hook up the trailers, then performed a walked-around inspection and kicked the tires.

Ten minutes after they had arrived, the trucks pulled out of the lot. Caroline rolled out from under the cover of the utility truck and breathed a sigh of relief. She was thankful to be off the gravel and glad the truckers hadn't spotted her. The stakeout had been a success, and her phone was full of images of the two truck drivers, their tractors, and the license plates on each. Darting to the Civic, she started it up, then pulled out to follow the trucks.

As she suspected, the semis led her to the Liberty Brigade compound after taking a circuitous route through the countryside. Once she had confirmed the final destination of the semis, Caroline turned off on another road and drove rapidly toward home.

Before she made it to her house, Caroline pulled off to the side of the road and killed the engine. Taking a deep breath, she forced herself to calm down. More deep breaths helped to slow her heart rate and recenter her focus. She hadn't been in this much danger since she'd left active duty.

Once she felt more in control of her emotions, Caroline composed an email to Rybeck, having found his work email on the FBI's website. She attached all the photos she'd taken of the guns, trucks, and drivers, knowing the images were inadmissible in court. Caroline had broken the law in obtaining the photographs of the firearms in the trailer. However, the intelligence she'd gleaned proved that her suspicions about Dombek had been correct. At least, she could turn the serial numbers of the rifles over to Rybeck and let him trace their origins.

With a sense of pride, Caroline hit the send button. The investigation was in Rybeck's hands now.

CHAPTER TWENTY-ONE

FBI Resident Agency Office
Lima, Ohio

Parker Rybeck sat at his desk with a cup of coffee in one hand and a stale bear claw in the other. Normally, he ate a decent breakfast, but he'd woken up late this morning. He had been in a hurry to attend a weekly all-hands staff meeting, with SAC Talbot in attendance via video conference.

He set the half-eaten bear claw on his desk and clicked open his email. He read through interoffice briefings and then clicked on the email from Caroline Thurmond, having, in his mind, saved the best for last.

As he read the email and scanned the photos, his eyes widened. Reaching for the phone, he dialed Caroline's number, not caring that she might be asleep after working the night shift.

"Where did you get these pictures?" he demanded after Caroline answered.

"I took them last night," she replied groggily.

"You found those guns in the trailers on Dombek's car lot?" Rybeck pressed.

"Yes." Her voice was clearer now that she was fully awake.

Rybeck motioned his partner over to look at the pictures.

"And they moved the guns to the Liberty Brigade compound," Rybeck said, confirming what she had written in her email.

"Yes, Parker. I followed them there," Caroline replied.

"Throw out the pictures of the guns, and all we have is a couple of guys moving some trailers around," Pratt pointed out.

"I realize that," Caroline said, having overheard Pratt, "but at least you can trace where the guns came from, and if nothing else, it implicates Moran, the militia, and Dombek in receiving, transporting, and distributing stolen goods."

"What you did could have cost you your job, Caroline," Rybeck warned. "If Dombek caught you, he could have pressed charges against you for trespassing and breaking and entering."

"I know, Parker," she said in exasperation. "I don't need a lecture. What I need are answers. I want this militia out of my town."

"We'll run the plates and the serial numbers, but we can't use any of this in court," Pratt said to both.

"But it's a start, and it seemed like you guys were kinda floundering around … I mean, based on the questions you asked me at Skinny's."

"Thanks for the vote of confidence," Rybeck shot back.

Caroline sighed. "I'm just trying to help, Parker."

"I know," he replied softly. "Thank you for what you did. We'll do what we can from this end. How about dinner this evening, and you can tell me the whole story?"

"Absolutely, I'm off tonight."

"Good," Rybeck said. "I'll call you later, and we can figure out the details. Right now, I need to get back to work."

Caroline yawned. "Talk to you later."

When Rybeck hung up the phone, Pratt was already running the firearm serial numbers through the ATF's federal database. Rybeck opened the Ohio Department of Motor Vehicles website and input the license plate numbers from the semi-trucks. They came back almost immediately as being registered to a trucking firm called Conner Enterprises. Another search revealed that Tim Conner owned Conner Enterprises, and his business was just down the road from their field office.

As they were grabbing their suit jackets and about to head out the door, the phone on Pratt's desk rang. He glanced at Rybeck, then picked up the phone.

"Agent Pratt," he said. He listened momentarily, and then his face turned a shade whiter. "Ukraine? They're not in Ukraine. My informant took those photos in Kenton, Ohio." Wide-eyed, Pratt turned to face his partner. "I'll call my agent in charge right away."

He hung up the phone and then picked it back up, punching in a new number. As he placed the phone on speaker and listened to the line ring on the other end, Pratt said to Rybeck, "We've stepped in it now. Those guns were part of a shipment to Ukraine. The ATF is dumbfounded as to how we came across them."

When Talbot's secretary came on the line, she informed them that Talbot was out of the office. Pratt gave her the gist of his conversation with the ATF agent and asked her to have Talbot call him as soon as possible.

After ending the call, Pratt straightened. "Nothing we can do about it now, but wait for the big man to call us back and tell us what he wants us to do."

Rybeck shrugged. "In the meantime, we might as well

visit Conner Enterprises while we wait for our tongue-lashing."

———

FIFTEEN MINUTES LATER, Pratt nosed the government-issued sedan into the parking space outside the small office of Conner Enterprises in a rundown industrial complex on the outskirts of Lima.

Inside the cramped office was a reception area with an overweight blonde woman behind the desk, guarding a closed door that Rybeck assumed was Tim Conner's office.

Both agents flipped open their badges and identified themselves to the secretary, who squirmed in her chair as she pressed several buttons on the desk phone. They could hear the phone ringing through the flimsy interior office door before a man's voice answered with, "Yeah, Darcy."

Darcy glanced up at the agents, clearly uncomfortable. In a nasally voice that grated on Rybeck's nerves, she informed Conner of the agents' arrival.

Conner opened the door. "Come on in, fellas."

He was a short man with a wide face, thick eyebrows, and deep-set blue eyes. He pushed his black cowboy hat back on his head as he examined their identification badges.

"Tell me what I can do for you?" Conner asked, returning to the desk to plop himself into his chair.

Rybeck and Pratt took seats in folding steel chairs across from the desk. The office had seen better days, and Rybeck hoped the man kept better records than his overstuffed filing cabinets suggested.

Pratt motioned for Rybeck to take the lead, and the younger agent pulled a notebook from his pocket and clicked open his pen. "Last night, two of your tractors—Fifteen and Twenty-one—picked up some trailers at Kenton

Truck and Machine. Who contracted with you for that job?"

"No one," Conner replied.

Rybeck and Pratt exchanged dubious glances.

Seeming to read their thoughts, Conner explained. "You see, times have been tough, and I've had to contract out several of my rigs. I have a fleet of twenty-five, but nine are offsite on lend-lease arrangements."

"Can you tell us who is using those trucks?"

"JP Transit from Kenton has Thirteen, Fifteen, Nineteen, Twenty, and Twenty-one, and Archer Transport out of Wapakoneta has Seventeen, Twenty-two, Twenty-three, and Twenty-four."

Rybeck scribbled down the numbers and company names in his notebook before asking, "How long has JP Transit been leasing the rigs?"

"Oh, about seven months," Conner said. "They're pretty good customers. They pay on time and take excellent care of the rigs. I've never had any problems with them. What's this all about?"

"Have you seen either of these men?" Rybeck held up his phone to show Conner pictures of the men Caroline had photographed driving the trucks.

While looking at the first photo, Conner said, "I've never seen him before." Rybeck flipped to the second, and Conner's eyebrows rose as he spoke. "But that's Wayne Patterson. He's the owner of JP Transit. What's going on here, fellas?"

"I guess that wraps it up," Pratt said. "Thanks for your help, Mr. Conner."

Still puzzled about what his trucks were involved in, Conner said, "Glad to be of service."

———

Once the two FBI agents had returned to the office, Rybeck decided he would head for Kenton to look at Dombek's operation and maybe stop by the gun store.

"Say hi to your girlfriend," Pratt jibed as Rybeck headed out the door.

He called Caroline from his truck, and she told Rybeck to meet her at Jitterz Coffee Company on the square across from the courthouse.

It didn't take Rybeck long to find the place, and Caroline was waiting inside when he arrived. They ordered coffee and found a table near the front window. As they passed a table with a paraplegic hunched over a computer, Caroline waved.

"You know him?" Rybeck asked, glancing over at the guy.

"That's the owner's son-in-law."

"What's he doing?" Rybeck asked.

"Trying to write the next great American novel, I guess," Caroline replied, then sipped her coffee and turned her attention out the window.

Rybeck studied her profile, waiting for her to speak.

"What about the guns?" she asked softly, leaning forward so as not to be overheard. "Have you heard anything back from the ATF?"

"They were part of a shipment headed to Ukraine. I guess they're scrambling to figure out how they fell off the truck and landed in Kenton."

She nodded as if expecting it to have happened that way. "What about JP Transit? They own those trucks, right?"

"No," Rybeck replied. "A company called Conner Enterprise owns them."

"But Wayne Patterson was driving the truck. I saw him with my own eyes."

"And Conner identified him," Rybeck added.

"Do you know what the 'J' in JP Transit stands for?" Caroline asked.

Rybeck shook his head.

"'Jackson,' as in Steven Jackson. He and Patterson have been partners for years. I bet they're helping Moran run guns."

"It stands to reason," Rybeck agreed. "Jackson set Moran up with land and money."

Caroline sat back and stared out the window again, shaking her head in disbelief. "I can't believe this is happening in my little town."

"We have to follow the evidence, which means finding a way to track the semis and find out where they've been?"

"Traffic cameras?" she suggested.

Rybeck wasn't sold on the idea. "Too many, and it would take too long to sift through all of them."

They both lapsed into thought as they sipped their coffee.

Suddenly, Caroline looked up from the table, her eyes glowing. "Weigh stations!"

"Weigh stations?" Rybeck repeated, not following her train of thought.

"Patterson's operation is small. I don't know if they use GPS tracking for their rigs, so maybe we can track them through the weigh station. The stations keep a record of all the trucks that pass through them. All we need is the license plates for the trucks, and we can track them anywhere they go."

"As long as they went through a weigh station," Rybeck replied hesitantly.

"Patterson ships up and down the east coast. He has to have the trucks registered to go through the weigh stations. Each truck has a transponder that transmits the truck number, carrier name, and weight of the vehicle. If they go past a weigh station, the transceiver reads the truck, checks the vehicle safety and compliance record, and verifies the weight as it goes over a scale built into the road."

Rybeck nodded. "We can check them out, but if the semis bypassed the scales or didn't go near them, we might not get anything."

"But you might get *something*."

"We can only hope," Rybeck said.

CHAPTER TWENTY-TWO

FBI Resident Agency Office
Lima, Ohio

"Where have you two been?" Roger Talbot barked as Pratt and Rybeck entered the office the following day.

"We just got in," Pratt said, holding up a cup of coffee.

Rybeck understood immediately that their investigation had become intriguing enough for Talbot to drive down from Cleveland. The SAC was a pasty white guy with graying hair and rectangular glasses. He wasn't easily excitable, but today, he seemed flushed.

"Get your butts into my office and tell me why I've got the ATF breathing down my neck."

"Yes, sir," Pratt said, leading Rybeck toward the SAC's office.

Rybeck shut the door, and the three men found seats.

Talbot leaned forward, placing his arms on the desk. "What's going on?"

Pratt cleared his throat. "We got a tip about some illegal firearms being trafficked into the Liberty Brigade compound."

"Who's the source?" Talbot asked.

Pratt glanced expectantly at his partner.

Rybeck fidgeted in his chair, choosing his words carefully. "I'd rather not say."

"You're not a journalist, Rybeck," Talbot growled. "You don't get to protect your sources."

Rybeck relented, knowing he had no other recourse. "The source is a fellow law enforcement officer who we feel would be put in danger if it was leaked that they were assisting our investigation."

"Fine, I'll take that answer," Talbot retorted.

"You shouldn't," Pratt said, looking pointedly at his partner.

Talbot's gaze shifted between the two men, silently letting them work out their issues as Rybeck glared at Pratt.

When neither man spoke to follow up on Pratt's statement, Talbot turned to Rybeck. "Confession time—and I want *full* disclosure."

Rybeck sighed and then detailed his first encounter with Officer Thurmond to their date last night.

"So, none of this gun stuff is admissible in court?" Talbot said, shaking his head. He looked up sharply at Rybeck. "Are you screwing this deputy?"

"No, sir," Rybeck replied. "It's merely a platonic relationship I'm using to gather information about the Liberty Brigade. I did not coerce her into breaking into those trailers."

Talbot swore under his breath as he rubbed his face with

his hands. "I'm going to regret this, but show me the email. The ATF is still hot to trot about these guns."

Rybeck borrowed the SAC's computer and pulled up his email account, showing his boss the pictures Caroline Thurmond had taken.

"Next time, keep me in the loop," Talbot said. He started to say more, but the phone rang, interrupting him. The SAC answered sharply, then handed the phone to Pratt. "It's the ATF. You started this mess; you clean it up."

While Pratt handled the call, Rybeck launched into an explanation of tracking the semis from JP Transit. Talbot agreed to give them some leeway to investigate. It didn't thrill the SAC that Rybeck's attention was starting to divert from the original investigation into Liberty Brigade.

Once Pratt was off the phone, Talbot shooed them out of his office. "I have to get back to Cleveland. Next time I come down here, it better be for something good."

Even though Pratt had called Talbot to tell him about his conversation with the ATF, both agents promised to keep their boss better apprised of the investigation before heading for their office.

Rybeck contacted the Ohio State Highway Patrol to better understand how to track the semi-trucks. The patrol referred Rybeck to the Public Utility Commission of Ohio (PUCO) Motor Carrier Enforcement Unit.

Brenda Sellers, a PUCO employee, became Rybeck's contact, running checks based on the transponder units registered to JP Transit and Conner Enterprises. Since this was an FBI investigation, she was given priority over other jobs and immediately began pulling the necessary data.

———

THE FOLLOWING AFTERNOON, Brenda Sellers called Rybeck back. "There's a warrant in your email inbox. I need you to sign it so we can proceed."

Rybeck opened his email and quickly scanned through the warrant documents. "What am I looking at, Brenda?"

"JP Transit uses a company called Digital Truck Route for their tracking services. We need access to their servers, and they won't allow us in without the warrant."

Before he e-signed the paperwork, Rybeck said, "A search warrant might tip them off."

On the other end of the phone, Brenda let out a sigh of exasperation. "JP won't know that we looked at their records. The warrant comes with a gag order not to discuss the requested information. PUCO has dealt with Digital Truck Route before, and they've never given us any problems. They are a by-the-book organization."

"Let's hope they keep their mouths shut," Rybeck said as he e-signed the warrant and returned it. "I just sent it back. What did you find out about the weigh station tracking?"

"We've collected all the information we can on the weigh stations. Those records won't be complete, however, because it's not exactly difficult to avoid the weigh stations and most of the trucks JP Transit operates don't travel near a weigh station—as in, they're operating in farming country and on rural routes."

"Thanks, Brenda," Rybeck said. "How soon will the warrant come through?"

"A couple days," she replied, trying not to get Rybeck's hopes up that this would be a fast process.

———

SEVEN DAYS LATER, Brenda Sellers called Agent Rybeck again. "I just emailed you all the files we collected from

Digital Truck Route. You can look at every truck JP Transit has driven with a tracker on it, all the way back to when they started using DTR in 2013."

"Did you see anything strange?" Rybeck asked.

"No," Brenda replied. "Most of what I saw were routine shipping routes."

Rybeck opened his email and clicked on the first file. "I guess I'll start with Truck One."

"I'm already into One," Brenda said. "You get Two."

Rybeck opened the second file and had to ask Brenda what the various acronyms meant and how to interpret some of the data points.

Once Rybeck was off the phone, he sent Pratt the file for Truck Three, and the three of them began combing through the digital files, looking for anything to implicate JP Transit in the trafficking of illicit firearms.

It was Brenda who called to report her discovery that Truck Five had received a red light ticket in Port Arthur, Texas, that had yet to be paid.

"And that's *way* off JP's normal route," Brenda said. "The funny thing is that there's no tracking information for Truck Five between Ohio and Texas and back, but the City of Port Arthur filed the red light ticket against the truck's license plate."

Rybeck took down the information for Five and then called the Port Arthur Police Department. He requested they send the red light ticket information to his email. The dispatcher sent it immediately.

Opening the email, Rybeck printed out the pictures of the tractor-trailer rig and a copy of the ticket. The enlarged photos clearly showed the front license plate of a Kenworth T2000 and two men in the cab of the truck. The driver was none other than Wayne Patterson, but Rybeck didn't know the identity of the passenger.

While it felt like a eureka moment, Pratt and Rybeck continued to comb through the records, looking for more anomalies. They ordered lunch and eventually called it quits at five that evening.

Rybeck went to the gym and spent an hour working out before driving to his apartment. He couldn't get his mind off the truck records, however, and after grabbing some leftovers from the fridge for dinner, he drove back to the office.

He was changing the filter to make a fresh pot of coffee when the phone on his desk rang. It was after seven in the evening, and he wasn't expecting any calls. Rybeck hurried into the office and bumped into the desk, sending an avalanche of old file folders sliding across its wooden surface. He grabbed the phone and clamped it between his shoulder and ear, still holding the filter.

"Agent Rybeck here. How may I help you, sir or ma'am?"

"Navy or Marine Corps?" The person on the other end of the line asked.

"Coast Guard."

The stranger chuckled. "I could tell by the way you answered the phone with the sir and ma'am stuff. Old habits die hard, don't they, Puddle Pirate?"

"Yeah," Rybeck said. "They kinda do. Now, who do I have the pleasure of speaking with, *sir*?"

"This is Detective Bryce Nixon, Port Arthur PD."

"What can I do for you, Detective?"

"You're the guy looking into a red light ticket for a semi-truck down here, right?"

"Yes," Rybeck replied. "Do you have more information than what they emailed me?"

Nixon chuckled. "Not on the ticket. But boy, do I have a story for you."

Begrudgingly forgoing the coffee, Rybeck tossed the filter

on his desk and leaned back in his chair, interested in what the detective had to say. "Go ahead, Nixon. Tell me a story."

"On the night your semi-truck busted through the red light, I got a tip from a homeless guy that he'd seen some guys loading a cruise missile into the back of a truck that fits the description of our red light runner."

"A homeless guy? Was he drinking?" Rybeck asked.

"He was sober when I talked to him," Nixon said. "He used to work on cruise missiles on submarines in the Navy before he got busted out. If the guy says he saw a cruise missile, I believe him. When the boomers, those are submarines that carried ballistic missiles, transitioned from ICBMs to cruise missiles, my guy helped with the changeover on his sub."

"Did you file a report?" the FBI agent asked.

"I did," Nixon said, "but my chief just laughed at me. I sent it to the FBI office in Houston but never heard anything back about it."

"Can you send me your report?" Rybeck asked.

Nixon reached for a pen. "Give me your email and I'll send it to you."

Rybeck gave the detective his email address, then leaned forward, expecting his computer to chime at any moment. As he waited, he asked, "What do you make of the story, Nixon?"

Nixon paused. "I think it has legs. Call me if you need anything else."

Rybeck set the receiver back in its cradle, got up, and finished making the coffee he'd started earlier. As the pot brewed, he returned to his computer and studied the file on Truck Five.

As a passing thought, Rybeck pulled up the red light photo and cropped the image so only the passenger's face was visible, then fed it into the FBI's facial recognition database, hoping for a clue as to the man's identity and what he was doing in Patterson's truck. Rybeck knew it would take some time for the software to match facial nodes and didn't expect a hit any time soon.

He also made a copy of the photograph, attached it to an email to Caroline Thurmond, and asked her to keep an eye out for the stranger. Then he printed the email Bryce Nixon had just sent to him.

As the printer spewed out sheets of paper, Rybeck finally poured piping hot coffee into his old ceramic Coast Guard mug that he had carried with him since graduating from boot camp. Back at his desk, he found Nixon's report and a brief, handwritten history of the source, Allen Montgomery.

Rybeck reread the sheets of paper, preferring to hold them over staring at a computer screen. He had been an outdoor kid, and while Rybeck had been around computers, he'd never much cared for them.

The line that struck him from Nixon's report was that Patterson had covered the missile with corn. Rybeck pulled up the file on Truck Five, but there wasn't a single weigh station slip from a run to Texas and back. Like Brenda Sellers, he found no GPS data for the run to Texas, but a brief entry caught his eye. According to Digital Truck Route's records, the truck had been idle in JP Transit's yard instead of on the move between Texas and Ohio.

Rybeck sat back and sipped his coffee, pondering the reason for the deception. He wondered if someone had temporarily removed the transponder from the truck.

If they had, then JP Transit was definitely up to no good.

Rybeck's spine tingled. In Nixon's report, Allen Montgomery had stated that the cruise missiles had not been of U.S. design. "So, where did they come from?" he asked the empty office.

When Rybeck dialed the number for the FBI's National Security Branch in D.C., he didn't anticipate anyone answering at this late hour. He was pleasantly surprised, however, to hear a female voice on the other end. "Shandra Everhart speaking."

"Hi, Shandra. My name is Special Agent Parker Rybeck. I work out of the Cleveland, Ohio, Field Office. Can you tell me if there have been any reports of cruise missile thefts in the past six months?"

"May I have your badge number, please?" Shandra asked.

Rybeck recited it. He could hear typing on the other end of the line and figured she was checking his credentials.

"Hold on," Shandra said. "The computer is a little slow this evening."

"I understand. They always are when you're in a hurry."

She clicked more buttons. "Okay, Agent Rybeck, there was a report issued on February fifth of this year about the hijacking of an Estonian cargo vessel in the Caribbean Sea."

Excited to make a connection between the hijacking and the red light ticket, Rybeck said, "Can you send me the report?"

"Yes, hold on ... Ough! Stupid computer!" She sighed in exasperation. "Finally! Okay. What's your email address?"

Rybeck's computer chimed a minute later, signaling he had a new email. He opened the file and told Shandra it had arrived, and they both signed off.

Rybeck poured more coffee and read the report by Commander Jim Booth, captain of the USCGC *Valiant*. Rybeck smiled to himself as he sipped his coffee. He knew Captain Booth from when they'd served together on a different ship during Rybeck's time in the Coast Guard.

According to Booth, upon intercepting the drifting *Alexsander Ushakov,* his crew had found four empty missile crates on board, and a civilian passenger was subsequently missing. Booth had also included the rumor circulated by the *Ushakov* crewman that the missing passenger was actually a Russian engineer for NPO Novator, and the empty crates had contained cruise missiles bound for Venezuela.

Slowly, leaning back in his seat, Rybeck contemplated the report made by Allen Montgomery and wondered if the man in the semi with Patterson was the missing engineer.

If Wayne Patterson had picked up one missile, other JP Transit trucks might have also picked up missiles.

While there were multiple reasons as to why Moran had acquired the Sampsons, from trafficking them to fund his militia to putting a crimp in Venezuela's supply chain, Rybeck believed, based on the man's rhetoric, that he planned to use the missiles as a first-strike option against the government.

Putting two and two together, the only logical place for the missiles to end up was the Liberty Brigade compound in Kenton.

"Looks like Moran might be a bigger threat than we thought he was," Rybeck muttered.

CHAPTER TWENTY-THREE

R ybeck summoned Brenda Sellers to the office early the next morning. Since neither he nor Pratt were well versed in the program used by Digital Truck Route, he wanted Brenda's expertise.

Once she arrived, he asked her to search through the records from December of the previous year to February of the current year to ascertain if any trucks had been idle.

It didn't take long for her to determine that Trucks Five, Seven, Eleven, and Twelve had been idle during the requested period.

"I have to say, I'm a little confused. Truck Five ran the Port Arthur red light on February ninth, but this data doesn't support that," Brenda noted.

"*Exactly*," Rybeck replied, continuing to ride the rush of euphoria he'd been on since last night. Even the thought of Moran possessing four rogue cruise missiles could not temper his excitement.

"So, how did they make the trucks appear idle?" Pratt asked. "Did they take the transponders off?"

"It certainly looks that way," Brenda replied.

"Can they do that?" Pratt asked.

"Doesn't matter whether they can—it's what they did. They made it look like the trucks were sitting at JP Transit's headquarters," Rybeck replied. "But the red light ticket blew the entire scheme."

"I think we need to talk to Digital Truck Route and find out what's going on," Pratt stated.

"I agree," Rybeck said, "but let's concentrate on those three trucks and see if we can come up with something for them first."

Each took a record and dug through it carefully, looking for any helpful clue.

———

AN HOUR LATER, Pratt announced, "A Florida State Trooper pulled over Truck Twelve for trying to avoid a weigh station. It was two thousand pounds over the weight limit when a trooper stopped it, and he cited it accordingly. No safety violations."

"What was it carrying?" Rybeck asked.

"Corn," Pratt replied.

Rybeck smiled. "Do you have the number of the trooper who pulled that truck over?"

"Yeah, it's listed right here." Pratt read it off as Rybeck punched numbers into the desk phone. He left it on speaker as it rang. The call eventually went to the voicemail of Trooper Kyle Smoot. Rybeck left his phone number and asked him to call back.

Holding the phone, Rybeck said, "Okay, next call. Brenda, what's the number for Digital Truck Route?"

She read off the number while he dialed. When a secretary answered, Rybeck identified himself as an FBI agent, and she passed him up the line to James Stokes, DTR's director of operations.

When he came on the line, Rybeck introduced himself again and said, "Mr. Stokes, I need to ask you a few technical questions about your GPS tracking devices."

"Go ahead," Stokes replied.

Rybeck cleared his throat. "If a truck is equipped with one of your tracking devices, is it possible to defeat it somehow?"

Even over the phone, Stokes sounded genuinely puzzled. "What do you mean by 'defeat?'"

Rybeck clarified his question. "Can a truck be driven while the GPS says it's stationary?"

"I don't see how it could," Stokes replied. "If a GPS receiver moves, then it will record that movement. We plug our transmitters directly into the truck's electrical systems, and they send data to a recorder every thirty seconds. We can tell exactly where the truck is to within ten feet so that we can monitor speeds and excessive time spent at idle. Plus, we can use that data to alter routes according to the needs of a company."

"Is it possible to disengage the tracker from a truck and attach it to a battery so it still reports to your company?" Rybeck asked.

"It *might* be possible, but it would take some effort. We would know if a truck went offline."

"The reason I ask, Mr. Stokes, is that I've been searching through records that we subpoenaed from your business, and those records show four trucks that went on extensive trips while the GPS trackers say they were idle."

"That's impossible," Stokes said indignantly.

"Well, it is possible," Rybeck said. "One truck received a red light ticket in Texas, and a trooper in Florida issued a citation to another for being overweight."

"I guess it's possible to remove the trackers from the

trucks and then hook them to an external power source to appear stationary, but why would they want to go through all that effort?"

"That's the million-dollar question, isn't it?" Rybeck replied.

"I'm afraid I don't have the answer for you, Agent Rybeck. Is there anything else I can do for you?" Stokes asked.

"That was it, sir. I appreciate your time."

"You're welcome, Agent. I'm sorry that I couldn't be more helpful," Stokes said as Rybeck hung up the phone.

Rybeck turned to his colleagues. "I think we have all the information we'll get on these trucks. Thanks for helping us out, Brenda."

"Before you dismiss me so quickly, I'd like to know what's going on," she said to Rybeck.

"The owner of those trucks is using them to smuggle some high-tech weaponry, and now it's up to us to figure out where those weapons are."

The PUCO officer raised her eyebrows. "Should I alert the Highway Patrol?"

"No need. I think they've already delivered the weapons," Rybeck replied. He saw Pratt eyeing him, begging to ask what weapons his partner was talking about.

Brenda picked up her purse. At the door, she paused. "Well, thanks for letting me play with you boys. If you need anything else, let me know. I'm just a phone call away."

No sooner had the door closed behind her than Pratt leaned forward and hissed, "Spill the beans, Parker."

"Give me ten minutes," Rybeck said. "I need to email Talbot."

After typing a message and clicking send, Rybeck picked up the phone and dialed Talbot's extension in Cleveland. The SAC had given the two agents a direct line of access since the ATF and Talbot's boss in Washington were breathing down his neck for updates. Talbot answered on the fourth ring with, "This is Talbot on a secure line."

"Rybeck here, and I've got Pratt with me. You're on speaker, sir."

"This better be good, Rybeck," the SAC chastised.

"Sir, there should be an email in your inbox with photos and reports to back up what I'm about to tell you. I think we've uncovered something bigger than Moran smuggling firearms into the Liberty Brigade compound," Rybeck said.

"What do you mean?" Talbot demanded.

Rybeck took a deep breath and plunged in, knowing he had only a thread of facts to work with. He quickly summed up the report from Captain Booth, ending with, "On February ninth, a semi-truck driven by Wayne Patterson ran a red light in Port Arthur, Texas. The camera shows Patterson with a second man in the cab. I think he's the missing Russian engineer. I sent you the photo."

"I'm looking at his ugly mug right now," Talbot replied. "What makes you so sure these two incidents are connected?"

"The same night Truck Five ran a red light, a man named Allen Montgomery, a former Navy machinist's mate, reported to the Port Arthur PD that he saw some guys loading a cruise missile into a tractor-trailer rig that matches the description of Truck Five in the JP Transit fleet. They backfilled the trailer with corn to hide the missile."

"How credible is this eyewitness?" Talbot asked.

"He's a homeless veteran, sir," Rybeck replied. "Based on his past experience, I'd say Montgomery makes an excellent witness."

"And you'd be willing to put the man on the stand in court?" Talbot asked.

"I'm not worried about taking this case to court, sir," Rybeck said confidently. "I'm trying to build a case that says Paul Moran took possession of four cruise missiles. If he's planning to launch them to kick off his militia war, then we need to stop him."

"You honestly believe Moran is capable of acquiring cruise missiles?" Talbot asked dubiously.

"Why not? He has plenty of military contacts and trained militiamen to do his dirty work. If you listen to anything he has to say, you'd know he would dearly love to take down the sitting government. What better way to do that than to use those cruise missiles as a first-strike option? But I want to put a little more flesh on the bone and talk to Montgomery myself."

"What happened to the arms trafficking?" Talbot asked.

"The ATF can take that over," Rybeck said. "What we have here is far bigger than a few stolen rifles."

"Only if your source checks out, Rybeck," Talbot countered.

"I think we should let Parker run with it, sir," Pratt cut in. "I can work the gun angle while he's gone. And if he kicks over the hornets' nest in Texas, then we can jump on it."

"Fine, but don't waste time on it if the story turns out to be a bum—no pun intended."

"Yes, sir," Rybeck replied.

Rybeck hung up the phone and stood, eager to get moving.

Pratt put a calming hand on the younger agent's shoulder. "You've done an excellent job of putting all this together, Parker. I'm not sure I would have been able to do the same, but if this thing is real, a lot is riding on us finding those missiles and proving Moran has them."

Rybeck nodded. "I know."

"So, what do you want me to do?" Pratt asked.

"See what it would take for Moran to launch the missiles. He has to build a launch facility or have launch controllers built. Those missiles won't fire on their own," Rybeck said.

Pratt nodded in agreement as he pinched his lower lip with his fingers. "I'll see what I can come up with. Good luck in Texas, partner."

Rybeck was halfway out the door when his desk phone rang. He considered not answering it, but then went back since Pratt had stepped out of the office on a coffee run. Sitting back down, Rybeck picked up the phone, immediately thankful he'd answered when the caller identified himself as Trooper Smoot.

"Thanks for getting back to me," Rybeck said.

"Sure thing. How can I help you, Agent Rybeck?"

"Do you remember ticketing a semi-truck from Ohio last February for being overweight?"

Smoot seemed to need a moment to think about it, then said, "Well, yeah. Sure, I do. The driver tried to avoid the scales on I-10 as he headed into Georgia. I thought he looked suspicious, so I pulled him over and weighed him using my portable scales. The truck was several thousand pounds overweight, but other than that, everything was in order."

"Your report said he was hauling corn. Is that correct?" Rybeck asked.

"I thought it was a little strange coming out of Florida. Not much corn grown down that way."

"You also reported the trailer was only partially full. Do you know what caused the truck to be overweight?"

"I'm not really sure, but something was off. I couldn't put my finger on it before, but the guy seemed jumpy, nervous like ... But now that I think about it, there's no way he should have been overweight."

"You didn't poke around in the corn?"

"No," Smoot replied. "Just as I got done writing the ticket, I got a call to help another trooper, so I let the guy go. Is there something going on?"

Rybeck figured he should let the trooper know he'd

missed catching an arms trafficker and wanted him to be more careful. "I think he was smuggling weapons," the FBI agent said.

"That makes sense," Smoot replied. "It would explain why he was overweight with half a load of corn. I'll keep a better lookout from now on."

"You do that, Trooper," Rybeck said, ending the call.

Smoot hadn't provided any more information about the puzzle. Instead, he only confirmed details Rybeck had already known.

Rybeck sighed and rubbed his face with his hands. He had stumbled into an arms trafficking deal had the potential to set America's Heartland on fire.

CHAPTER TWENTY-FOUR

While Rybeck boarded a commercial flight to Texas, Ralph Pratt strolled across The Ohio State University campus. He had called the engineering department and arranged to meet aerospace engineer Dr. Robert McMahon when he was between classes. Pratt found the engineering building and still had to ask two students for directions before he finally located McMahon's office.

Settling into a chair across from the professor's cluttered desk, Pratt consulted his notebook. "I need to know about Sampson cruise missiles."

McMahon removed his glasses and rubbed his nose. "May I ask why?"

"I have reason to believe that a terrorist group is in possession of some of these missiles and may attempt to launch them at targets across the U.S."

"That is a conundrum." Leaning back in his chair, McMahon stared at the wall above Pratt's head and fixed his gaze there for so long that Pratt was tempted to turn to see what the man was staring at. Finally, the professor returned his gaze to Pratt. "As I recall, the Sampson is a submarine-launched, nuclear-tipped cruise missile designed to fly a distance of 1,800 miles at 447 miles per hour. After the United States and Russia signed the START I treaty, which restricted the use of sub-launched nuclear cruise missiles, the Russians converted the Sampson to carry a conventional payload."

"You have all that stored in your head?" Pratt asked, amazed.

"Yes. You see, before I became a professor, I worked first with the Navy and then for an agency in D.C. that dealt with such things. It was my job to learn about Russian and U.S. cruise missiles."

Pratt nodded as he jotted down a few notes. "How easily could they launch them if the terrorists didn't have a submarine?"

The professor swiveled from side to side in his office chair, steepling his fingers beneath his chin. "That would depend on how creative the terrorists are, Agent Pratt. If the terrorists build a proper launch facility and install the necessary launch, targeting, and guidance electronics, then, yes, they could certainly launch the missiles.

Pratt glanced down at his notes. "How hard would it be to build a targeting and guidance system?"

"Building a launch facility wouldn't be hard. In this case, I would build a tube that simulated the launch tube on a submarine. Then there is the problem of the electronics. If the terrorists could get their hands on the original electronics suite from either a submarine or one of the ground-based variants, it would make the job much easier. If those weren't available, they would need to build a complete control unit."

"What if the terrorists had the help of an engineer from Novator, the manufacturer of the missiles?" Pratt asked.

"If the engineer's already familiar with the equipment, then he could quite easily build what they need," McMahon replied. "When I worked in D.C., my employer tasked a group of us with building a homemade cruise missile to see if we could do it. We built—and successfully launched—a missile using off-the-shelf components from a local hardware store."

Pratt pinched his lip. "You didn't need anything special to do that?"

"No, we were able to build everything ourselves. It was actually quite easy, and several others have done it since. You can find plans for a homemade missile online if you search the right forums."

"What about converting the Sampson to an improvised guidance system?"

The professor furrowed his brow. "It would be difficult, especially if you didn't have the proprietary software Novator uses. That software connects the missile to the satellite guidance system and nose camera feeds. They could bypass the internal system by wiring a handheld GPS unit inside the missile, but if the terrorists have one of Novator's engineers working on it, he might know how to connect to the satellite system."

Pratt looked down at his notebook. He'd been more engrossed in what McMahon had to say than in taking notes. The summary he'd scrawled upon the page was pathetic. While Pratt had learned it was possible to launch the missiles, he hadn't learned anything that would help locate them.

"Is there anything specific I need to be aware of so I can find these missiles?" Pratt asked. "I guess what I mean is, what do I look for—some Joe Blow walking into RadioShack and purchasing the equipment to build a launch and guidance system?"

"There are several things you could look for," McMahon said. "The first would be high-quality steel for the launch tubes and mass purchases of electronics, wiring, and solder. To be honest, Agent Pratt, I think it would be like searching for a needle in a haystack."

The professor's sentiments matched how Pratt already felt. Getting to his feet, the agent said, "Thank you for your time, Professor."

"Not a problem, Agent. I wish you all the best. Please let me know if I can be of further assistance."

The two men shook hands. As Pratt turned to leave, he glanced up at the wall the professor had stared at for so long.

There was nothing there.

It was a dead end, just like this trip.

CHAPTER TWENTY-FIVE

Inside the lobby of the Port Arthur police station, Rybeck showed his ID and asked to speak to Detective Bryce Nixon. After being buzzed through the security doors beside the front counter, an officer led Rybeck to a bullpen of desks and partitioned offices where Nixon sat, typing a report. He looked up as the two men approached, and the escorting officer made the introductions as Rybeck flashed his credentials.

"I want to talk to Allen Montgomery. I figured you would know where to find him."

"Sure. Have a seat, Coastie," Nixon said with a grin. "I need a minute to finish this report, then I can give you my full attention."

With no other choice, Rybeck sat down and waited.

Once he finished his report, the detective stood and picked up his suit jacket. "Okay, Special Agent. Let's go find our rummy."

The two men walked out into the heat and humidity of the south Texas summer. Nixon led Rybeck to an unmarked Dodge Charger that Rybeck thought screamed "Police" with its hidden lights and trunk-mounted antenna array, but the air conditioning was a welcome touch.

It took two hours of rolling down trash-filled alleys, searching abandoned buildings and empty industrial lots before they found Allen Montgomery huddled in a doorway. He wore ragged cutoff jeans, a dirty T-shirt, and a shabby pair of tennis shoes with loose soles. His bicycle had an attached trailer laden with aluminum cans and other items he'd collected from the streets.

"Hey, Allen," Nixon greeted him.

"Detective," Montgomery replied sullenly, keeping a wary eye on Rybeck. "Who's your friend?"

"This is Agent Parker Rybeck with the FBI."

Montgomery squinted at the far end of the street, like he was thinking of running, then seemed to think better of it. "I always wondered if you turned in my report."

"Yeah, I turned it in, but it took a while to filter up to Agent Rybeck."

Montgomery nodded and glanced down at his shoes.

Rybeck wondered why the man was homeless and why no one was doing anything to help him. *He's a veteran. He shouldn't be on the street.*

Rybeck squatted down beside his witness. "I want to talk to you about the night you filed the report. Is that okay?"

Montgomery shrugged.

"Will you go out to the shrimp docks and walk me through it?"

The homeless man looked blankly at his bike and cart. "Can't leave my bike."

"We can take it with us," Rybeck offered.

Nixon rolled his eyes and was about to protest when Rybeck told him to pop the trunk. It took some work, but they got the bike and the trailer into the Charger, although they had to drive with the trunk lid open.

At the shrimp docks, Montgomery walked the two men through what he had seen, recalling in precise detail the men in the semi, the boat, and the missile. He showed them where he had hidden in the weeds, stored his bike, and even picked up some scrap metal along the way.

Rybeck brought up a picture of a stock image of the Sampson cruise missile on his phone and showed it to Montgomery. The homeless vet rubbed his stubbly chin for a moment before he confirmed it was the type of missile he'd seen.

On the way back into town, Rybeck had Nixon stop at a store, where he bought Montgomery a new pair of shoes and gave him fifty dollars. "Thanks for your service, Allen."

The homeless vet issued several vulgar oaths against the United States Navy and then climbed out of the car.

"You know he's just going to blow that money on booze, right?" Nixon asked skeptically.

Rybeck shrugged. How the man spent the money didn't matter to him. He'd gotten confirmation from Montgomery that he had seen Wayne Patterson load a Sampson cruise missile into his semi-truck.

But Rybeck felt time was slipping away from him.

Rybeck could feel in his bones that the only reason Moran had smuggled cruise missiles into America was to launch them. He had to find the missiles before Moran struck first.

CHAPTER TWENTY-SIX

Caroline Thurmond's house
Kenton, Ohio

CAROLINE PULLED on her duty belt, charged her service weapon, and then slipped it into her holster before fastening the retention strap. It was going to be another long night on patrol. The department was short-staffed, and as a result, she had to take more shifts. While Caroline was grateful for the overtime, she looked forward to a few days off to recharge her batteries.

As Caroline navigated out of her driveway, the gravel crunched beneath her tires and pinged off the fender wells. Turning onto the road, she slipped through the twilight, admiring the setting sun as the Ford carried her to work. Her first stop was the sheriff's station.

She remembered when the building had once been a National Guard motor pool base until the government realigned the guard bases and left it empty. Hardin County had turned it into a state-of-the-art law enforcement facility a few years later. Still, they couldn't recruit enough deputies to fill the vacant jobs.

After checking her mail and talking to Angela in dispatch, she learned that not much out of the ordinary had happened while she had been off duty. Caroline told the dispatcher that she would cruise around Jackson's land and then park south of town on State Route 68 to see if she could pick up some speeders. Her ticket numbers were down for the month, and she needed to pad her account.

The old cruiser took Caroline on a tour of the land on the eastern side of the county, through stands of corn and beans, crisscrossing over the Scioto River under canopies of trees, and through cones of light from security lights shining on households bedding down for the night. She loved driving the old back roads. She knew, for instance, how long it took to get from one side of the county to the other and which roads would take her there the fastest. She knew which roads had curves and which terminated in dead ends. Caroline drove them throughout every season, checking conditions, responding to calls, and lending a helping hand anytime she could.

At eleven p.m., there were few cars on the road. The dispatch radio remained silent, and Caroline was alone with her thoughts.

She drove past the quarry where she had first met Rybeck and was temporarily blinded by a car's headlights as it turned toward her.

As she passed the car, the headlights on her cruiser illuminated the passengers, and something clicked in her memory. Caroline drove on, thinking about what had triggered her thoughts until she suddenly remembered the photo Rybeck had emailed her in his be-on-the-lookout message.

Caroline swung the cruiser south at the next road and then headed east, parallel to the road the other car was now driving along. She could see the car's lights across a field of beans. Caroline leaned on the accelerator, increasing her speed to draw even with the other vehicle. She turned north again to rejoin the road behind the car, thankful the streets had been laid out in a grid pattern. She stayed a mile or so back so she could follow without attracting too much attention.

As they neared town, Caroline closed the gap, pulling up behind the car at a traffic light. The driver glanced in his rearview mirror and then turned into a parking lot. Caroline watched them park in front of a grocery store as she waited for the red light. Once it turned green, she entered the parking lot, observing the two men exit their vehicle and head for the store. Deciding to follow them inside, Caroline wished she wasn't in a patrol car or uniform so she wouldn't look as conspicuous.

Pulling the cruiser to a stop, Caroline waited until the men had entered the grocery and then walked into the store herself. Once inside, she wiped her sweaty palms on her pants. Her heart was racing, and Caroline had to admit that apprehension coursed through her in waves.

Moving through the aisles, Caroline quickly spotted the two men she'd been tailing. She pulled out her phone and scrolled to the photo Rybeck had emailed her.

The stranger matched the photo!

The man with him, however, was Greg Allende, an officer with the Kenton Police Department. Caroline walked past them to the glass case where the store kept fresh doughnuts. She pulled a box of a dozen assorted out of the case and headed for the checkout.

On her way past the two men, Caroline said, "Hi, Greg. How are you?"

Greg beamed. "I'm fine, Caroline. You getting doughnuts for the night shift?"

"You know how us cops are," Caroline replied, trying to be charming and disarming. As Greg chuckled, she turned to the Russian. "Who's your friend, Greg?"

The police officer looked momentarily puzzled, as if he couldn't remember the man's name, but recovered quickly. "This is Roger Kozak."

Caroline shifted the doughnut box into her left hand and extended her right. "Nice to meet you, Mr. Kozak."

Kozak took her hand with a firm grip. In a heavy accent, he replied, "It is pleasure to meet such beautiful woman."

"Nice to meet you, sir," Caroline said. "What brings you to America?"

"I am engineer for John Deere. They send me to work for Mr. Jackson to get hands-on experience before I return to Belarus."

Caroline smiled at the plausible story. *Nice try,* Roger, *but we both know you're not here for the harvest.* Feeling the conversation had run its course, Caroline said, "Good luck to you, Roger. See you later, Greg."

The police officer waved as Caroline walked away. She picked up a sweet tea before paying for her goods at the register.

Once Caroline had returned to the parking lot, she hurried to her cruiser. Sitting in the driver's seat, she shoved a glazed doughnut in her mouth, chewing rapidly and washing it down with the tea. Caroline hadn't felt this nervous since losing her virginity at her senior prom.

After getting the doughnut down, she picked up her cell phone and dialed Parker Rybeck's number. As the phone rang, she fired up the cruiser and headed for headquarters to drop off her box of doughy sugar.

Rybeck's voice was full of sleep when he answered.

"Hi, Parker," Caroline said.

At the sound of the tension in her voice, Rybeck was instantly awake. "Hey, Caroline. What's up?"

"I saw that Russian guy you've been looking for. He's using the name Roger Kozak and claims to be an engineer from Belarus."

"Great work, Caroline. Talk me through it."

Caroline recounted the events as Rybeck took notes. When she finished, he said, "Finding this guy proves the missiles and the Russian engineer are all in the same place: Liberty Brigade."

CHAPTER TWENTY-SEVEN

FBI Resident Agency Office
Lima, Ohio

Rybeck sipped coffee from his Coast Guard mug as he and Pratt briefed Talbot.

SAC Roger Talbot had driven from Cleveland to have a sit-down with him, Ralph Pratt, and Caroline Thurmond.

Ahead of the SAC's arrival, Rybeck and Pratt had compiled a brief containing all the information they had collected over the past five days, including the positive confirmation from the FBI's facial recognition database that Roger Kozak was, in fact, Kostya Dragomirov, and Rybeck's hypothesis that Moran intended to launch the Sampson missiles at U.S. targets. Thurmond was in attendance purely because she had been Rybeck's eyes on the ground in Hardin County and had spotted the missing Russian in the company of one of Kenton PD's finest.

The SAC held up a hand to stop Rybeck. "Based on the

testimonies you have so far, I think we can safely assume that someone brought weaponry into the country. Whether it was Russian cruise missiles has yet to be seen. All the evidence you have here is circumstantial at best.

"Fortunately, if what Dr. McMahon says is true," Talbot continued, "it could take Moran a long time to build a functional launch system—if he can do it at all. And that doesn't include directional guidance, either. Plus, we have no evidence that Moran has built a launcher or is launch capable."

Rybeck looked down at his hands. He knew exactly where Talbot was taking them. He was picking apart their evidence, looking for holes in the theory. And even Rybeck had to admit that there were some big ones.

Caroline cleared her throat. "Sir, when I told my boss I was coming here to meet with you, he gave me this file folder." She pushed it across the table to Talbot.

The SAC opened the folder and focused on a list of names printed on a sheet of paper. Under one heading, a column read: "Police," with a second heading titled: "Sheriff's Department."

"The names on that list are all law enforcement connected with the Liberty Brigade," Caroline explained.

The other items in the folder were a series of photographs. The first was a screenshot captured from Google Earth, followed by a sequential series of photographs showing the progressive buildup of Liberty Brigade's headquarters since Moran had set up camp at the old quarry.

"These from Moran's compound?" Talbot asked.

"Yes, sir," Caroline replied. "The Google Earth printout shows the quarry before Jackson purchased it in its original condition. Sheriff Marker doesn't like Moran or his militia, and he's had his fair share of run-ins with Jackson when he was a county commissioner. Anyway, Sheriff Marker is convinced something funny is happening at the Liberty Brigade compound, so he hired a local pilot to fly over the property twice a month to photograph it."

Talbot sifted through the pictures. They started with the old stone-crushing and quarrying equipment still in place, and, over time, the militia had torn down the old buildings, leaving pits in the landscape. The next photo showed that someone had covered the pits, and gradually, the images displayed the development of the militia compound to present day.

As Talbot finished studying one photo, he passed it to Pratt, who passed it to Rybeck so they could all observe the pictorial timeline.

"Did they turn those pits into bunkers?" Pratt asked.

"According to what we've overheard, yes," Caroline replied. "The rumor is that Moran's people reinforced the walls with concrete, capped the old pits with precast concrete plates, and covered the whole thing with dirt. One of our sources told us they store everything from food to guns in them."

"It appears Moran has done some pretty substantial underground work," Pratt said, laying a photo on the table that showed more deep pits and the trenches that connected them.

"They could be more bunkers," Caroline agreed. "Sheriff Marker didn't want to tip off Moran with too many over-flights, so we don't have photographs of every stage of the building process. He also tried talking to the guys who did the excavation and concrete work until their boss showed Sheriff Marker the confidentiality agreement Moran had forced them to sign."

"My inner conspiracy theorist tells me Moran has built bunkers under the barn to house the launch control systems," Rybeck stated. When no one rose to his bait, he tried a different tack. "What about these grain silos beside the barn? Could they be used to hide the missiles?"

Pratt answered with, "They could be. According to Dr. McMahon, just about anything could be used. Whoever has the missiles just needs to build vertical launch tubes for them and stand them upright. Since my chat with McMahon, I looked around for any unusual purchases Moran or Jackson might have made, but I couldn't find anything. Much of what Jackson buys is for farm use, and we can't look at his purchases without getting a warrant."

"Allen Montgomery told me that the missile Wayne Patterson loaded into the back of his truck looked like it was in a special cradle, which seemed rather odd to him. He drew a picture for me." Rybeck sifted through the paperwork he'd compiled for the SAC and found the sketch. Pointing to it, he said, "That could be half of a launch tube."

Talbot studied the illustration and then placed it back on the table. "All this evidence is circumstantial, and I can't go to a judge and ask for a search warrant based on what we now have. Keep pulling the threads, but in the meantime, Moran has a rally coming up. What do we have planned?"

"Both Pratt and I are going in as militiamen," Rybeck said. "I suspect other undercover federal agents will also be there."

"What's the latest prediction of the number of people who will show up?" Talbot asked.

"We're hearing at least two thousand people," Caroline replied. "Moran has to file permits with the county to have a gathering of this size."

Talbot whistled as he sat back in his chair. "That's a lot of hotheads in one place."

"Like AA for conspiracy theorists," Pratt said with a laugh, and they all chuckled at the joke.

"Has Sheriff Marker appointed you as our liaison, Deputy Thurmond?" Talbot asked.

"Yes, sir."

"Good. I'm glad to have you on board. Gentlemen, contact the other agencies and see who's sending people to this shindig. We need to have a sit-down so everyone is on the same page."

"Good idea, sir," Pratt said. "I've already contacted ATF and Homeland."

"What about the U.S. Marshals?" Talbot asked.

"I'll call them," Pratt replied. "Who else do you want here?"

"Do you have anyone to conduct diving operations?" Caroline asked.

All three men glanced her way.

"Well," she replied defensively, "it is a quarry, and they could hide the missiles underwater. They are submarine-launch capable."

"Good call, Thurmond," Pratt said supportively, adding a note to his already lengthy list of things to do on his legal pad. "I'll contact the FBI dive team."

"Rybeck, I want you to dig into this gun dealer, Dombek," Talbot instructed. "This time, I want you to draw up a National Security Letter so we can gather information without getting a warrant or going to a grand jury."

"But, sir, aren't NSLs for foreign counterintelligence operations?"

While Rybeck was correct in that National Security Letters were typically issued to collect information on foreign agents suspected of espionage against the United States, government agencies also used them against American citizens considered to be acting against American interests. An NSL allowed the FBI to view electronic communications, financial records, money transfers, credit records, and

Internet service provider logins, but did not provide for wire-tapping, electronic surveillance, and physical searches, which required a warrant signed by a judge.

Talbot sighed as if he had little patience for his junior agent. "Listen to me carefully, Rybeck. Write an NSL for Dombek's records. He acts as a conduit for firearms stolen from shipments to Ukraine, which means he acts as a foreign agent, facilitating the delivery of stolen property to Paul Moran and Liberty Brigade, which we have classified as a domestic terror organization."

Rybeck nodded. He was glad to have Talbot on his side. "Yes, sir. I'll write it up this afternoon."

"I'll sign it as soon as you finish," Talbot said. "And I'll have a financial analyst on standby to comb through Dombek's records and remind everyone involved they are under a gag order not to speak about the NSL or the records they surrender to us."

"Yes, sir," Rybeck replied.

Talbot glanced around the room at the others. "Is there anything else?"

The trio of law enforcement officers shook their heads.

"All right, I want an all-agency meeting in ten days," Talbot ordered.

Rybeck, Caroline, and Pratt walked to the office of the two agents, leaving Talbot to make phone calls from the conference room.

Pratt sat at his desk and picked up the phone to call the other agencies while Rybeck grabbed his laptop and the stack of files he would need to write the NSL for Roy Dombek.

Leading Caroline to a second conference room, Rybeck stopped to refill their coffee cups.

"How can I help?" Caroline asked as they took seats at the conference room table.

"Ralph and I are going to handle it," Rybeck replied.

"This is a federal case, and while we may still need help from the sheriff's office, I don't think this is the time to play that hand."

"I understand," Caroline replied, though she couldn't completely disguise the disappointment in her voice.

"You've done enough already," Rybeck said sympathetically. "You put us onto Dombek, found his illegal arms shipment, and spotted Dragomirov. I think you deserve a medal."

Caroline smiled and leaned in closer. "And I think you're just trying to butter me up."

"No, I mean it. You've done a wonderful job. I think you should apply to the Bureau."

Caroline laughed involuntarily. "And become a Fed? No, thanks. I like my county job."

"I hope Sheriff Marker appreciates you," Rybeck replied.

"I doubt it, but I'm happy with my life, and that's all that matters to me."

"Good to know," Rybeck replied, wondering if it was worth pursuing a relationship with Caroline. He glanced at his watch and said, "How about we grab lunch after I get this NSL written?"

Caroline smiled. "Sure. I've been jonesing for a Kewpee burger. I'll give you some space to work. Call me when you're ready for lunch."

Rybeck opened his laptop as Caroline left the conference room. It took him several hours to complete the NSL and email it to SAC Talbot, who immediately kicked it back as needing more information. After spending another two hours researching previously written NSLs and applying their language to his, Talbot signed the NSL. While one of the Bureau's forensic accountants collated Dombek's banking information, Rybeck was to help Pratt coordinate with the other agencies.

He decided that helping Pratt could wait while he took

Caroline to lunch. Rybeck called Caroline, who said she would meet him in the parking lot outside his office, so he left the conference room to get his partner's lunch order.

Rybeck found Pratt in their office, and when the younger agent stuck his head in, he said, "Caroline and I are going to Kewpee. You want to go with us?"

Pratt looked up with a grin, still clutching the phone to his ear. "Absolutely! But I can't. I'm on hold with Homeland."

The Kewpee burger chain had arrived in Lima in 1928, opening its first restaurant in the downtown district. The place still maintained the original exterior and diner-like atmosphere inside. Since the restaurant was one of Pratt's favorites, so Rybeck had eaten there frequently. And a trip to Kewpee was also part of any visitor's initiation into Lima's culture.

Pratt turned serious. "Did you get that NSL written?"

"And signed. We're in a holding pattern while we wait on accounting. I'm supposed to help you, but I know how cranky you get when you don't eat, so I'm making a food run first."

"Yeah, fine," Pratt said. "Grab me a cheeseburger with everything. You know what I like."

Rybeck pulled his suit jacket from the hook in their office and headed for his truck. The temperature had reached the low eighties, and Rybeck started to sweat under his jacket almost as soon as he stepped outside. However, he didn't take it off as it concealed his gun and badge, and Rybeck didn't want everyone to know he worked for the FBI.

Caroline was waiting for him, and they climbed into his truck for the short drive to the hamburger stand. Once there, they went through the Kewpee drive-through and ordered two hamburgers with everything but relish and green olives to go with their fries and soft drinks. Then Rybeck added Pratt's cheeseburger, which included the relish and green olives.

Once they had their food in hand, Rybeck drove them through town to Schoonover Park, a large lake surrounded by green space with plenty of walking and cycling paths and an old observatory that contained a modern telescope.

Rybeck parked the truck, and he and Caroline ate their sandwiches in silence as they stared out across the pond's glassy surface.

Caroline was the first to break the lull in conversation. "You think Dombek will roll over once you get his financial records?"

"Let's hope so," Rybeck replied.

Caroline wadded up her trash, stuffed it into the burger sack, and then slid out of her seat. "Let's go for a walk."

Rybeck followed the deputy down a paved path toward the muddy brown water of the Ottawa River that bordered the park as it meandered through Lima on its way north to feed Lake Erie. The path the two law enforcement officers walked along would eventually take them all the way across town, but they had no plans to go that far.

As they strolled along the tree-shaded path, Caroline slipped her hand into Rybeck's. He wondered if he was interpreting Caroline's signals all wrong. In the office, she had said she was happy with her life, and Rybeck had felt slighted. He wondered now if she was happy because he was a part of it. Despite the pressure of the Liberty Brigade investigation, Rybeck felt carefree as he walked with her under the canopy of trees.

"This is nice," he commented. "I like spending time with you."

"That's good," she replied. "I like spending time with you, too."

They silently walked on until Caroline asked, "When are you going to Dombek's?"

"It will be a few days. The NSL has to clear the channels

in Washington. After that, a forensic accountant will dig into Dombek's banking info. Once we move on Dombek, we might need local help. Is there anyone in the KPD that we can trust who isn't involved in the militia?"

Caroline laughed. "I think trust will be hard to come by there."

Rybeck agreed, adding, "It's courtesy to let the locals know if we do an investigation in their area."

"I'm well aware of that, Parker. I'm not saying the department has a leak. I'm saying it's a sieve."

"What about the Sheriff's Office?" he asked.

Caroline counted on her fingers. "One, we don't operate inside the city limits—and two, we would be happy to help, but we have militia members in our ranks."

Rybeck shrugged. "Despite the gag order accompanying the NSL, I think someone will still tell Moran that we're investigating Dombek and, by extension, him."

Gripping his hand, Caroline asked, "Parker, how do you know I'm not the leak?"

He smiled. "I guess I'll have to take your word for it, but I also don't think you'd risk your career searching Dombek's trailer if you were loyal to Moran."

They paused on a bridge to watch the river flow along its green banks. At that moment, Rybeck wished he could take the day off and keep strolling. He could take Caroline to Old City Prime for medium-rare New York Strip and then back to his apartment for a different kind of strip.

Caroline leaned her head against his shoulder. "I wish you didn't have to go back to work."

Rybeck turned to her, and she looked up at him, holding his eyes with hers. He leaned in and kissed her. The kiss was long and lingering, and Rybeck didn't want to let her go, but after a few moments, she stepped back, her eyes searching his face.

"Now, I *really* don't want to go back to work," Rybeck said.

Caroline smiled wistfully. "I don't have to, but you do. Besides, Ralph's food is probably getting cold."

He knew she was right, and Rybeck had to admit, he was eager to bring Roy Dombek in. He knew the entrepreneur would have dirt on Moran and the Liberty Brigade. It was just a case of working out how much pressure he needed to apply to get Dombek to give it up.

CHAPTER TWENTY-EIGHT

Two days after SAC Talbot had signed the NSL, a woman in her mid-thirties, her brown hair pulled back in an officious bun, walked into Rybeck and Pratt's office armed with a stack of paperwork.

"Which one of you is Agent Rybeck?" she asked coolly, glancing between the two men.

Pratt pointed at the same time Rybeck said, "I am."

The woman sat, uninvited, across from Rybeck's desk and introduced herself as Agent Maria Hill, a forensic accountant for the Bureau. "Agent Rybeck, I have the research you requested on Roy Dombek." She set the stack of papers on Rybeck's desk and adjusted her glasses, which had slid down the bridge of her nose. "As I'm sure you were expecting, I couldn't account for all the money coming in and out of the bank accounts that Mr. Dombek holds in both his personal and business names. Sometimes, it's common for a business owner to skim a little petty cash off the top to pay his personal expenses, but this was too much cash. It wasn't large deposits, just little bits here and there, so I searched for accounts Mr. Dombek might have elsewhere."

"Like overseas?" Rybeck asked, hoping he was keeping up with her.

"Precisely," Agent Hill replied. "After a lot of checking, I found he had two, one in the Cayman Islands and another in The Bahamas labeled Tahoe Unlimited." She pulled a piece of paper from the stack and handed it to Rybeck. "As you can see, an attorney in Columbus established for Mr. Dombek both Tahoe Unlimited and a company called Ammunition USA."

Rybeck read over the statement several times. The account balance was just north of a million dollars. Despite Agent Hill's earlier assertion, there had been several large deposits in the past two years, which Rybeck was positive Dombek couldn't account for if the IRS were to audit his businesses.

"Roy's Guns and Ammo wires deposits to Ammunition USA for the legitimate purchase of ammunition and firearms, but all of AUSA's wire transfers to Tahoe Unlimited are for consulting fees. I have yet to determine who owns the account that sends the larger deposits since it's buried in multiple layers of shell corporations. Whoever set it up was very good at their job, but I don't believe it belongs to Mr. Dombek."

"Is this enough evidence to bring Dombek in?" Rybeck asked.

"I don't know, Agent Rybeck. That's not my department, but I can tell you the IRS doesn't know about Mr. Dombek's overseas account."

"Any other financial missteps by our gunrunner?" Pratt asked.

"Not that I found, but there may be something we don't know about. We looked at Dombek's ISPs and phone records, but as you know, we can't see numbers or text messages without getting a warrant for that information."

"They probably used burners, and we'll never know who Dombek was talking to," Rybeck stated.

"Anything else, agents?" Hill asked.

Neither man had any more questions for the accountant. The financial information was enough for them to apply leverage to Dombek. Rybeck just hoped the broker had kept a record of his transactions with the Liberty Brigade.

"Thanks, Agent Hill. We appreciate your hard work," Pratt said.

Agent Hill left her business card on Rybeck's desk, then stood and left the office.

Rybeck handed the bank statement over to Pratt. "What do you make of that?"

"Offhand, I would say Dombek is hiding payments from his illegal gun shipments." He flicked the sheet with his finger and smiled. "Now is the perfect time to talk to this joker."

———

An hour later, Rybeck parked the government-issued sedan in front of Kenton Truck and Machine.

As they stepped out of their vehicle, a flock of salesmen immediately accosted the two agents. Ignoring the overzealous pitchman, Pratt and Rybeck walked into the dealership building and asked for Roy Dombek.

The secretary had seen enough men in suits come and go from Dombek's office not to ask questions. She just pointed up the stairs, and as the men ascended, she called Dombek to let him know he had visitors.

The door to Dombek's office was open, and Rybeck led the way inside.

"What can I do to help you, gentlemen?" Dombek asked, rolling a cigar between his fingers.

Rybeck and Pratt took turns showing the car dealer their

badges and identifying themselves before sitting down in Dombek's visitor chairs. The room smelled of pine air freshener, doing a poor job of masking the pungent odor of stale smoke. Rybeck eyed the oversized gun safe in one corner, the televisions, and the Caribbean artwork.

Since Pratt had said in the car that he would defer to his partner, Rybeck took the lead, but it would still be a tag team affair.

Rybeck leaned forward, adjusting his suit coat as he said, "We want to discuss your relationship with Paul Moran."

Dombek removed the cigar from his mouth and stroked his chin. "Sure, Paul and I have a business relationship."

Pratt glanced at Rybeck. Both men had expected Dombek to be cagey.

"Let's talk about the things you ship for Moran," Rybeck suggested.

"I contract with couriers to move things for him. I'm a facilitator," Dombek said.

"Why doesn't he use JP Transit?" Pratt asked.

Dombek shrugged. "I don't know. He asks me to help him out, and I do." He smiled smugly. "For a fee, of course."

"Of course," Pratt mimicked.

While Caroline had spotted the firearms in Dombek's trailer, Rybeck still wanted to pin the theft of the cruise missiles on Moran. He'd reviewed Pratt's report from his interview with Dr. McMahon, learning Moran would need to transport the launch controls and guidance systems to the compound via truck. If Moran hadn't used JP Transit, Dombek would be the next best source.

"Look, Mr. Dombek," Rybeck said, "I'm particularly interested in any type of electronics Moran might have shipped in."

The car salesman puffed on his cigar then shook his head.

"I don't know anything about any electronics. Like I said, I'm just a facilitator."

"Yeah, we figured you would say something like that," Pratt said. "Everything has a nice label, like crock pots or toilet seats. What did you call the M4s you shipped in here? You know, the ones that fell off the truck on the way to Ukraine."

"Whoa! Hold up there, Agent," Dombek said derisively as he held his hands up, palms out. "Are you angling for a slander suit?"

"No, Mr. Dombek, we're not angling for a lawsuit. What we *want* is your help," Rybeck replied, trying to keep his anger in check. Questioning Dombek felt like they were pulling teeth. *Why don't people just cooperate with us?* he wondered.

Rybeck glanced at his partner, who nodded his head as if to say, "Keep going."

"On May fourteenth, two semi-trailers showed up on your lot across the street." Rybeck hooked a thumb over his shoulder to indicate the location. "They contained a shipment of M4 rifles stolen from the New York Port Authority. The night of May fifteenth, JP Transit picked up the trailers and took them to the Liberty Brigade compound."

"That's a fascinating story," Dombek declared as smoke trailed from his lips.

"Look, Dombek," Pratt said wearily, "you can cooperate with us, or we can get a warrant and take this place and your gun shop apart. If we have to go there, we'll seize all your assets, including the contents of the two undeclared offshore bank accounts you probably wish we didn't know about."

Shell-shocked, Dombek stuttered, "I-I-I don't know what you're talking about."

Pratt shook his head and held up a hand to stop Dombek from making any more excuses. He opened the file folder he carried and flipped through the pages to find the document he wanted. "About five years ago, a lawyer named Todd Grafmiller set up a dummy corporation called Tahoe Unlimited at the Grosvenor Limited bank in Nassau, Grand Bahamas. That account, including your last deposit from Ammunition USA, brought the total to just over one point two million dollars. Sound familiar?"

Dombek nodded. His face had gone from smug to a sickly shade of green as he stubbed out his cigar in a crystal ashtray.

Pratt consulted the folder again. "You also have an account at the RBC Royal Bank in Grand Cayman with one point five mil in it. You're not doing too bad for a car dealer."

Pratt laid the bank statements side by side on Dombek's desk. His face faded from green to a shade of white that matched the sheets of paper he now stared at.

"Here's the deal," Rybeck began. "We know about your offshore dalliances, but the IRS does not. Most of the money you've put into the Grand Cayman account appears to have been after-tax money, so we're not too worried about that one. However, we suspect you're using the Tahoe Unlimited account to collect your 'facilitation' fees from helping Moran solve his transportation issues."

Dombek, normally unflappable in the face of controversy, simply stared at the two agents.

"We've been through this before," Pratt said knowingly. "You're feeling numb inside, like we just exposed your innermost secrets. That's okay. It's just reality setting in. What you need to do now is play ball. You do that, and we can grease the skids on this IRS beef."

Dombek shook his head as if trying to clear it, realizing that a single stroke of a pen could crush everything he had built. Finally, he gulped. "I can play ball. What do you want to know?"

"It's pretty simple, really," Pratt said. "We just need you to answer our questions, and we need access to any shipments Moran may make in the future." He snapped his fingers as if forgetting something. "Oh, and we also need copies of any files you've kept on past shipments."

The facilitator nodded. "Okay. And if I cooperate, what will you do about my accounts?"

It was Rybeck's turn to speak. "I've already spoken to the IRS, and they've agreed to allow you to disclose your accounts voluntarily. You'll need to pay taxes on any interest the accounts have earned, and you'll have to pay a penalty of ten percent."

"That's outrageous!" Dombek shouted.

"It's better than going to prison for ten years for theft of government property," Pratt said. "I'm sure we can come up with a few other charges to extend your time behind bars."

Holding his hands up to calm the situation, Rybeck said, "The IRS can claim up to fifty percent of your money as a penalty, and based on what I've seen, they'll be hitting you where it hurts the most. I'm sure your attorney walked you through all that when he set up your accounts, so we're being more than reasonable here. Cooperate, and you get a lighter sentence, but if you don't, then the IRS will have a field day. Trust me: they'll dig through all your accounts, receipts, records, and inventories and find enough discrepancies to take *all* your money."

Rybeck could see the light dawning in Dombek's eyes as he slowly realized they had him over a barrel of his own making.

"I've got records," Dombek stated. He stood, balanced unsteadily for a moment, then walked to the gun safe.

Rybeck jumped from his chair, placing his hand on his Glock 19 service weapon. The older man could open the safe, pull out a gun to shoot both agents, or use it to commit suicide. Either way, Rybeck didn't know Dombek's intentions and felt it prudent to be ready.

After punching in a code to open the safe, Dombek stood back from the door and opened it slowly, keeping one hand raised. "I'm going to retrieve a file box from the bottom of the safe."

Rybeck didn't move his hand from his gun but nodded for Dombek to do as he'd said. From where Rybeck stood, he could see the safe contained stacks of money in paper wrappers, boxes of records and file folders, multiple packages of ammunition, and at least four long guns in the rack, while several handguns hung in custom holsters on the back of the door.

Dombek plucked a file box from the safe and set it on his desk. "Most of my deals with Moran were verbal, but I took some notes. There are invoices from various shipping companies that I used, but they either don't list what was being shipped or someone intentionally mislabeled the shipments."

"Let's circle back to the electronics," Rybeck urged. "Do you know if Moran shipped anything like that?"

As Pratt stood to examine the contents of the box, he swung the safe door closed and locked it to prevent Dombek from retrieving a weapon.

Dombek noted the agent's movements but concentrated on what Rybeck had asked. "Most shipments were black-market arms deals. During the first year, everything Moran wanted came through me, and I kept an inventory of every shipment. Then, he started using his own sources for weapons. After that, I just managed the shipping."

"Do you know what Moran does with these arms shipments?" Pratt asked.

Dombek shrugged. "I assumed most of them go out to their little compound. I heard his militia has bunkers full of guns and ammo."

"Were there any strange shipments?" Rybeck pressed.

"Most of them were strange. I would ship the guns to an address in a warehouse district in Columbus or Cleveland or Cincinnati. Patterson's guys would meet the other driver to exchange trailers."

"Where did the shipments come from?" Pratt asked.

"East Coast and Gulf Coast, mainly," Dombek replied. "I only remember one shipment from California. Moran arranged it himself. He told me it was a cargo container, and I would need a flatbed instead of a van body."

Dombek dug through the file box and produced a receipt with an expediter address in Long Beach, California, one of the largest container ports in the world.

"Any idea what was in it?" Rybeck asked, his interest piqued.

"Funnily enough, the driver asked me what I was going to do with a shipping container full of Ural motorcycle parts." The two agents looked confused, so Dombek explained. "Urals are Russian-made motorcycles, usually equipped with a sidecar. During World War II, they copied BMW's design and never changed it. People say it's the only brand-new motorcycle you have to rebuild before you can ride it."

Pratt chuckled. "Maybe Moran's building a motorcycle regiment."

"I doubt Moran is doing anything with motorcycles," Rybeck said. "Most likely, they mislabeled the shipment as Mr. Dombek has suggested, hoping no one would be the wiser. Customs can't look at every shipping container that comes through the ports, especially in Long Beach."

During his time in the Coast Guard, Rybeck had witnessed how thinly spread Customs was and how futile their job could be.

"Any idea where the container came from?" Pratt asked.

"I don't know where it originated," Dombek said.

"What about a container number?" Rybeck asked, picking up the receipt.

"It's probably on the receipt, but I know it was a Maersk container," Dombek remembered. "After Moran emptied it, one of Patterson's guys dropped it back here, and I had a driver take it to the New York terminal."

Rybeck found the container number on the receipt, hoping he could use it to track the cargo container from its point of origin to the Liberty Brigade compound and wondering if he could discover what it had really contained. He might finally be ahead of Moran's game if he was successful.

Seeing his partner consumed with studying the Ural shipment, Pratt asked Dombek, "Does Moran have any other shipments in the works?"

"Not that I'm aware of," Dombek said.

Pratt handed him a business card before picking up the carton of files. "Okay. Looks like we're off to a good start, Mr. Dombek. Please call us when Moran plans to make another shipment."

Rybeck slipped the shipping manifest into the pocket of his suit jacket. "As of now, Mr. Dombek, we consider you a confidential informant, but if you fail to report any shipments, we'll hold you liable."

"What's next?" Dombek asked, straightening as if the weight had eased off his shoulders.

"Keep in contact with us and call the lawyer who set up your offshore accounts. The IRS is expecting his call."

Dombek nodded as Pratt and Rybeck made their way down the stairs, then through the row of salespeople who didn't even bother to look up at them this time.

Rybeck didn't care. Ural motorcycles came from Russia, just like the Sampson missiles and Kostya Dragomirov. It was time to connect all the dots.

CHAPTER TWENTY-NINE

B ack at the car, Rybeck asked Pratt to drive as it would take at least an hour to get back to their office in downtown Lima. Rybeck wanted to put that time to good use by researching the Maersk cargo container Dombek had told them about.

Pratt kept the sedan at the speed limit while Rybeck investigated Maersk on his smartphone. He already knew from his Coast Guard days that Maersk was one of the largest shipping companies in the world. He'd seen many of their containers being transported all across the country via road and rail. His Internet search revealed that the company had its headquarters in Copenhagen, Denmark, and employed over six hundred ships.

Next, Rybeck clicked on a link at the bottom of the search engine page labeled "Maersk Tracking" and then clicked on a link for container tracking on the Maersk website. The page opened with a box to type in the container number. Rybeck idly wondered if the tracking number would produce a result since it was more than a year past the container's delivery date.

Rybeck learned his assumption was correct when he typed in the container number and received an error message that told him the number was invalid. Clicking the "Contact Us" button redirected Rybeck to the main Maersk website. A few more clicks into his search quickly led to frustration at his inability to find a phone number, and he complained bitterly to Pratt.

Pratt scoffed. "A dollar says that even if you found a number, it would be an automated line."

"I'm not willing to take that bet," Rybeck replied, dialing a new number and lifting the phone to his ear.

"Federal Bureau of Investigations, Cleveland Office. How may I direct your call?" Richelle Stump asked.

Rybeck pictured the attractive woman on the other end of the line. She had thick red hair and a waistline that bulged at the hips from countless hours of sitting behind a desk as the receptionist for the Cleveland office.

"Richelle, it's Parker Rybeck. Do you know if we have a phone number for the shipping company, Maersk?"

"Let me look."

He heard her typing on the computer and then leafing through a binder. Rybeck knew Richelle kept a large binder under her desk that contained phone numbers, addresses, business cards, and other contact information on various businesses she might need to connect with during the course of her duties. It was a resource many of their colleagues used daily instead of endlessly searching the Internet.

"I need to make a call. I'll get back to you in a few minutes," she told him adroitly.

"Thanks, Richelle," Rybeck said before ending the call.

The two agents rode silently in the car as they sped west, staring at the passing fields of soybeans and corn.

They had just entered the outskirts of Lima when

Rybeck's phone rang. After answering, he listened to Richelle give him a rundown of what it had taken for her to find the number he needed for Maersk. When he finally got off the phone after her long dissertation, Pratt was pulling into the parking lot of their office.

Inside, Rybeck sat down at his desk and dialed the number Richelle had given him, figuring the call might appear more official if he used an FBI-assigned phone line. The call rang five times before a female voice at Maersk picked up the line. Rybeck was pleasantly surprised to get a human on the first try. After he explained who he was and what he needed, the woman was very accommodating and looked up the old tracking number.

"Sir, that order originated from our offices in Novorossiysk, Russia. According to the manifest, the client loaded the container in Murmansk before shipping it to the Port of Long Beach. From there, it went to Kenton, Ohio, then returned to our New York Port Authority office."

"Does it say who paid for the container?" Rybeck asked.

"A company from Singapore called Blanden Transglobal." The Maersk representative spelled the company name for Rybeck, who wrote it on a notepad.

"What cargo did they list on the manifest?" he asked.

"Ural motorcycle parts," the woman replied, as expected.

"Can you email me a copy of the manifest?" Rybeck asked, hoping he wouldn't need a warrant.

"Certainly."

Seconds later, the email was in his inbox after he gave the woman his email address.

"Thanks for helping me out," Rybeck said. "Can I call you if I have more questions?"

"No worries, Agent Rybeck. Please, call anytime."

Rybeck hung up and used his search engine to look up

Murmansk, Russia. He shivered when he saw the location of the town near the tip of the Scandinavian Peninsula. Other than its submarine base, the town's only other claim to fame was that it was the home port of the *Lenin*, the world's first nuclear icebreaker, which was now a dockside museum.

Rybeck turned to Pratt. "Did you know that you can take a seven-day cruise on a Russian icebreaker from Murmansk to the North Pole for thirty grand? They'll drive you right up to it."

"Robert Peary would be so proud," Pratt replied sarcastically.

"Who's Robert Peary?" Rybeck asked.

"The first guy to reach the North Pole, numbnuts," Pratt retorted, smiling at his joke. "And what's this got to do with our investigation?"

"Murmansk is an active Russian submarine base. They also have a lot of old subs there that the Russian Navy has decommissioned and are cutting up for scrap. Moran could have bribed some dockworkers to load the missile launch equipment into the shipping container and send it to him."

"A lot of theorizing, Parker."

"Sure, it is," Rybeck admitted, "but it makes more sense than buying Ural parts. We've had no reports of motorcycles running around the militia compound, nor does Moran have a website to sell the parts."

"Maybe he bought them, shipped them over, and sold them before he took delivery," Pratt theorized.

"But Dombek said JP Transit took the container to Moran's compound. Why would they do that if they sold the parts before they took delivery? Why not ship them directly to the customer who purchased the parts?"

"I don't know, Parker," Pratt said in frustration. He stood and picked up the file box Dombek had given them. "I'm going to the conference room to sort through this."

After his partner left, Rybeck pondered whether all the clues added up to Moran having cruise missiles at his compound. His gut told him they did. The only way to prove it was to keep digging until he had enough evidence to convince Talbot that they should raid the compound.

Rybeck turned to his computer and searched for the Singapore-based shipping company Blanden Transglobal. He found an obscure reference to it on the third page of the search, and then he called the number for Maersk again. Fortunately, the same representative answered the phone.

"This is Agent Rybeck again," he said. "Can you give me the contact information for Blanden Transglobal?"

"Certainly," she replied. "Hold on while I bring that up." After a moment, she said, "I'm sorry, sir. I need to check the file," and put Rybeck on hold. He listened to the classical music piped over the line until she returned. "Sir, I have a phone number and an address for you."

She read them off, and Rybeck copied them on paper and then read them back to ensure they were correct. Once he'd confirmed they were, he ended the call and tried the number in Singapore.

An agent at the Blanden Transglobal helpdesk answered the call, having a twenty-four-hour service line. Rybeck promptly asked for information about the container. The first guy passed Rybeck to another representative, who informed Rybeck that a company in Seychelles had ordered the container and handled the pickup and delivery in Russia.

The Seychelles, Rybeck learned from a quick search, were a group of 115 islands off the coast of Africa in the Indian Ocean. According to the Blanden rep had given him, the Seychelles company was nothing more than a solicitor's office with a post office box address, leaving Rybeck to speculate that someone had set up the Seychelles company with the specific purpose of handling the shipment of the Ural parts.

Despite the dead end with the container, Rybeck felt like he was making progress, even if he was just sniffing the edges. Eventually, he would find a hole and blow the case wide open.

CHAPTER THIRTY

Liberty Brigade compound
Kenton, Ohio

Paul Moran looked up as Dragomirov walked into his office. It galled Moran's sense of standards that the Russian never bothered to knock.

The engineer dropped into the chair across from the militia leader, took a drag on his cigarette, and then crushed it on the heel of his shoe. When he'd first arrived at the compound with Wayne Patterson, the man had seemed intimidated, a little cowardly, in a nerdy sort of way. Now, though, as he tossed the cigarette butt in the trash can, Dragomirov was openly brazen, maybe spurred on by the fact that he knew he was the only person on-site who could turn the pile of junk Moran had sourced from a decommissioned Russian submarine into a workable launch control system.

"It is done," Dragomirov said proudly.

"What's done?" Moran asked, still taken aback by the abrupt interruption.

"The missiles are ready. I have built guidance system."

Moran had to admit that he was surprised. The engineer had been insufferable to work with. Moran's questions were always met with a shrug or a smattering of Russian, and now, out of nowhere, he was claiming that he'd completed the job.

"You look ... how you say"—Dragomirov paused, searching for the right word—"puzzled?"

"For six months, I have asked you when you would have the guidance system built, and you couldn't tell me. Now, it is just done?"

The Russian shrugged. "All we need is coordinates for target."

Moran nodded. "I have them. I will program them myself, but you will show me how right now."

Again, the Russian shrugged. "What do I care? You pay me to do job."

Your arrogance is irrelevant, Moran thought. *After we fire the missiles, I'm going to kill you.*

It was a pleasant thought for Moran now that Dragomirov had finished with the system. He was just one more loose end to tie up, and Moran had known all along that the Russian planned to escape once he had launched the missiles.

Through keystroke loggers, phone taps, and screen capture malware installed on the engineer's devices, the militia's IT guys had been keeping track of Dragomirov's every move, from his money transfers to buying clothing online to emails traded with the Kenton police officer Moran had hired to help babysit the Russian. Moran knew Dragomirov's thoughts as if they were his own.

He smiled at Dragomirov as he stood from his desk. "Let's go. I've been waiting for this day for a long time."

The two men walked through the underground tunnel to

the missile command bunker. Every time Moran stepped into the tunnel, it reminded him of being in a James Bond movie—except he, not Blofeld, had built the supervillain's lair. He often wondered who would play the spoiler role. Someone out there would inevitably try to stop him before he could implement Liberty Brigade's action plan.

Truthfully, though, Moran welcomed the challenge. Soon, he would be chief of staff to the next commander-in-chief, and no one would be able to touch him.

Dragomirov led Moran into the control bunker and stopped in front of the launch control panel. Despite the engineer's challenging nature, Moran had tried to stay away from the bunker to let the engineer work in peace, so he was immediately impressed by what he saw. Dragomirov had lined up the equipment Moran had purchased from the defunct Russian submarine in Murmansk on racks.

The electronics had arrived in jumbled disarray. It had taken Dragomirov six months to rebuild the system, setting each box on a rack and connecting them using the supplied cables, building new cables to replace missing ones, and then attaching the launch controller to the four missiles in the grain silo above.

In order to complete the momentous project, Dragomirov had built a computer control center that had not been shipped with the other parts. He'd spent hours getting each component to interface and function as a unit. Dragomirov had only deemed the job successful when he could finally power up the missiles. From there, the engineer had hacked into the Russian satellite guidance system to allow for accurate delivery of the payload.

Now, all the gear was neatly aligned on the racks with each part, cable, and box labeled in Russian and English. Two racks of computer servers used to access the Russian satellites hung on the wall beside the guidance systems. Four flat-screen televisions, each displaying a map of the United States, hung on the wall above a computer with dual monitors.

"These screens show missile path." Dragomirov pointed to the top four. "Monitor on left for access to guidance satellite, and this monitor for tracking stock portfolio and buying from Amazon."

Moran shook his head in amazement. "How hard was it to hack into the guidance satellites?"

"Very easy. Morons left my access code operational at Novator. I got in, accessed friend's account, and set up a partition so my program run in background undetected. Program will not come on until you press button to launch, then it will sync with satellites and provide guidance."

The militia leader glanced at the open hatch above his head that led to the makeshift missile silo. "And the missiles are ready? Everything is connected?"

"*Da*. Everything is ready. Put in coordinates here." Dragomirov pointed to eight blank boxes on the guidance screen: one for longitude and latitude of each target.

"The computer will store GPS data for each missile unless you make change. The screen will go blank when inactive. Press space bar to wake computer. Once you put the coordinates in, click box beside each to arm missiles."

Moran pulled out the chair in front of the monitors and sat down as the engineer continued with the technical explanation of the launch system. "But how do I launch them, Dragon?"

Dragomirov pointed to four red buttons mounted on the wall several feet from the computer station. Above them was a key lock. The engineer took a key on a chain from around his neck and handed it to Moran. Pointing to the lock, he said, "You insert key and turn to activate missile launch system. Press button, and missiles launch."

Moran studied the bank of buttons—each about two

inches in diameter and spaced far enough apart to slap each one individually with his palm. He turned in the swivel chair and took in the entire setup that Dragomirov had created. To him, it was a thing of beauty. Moran had worked hard to accomplish this goal, and, finally, he could strike a devastating blow against the Deep State.

"After I put in the coordinates, I want them password-protected so no one else can change them," Moran ordered.

"Then you will have to enter password before activation," the Russian replied.

"So be it. The fewer people who can tamper with the system, the better."

Dragomirov shrugged. "I will need to write new program for password protection."

"Call me when you're done," Moran said. He left the bunker, walking up the stairs to the barn above.

Everything was finally coming together.

Leaving the barn and crossing the stone-packed drive, he stopped to look at the sun glistening off the deep blue water in the quarry. He drew in a long breath and slowly exhaled. The wind carried the pungent odor of cow and hog manure from the neighboring farm. Jackson had been steadily buying up the land around the compound, but he hadn't been able to purchase it all. As a result, the militia compound still had neighbors—smelly ones, too.

Moran walked along the quarry, deep in thought about the missile project, his arms trafficking, the upcoming militia gathering, and what the world would think of him when he finally pressed those four buttons deep in the bunker.

Will I be a savior or a lunatic?

He immediately shook himself from that line of thinking. He had to focus and keep pushing. He couldn't afford to let doubts prevent him from going through with his audacious plan.

His mind turned to the motto of the Army Special Forces: *"De oppresso liber,"* which, loosely translated, meant "Free the Oppressed." That had been Moran's mission during his time in the Army, and it was still his mission now. He was going to free the oppressed people of the United States by liberating them from a tyrannical government.

The former Green Beret left the idyllic scene of the quarry behind, climbing the steps to his office before stopping to see his head of security, Jonas Temple, a skilled fighter with a fastidious attention to detail. Short and bald with an overly large nose and a ruddy complexion, Temple had first worked for Halberd Security before joining Moran's inner circle.

"Dragomirov has completed his job," Moran said, leaning against the doorjamb of Temple's open office door.

"That's great news."

"I'm going to call Jackson. Once he arrives here, I want you to discreetly follow us into the tunnel. I'll signal you, and we'll take Dragomirov into custody. We'll put him in one of the tunnel bunk rooms for now."

Temple's smile told Moran that the security chief would enjoy imprisoning the Russian.

Leaving Temple's office, Moran entered his own, picked up one of his multiple burner phones, and dialed the number for his benefactor, Steven Jackson. Listening to the phone ring, he thought about the man who would answer.

From an early age, Jackson had wanted nothing more than to join the Navy and become a SEAL. He'd dedicated his life to the training needed to pass Basic Underwater Demolition Training/SEALs (BUD/S), pursuing every sport from football to track to martial arts. He'd studied hard, knowing that he needed to be a student of history and a master of body and mind.

During a high school track event, Jackson had collapsed

as he'd neared the finish line of a long-distance run. An event organizer had called an ambulance when he learned Jackson had severe chest pains, and they'd rushed him to the hospital. The doctors diagnosed Jackson as having heart arrhythmia that required immediate surgery to repair. The heart condition had automatically disqualified him from joining the military, and the recruiter dropped him from the delayed entry program. It was a crushing blow for a young man in the prime of his youth.

Jackson had spent much of his senior year of high school recovering from his surgery and trying to find a different path in life. Eventually, he entered college at The Ohio State University, where he'd met his wife, Cheryl. She'd brought life back to the despondent young man. After graduating from OSU with a degree in economics, Jackson began working for a small boutique investment firm.

It hadn't taken long for Jackson to realize that he had a passion for building businesses. He invested the profits he'd made from them into the family farm, growing it substantially from the meager plot once tilled by his great-grandfather to the thousands of acres now owned by Jackson Farms. Then, Jackson invested in real estate, buying single-family houses and apartment buildings, forming companies to manage the real estate, and growing those businesses by offering their services to other customers and investors.

But the need to serve his country had never left Jackson. It was the one resentment he had in his life. His passion for the military had led him to the local militia movement, which embraced all supporters regardless of their health, age, or experience. In the militia, Jackson had learned things that any basic infantryman would need to know, and he'd met men and women willing to stand up against the tyranny of a radical government. Jackson had studied their ideals and training methods, quickly rising through the militia ranks.

Eventually, Jackson had established his own militia before becoming the founding benefactor of the Liberty Brigade. If he couldn't physically fight a war, he could undoubtedly help fund one.

The ringing on the other end of the line stopped as Steven Jackson picked up the phone.

Without pretext, Moran said, "Sampson is ready to pull down the pillars."

———

THE LEADER of Liberty Brigade stood in the shadow of the barn as Steven Jackson pulled his Chevrolet Tahoe to a stop, raising stone dust that drifted in the still afternoon air. The two men walked down the stairs to the bunker where Dragomirov remained hunched over the computer, streams of code passing across the screen. Music from the Russian rock band Night Snipers blasted from his earphones, loud enough for Moran and Jackson to easily listen along.

"He's probably deaf if he has to listen to it that loud," Jackson shouted.

"What?" Moran replied.

"I said, he's probably ... Oh, never mind." Jackson waved off his friend when he saw Moran's mischievous grin.

Moran tapped the Russian engineer on the shoulder, startling Dragomirov enough to cause him to spin around in the chair and shout in incoherent Russian. The cord attaching his earphones to the computer snapped taut, and the earphones flew off his head.

Both Jackson and Moran laughed at Dragomirov's reaction.

"Not funny!" the Russian said, turning down the music.

"Are you ready for the password?" Moran asked.

"Ten minutes," the engineer replied.

The two militia leaders waited impatiently, staring over Dragomirov's shoulder.

Finally, Dragomirov completed his task and stood from the desk. "It is all yours, my supreme leader."

Moran smiled. It was better than being called comrade.

He motioned for Jackson to take Dragomirov's place at the computer console. The man sat in the chair and spread his fingers across the keyboard. Moran laid a sheet of paper on the desk, and slowly, the mega-farmer input the GPS coordinates for their intended targets with Moran double-checking his work.

Missile One targeted the NSA Data Center in Saratoga Springs, Utah; Missile Two, the U.S. Capitol Building; Missile Three, the United Nations complex in New York City; and Missile Four took aim at FEMA's Mount Weather Emergency Operations Center in Bluemont, Virginia.

The two men had discussed these targets at length. One of the first suggestions had been to aim at the White House, but neither man wanted to destroy such a defining symbol of American pride and heritage. The only other time the White House had been set ablaze was by the British in 1814, during their twenty-six-hour siege of the city.

The day after they set it on fire, a hurricane stormed ashore, bringing heavy rains and driving winds that had lifted houses off their foundations and swirled cannons around in the air. Spooked British soldiers had rapidly abandoned their occupation of the capital amid the chaos.

Moran didn't know whether it had been a coincidence or the hand of God protecting a young nation. Neither he nor Jackson desired to repeat the disastrous steps of the British. So they'd decided to the U.S. Capitol Building instead, hopefully striking it while Congress was in full session.

Once Jackson had entered the coordinates into the computer, password-protected by a code that only Moran and

Jackson knew, Jackson stood and tucked the GPS coordinates into his pocket. "Where's our mad Russian?"

"Probably smoking one of those foul cigarettes," Moran commented, then roared, "Dragon!"

The engineer stepped back into the room. "I want to give privacy. For codes, you know."

"Excellent work," Jackson said, extending his hand.

Dragomirov shook the man's hand. "I am glad you are pleased. I make one other modification I must inform you about." He swept his hand around the bunker, smiling conspiratorially.

"Tell us," Jackson said, glancing at Moran, who lifted a shoulder to signal he didn't know what Dragomirov was talking about.

Grinning like a happy schoolboy, Dragomirov said, "I make room into Faraday cage."

Both men stared hard at the engineer. Each knew Faraday had designed his cage to protect electronic equipment from damaging electromagnetic radiation. In the event of an electromagnetic charge, the current was distributed around the metal framework, preventing it from reaching the sensitive electronics stored within.

"You think Faraday cage not good against EMP," Dragomirov continued, smiling proudly, "but in Russia, we test cage against all electronic fields and EMPs. We make modifications to Faraday's work and now block EMP. We Russian engineers more advanced than any other in Faraday technology."

"That's great, Dragon," Moran stated, though he doubted the compound would need protection against a nuclear or EMP attack. Nevertheless, an additional layer of protection for the sensitive electronics gave him peace of mind that the system wouldn't shut down because of static discharge or power surges.

"Now, you can launch missiles in peace. I leave now."

"We have a parting gift for you." Moran signaled to his head of security, who was waiting nearby. Temple and another security force member stepped inside the control room and seized Kostya Dragomirov by the arms.

"We have deal!" Dragomirov screamed, thrashing against his captors. "I did what you asked! Let me go!"

"You're a security risk, Dragon," Moran said flatly. "Maybe when this is over, I'll let you go."

Dragomirov lashed out with his feet, trying to shake free. "I swear I won't talk! We have deal! I build system. You give me money!"

"The deal has changed. Take care of him, boys," Jackson said as he left the bunker.

Moran stood alone in the control room, listening to Dragomirov plead for his life as Temple dragged him down the tunnel. He wasn't through with the Russian just yet. If the missiles failed to launch, he would haul him from the little cell and make him repair the system.

But once the missiles were in flight toward their targets, Dragomirov was expendable.

The leader of the Liberty Brigade smiled mirthlessly. They were all expendable when it came to watering the tree of liberty with the blood of patriots. Moran fully expected to die for his cause.

But between then and now, there was still a lot of work left to do.

CHAPTER THIRTY-ONE

The Woodlot
Arbuckle, West Virginia

The bright red Peterbilt 362 cabover semi-truck, towing a heavily modified fifty-three-foot van body trailer, barreled through the trees, raising a plume of dust behind it.

Paul Moran watched as it slid to a stop in the dirt. A massive brush guard protected the radiator, and steel plates hung over the windshield and side windows, with slits for the driver to see through, making the truck seem to the militia leader like something out of a *Mad Max* movie.

Before the dust had cleared, a group of men swarmed out of the trailer, all wearing tactical gear and armed with M4 rifles. Several more troopers appeared on the roof of the trailer, flipping an M60 machine gun into place from its hiding spot. One of the men jumped into the seat behind the weapon and, using corresponding foot pedals, slewed the gun left and right through a one-hundred-eighty-degree arc.

A member of Halberd Security ran up to where Moran stood and saluted. The man's black battle dress uniform (BDU) appeared impeccably ironed, with stiffly starched military creases in both the shirt and pants, his battle rattle freshly cleaned and neatly arranged.

Moran returned the salute. Kenny Orlando, who had stood beside his boss during the demonstration, introduced the team leader. "This is Tim Green."

The head of the Liberty Brigade shook Green's hand and gazed deeply into his brown eyes. "You ready for battle, Green?"

"Yes, sir!" Green cried.

Moran nodded. "Are the other two trucks ready?"

Orlando nodded. He raised a radio to his lips and issued an order. Moments later, two more cabover Petes raced into place. They were identical to the first, save for one was blue and the other black. When the men had disembarked from their assigned trucks, Orlando introduced Bubba Ray Jefferson, the second team leader, a stocky man who grunted like he was still in the Louisiana bayou. Orlando would command the third team in the blue truck.

"Let's see the inside of these impressive machines," Moran said.

"This way, sir," Green replied. He performed an about-face and led Moran toward the steps into the trailer. The militiamen had reinforced the interior walls with half-inch steel plating to deflect incoming rounds and mounted sling seats for the ride between their Bluemont Farm base and Mount Weather. A weapons locker had been installed on one side and a gear locker on the other, leaving room for a double row of cardboard boxes loaded with powdered soap between them and the rear doors. If law enforcement were to stop the trucks and open the trailer doors, the boxes would conceal the true purpose of the trailer, and the driver would have a manifest to match.

A simple metal ladder led to the overhead gun mount. When not in use, the contraption folded into the trailer, leaving the roofline intact. But once pulled into place, the M60 would provide protection for the dismounted troops.

Moran had an excellent view of his property from atop the trailer, where he was inspecting the M60. What had once been a former lumber company comprising thirty-five acres, the Woodlot compound was now a state-of-the-art training facility for Liberty Brigade members tasked with attacking Mount Weather after the initial missile strike. Kenny Orlando had overseen the transformation and had hand-picked the mercenaries for the fight. Together, they had turned the on-site warehouse and two office buildings into barracks, mess facilities, a shoot house, and mocked-up tunnels. An eight-foot-high chain-link fence topped with razor wire protected the perimeter, and a small placard at the front gate read: ENTER AT YOUR OWN RISK. PROPERTY OF HALBERD SECURITY.

The militia members used the shoot house to train for various urban combat scenarios while permitting them to use their full-power service weapons. These scenarios included room and apartment clearing, door breaching, and rescuing hostages. While the militia members knew they would face heavy resistance from FEMA's Cadre on Call Response and Recovery Employees (CORE), they did not plan on taking captives.

Moran approved the truck modifications and climbed down from the trailer. He and the team leaders walked to Orlando's office, where the battle plan awaited.

On a large table, Orlando's men had constructed a model of Mount Weather using Google Earth, topographical maps, and any human intelligence (HUMIT) Moran's analysts could gather. To secure the HUMIT, several team members had canvassed local bars and other establishments around Mount Weather. They had talked to people who lived in the area and those who worked inside the facility. They'd also hiked through the surrounding woods, photographing and sketching the above-ground facility.

Moran looked over the three-dimensional model. Despite the many unanswered questions about what the men would face once they arrived on-site, they were committed now, and there was no turning back. He flipped open the folder containing HUMIT summaries. Sifted through it, Moran thought about what he personally knew about the government facility perched on the edge of the Shenandoah Valley just forty-eight miles from Washington, D.C.

Construction on Mount Weather had started in the late 1800s as an observatory. It had functioned as President Calvin Coolidge's summer White House in 1928. In 1936, the Bureau of Mines took control of the site to test new mining techniques by boring into the rock. After a favorable evaluation of the hardness and integrity of the rock, the Army Corps of Engineers built an underground bunker for the continuation of government, completing it in 1958.

Mount Weather passed into the hands of FEMA in 1979 and now sprawled across 564 acres. While FEMA maintained the compound was purely their operations center, the true secret lay in the underground tunnel complex deep in the bowels of the mountain. According to open-source documents, the place was a veritable underground city, complete with hospitals, apartments, schools, and cafeterias, all with their own power supplies, freshwater resources, sanitation, transportation, and communications facilities.

FEMA's initial mandate was to ensure the succession of power and, as such, had built a facility that would allow the president and his cabinet, as well as handpicked members of society, to survive a nuclear holocaust. If the command staff could not reach the bunker, those inside Mount Weather's tunnels would function as a parallel government.

The two main functions of the compound were to play war games and test crisis management. FEMA intended for the war games to train the Mount Weather bureaucracy to manage a wide range of problems associated with the next world war and foreign and domestic political crises. In conjunction with the NSA Data Center in Utah, FEMA was to track large numbers of American people, monitor crises, and respond to them accordingly before they became emergencies. This function also worked reversely, allowing the facility to start crises and monitor them closely to see how the American people would react.

Through these management techniques, the cabinet heads at Mount Weather had assembled and maintained a list of people deemed vital to the survival of the nation and who could assist in essential and non-interruptible services. Conversely, FEMA also kept a list of people considered harmful to their plans should they enact martial law or other contingencies.

For Moran's insurrection to succeed, it was crucial to remove both the visible and shadow governments. For this reason, he had set in motion plans to send in an elite strike force to penetrate Mount Weather and eliminate any behind-the-scenes threats to the Liberty Brigade as they established a new government. Moran believed a combined attack by cruise missile and the Halberd Security strike teams should overcome Mount Weather's defenses and cut off any communication in or out of the facility.

Planning an attack on the top-secret government installation had proved extremely challenging due to the limited information available about the target. While satellite photos of the above-ground portion of the facility were widely available, the team did not know the exact layout of the tunnels nor what they would face if they made it past the giant blast doors that guarded their entrances. Few people who had been inside Mount Weather ever spoke about what they had seen or done there—those who did often wanted to remain anonymous and rarely shared exact details.

While Moran had been working for JSOC, he'd tried to wrangle a spot on a team sent to Mount Weather for training. Yet, he had been unable to do so, having to remain in Tampa to help coordinate a top-secret SEAL team mission. Those he talked to about the training afterward quickly dropped the subject without sharing vital information.

Orlando's infiltration teams identified the two tunnel entrances using satellite imagery and analysis. According to Internet articles, the base would go on lockdown if any threats were made to the facility. FEMA would seal off the tunnel compound using massive blast doors measuring ten feet tall, twenty feet wide, and five feet thick, weighing over thirty-four tons each. Based on that information, the team guessed the doors would take approximately ten to fifteen minutes to close.

Their attack plan began with the Halberd strike teams positioning themselves close to the facility in the early morning before the missile launch. Right after the missile strike, the teams would drive through the compound gates.

The preprogrammed missile coordinates would take out the cluster of buildings in the center of the facility, eliminating many of the six-hundred-fifty employees and two hundred-plus CORE troops, leaving a clear path to the targets for the strike teams. Two teams would secure the tunnel entrances while the third team would sweep through the compound, eliminating the remaining CORE troops and any other resistance that posed a threat.

"Sir, will you be addressing the troops?" Shawn Divert

asked from the office door. "They're gathered in the mess hall."

"Yes. Thank you," Moran replied.

"I have a PowerPoint presentation for them, sir," Orlando stated. "Would you like to see it? It's our battle plan."

"I trust you, Kenny," Moran said, laying a hand on the younger man's shoulder. "You prep these guys for battle at Mount Weather, and I'll take care of the rest."

Orlando nodded and then led the way to the mess hall in the old warehouse. Moran stopped to pour himself a cup of coffee into a paper cup at a refreshment table before climbing to the podium. He looked out on the men gathered in steel chairs, calmly waiting for his words of wisdom and the order to execute the operation they'd trained so hard for.

Moran sipped his coffee and then set the cup on the podium. "You have all done excellent work, men. I believe we're ready and well-prepared for this attack. As of three days ago, the missiles are online and operational." The men bobbed their heads, and some grunted in approval.

"Everything is set for the rally over the Fourth of July weekend. I want those of you not working security there to feel free to join the festivities. Before you head for your next duty station in Virginia, you must destroy everything relating to our operation, from the wall maps to the shoot house. Leave no trace of the plans we've made except for the ones you carry in your heads. Clear?"

"Crystal!" the men responded.

"Excellent," Moran said. "The plan is to launch the missiles on July twelfth, but I want everyone in place on July sixth, so if we have an issue, we can launch our operations early, and we'll be in communication with you if that occurs. Set up a rotating watch so there's always a crew on standby to get the ball rolling."

"Already done, sir." Like most good leaders, Orlando had anticipated his commander's request.

Moran shook hands with the men as he left the mess hall and walked to the waiting helicopter. The pilot began the start-up procedure for the Defender as Moran climbed inside.

As the helicopter rose off the ground, Moran turned to look at the men who stood in ranks at attention in front of the warehouse, saluting the departing aircraft. Moran returned the salute, knowing he might never see most of them again. They were true patriots, ready to die in battle for their country.

CHAPTER THIRTY-TWO

FBI Resident Agency Office
Lima, Ohio

Standing beside Caroline, Parker Rybeck watched as a group of men entered the conference room, shaking hands with SAC Talbot or helping themselves to the coffee and doughnuts on a table at the rear of the room.

Talbot was in his element, schmoozing ahead of the all-agency briefing he had called for on the Militias for a Free America rally. Since Rybeck and his partner Ralph Pratt were the lead investigators on the case, the FBI resident office had become the designated contact and meeting point for all agencies involved in surveilling the rally. Despite the headway they had made on the case, Rybeck knew Talbot hated seeing his agents pulled away from other ongoing investigations to keep tabs on the militia movement, and he'd asked FBI Director Keith Scoda to implement a dedicated Domestic Terrorist Task Force that would take over the duty of surveilling militias. Unsurprisingly, someone had vetoed his request.

Once the men from the other agencies had their refreshments and were seated at the table, Rybeck took his place at the podium at the front of the room, causing the buzz of conversation to die.

Clicking the remote to start the PowerPoint presentation he and Pratt had prepared, Rybeck brought up the first slide, which glowed on the screen behind him. It displayed the Liberty Brigade logo: a skull painted like the American flag, with the blue field and stars at the upper left-hand side and red and white stripes running vertically down the skull. Behind it was a pair of crossed M16 rifles, and curved around the skull were the words: LIBERTY BRIGADE.

"Before I get started with the briefing," Rybeck said, "I want to go around the room and have everyone introduce themselves. I'm Special Agent Parker Rybeck, and my partner at the back is Ralph Pratt." Pratt waved to the crowd. "We've been on this case for the last few months, and we'll share our developments as we progress through the slides."

Pointing to the man on his right, Rybeck indicated he should go next.

The man stood to his full five-nine height. He was bald with a long beard. Tattoos covered his arms, and he had several rings on his fingers. "I'm Carl Crane, U.S. Marshals Service, Fugitive Operations."

As he sat back down, John Hoffman with the Homeland Security Counterterrorism Unit introduced himself but stayed in his chair. He wore an expensively tailored suit with a sharp haircut. For some unknown reason, his relaxed demeanor irritated Rybeck.

"Steve Fisher, ATF," said a man with sandy blond hair that hung almost to his shoulders.

The next man spit tobacco juice into a Styrofoam cup

before he spoke. "Dan Marker, Hardin County Sheriff. The young lady with me is my deputy, Caroline Thurmond. She's my liaison between you fellas and my office. I'm available to any of you gentlemen, but please coordinate with her."

As Marker finished speaking, a thin man with a small mustache and round glasses stood. Rybeck had worked with Marion County Sheriff's Deputy Devon Lake before and knew the young man was more of a politician than a dedicated law enforcement officer. However, his counterpart from Wyandot County, who was also present, had a reputation as a bit of a gunslinger. Deputy Carson Whitman was a product of the Army's Military Police training. He kept his hair in a buzz cut and still habitually ironed military creases into his uniform.

Talbot was the last to address the room. "I know most of you, so I'll keep this brief. The mission is to observe and report. We want to know what's happening at Moran's birthday bash, so keep it low-key." Changing gears, Talbot took the time to point to two men at the back of the room. "We have two other guests with us today—Andy Burke and Harry Jacobs with the FBI's Underwater Search and Evidence Response Team. They have a truckload of equipment ready to go, should we need them."

Rybeck had once applied to the dive team, but they hadn't selected him due to his lack of time in the Bureau. He took a moment to look the two men over. Burke was stocky, with blond hair and blue eyes, while his partner was taller, with close-cropped brown hair. Both were weathered by the sun and from years of working on and around the water. From reading their files before the meeting, Rybeck also knew both men had extensive experience as military divers and had come to the FBI specifically to join the dive team. But before they became divers, they'd had to pass the course at Quantico and then spend at least two years as conventional special agents. Once accepted into the USERT program, they'd undergone rigorous dive training from instructors inside and outside the Bureau. Every member of USERT was a highly trained criminal investigator and on-call diver twenty-four hours a day, seven days a week, ready to investigate a crime scene, combat terrorism, and conduct underwater search and rescue or retrieval operations.

None of the people in the room were newcomers to law enforcement. Many had served in the military or some local police department before joining their respective federal agency. The only person in attendance Rybeck didn't care for was Hoffman, whose training was as a lawyer. Lawyers and lawmen often thought along completely different lines, and Rybeck knew those lines didn't always serve the same purpose.

"Okay," Rybeck said, calling the room to order again. "Now that we've had a meet and greet, I'll begin the presentation."

He gave a cursory rundown on Paul Moran's background and the establishment of the Liberty Brigade.

The following slide brought up an overhead shot of the Liberty Brigade compound. "This quarry first operated as Tri-County Stone because it sits on the borders of Hardin, Wyandot, and Marion Counties, hence the need for each of their deputies to be on hand."

Rybeck detailed the roads surrounding the compound and who would have jurisdiction over the area. He glanced around the room periodically to see if anyone had questions. Caroline always gave him a quick smile.

Rybeck clicked to the next slide, which showed a closer view of the compound. He listed what he and Pratt knew about each building and explained why they thought bunkers and tunnels crisscrossed the property.

"Where did you get this information?" Hoffman asked as he clicked a pen and swiveled in his chair.

"The Hardin County Sheriff's Office and the Kenton Police Department employ personnel who associate with the militia," Rybeck said. "While we've interviewed them extensively about the compound, most didn't know about the tunnels. We believe the tunnels exist because Sheriff Marker had a series of photographs taken by a pilot who routinely flew over the compound."

When no one had a follow-up question, Rybeck clicked to the next slide.

"This is a picture of the pole barn Steven Jackson erected last year. As you can see, large mounds of dirt are piled here and here." Rybeck used a laser pointer to locate several large mounds of dirt near the southeastern side of the building. "There are also indications that tunnels were dug from the pole barn to the HQ if you look at these faint lines here. We had photo analysis done, and our experts believe the militia excavated the tunnels using heavy equipment, then capped them and recovered them with dirt."

"What's in the bunkers?" Crane asked, leaning forward to put his arms on the table. "I'm a little late to this show."

When Talbot had suggested that Pratt contact the Marshals Service, the organization hadn't wanted to send anyone to the meeting. Pratt had convinced them that it was possible some of their fugitives would turn up in Hardin County for the rally.

"Since militias are into disaster preparedness, we believe Moran has stockpiled food, water, ammunition, clothing, chemical suits, firearms, and anything else he believes he might need for the coming apocalypse," Rybeck replied.

Crane nodded and stroked his beard in thought as Rybeck continued with his presentation. He sipped coffee and clicked to the next slide, showing an RV.

"Wait. Go back to that slide with the buildings on it," ATF Agent Fisher said.

Rybeck backed up several slides until Fisher told him to stop. "What's that little house over there in the woods? The one by the water?"

"That is Moran's personal home," Rybeck replied. "We don't think we need to be concerned with it right now. If you can get into it, we'd like to know what you see, but it's not a priority." When Fisher didn't ask another question, Rybeck glanced around the room and asked, "Anything else?"

All eyes swiveled to look at Andy Burke when he asked, "What's in the water? I've got a truckload of gear waiting for you guys to tell us what to do. What's in the water that we need to look at?"

Rybeck took a deep breath before glancing over at SAC Talbot, who nodded, telling Rybeck to inform the group of their suspicions that Moran had cruise missiles located somewhere on the Liberty Brigade compound.

Witnessing the silent conversation between his partner and his boss, Pratt explained, "You're on standby because we believe there may be ordnance stored in the water."

"What kind of ordnance?" Jacobs asked, his voice full of skepticism.

Rybeck cleared his throat and rapidly clicked through the PowerPoint slides until he came to a stock photo of a Sampson cruise missile he'd sourced from the Internet. "We have reason to believe that Moran has acquired four Russian cruise missiles."

There was an audible gasp and some swearing as the men absorbed what Rybeck had just told them.

"How did a militia get their hands on Russian cruise missiles?" Hoffman asked skeptically.

"Glad you asked, Homeland," Rybeck said, involuntarily looking pleased. "We believe Moran is connected with the theft of four SS-N-21 Sampson cruise missiles from an Estonian freighter back in February of this year. A Coast Guard cutter discovered the theft after they received a distress signal from the hijacked ship."

Rybeck explained about the red light ticket, the discovery of Kostya Dragomirov living at the Liberty Brigade compound, and the shipment of Ural motorcycle parts from Murmansk.

"Impossible." Hoffman chuckled. "You think this happened right under our noses?" He pointed at Rybeck. "*Your* noses."

"We all missed on 9/11 and a bunch of other terror plots," Talbot interjected. "The information Pratt and Rybeck gathered shows this could be a valid threat. And we're treating it as such."

"Why weren't we briefed on this before?" Hoffman shot back.

"Honestly, I didn't know if I was going to tell you," Rybeck replied. "My evidence has a lot of holes in it."

"I need to report this," Hoffman stated.

"I'd rather you didn't," Rybeck said.

"Why?" Hoffman demanded. "We need more eyes on this if what you say is true."

"The more eyes on it, the sooner it will get back to Moran," Rybeck stated. "We know he still has contacts in the government. If word gets back to him that we think he is in possession of these missiles, he could move them or, worse, launch them. I want to get into his compound and see if we can find them first and then decide how to take them out."

"Ludicrous," Hoffman scoffed. "Either you're tilting at windmills, or this is the worst security breach in our nation's history." He turned in his chair to face Talbot. "This is on you if this goes sideways."

Talbot nodded. "I understand your point of view, John, but the decision has been made—and it's FBI jurisdiction."

"How so?" Hoffman asked. "This is clearly counterterrorism."

"I've already kicked it up the chain of command," Talbot replied. "The FBI has jurisdiction because it involves the militia." He nodded to Rybeck to move on.

"Wait. You just said you hadn't run it up the chain of command," Hoffman said, glancing between Rybeck and Talbot. "Now, you're saying you have."

"That's right, Homeland," Talbot answered. "Agents Pratt and Rybeck didn't know I'd spoken to Director Scoda last week about the missiles. He's new to the directorship and, as far as we can tell, has no connections to Moran and his militia."

"You vetted your director?" Carl Crane asked incredulously.

"We need to play this close to the vest, and I don't want to talk about it anymore," Talbot stated. "What you've heard is sensitive information and does not need to be discussed with anyone outside this room. Am I clear on that?"

The group reluctantly consented, as they were all eager to report the possible threat up their chain of command.

Again, Talbot nodded to Rybeck to continue.

"Are those cruise missiles submarine-launch capable?" USERT member Jacobs asked from the back of the room. He was upright now and fully attentive to the conversation.

"Yes," Rybeck said.

"Nuclear or conventional warheads?" Burke asked.

"According to our information, they're loaded with conventional warheads." Rybeck watched as Jacobs turned to his colleague and engaged in a whispered conversation. When it appeared that they wouldn't share, Rybeck continued with his briefing. "During the Fourth of July weekend, I want all of you to be on the lookout for Kostya Dragomirov." He displayed a photo on the screen of Dragomirov provided to them by NPO Novator. "He now goes by the name Roger Kozak and is posing as an engineer from Belarus.

"The second order of business we need to consider is Moran's acquisition of illegal weapons. We know from a confidential informant that Moran has been purchasing large quantities of black-market firearms and ammunition. Last week, we received a phone call from our CI about a new shipment of rifles headed for the Liberty Brigade compound. With the help of Steve Fisher and the ATF, we intercepted the shipment and put trackers inside the butt plates. I'll hand that portion of the brief over to him."

Steve Fisher cleared his throat and sipped some water. "We stopped the shipment in Cincinnati before JP Transit picked up the trailers. I posed as the semi-driver and made the switch after we put the trackers on. We tracked the guns straight to Moran's compound and then lost the signal. We think they're in one of the bunkers, and the concrete is blocking the signal. Once we're in the compound on the Fourth, one of my goals is to locate those firearms."

"What's Moran doing with all those weapons?" Deputy Whitman asked. The Wyandot County Sheriff's Department had kept track of the militia news, but with Moran's compound in another county, the goings-on there didn't affect their daily operations.

"We think Moran is either sitting on them or distributing them," Fisher replied. "If I were to guess, he'll sell some during the rally."

"What we have here is a possible combination of Waco and Timothy McVeigh," Dan Marker said to no one in particular. Then, he was more direct. "This affects a lot of locals. There are lots of folks who live around that compound, and it's our duty to protect them. We need to make sure this rally is peaceful. I don't want to see this thing end in bloodshed on the evening news, and I'm guessing neither does Moran. You boys are interested in securing these weapons. My primary concern is safety. Moran has hired a private security firm to keep the peace. I know of several of my deputies and KPD officers who will work there in uniform on the taxpayer's dime."

Rybeck spoke up, trying to take control of the meeting once again. "We're all concerned about safety, Sheriff, and I will stress again that our goal here is to observe and report. No one wants to be on the five o'clock news." He clicked to the next slide, showing a large RV. "The Marshals Service was kind enough to allow us to use an RV and a four-door Jeep Wrangler in case we need another form of transportation. Pratt and I outfitted the RV with radios, listening equipment, and other items we might need to make it a base of operations. We'll be attending under the guise of militiamen from Tennessee. We'll carry Tennessee driver's licenses when we go undercover. This will allow us to come and go from the RV and not arouse suspicion."

"How many people does that thing sleep?" Steve Fisher asked.

"Not all of us," Rybeck replied. "Deputy Thurmond and I have spots in the RV. There's room for four more, depending on how cozy you want to get. The rest can sleep in tents. Agent Pratt will stay in Lima to coordinate our activities and provide backup if needed."

"Doesn't sound like much fun," Hoffman muttered, then said, "I'm calling a bed right now."

"What about her?" Crane asked, pointing at Caroline. "You just said she's coming with us. If there are local PD there, they'll recognize her."

"It's not an issue," Rybeck replied. "Our cover is that she

and I are dating and that we met during another militia gathering."

Crane nodded. "A plausible cover since she's sweet on you. I've been watching her make eyes at you this entire meeting."

Rybeck chuckled nervously. "Full disclosure: Caroline and I are dating."

"Any more bombshells you want to drop, Rybeck?" Hoffman asked.

"No. Moran issued paperwork for all the Liberty Brigade militias, stating what they should bring. We have loaded packs for each of you and your choice of firearms—mostly M4s and your own sidearms unless you have a preference when it comes to long guns."

Pratt passed out Liberty Brigade pamphlets and loadout lists for everyone to study.

"As I said earlier, our primary mission is to observe and report," Rybeck reiterated. "There will be a lot of people at this rally, and we *do not* want to start a shooting war. Everyone will be well-armed, and a shooting match will not be well-received by our bosses or the media. It will probably rally even more support to Moran's cause. We need to be very careful how we conduct ourselves."

Everyone at the table agreed they didn't want to appear on the news for disrupting Moran's Fourth of July militia rally.

"We plan to drive to the rally tomorrow evening," Rybeck said. "We'll meet at Deputy Thurmond's house." He posted her address and directions on the PowerPoint screen. "Any questions?"

No one at the table had any, so Rybeck dismissed the meeting.

As Rybeck wrapped up his computer cord, preparing to return to the office, the two divers approached him.

"What's the plan for us?" Burke asked.

"We want you on standby for now," Rybeck replied. "We have a place to park your truck, and we'll put you up in a hotel until you get the call."

"How long do you expect us to be here?" Jacobs asked.

"Depends on what we find during the rally," Rybeck replied.

"Two weeks?" Jacobs asked, gauging Rybeck for a reaction.

Rybeck shrugged. "I'll be honest, I don't think we need you guys here, but we were told to bring you in. This could be a nice break for you guys."

"I have other work I need to get done," Burke argued. "We can leave the truck here and go back to D.C. until you need us."

Talbot cut in. "Sit tight for now, guys. We don't know if or when we'll need you. As Rybeck said, think of it as a vacation until further notice. Maybe drive past the compound and get a feel for things. Rybeck says you can get a good look at the quarry from the road."

Reluctantly, Burke agreed, and he and his partner left the conference room.

Caroline approached Rybeck next. "Parker, we need to go grocery shopping. If we'll be there for four days, we'll need lots of food and drinks."

Talbot agreed. "You two go get what you need. Ralph and I will make the rest of the arrangements and ensure the others are ready."

After the Marshals had agreed to loan the team an RV, they had sent an Entegra Coach Reatta XL that a guy had used to smuggle drugs across the Mexican border. Since there was no place to keep the RV near the downtown Lima office, Rybeck had placed it in a storage lot on the edge of town. He and Pratt had been to the RV several times over the past few days, using the hidden compartments to install a sophisticated electronic surveillance package.

When Rybeck and Caroline walked into the Reatta XL a half hour after leaving the all-agency meeting, she glanced around with approval at the modern décor, including vinyl plank flooring and granite countertops. Instead of a tiny fridge like most campers had, the Reatta XL contained a full-size fridge and freezer, which would come in handy over the weekend.

Opening the cabinets, Caroline confirmed they were all empty. "We also need blankets, towels, dishes, silverware, and bed sheets. This is going to be an expensive shopping trip."

Rybeck hadn't even thought of all those things. *Leave it to a woman to ride herd on a bunch of guys to get us through the weekend.*

"I don't think we can get away with buying everything we need," he said. "We don't have a big budget for this operation."

"Then we can take the RV to my place and load the things we need," she suggested. "Let's make a list so everyone will know what to bring."

They made a list for each person, and Rybeck called the other agents.

With the Jeep attached to the tow bar, Rybeck drove the camper to the nearest grocery store. They filled two shopping carts with supplies before storing their purchases in the camper.

"This is like setting up a house," Caroline said, giving Rybeck a mischievous smile.

"I'm not ready to move in together," he replied bluntly.

Caroline looped her arms around his neck as they stood in the Entegra's kitchen. "If we're going to pull off the happy couple routine this weekend, you'd better be ready."

Rybeck kissed her deeply, then said, "I think I can manage that."

CHAPTER THIRTY-THREE

FBI Headquarters
Washington, D.C.

Director Keith Scoda scanned the written report he'd just received from SAC Roger Talbot detailing the all-agency briefing about the upcoming Militias for a Free America rally at the Liberty Brigade compound.

Talbot had sent the report straight to the agency's newest director, confessing that he didn't know who he could trust in the administration to keep the information confidential as Talbot and his team were concerned their investigation would leak back to Moran.

Initially, Scoda had acted like it was a far-fetched fantasy that someone could steal cruise missiles from an Estonian cargo vessel and smuggle them into the United States, but he knew it was true. Paul Moran had briefed him on the plan just after the Senate had confirmed Scoda as the new director of the FBI. It was a fantastic tale and an excellent piece of detective work by Rybeck to piece together the splinters of information into a coherent case against Moran.

Scoda poured himself a glass of water from a crystal pitcher on the small side table. Standing at the window, he stared across the city landscape as he sipped the ice-cold liquid. Looking to his left, he could see all the way down Pennsylvania Avenue to the U.S. Capitol Building. To his right, he could see the green grass of the National Mall.

Scoda had witnessed the corrupt, two-tiered justice system firsthand in his years as a federal agent. Cases that should have been prosecuted slipped through the cracks due to influence peddling. In contrast, others, such as the Steele dossier that supposedly showed collusion between former President Trump and Russia, were pursued with religious fervor. It saddened Scoda to see the once proud institution become another puppet of the Deep State.

In fact, Scoda's nomination to the directorship had come as a complete surprise to him. While he had earned a law degree from Mississippi State before joining the Bureau, been SAC of the Los Angeles Field Office, and headed the National Security Branch, Scoda believed he would retire as the counterintelligence chief. But it had been Diane Warrick's direct influence on the Senate that had led to his confirmation. Scoda would later learn that Chet Gravely had loosened his purse strings of special interest. At first, Scoda had resisted meeting with Gravely, but once the two had sat down to talk, Scoda learned they had much in common and was soon playing his part in the militia drama.

After a few minutes of quiet contemplation, Scoda turned away from the bright summer's day and pulled on his jacket then picked up Talbot's report. Walking out of his office, Scoda told his secretary he was going to the White House. From the lobby beside his office, he took an elevator down into a tunnel system that ran beneath Pennsylvania Avenue, connecting many of the government buildings in D.C. with the White House.

Once in the tunnel, Scoda stepped onto a small platform and flagged down one of the electric carts used to shuttle people between buildings. When Scoda stepped off the cart onto the platform at the White House, a member of the Secret Service ushered him straight to the office of Arnold Gottfried, the president's chief of staff, instead of the Oval Office as Scoda had expected.

Gottfried looked up from his desk, his glasses slipping off his long, slim nose and the light reflecting off his bald head. "What can I do for you, Director?"

"I need to see the president."

"Can it wait? We have a meeting with the House Subcommittee on Energy and Mineral Resources."

"No," Scoda said. "I need to see him now. It's a matter of national security."

Gottfried leaned back in his chair and looked Scoda up and down, taking in all six-three of Scoda's muscular frame, his thick head of wavy blond hair, and piercing blue eyes. The two men had never seen eye to eye, being from opposite sides of the political aisle. Scoda always felt a little dirty after speaking with him. But that was part of doing the job—dealing with all types of people and playing the game by buddying up to those who could help you gain power.

"What's this about?" Gottfried asked.

"I don't want to explain it twice, Arnold."

Gottfried stared at him, his elbow on the armrest and his chin resting on his thumb. He swiveled slightly in the chair as he stared at the director.

Scoda hated that this man held the keys to the president. He had entirely too much power, and Gottfried knew he held that power. He frequently used it to curry favor and leverage advantages. Scoda turned and walked to the door leading into the Oval Office. He placed his hand on the knob and had just started to turn it when Gottfried leaped out of his chair.

He pushed his thin frame between the director and the door, whining, "This is the thanks I get for helping you get appointed?"

Gottfried had his own skeletons, and Scoda suspected someone had pressed the right button to get Gottfried to support his nomination. It didn't matter what Gottfried had done in the past. He would soon be out of a job, and that thought didn't bother Scoda one bit.

Wearily, Scoda stared back at the shorter man and replied, "This is me doing my job, Arnold. I need to see the president."

Gottfried was the first to blink and, in a whisper, said, "Fine." He turned the doorknob and led the way into the most famous office in the world.

President David Thomas Cross looked up as at his chief of staff and the director of the FBI tumbled into the room. They spread out and flanked the president, who was seated on one of the blue couches. Cross pulled off his glasses and ran a hand through his salt-and-pepper hair as if he knew something bad was coming. He put his glasses back on and slid to the edge of the couch cushion. At fifty-five, the man resembled a young Ronald Reagan, which, in Scoda's opinion, probably explained his popularity more than his progressive liberal policies. Despite his handsome looks, Cross was vain, and he wore a girdle under his modest blue suit to hide his slowly developing belly.

"What can I do for you two?" Cross asked.

Moran held out the file he'd been carrying. "We have a developing situation, Mr. President."

The president's eyebrows rose slightly as he accepted the documents.

"May I sit, sir?" Scoda asked.

The president waved a hand, indicating any of the pieces of furniture that formed a rectangle around a central coffee table.

Scoda took a seat across from the president and leaned forward, his elbows on his knees. "Retired Army colonel Paul Moran is in the process of uniting the unorganized militias under the banner of Liberty Brigade." He continued to explain Moran's ideology and the threat he posed to the state of the nation by acquiring the Sampson cruise missiles.

"This is news to me," Cross said. "I've heard of Moran, but I had no idea he was such a polarizing figure."

Scoda said, "I included part of it in the daily brief about two weeks ago."

"I must not have attended that one."

Scoda let his head drop between his arms and shook it in disbelief before looking back up. The president was notorious for skipping his daily briefing about the serious or perceived threats to the country.

"How did Moran acquire cruise missiles?" Gottfried asked incredulously.

"Everything is in the folder," Scoda said. "But since you probably won't read it, I'll tell you what happened."

Scoda painted the broad picture from the Coast Guard locating the *Alexsander Ushakov* adrift on the high seas to the red light ticket and the shipment of Ural parts.

"None of that was in the previous briefing," Gottfried observed, stunned by the news.

"No, it wasn't," Scoda concurred. "I just received this information myself from the Cleveland SAC."

"Do you know where the missiles are?" Cross asked.

"We're not sure at this time, Mr. President, but we suspect they're being kept at the Liberty Brigade compound."

"'Suspect,' but don't know for sure," the president replied. "Do you even know for certain that Moran has the missiles?"

"Not one hundred percent," Scoda replied, "but the possibility is very strong."

Cross pondered this momentarily, then asked, "What's the next step?"

"The Liberty Brigade is hosting a rally called 'Militias for a Free America.' We're putting a joint task force of undercover agents on the ground to see if we can verify whether the missiles are there and try to locate the engineer that accompanied them."

"What happens if you find the missiles?" Gottfried asked.

Scoda spoke matter-of-factly. "We execute a raid on the compound and hope Moran doesn't launch them between now and then."

"Wonder what his targets are?" Cross asked absently.

"There's really no way of knowing," Scoda replied, "but if I had to hazard a guess, at least one of them is pointed at the U.N. Building in New York." He had no idea what the actual targets were, but he could make an educated guess based on Moran's rhetoric. While Moran had briefed him on the plan to dismantle the sitting government and enact a new one, Scoda was not privy to the precise timing of the operation nor targets of the missiles.

A secretary knocked on the Oval Office door and then entered to inform the president that the energy committee was waiting outside.

"Thanks, Stacey," Cross said to her.

The president stood and buttoned his suit jacket, preparing for the next meeting. "Keep us apprised of the situation, Director."

———

SCODA TOOK the tunnel back to the J. Edgar Hoover Building. Instead of returning to his office, he walked to his car in the parking garage. He climbed into a black Cadillac CTS-V and drove away from the building, taking a winding, fifty-minute drive through the city to Chesapeake Beach, Maryland, beside the muddy waters of Chesapeake Bay.

He parked in front of the Chesapeake Beach Railroad Museum. Scoda buttoned his suit jacket as he crossed the street to a small café on the riverfront boardwalk. Entering the restaurant, Scoda spotted Phillip Upton alone at a corner table. The reporter gave Scoda a curt nod when their eyes met.

Scoda glanced around to see if anyone had recognized him. Satisfied he was in the clear, he made his way over to the table and sat down. Upton had been kind enough to order a glass of water for him, and Scoda took a long sip, grateful to slake his thirst.

"What do you have for me?" Upton asked.

"Lots of fun stuff." Scoda pushed a copy of the file he'd given President Cross across the table to the *Washington Post* reporter.

Upton didn't bother to open it as he slipped it into his backpack. "What do you want me to do with it?"

"Sit on it until we have confirmation," Scoda replied.

The reporter rolled his eyes. "When will that be?"

"We're placing undercover agents at the Liberty Brigade's Fourth of July rally. We should have confirmation after that."

The waitress delivered two draft glasses of ice-cold Coors Light. Upton took a long drink of the beer and set it down on the table. Scoda sipped his gently.

The reporter and Scoda shared a fondness for the beer brewed in Golden, Colorado. The two men had been associates for almost twenty years when Upton had been a beat writer, and Scoda was just a special agent, working insurance fraud cases.

Back then, Scoda and Upton had pooled their resources to

track down a perp who had bilked an insurance company for over ten million dollars and fled to a non-extradition country. Together, they had set up a sting to lure the man back to the United States, where Scoda had arrested him and recovered almost eighty percent of the insurance company's assets. That case had been the cornerstone of Scoda's career, and the two men had continued to pass information back and forth when it benefited their careers.

Scoda took another sip of beer, then slid from the booth. He tossed a couple of dollars onto the table and said, "Just be ready to publish an expose on the material I just gave you. Things should start happening quickly."

CHAPTER THIRTY-FOUR

Caroline Thurmond's home
Kenton, Ohio

Parker Rybeck pulled the RV into Caroline's driveway and parked it close to the house. She began gathering items from inside her home and piling them beside the front door while Rybeck made trips to the camper and put things away. Getting sheets, blankets, pillows, and everything else they might need for a weekend stay at Moran's rally.

When they finished, Rybeck unhooked the Jeep and stowed the tow bar. "The rest of the guys won't be here until this evening. While we wait for them, I thought we could look around before we drive the camper down to the LB compound."

Caroline shrugged and started for the passenger seat, but her beau tossed her the keys. "You drive. You know your way around, and no one will recognize us in the Jeep."

Pulling out of her driveway, Caroline headed south. "I'll

take you on some of my favorite roads in the county. This road is what we call 'Devil's Backbone.'"

Rybeck held onto the grab bar just above the door and allowed Caroline to put the Jeep through its paces on the winding road.

After making several turns onto other roads, Caroline said, "This is County Road 265. It runs from Ohio 292 just south of here and passes the Liberty Brigade compound shortly before ending in the north. It's called the Old Sandusky Trail. Indians followed this route from Cincinnati to Sandusky on Lake Erie. Later, it became a stagecoach road, and now it is home to one of the largest Old Order Amish populations in the state."

Again, they drove in silence until they reached a tiny settlement called Pfeiffer Station, where Caroline pulled into the parking lot of the Pfeiffer Station General Store. They went inside and bought sandwiches and sodas.

Caroline knew the pleasant-looking woman working behind the counter. "Have there been many people through here?" she said conversationally.

"Yes," the woman said, wiping her hands on her apron. "Business has been fantastic with everyone coming to the militia rally. We're almost out of baked goods."

Rybeck glanced at the shelf of pies and freshly baked bread, spotting one of his favorite desserts, a Dutch apple pie. He slid it onto the counter and paid for it.

Outside, they walked across the street and read the historical marker about Wheeler Tavern. The old brick house had once been a layover on the stagecoach line Caroline had mentioned earlier and then later served as a stop on the Underground Railroad. Today, the old inn was a private residence and a small horse ranch.

From Pfeiffer Station, 265 straightened, with one sharp curve where it intersected with County Road 245. "I call this curve 'Truck Stop' because of the cement factory there," Caroline shouted over the roar of the wind through the Jeep's open windows and roof as she took the curve at sixty.

Rybeck nodded and watched the road fly by.

Several miles later, they slowed and turned right onto County Line Road 255, which bordered the western edge of the Liberty Brigade compound. A line of RVs, campers, cars, and trucks waited to turn into the quarry compound.

Driving slowly past the line of vehicles, Rybeck and Caroline looked to the east and saw the field by the large barn was filled with tents and RVs. They turned left on Rubins Road, where another line of traffic waited to enter the second driveway into the compound.

Rybeck tried to see as much as he could by standing in the seat with his head above the Jeep's roll bar. He couldn't see much, as trees and saplings growing along the ditch blocked his view.

Past the traffic, Caroline continued to cruise slowly up and down the rolling hills of the Little Tymochtee Creek bottom. At Fail Road, she turned left. Rybeck's head was on a swivel, looking at the passing scenery. Farmers were paid not to grow crops as part of the government's "set-aside" program designed to give the land a break. As a result, large fields were overgrown with weeds. Old houses stood among ancient trees, and empty barns built during a bygone era appeared on the verge of falling down. The scenery caused Rybeck to reminisce about his home in North Dakota.

As they entered the rundown village of Marseilles, Rybeck saw houses rotting away with neglect, a boarded-up gas station, a church, and the Angle Back Just One More bar. The parking lot was full of beat-up trucks and some newer cars, with campers pulled off to the side of the road.

"Looks like a popular spot," Rybeck remarked.

"They do a booming business on training weekends," Caroline replied. "They're the closest thing to a restaurant around here. This is Wyandot County, so I don't come over here on duty, but I hear things can get pretty tense." She laughed. "Carson— you know, the kid you met at the meeting—told me a story the other day about that place. He said a concerned citizen called 9-1-1, reporting someone trapped in the trunk of a car in the parking lot. Carson rolled lights and sirens and quickly located the car. He said it sounded like someone was trying to beat the trunk lid off with hammers from the inside. After assuring the victim he would be right back with help, he ran into the bar and asked who owned the white Buick. After some interpreting, this Mexican guy stands up and admits it's his. Carson escorted him to the car, and when the guy opened the trunk, out pops a sheep!"

"A sheep?" Rybeck asked.

"He told Carson it was the only way he could get the sheep home. I guess he'd bought it and was taking it home when he stopped for a few drinks."

"I am so glad I work on a federal level and don't have to deal with crap like that," Rybeck said.

"You'll have to ask him about it," Caroline said, belly laughing. "All the guys in his department give him a baaad time."

Rybeck rolled his eyes at her poor imitation of a sheep, but he had to admit, the story was pretty funny.

Outside of Marseilles, they rejoined County Road 265, having made a complete circle around the Liberty Brigade compound. Caroline braked to slow the Jeep as they dipped into the valley formed by Little Tymochtee Creek, their nostrils flaring from the acrid stench of oil being pumped from the ground. Oil storage tanks lined the road along the creek bottom, collecting crude from the pump they had just passed at the top of the hill.

The road rose from the creek and ran along the northern

edge of the quarry. Rybeck stood up in the seat again as Caroline came to a stop for traffic turning onto 255. He could see the layout of the compound and part of the bright blue water in the quarry.

Sliding back down into the seat as they passed the place they'd first met, he said, "This brings back memories."

Caroline smiled. "Best trespassing call I ever responded to."

With a grin, he said, "Let's roll past Jackson's house, then go to Skinny's so I can say hi to Marge."

As she drove, Caroline told Rybeck about various events that had taken place on the roads as she drove. Some stories were funny, and a few were sad. Rybeck was sure she kept the worst locked up inside.

Approaching the Scioto River, Caroline said, "This is Jackson's place on the left. Although pretty much all the land we've driven past belongs to him. He's been on a buying spree for the last few years. I think he's one of the top landowners in the state."

Rybeck stood in the seat again as she slowed. Jackson's property was impressive, with a multi-acre figure-eight-shaped pond and a garden shed for a lake house at the far end. A small beach area beside the lake house provided a break in the stones that lined the rest of the pond. Just past the pond was a custom-built, two-story brick home with an attached three-car garage. Across the road from the house sat a cluster of silos and a massive grain leg to feed them all. The yards were well-maintained and landscaped, though Rybeck expected nothing less from a wealthy farmer.

Caroline pulled into the driveway by the grain bins and then backed out onto the road, heading back in the direction they'd come from. As they slowly cruised past the homestead this time, Rybeck could see a cement helicopter pad and, beyond, a shiny black MD 500 Defender through the hangar's open doors.

Dropping back down into the seat, Rybeck wondered why a farmer would need a military-grade helicopter. After seeing all the grain silos at the Liberty Brigade compound and at Jackson's house, Rybeck couldn't help but think how easy it would be to conceal a batch of cruise missiles inside them. The military didn't need to build top-secret bases, they just needed a few grain silos in the Midwest.

CHAPTER THIRTY-FIVE

Liberty Brigade compound
Kenton, Ohio

The sun was high in the western sky when Hoffman, the last undercover agents, arrived at Caroline Thurmond's house. They spent some time getting their gear situated, then crowded into the RV for the drive to the Liberty Brigade compound.

Everyone stared out the windows as they approached the site.

Traffic had been steady since Rybeck and Caroline had driven around the trapezoid of roads that framed the quarry compound last evening, and they could see the compound's population had swelled in size. Groups of men and women gathered around tents and RVs, talking, laughing, drinking beers, and enjoying campfires. The smell of wood smoke hung heavy in the air as Rybeck navigated the RV down the long driveway.

ATF Agent Steve Fisher let out a low whistle. "Look at that quarry. It's massive."

"I wasn't expecting it to be so large, either," U.S. Marshal Carl Crane agreed.

"I can't believe how many people are here already," Caroline said from the front seat.

Rybeck brought the RV to a halt and slid open the window beside a security guard, wearing a uniform with a Halberd Security patch on his shoulder and a holstered pistol on his thigh.

"Where are you from?" the guard asked, looking up from a clipboard.

Rybeck said proudly, "Militia of East Tennessee, 3rd Brigade."

The man shuffled through a stack of papers. "I don't have you on the list."

Rybeck exchanged a glance with Caroline before turning back to the security guard. "I registered on the website. I was kinda late on the deadline."

"When did you register?" the guard asked.

"Two weeks ago." Rybeck pulled a piece of paper from the dashboard and handed it to the burly man.

The guard copied the information onto his list with a pen and then returned the registration sheet to Rybeck. "Straight ahead. Joe will tell you where to park."

Following the instructions, Rybeck pulled ahead to a man holding wands, who directed him to turn right into the field. A second man with wands guided him into a parking spot.

With the RV parked, Rybeck and Caroline set about leveling it, extending the slide-outs, and unhooking the Jeep.

Twenty minutes later, they had everything set up. The men offloaded lawn chairs and quickly got a small campfire going in a provided fire ring, then began cooking dinner.

Glancing around, Rybeck saw almost everyone either

carried a sidearm or had a rifle slung over their shoulder. Most wore some type of garb to distinguish which militia they represented. Others wore apparel with the Liberty Brigade logo on it, and the undercover agents followed suit, purchasing merch from a booth near the barn.

"What is it?" Caroline asked, sensing Rybeck's growing unease.

"I just can't shake the feeling that something's about to go very, very wrong."

———

RYBECK LAY awake in the RV, listening to the sounds coming from inside and outside the camper. One of his companions was snoring peacefully, and somewhere, a rooster crowed. Rybeck's back ached from lying on the paper-thin mattress. During the night, Caroline had curled up beside him, taking up most of the bed and covers.

Accepting he would not get more sleep, Rybeck got up and pulled on shorts, a T-shirt, and running shoes, careful not to disturb anyone else in the early morning darkness.

His muscular legs carried him along the driveway, deeper into the Liberty Brigade compound, past sleeping campers, alert security guards who gave him a nod or a wave, and the massive barn that dominated the compound. He followed the road to the east side of the quarry, which afforded an excellent view of Moran's house perched on the edge of the water.

When the militia leader stepped out onto the back deck with a cup of coffee in his hand, Rybeck hightailed it around the rest of the quarry, returning to the RV.

Since their temporary domicile didn't have running water, Caroline and the federal agents used the showers and toilets inside the barracks. After a quick shower, Rybeck returned to fix breakfast and rouse the troops.

Rybeck found Carl Crane in front of a laptop and gave him a nod as Rybeck headed for the master bedroom where he and Caroline slept. Closing the door behind him, Rybeck bent over the bed and gave her a gentle kiss on the forehead. Caroline stirred, pulling herself from sleep, and stretched her arms over her head.

"Up and at 'em, sunshine," Rybeck said.

She rubbed her eyes against the sun that stabbed through the gap in the curtains. Sleepily, she said, "Sorry, I'm not used to the day shift."

Rybeck stepped back out of the bedroom to afford her some privacy as she dressed.

He was getting a bottle of water from the fridge when Crane called out, "Bingo! Got another hit." Crane glanced up at Rybeck. "This fancy camera on top of this RV works wonders. I've spotted two people who are on our Most Wanted list."

Part of the electronic surveillance package provided by the FBI included a camera that allowed the team to photograph anyone within range and then run those images through the federal government's facial recognition program. When the software identified a fugitive, the agents placed trackers on the vehicles they saw them using, with a plan for a joint task force to arrest the fugitives after the rally was over.

Crane fired off a warrant to a friendly judge who had to sign off on all tracking devices. He rubbed his hands together in anticipation. "I've got to get a tracker on my boy. I'll see you clowns later."

CHAPTER THIRTY-SIX

Paul Moran glanced around at the militia leaders gathered in his headquarters building. Most were solid family men who wanted nothing more than to ensure the safety of their families and place limits on the government. They all watched him eagerly, waiting for his advice, knowledge, leadership, and, most of all, a plan.

He cleared his throat to get everyone's attention. Once things had quieted down, he said, "First, thank you all for coming. Next, I want you to tell your people that this is a peaceful gathering. We don't want any fistfights, gunplay, or anything else that can give the press or law enforcement a reason to give us a black eye. We have to assume that every alphabet agency in this country has an undercover agent or two in our midst."

The other militia leaders in the room agreed. They had already said as much to their people. Just about every one of them was on the lookout for a Fed, especially after FBI agents had helped to organize the J6 riots at the Capitol Building.

"With that being said," Moran continued, "this weekend

is also about fun. We have training events and entertainment scheduled. We want everyone to socialize, train, learn, and have fun."

"What about the plan?" Garry Dart from the Idaho Free Militia asked.

Moran held up his hand. "Many of you want to discuss the timetable for our revolution, and some just want help with your own causes. Now that I've said my piece about keeping things peaceful, let's address those concerns."

"What is the plan?" Spencer Tyson, leader of the Michigan Militia, asked. "You've been stumping all over the country like a politician, bringing us all together, but there's never been one word about a plan of action."

Once the largest militia in the country, Tyson's numbers had dwindled since Timothy McVeigh had bombed the Alfred P. Murrah Federal Building in Oklahoma City in 1995, but Tyson still held considerable sway.

Moran took a sip of water and set the glass atop the water ring that had already formed on the coaster's surface.

"I'm glad you asked, Spencer." Moran smiled at the man, meeting his brown eyes with his steel blues. "As we know, marching on Washington leaves much to be desired because marches and rallies fail to attract the attention of our representatives. We can't assault Washington without risking an all-out war with whatever federal agencies the Deep State wants to throw at us—and after the events at the Capitol on J6, I know they would come in with guns blazing. So, that leaves what—voting?

"We all know the system is rigged. The last two elections saw electronic ballot stuffing, dead people voting, and glitches with the software. And since we don't have enough money to buy the number of representatives it would require to force through legislation, that leaves us with doing something drastic."

Moran paused, gauging the reactions of his fellow leaders. Their responses were mixed: some groups were built around working with the government to enact change through legislation, while others stood for border protection. However, there were also those who wanted to fire a gun in anger. And Moran could see the glint in their eyes now as he continued. "We must strike a radical blow against the government, and when that happens, the militias will secure their local governments and borders and help to control emerging crises."

"What do you mean by 'radical blow?'" Shane Albertson of the Texas Militia Movement asked from behind crossed arms.

Since the meeting at Chet Gravely's California Vintage Estates, Moran had pondered just how much to tell the other militia leaders about the plan. He trusted them, but not enough to reveal the master stroke. As dedicated to changing the landscape of American politics as they were, he was pretty sure that at least one of them, if not more, would run straight to the FBI or Homeland to blab that their pal Paul Moran had his thumb on the launch button of four cruise missiles.

"What I'm saying," Moran continued, "is that we cannot continue to rely on the status quo to enact the change we seek. Our battle is against the liberal progression of our country, where people are conditioned to accept big government and question the Constitution. We're up against some of the wealthiest people on the planet, who are constantly purchasing influence and shaping policy in the U.S. and the U.N.

"Paul, we're all on the same page with that," Gaston Price said. "What we disagree on is how to enact the change. You seem to have a plan, but you're unwilling to share it with us for whatever reason. We each have a different level of dedication to the cause, but we're willing to work together to achieve our goals." As leader of the John Birch Society, Price wanted to strike a revolutionary blow, not with the hot barrels of rifles, but with the stroke of the pen. "Now that we're all in the same room, just tell us the plan already."

"I do have a plan," Moran conceded, "and it involves each and every one of you. The time is coming when we will strike, and when you look to the skies, you will know the strike has happened."

Every face appeared puzzled by Moran's reference.

"What? Like a Bat-Signal?" Dart scoffed.

Moran smiled, and several people laughed. "Something like that. You'll know exactly what it is when you see it, and the media will broadcast the signal on every television around the world. When that time comes, you'll mobilize your forces and assist local law enforcement in upholding the rule of law. In some cases, you may need to be law enforcement, or overthrow corrupt local governments. Those of you operating on the borders will need to secure them to hold back the tide of illegal immigrants that may want to take advantage of a time of turmoil in our country."

"Can't be any worse than it is now," Albertson commented. "I mean, the current administration is blindly letting them in and escorting caravans across the border."

Isaac Kemp from California's Cottonwood Militia sat forward like everyone else, intrigued by Moran's words. "Will there be an assault by our troops?"

"Not with our militia forces."

"So, Liberty Brigade will get all the glory?" Dart stated indignantly.

"No. Gentlemen, please," Moran pleaded. "We will all share in the glory of a renewed republic. Please hang tight for a little longer. Things are about to change soon, I promise."

"And just what are you planning to do that we'll need to assist law enforcement?" Kemp asked.

"I plan to cause turmoil and unrest that will spark the engine of change," Moran stated.

Several men shifted nervously in their seats while others eyed the Liberty Brigade leader suspiciously. They could read between the lines, and they all knew there was *a lot* he wasn't telling them.

"What happens after you strike and we mobilize?" Heather Butcher, a solidly built redhead, asked from the back of the room. She was part of The Alabama Regulars and had been in Moran's camp since he'd started stumping for unification.

Moran smiled. "We'll cast out all the old politicians and put a dictatorship in place to pare down the government, eliminating unnecessary programs, departments, and regulations."

A collective gasp passed through the room. A dictatorship flew in the face of everything they stood for. Nowhere in the Constitution was there room for a dictator. Every dictatorship around the world had proven to be an abject failure or led to ruthless violence to ensure the dictator remained in power.

"Should we start calling you Kim Jong Il or Saddam Hussein?" Dart asked irreverently.

Moran held up his hands to quell the tide that seemed to be turning against him. He understood the collective leaders' feelings. He sipped his water and wished it was something stronger, remembering the hint of vanilla on his tongue from the whiskey he'd been sipping in Gravely's study while ogling Diane Warrick.

"Listen to me," Moran said, standing. "A dictatorship creates a stable base with one person running the government, allowing us to focus on our objectives. There will be no opposition to delay our changes, so we can get everything done quickly and efficiently. If we put in newly elected leadership, chances are they'll do exactly as their predecessors and seek money and power for themselves. I promise this will be a good thing, guys."

"And who will be our great leader?" Albertson asked. "You? Is that why you've put all these plans in place—so you can be a dictator?"

"No!" Moran objected. "I will not be the head of the government."

"Who do you have in mind?" Butcher asked.

Moran hesitated. Before he could speak, Kemp complained, "But like your master plan, you're not going to tell us who it is?"

"I can't," Moran replied. "But rest assured, they will do what is best for our country."

Several of the men scoffed or swore under their breath. None of them seemed thrilled with Moran or his obfuscations.

"How long will this dictatorship last?" Kyle Fuller asked.

Moran eyed the leader of Colorado's Mountain Men. "The plan is to elect new senators and representatives at the next election cycle. When they come into session, we will limit them to two terms in the Senate or three in the House. We'll also ask the states to address term limits within their governments. The dictator will remain in office until the next presidential election cycle."

"Is this for real? You're really planning to do this?" Carter Ashton from the Granite State Irregulars of New Hampshire asked from the back of the room.

"I can't say if it will happen," Moran replied, "but I think it's the best way to create the change we so desperately want and need."

"You're just spitballing here?" Price asked with incredulity.

Moran opened his arms and turned his palms upward. "I'm just running it up the flagpole to gauge your reactions."

"I'd say it's polarizing," Price observed. "And I'd say our reaction isn't causing it to flap in the breeze."

Carl Jenkins of the Minnesota Militia chimed in from the back, "While we're shooting for pie-in-the-sky wishes, can we get rid of those irritating medical commercials on TV? Especially all the ones about male performance or anything dealing with painful menopause."

Someone called out, "I'll second that!" and laughter rolled through the room.

Moran was happy to escape the conversation with his scalp intact. The laughter had broken the tension, and the militia leaders began freely talking amongst themselves. It was the first time many of them had ever met. Moran felt it was vital that they meet and interact so they could put faces to the names of other militia leaders across the country who would stand alongside them when the time came to fight for liberty. He had learned early on in his Army career that friendship and bonding went a long way toward getting men to work together—to fight and die together.

And the stronger the bond, the more likely they were to run into a hailstorm of bullets to save their comrades.

CHAPTER THIRTY-SEVEN

"I still can't believe how many people have turned out for this rally," Caroline commented.

She stood atop the RV with Rybeck, John Hoffman, and Carl Crane. They were watching the line of attendees still streaming into the event. The field next to the compound had filled to capacity, and campers were now setting up their tents or parking their RVs along the driveway leading out to Fail Road.

"A lot more than anyone predicted," Hoffman replied.

Hoffman had pleasantly surprised Caroline and Rybeck. When they'd first met him at the all-agency briefing, he'd been standoffish and arrogant. Now that they had gotten to know him, they liked his dry wit, sharp intelligence, and commitment to his job.

"See that man in the Cincinnati Reds ball cap and camouflage pants?" Crane asked.

"Yes," the other three replied.

"That's Fredrick Douglas Pascal. He's wanted in connection with three murders and two armed robberies. The computer flagged him this morning. I put a tracker on the truck by his camp, but I can't tell if it belongs to him." Crane smacked his fist into his palm. "Man, I'd love to bust that guy."

"The computer flagged two people on our watchlist, too," Hoffman said. "This militia craziness attracts all kinds."

"Lots of these militias are flashes in the pan, started by people who confuse patriotism with conspiracy theories," Rybeck pontificated before taking a sip of the beer in his hand. "Moran is just one of the few who hasn't been caught yet."

"Any sign of those guns you guys put tracers on?" Crane asked.

"Not yet," Rybeck said. "Fisher has been all over this compound, looking for them. He thinks they're in those two concrete bunkers by the bunkhouses and that the concrete is blocking the signal."

"Has anyone found a way into those bunkers?" Caroline asked.

The three men shook their heads and stood sipping their beers. All of them had been hunting for a way to access the bunkers or the tunnel system, but they'd come up short. Rybeck suspected Moran had hidden the entrances in plain sight and that they'd probably walked past them several times already.

"What about the main barn? Has anyone been through there yet?" Crane asked.

"I got into it this morning," Caroline said, and Rybeck shot her a look. "I haven't had an opportunity to tell you. I acted like I was looking for a bathroom and slipped in through a side door. The place is empty of farm equipment, but there appears to be a small apartment at one end."

"Any sign of our Russian?" Rybeck asked, concerned Caroline might have blown their cover.

"No. Security ran me out before I had a chance to look around. The place is well-guarded."

The foursome stood silently, watching the crowd move toward a large, open lot north of the main barn. The organizers had cordoned off part of the field to prevent RVs from entering, utilizing it as a gathering area for the attendees.

Crane glanced at his watch. "Looks like it's about time for our fearless leader to give his first speech."

"We should go see our leader and tell him we come in peace," Hoffman scoffed, and everyone chuckled.

Climbing down from the RV, they heard approaching rotor blades. A helicopter bearing the logo for CBS Channel 10 News arrived from the southeast and flew in a circular pattern above the compound. It came to a hover just south of the large barn and dropped to the concrete landing pad, where it sat for several minutes, rotors turning as it disgorged the news crew, then lifted off to fly in circles around the compound again.

Caroline slipped her hand into Rybeck's as they walked toward the gathering area. "What do you think Moran will say?"

"Death to the government. Down with the Deep State. Bring back Ronald Reagan. If he says, 'Respect the government and work within it to create change,' this was a lot of work for nothing. Working within the government hasn't accomplished much. How many of those senators and reps go to Washington penniless and come back millionaires? You can't tell me that special interest money didn't line their pockets."

"Careful, you're starting to sound like one of Moran's Marauders," Caroline said, using the nickname the assortment of federal agents had created for Moran's band of merry followers who seemed to shadow his every move.

"No, that's just common sense," Rybeck said.

They found spots near the stage and waited for Moran to appear. The CBS news crew had set up in front of the stage, and the reporter, a young brunette, was interviewing people in the crowd.

A hush descended as a confident-looking Moran walked from the barn to the stage and stepped to the microphone set up for him at a small podium. A wild cheer rippled through the crowd, and Moran waved and smiled, calling for calm.

"I want to welcome all of you to the great State of Ohio. Thank you for coming to Militias for a Free America and embracing Liberty Brigade. Like you, I have a deep love for my country and do not like the path we find ourselves on. We stand together to fight the policymakers dragging us down this slippery slope. We stand together against tyranny."

The crowd thundered with applause.

Moran waved his arms to silence the crowd and went on. "I ask everyone to be on their best behavior. We are here to have a good time, to learn, and to train. There's a news crew here to watch us—and I'm sure there are plenty of undercover officers among us."

Many in the crowd booed while others chanted, "Go home, Feds!"

"It's all right," Moran continued. "We want them to see that we are peaceful and law-abiding—to a point. That point is coming! We will rise up, take back our government, and reinstall the beliefs and values of our Founding Fathers to make this country great again!"

More cheers erupted from the crowd.

"We'll talk more soon, but for now, I want everyone to have a wonderful evening and a great weekend!"

Moran stepped away from the microphone and returned to the barn.

Hoffman leaned over to whisper in Rybeck's ear, "Did you see him come from his office in the headquarters building?"

Rybeck shook his head.

"Me, either, which makes me think there really are tunnels under that barn," Hoffman concluded.

Rybeck nodded. He had come to the same conclusion. In his mind, he felt that if he could find the entrance to the tunnels, he would find the missiles.

CHAPTER THIRTY-EIGHT

Steve Fisher had been waiting all day for a moment when he could go unnoticed.

As Moran gave his welcoming address, the ATF agent slipped into the men's barracks and began a methodical search of it. He had to make it fast because the militia's hired security performed roving checks of all the buildings, and he didn't want to arouse any suspicions.

After several thorough searches earlier in the day, Fisher concluded the hidden door to the underground tunnels and bunkers was not in the bathroom. So, he was bent on searching the rest of the building for a tunnel entrance, believing it extended from the bunkers to the barracks.

Like many military barracks rooms, it was a long, open affair, with steel-framed bunk beds that ran the length of the room and hanging lockers positioned between the beds. It reminded him too much of his days in the Army.

During his previous trips, Fisher hadn't been able to search the office, and he found the doorknob locked as he grabbed it now.

Pulling a set of lock picks from his pocket, the ATF agent

quickly unlocked the door and stepped inside. Positioned in the center of the room was a desk so the seated occupant could look out a window into the barracks. Along the rear wall were several steel cabinets.

Fisher thought there was something strange about the size of the room, but he couldn't put his finger on what it was, so he began his search by going through the desk. It was empty except for an assortment of pens and pencils and a pad of legal paper.

Next, he checked the filing cabinets, pulling them away from the wall and sliding them back into place. As he pushed back the one closest to the office door, he felt a cold draft on his shoulder. He placed his hand flat against the wall and felt the draft, which followed the outline of a door. Sliding his hand around the edge of the hidden door, he found a pressure switch that released a magnetic lock, allowing the door to swing open just enough for him to get his fingers behind it.

With one last look around, Fisher slid through the secret door and closed it behind him.

Now that he was on the other side, Fisher realized what had nagged him earlier. The dimensions of the office had seemed off as he walked through the barracks, and now he knew why. A three-foot gap between the bathroom and the office walls provided the hiding spot for the staircase down to the tunnel.

Fisher crept down the stairs and stood in the narrow alcove at the bottom. He was on the north side of a tunnel that ran east and west. To his left, he could see a staircase that he assumed led up to the women's barracks. To his right, the tunnel seemed to stretch into infinity.

Stepping into the tunnel, Fisher headed west, walking quickly along its length, thankful for the rubber soles of his combat boots that masked his steps. He figured the tunnel would lead him to the bunkers, and once he was there, he stood a better chance of hiding than in the tunnel proper.

He pulled out his cell phone and opened the tracking application. There was a faint flash, showing the trackers he had placed on the latest batch of stolen M4 rifles were transmitting, and the app was picking them up.

Four more steps into the tunnel, Fisher's phone lost service, but the trackers continued to flash. A few steps more, the tunnel opened into a room with a much higher ceiling. Fisher took it as the first bunker they'd spotted in Rybeck's aerial surveillance photographs.

Bright LED lights illuminated the rows of shelves that held canned goods, prepackaged food, and everything else a person would need to survive an apocalypse or a civil war, from first aid kits to plastic utensils. Large containers of water lined one wall, and Fisher estimated the tanks held least a thousand gallons.

There's enough food here to feed a small army, Fisher thought.

After a quick search, Fisher concluded the M4s had not been stashed in this bunker, and he crept back into the tunnel on the eastern side of the food bunker. The tunnel bent slightly to the left, and fifty more paces brought him to the second bunker, where the red dot on the tracking app glowed more noticeably.

Fisher stepped into the second bunker and paused to catch his breath. He hadn't overexerted himself, but he was stunned by the sheer volume of firearms and ammunition stored there.

The militiamen had stacked crates of ammunition and firearms from floor to ceiling, forming pathways through the bunker. He figured there were several million rounds of ammo, and he dared not hazard a guess at the number of firearms.

Fisher swept the tracker across the room. The M4s were in there somewhere.

The ATF agent began on his left, where stacks of wooden gun crates held M4s, AR-15s, AR-10s, bolt action hunting rifles, and more crates laden with pistols. He saw labels for Beretta, FN, SIG Sauer, Smith and Wesson, and Glock.

It took almost ten minutes of searching before Fisher located the stack of Colt Defense M4 carbines that he and Rybeck had planted trackers on. He used his phone to snap several photographs of the location of the M4s in the bunker.

After confirming the location of the stolen rifles, Fisher stepped out of the bunker. His attention was drawn immediately to the two stacks of long, dark green plastic cases in an alcove. He knew exactly what was in those cases, and seeing them sitting in the damp bunker frightened him.

Hoping he was wrong, Fisher snapped open the latches on the side of the case and raised the lid. It was as he feared. The cases contained Raytheon FIM-92E Stinger missiles.

Fisher snapped a picture of the missiles with his phone and tried to take a picture of the gun bunker. He couldn't capture all of it in one photo, so he took several. They still didn't do justice to the sheer number of firearms contained within the bunker. No one would believe him without photographic proof. *As the kids like to say, pics or it never happened.*

After closing the lid of the Stinger case, Fisher continued to explore the tunnel. It ran straight as an arrow. If someone stepped out of an alcove, they would clearly see him. He prayed no one was prowling the tunnels and that the militiamen were all upstairs, enjoying the concert. After Moran's opening speech, country music artist Randy Hogan had taken the stage. It was part of the draw to get people to attend the rally. Several big-name artists sympathetic to the Liberty Brigade cause would play for the crowd during the long holiday weekend.

In the tunnel, though, it was quiet, and Fisher tried his best to move with stealth, ears perked up, senses on high alert.

A low, shuffling sound caused Fisher to freeze in his tracks. He held his breath and debated whether to sprint back to the nearest alcove but decided against it. Fisher couldn't see anyone else in the tunnel. As he strained his ears, he heard a low moan and a muffled cough.

Fisher flattened himself against the cold concrete wall, feeling the adrenaline surge through his body. The shuffling and moaning continued, and Fisher figured it was coming from one of the doors up ahead. He crept forward, counting at least twenty doors—ten on each side of the tunnel.

The ATF agent paused at each door to peer through the mesh-reinforced window fitted into it. Through the windows, Fisher saw each room contained twin bunks, a metal desk, a chair, and a toilet.

To him, they looked like prison cells.

He was almost to the end of the bunk rooms before he saw a man lying crumpled on a lower bunk. The cell door was locked when Fisher tried it.

Instantly, the man came to life, shifting off the bed and rising to his feet.

Fisher froze. The man had seen him, and he would know that an intruder had entered the tunnel. Prisoner or not, the man might alert someone to Fisher's presence there.

Fisher cursed himself for trying the doorknob.

The room's occupant came toward the door, staring at Fisher with a puzzled expression. Suddenly, Fisher recognized the man as the missing Russian engineer, Kostya Dragomirov, feeling all his other discoveries paled in comparison.

After Fisher took a picture of Dragomirov with his cell phone, he pulled up a notepad application, typed a brief message, and held the phone screen up to the window.

Dragomirov read the note and nodded his head. "Let me out!" he cried, his voice muffled by the thick steel door.

I don't have the key, Fisher typed.

The Russian cursed in his native tongue and slammed his fist against the door. Fisher jumped at the sound and glanced up and down the tunnel.

The ATF agent pointed at the top message on the app. *Are the Sampson missiles here?*

The prisoner nodded and said, "In the silo."

What silo? Fisher typed.

Dragomirov struggled with his words, placing his hands against his head and pulling at his disheveled hair. "Missile silo."

No kidding, Fisher thought. He pondered what Dragomirov was trying to convey, then typed. *Grain silo?*

Dragomirov nodded and held up his hands in victory before shouting, "Get me out!"

I can't right now. Sit tight, and I will work on it.

Dragomirov appeared crestfallen, stepping back from the door.

Where's the control room?

Dragomirov pointed west. "Under barn."

Are the missiles operational?

"Yes."

Fisher paused, taking in a ragged breath. *That confirms it,* he thought. *If the Sampsons are operational, Moran intends to use them.*

Do you know what the targets are? Fisher typed.

The engineer shook his head.

A door slammed farther down the tunnel, causing Fisher to jump again. He stuffed the phone into his pocket. "I'll be back," he mouthed, then he turned and ran down the tunnel the way he had come.

Climbing the stairs back to the barracks, Fisher hoped no one was in the office so he could get out unseen.

At the top of the stairs, Fisher paused, ready to push open the door, when he noticed a small beam of light to the left of the jamb. He pressed his eye against the hole and saw two people sitting in the office.

Fisher cursed his luck. He couldn't get out.

He turned and crept back down the stairs. At the bottom, he removed his phone from his pocket and erased the messages he had used to converse with Dragomirov but kept the pictures. If the guards caught him, it didn't matter, anyway. Moran would know he had seen everything. If he got out, he would have proof that Moran was as dangerous as Rybeck and his team had led him to believe.

Needing to find a way out of the tunnels, Fisher headed for the women's barracks. He walked to the far stairs, climbed up, and found a gap between the door and the jamb to spy through. He didn't see anyone and, by pressing his ear against the door, couldn't hear anyone either. After pushing through the open door, he swung it shut, making sure he closed it all the way before beating a hasty retreat through the back door of the barracks.

Outside, the concert was still in full swing. Music blared across the compound, reverberating off the buildings and the stone walls of the quarry. Most of the attendees had spread out across the green space in front of the stage. Vehicles lined the edge of County Road 265, with people watching and listening on the dirt embankment that separated the quarry from the road.

Fisher crossed the compound, skirting the buildings and the crowd to get to the RV. Once there, he downloaded the pictures from his phone to his computer and composed a report. Thinking he should inform his fellow agents, Fisher paused before he pressed *Send,* but he didn't know where they were. Then he thought about the grain silo and climbed up onto the roof of the RV, holding a camera with a telephoto lens. Fisher examined each of the grain silos through the camera but couldn't see a difference in them. Just for good measure, he snapped a few pictures of the silos and, returning inside, added them to the email.

A couple of minutes later, Rybeck and Caroline walked into the RV. They'd planned to take advantage of the empty RV. However, they immediately put those amorous thoughts on hold as Fisher excitedly told them about his trip into the tunnels. He showed them the pictures and recounted the conversation with Dragomirov.

"I knew the missiles were here, but part of me hoped I was wrong," Rybeck said, shaking his head in disbelief.

"This is crazy," Caroline said, "but we haven't seen them yet."

Rybeck slammed his hand against the table. "That's the argument the brass will make, and they won't make a move until we confirm with absolute certainty that they're here."

"I grew up in the city and spent my entire career in one inner suburban hell after another, but even I know there's no getting into those grain silos," Fisher stated.

"Let's go up and have a look," Caroline suggested calmly.

The trio climbed the RV ladder to the roof, perching on top with binoculars and the camera.

Rybeck zoomed in on the closest silo, focusing on the bottom and working his way up each one.

Resisting the urge to point, Rybeck said, "Caroline, look at those roof hatches on the middle silo. Are those hydraulic arms attached to them?"

Caroline took the camera from Rybeck and focused the long lens of the DSLR camera on the top of the silo. She corrected the zoom to bring the picture into focus, snapped half a dozen photos, and used the wireless feature to transfer them to the laptop in the RV below.

"They're different from the hatches on the other two silos, right?" Rybeck asked.

Fisher lowered his binoculars. "I don't know. They all look the same to me."

Caroline snapped a few pictures of the tops of the other two silos, and then the trio descended back into the RV. Rybeck got sodas from the refrigerator and sat down at the table as Caroline enlarged images of the silos.

"Look," she said, pointing at the computer screen. "See how these hatches have hinges at the top and a handle at the bottom?" The men nodded. Shifting her finger to the photo of the middle silo, she continued, "The hatches here have a hinge on the side and what looks like a hydraulic cylinder on each to open them."

"They're also in a different location than on the other two bins—closer to the top and closer together," Rybeck observed.

"Why did they put hydraulics on them?" Fisher asked, looking over Caroline's shoulder.

"So they can open them remote—"

Caroline stopped Rybeck by slapping him on the arm. He turned to look at her, and she held a finger up to her lips and then pointed to the shadow of a figure lurking outside the Entegra's window.

Fisher reached across the table and pulled the blind back, but whoever had been standing there was gone. Rybeck darted out the door and ran to the back of the RV, trying to see who had been eavesdropping on them. While he saw several people walking between other RVs, he didn't know if any of them had been their lurker.

Back inside, Rybeck shook his head as the other two

looked at him expectantly. He sat back down at the table. "We need to develop a code."

They sat in silence for a few minutes until Caroline said, "We should call the things in the silo Budweisers. That way, we're just looking for some beer."

Fisher held up a thumb and forefinger like a pistol. "Okay, then those can be pop cans," he said, referring to the M4 rifles.

They nodded, agreeing to tell the others when they saw them.

"Save the brief to send later, and let's see if we can find the Budweisers," Rybeck said, standing up. "Come on, honey. Let's go for a walk."

The two lovebirds crossed the Liberty Brigade compound, weaving through trailers and occasionally stopping to talk with other campers. Caroline held Rybeck's hand in hers, feeling like she was growing closer to him with each passing moment.

"Let's see if we can score some Budweisers over by the silos," Rybeck said, leading the way toward the three steel towers gleaming in the late afternoon sun.

"A wonderful way to spend the Fourth of July," Caroline muttered.

"Where else would you rather be?" Rybeck asked in jest.

"Neck deep in a hot tub with you in some fancy little hotel," she replied.

Rybeck liked the sound of that.

Up close, the grain bins towered thirty feet above them and spanned twenty feet in diameter. A metal staircase wrapped around each bin, leading to the top, and a horizontal grain auger connected the conical tops of each bin with a vertical auger that led down to a large hopper where grain wagons could dump their loads.

"I wonder how much grain these things hold?" Caroline mused as they walked around them.

"My parents bought some the last time I was home. Dad told me that a grain bin this size can hold twelve hundred bushels of grain. Theirs cost about thirty grand apiece, and that didn't include the concrete for the pads or have the utility poles installed to run three-phase electrical wire to them."

"Hey, Parker, come here." Caroline motioned him toward where she stood by the barn, having ducked under a yellow banner of caution tape meant to keep trespassers out from around the bins.

After he had joined her, she pointed to a vertical seam in the metal and asked, "What do you make of this?"

"It looks like someone cut part of the silo open and then welded it back together."

Rybeck squeezed between the barn and the silo, and Caroline followed. They could see a matching seam on the other side.

Caroline was looking up when Rybeck hurriedly pulled her around and pressed her against the metal silo. He kissed her deeply, wrapping his arms around her waist, but she could see he had fixed his gaze on something in the distance.

"Hey, you two! Get out of there!" A security guard ordered.

Rybeck released his girlfriend and held up his hands.

Glumly, he said to Caroline, "Come on. I guess they don't want us making out behind the barn."

Caroline eyed the guard from Halberd Security, who stood ten feet from them, one hand resting on the butt of his pistol.

"Sorry, man," Rybeck apologized. "We just thought we'd found a quiet place to hang out for a minute."

"Stay out of there," the guard barked. "The owner doesn't want people messing with his grain bins."

"Guess he shouldn't have a militia rally on his farm then, huh?" Caroline shot back, feeling testy that the guard was harassing them.

Caroline held Rybeck's hand as they went around to the concert venue. They stood watching the band play as the crowd swayed and danced to the music, which wasn't what Rybeck had envisioned when he and Pratt had first heard about the rally. He'd pictured men with guns running through the woods, playing paintball, and chanting slogans. And he'd expected pushback from counter-protesters, but so far, the Halberd Security team had kept the crowd of thirty people at bay in a separate roped-off area across the road. If they chanted louder, waving their anti-militia signs and banners, the sound tech turned up the speakers for the band to drown them out.

But Rybeck's focus had never been on having a good time at the rally, and knowing what he knew now, he would find no enjoyment there. Dragomirov was in a cell below their feet, stolen rifles rested in a bunker, and all signs pointed to the Sampson missiles lurking in a grain silo, ready to fire.

The whole place felt like the lid could blow off at any second.

CHAPTER THIRTY-NINE

Saturday morning dawned brightly, with temperatures promising to rise into the high eighties. Paul Moran sat at his desk, staring at the notecards for his speech. He had written what he considered the best speech of his life, but he couldn't enjoy it. There were other things on his mind.

Moran took several deep breaths, then placed the speech cards in order, aligning the edges to match. It was at times like this that he missed his wife. Mary had been a rock for him throughout his Army career. She'd consoled him when he was sad or angry, given him advice in times of need, and had raised his children. And even when he'd turned away from the establishment in favor of the radicalism of the militia movement, she had tried to rein him in. Moran had shaken her off, seeing his leadership of Liberty Brigade as an extension of his military service and the oath he'd sworn to defend the Constitution.

Unable to reconcile his new beliefs with hers, Mary had left him three years ago. It had been devastating to Moran, but he'd put it out of his mind and concentrated on what he believed to be his greatest work. Now, sitting in his office and faced with the upcoming speech, the growing pressure from the government, and the ever-present thoughts of the missiles, Moran missed her guidance more than ever.

Getting up from the desk, Moran poured himself a cup of coffee, then stood on the back deck, watching the tranquil blue water of the quarry. The camp was just starting to stir. He could hear the sounds of laughter, the hum of a diesel generator, and smell wood smoke even though his house was some distance from the campground.

His thoughts returned to Mary and their two children—Gabriel, a Recon Ranger in the Marine Corps, and Shelly, a middle school teacher in Georgia. He missed them terribly. They had both sided with their mother in the divorce and had not spoken to their father since. Gabriel had chosen the Marine Corps to escape the Moran name in the Army, although the Moran name was now toxic because of his decision to solidify the militias. Shelly was expecting her first child and had not told him he would soon be a grandfather.

Moran had known there would be a price to pay when he'd started Liberty Brigade. The Founding Fathers had suffered even greater oppression. Some had lost their lives, their families, and their fortunes. As difficult as it was to accept, Moran's price had been his family.

He knew he was doing all of this so they could live in the land of the free and not be held hostage by ruthless politicians, terrorists, or illegal immigrants, even though his family couldn't see it.

Those who chose to subvert the American way of life wanted to drag Lady Liberty down to be like the rest of the Third World nations. Moran knew there was no way to make everyone equal. It had never worked before, and it wouldn't work now. Even the Pilgrims, striving to create a new home for themselves, had found that socialism didn't work. It allowed naturally lazy people to avoid work in favor of riding on the coattails of those who worked hard. They had prospered only when the Pilgrims changed to a system where everyone had to fend for themselves. Turn a man loose to his own devices, and he would either succeed or fail.

What Moran couldn't comprehend was how the thinking of those who had succeeded in America, those who had made real wealth through acting, investing, or building businesses, could turn from the capitalistic system that had allowed them to gain their wealth and then insist that others didn't have the right to follow in their footsteps. How could the supposed elite believe they were better than everyone else now that they had acquired their wealth yet tell others they didn't have the right to rise above their stations?

Moran shook his head and sipped his coffee. A knock interrupted his thoughts.

Turning, he saw Jonas Temple, his head of security, and a knot of dread tightened in his gut.

Temple's raspy voice was little more than a low growl as he said, "We have a problem."

"What is it?" Moran asked, extending his hand for the folder Temple carried. He handed it to his boss. Moran opened it on the deck railing. It contained photographs of the federal agents his Halberd Security team had already identified.

Throughout the evening, Temple's team used software similar to the facial recognition program the undercover agents used in their RV to scan faces at the rally. Instead of looking for criminals, the militia had programmed their software to look for law enforcement agents.

The Halberd guards had been taking turns shadowing the agents and had overheard conversations in the RV. Although they didn't know what the Feds had been discussing, it didn't take a genius to conjure up their conversations.

"These two were spotted examining the middle silo." Temple pointed to Rybeck and Caroline. "They've been sneaking around the compound, taking pictures. Our facial recognition software identified FBI Agent Rybeck, and we know Caroline Thurmond is a Hardin County sheriff's deputy. We haven't identified the others with them, but rest assured, they're law enforcement."

"We knew federal agents would infiltrate our rally," Moran replied.

"That's not the problem I wanted to talk to you about," Temple stated. "Our problem is that video surveillance caught someone sneaking around in the tunnels yesterday. He talked to Dragomirov."

"Who was in charge of tunnel security?" Moran asked angrily.

"Not to worry, sir. I've already reprimanded the men. Apparently, they thought going to the concert was more important than guarding the tunnels."

"I want them fired," Moran growled.

Temple shook his head. "I would suggest, sir, that we don't do anything rash. Those four men are loyal to our cause, and they know our innermost secrets. We can't afford to turn them loose."

Moran ground his teeth together and sighed, trying not to take his frustration out on his head of security. He had to wonder, though, if he'd made a mistake holding a public rally on the same grounds as he'd secreted his missiles and constructed his emergency bunkers.

Tucking the folder under his arm for later perusal, Moran said, "Keep an eye on the agents and make sure they don't get into the tunnels again. Leave the folder on my desk."

"I'm worried about the security," Temple stated. "We can't guard everything even with the augmentation from Halberd

Security. There are way more people here than we ever dreamed would come."

"I know, Jonas. Just do your best. Keep on those agents." Whatever joy Moran felt about the larger-than-expected turnout had been tempered by Temple's unwelcome news.

"Yes, sir." Temple turned and went down the stairs off the back deck.

Moran slammed his hand down on the deck railing and cursed Wayne Patterson for getting the red light ticket in Port Arthur. Patterson had shown him the paperwork, including the clear picture of him and Dragomirov in the cab of the Kenworth. According to his sources in the military, the Coast Guard cutter that had assisted the *Alexsander Usakov* had also filed a report detailing the missing missiles and absent Russian engineer.

FBI Director Scoda had called him yesterday and briefed him on the report Talbot had turned over to him. With the document's author, Rybeck, at the rally, Moran was feeling a time crunch. Now that the FBI knew about the missiles, they would come for them. He needed to speed up his timetable.

Moran returned to his desk with his cup of coffee, wishing he could call Diane Warrick. He just wanted to hear her voice and be reassured that he was on the right track, but he would never endanger the plan for his own vanity.

Picking up his cards, Moran tried to rehearse his speech again, but he quickly put them back down. He had it down cold, but that wasn't what troubled him. Moran couldn't shake the feeling that someone was watching him and had discovered all his secrets. The FBI was watching, that was for sure.

Leaving the speech cards, Moran opened the folder containing the photographs Temple had shown him. He shuffled through the images, stopping at the picture of FBI Special Agent Parker Rybeck.

According to Scoda, the FBI had assigned Rybeck and his partner, Ralph Pratt, to investigate the Liberty Brigade. Moran studied the photo, memorizing the man's face, and then laid it on his desk.

The next photo showed Rybeck and Hardin County Sheriff's Deputy Caroline Thurmond in an embrace behind the silo.

Moran tossed the pictures aside and left the house, wondering just how much Rybeck knew.

———

MORAN HAD ALWAYS BILLED The Militias for a Free America rally as a training weekend, and it lived up to its advertising. Militia members could choose from various training packages, including patrol tactics, survival, underwater search and rescue, first aid, and a host of other options.

So many people had shown up for the rally that not all could participate in the training. Others actively chose not to, preferring to sit by their recreational vehicles or tents to socialize.

An incident during the day involving a group of skinheads attacking Black participants resulted in the skinheads being rounded up and evicted from the grounds by the Halberd force. Moran had wanted to send a clear signal to all the rally participants that he wouldn't tolerate hate speech by fringe groups within Liberty Brigade. Prejudice could not jeopardize unity against the government.

When training had ceased for the day, Paul Moran took the stage. The CBS film crew was back and poised to record his speech.

Moran strode to the podium, trying not to look at the red light on the camera, and set down his note cards. He took a sip of water from a glass under the podium, then surveyed the crowd, seeing the multitude of people gathered to celebrate freedom, ready to defend liberty, and enjoying the benefits of fellowship, training, and entertainment on a perfect Fourth of July weekend. That sight alone was heartwarming and inspirational.

His gaze moved to the small knot of four men and one woman standing to his left, close to the stage. From the photographs Temple had shown him that morning, Moran identified Parker Rybeck and Caroline Thurmond among them. Moran's lip curled slightly as he moved on. He'd known they would be there, watching him, from the moment he'd conceived of this rally, but the gall of their presence still infuriated him. He couldn't let it show, though. His audience was waiting, and he needed them to see him as a beacon of truth rather than a man easily distracted by such annoyances. He needed them to feel his rage at the government, not at four mere observers of the speech he hoped would underpin everything he had worked for.

Moran cleared his throat, picked up the cards again, and scanned the crowd again before speaking. "I want to thank all of you for being here and making this rally an enormous success. This country needs more patriots such as yourselves. If we can rally together here, we can rally together for even greater causes. The strength we possess when we stand together will topple governments and spark a revolution.

"But today, I stand before you to address a matter of utmost importance: extremism. People dare to say that *I* have become extreme! If this is the case, then let me declare my extremism to you. My extreme nature stems from my unwavering passion for American liberty. I am considered extreme because of my love for my God, my love for my country, and my love of the freedom we have here. I am extreme because I believe the Constitution limits the government's powers and grants the people the unassailable rights of 'Life, Liberty, and the Pursuit of Happiness.' I am extreme because I believe government is *by* the people and *for* the people. I am extreme because I believe there is a war raging against our rights, our liberties, our freedom, and our religion.

"This 'extremism' has branded me a traitor to my country, the bane of sedition, because I support the rights of the people over the tyranny of government.

"Ought not liberty be the direct end of our government? So it is that the Founding Fathers fought valiantly to establish a nation built on the principles of freedom, equality, and justice, and, in due course, left us with the Constitution, the one great power to limit government, starting the Preamble with three bold words: 'We, the people.' Those words mean that *we* tell the government what to do. And when they don't listen, we are emboldened to act through the commission of the Second Amendment to keep a well-regulated militia to save our beloved nation from the clutches of tyranny.

"Tyranny lurks at our doorstep, seeking to erode the values that have made America a beacon of hope and opportunity. It is incumbent upon each and every one of us to safeguard our nation's legacy and secure a future of liberty for generations to come.

"The seeds of tyranny have slowly taken root, often disguised as the promise of security or false narratives that prey upon our fears, such as demanding we take a vaccination that are not needed and condemning us for being unpatriotic for not doing so. They want us to sacrifice our freedoms and accept surveillance under the guise of fighting terrorism. They impose unlawful regulations on our Second Amendment rights. They silence our views in the news and on social media. All in the name of security.

"But *whose* security? Certainly not *our* security, but the security of the government entrenching itself against the people it was designed to serve. They listen to our conversations, track us through our computers, cell phones, and vehicles, frisk us in airports, strip us of our rights, attack our liberties, restrict our speech, and deny the unalienable rights given to us by the Constitution and the Creator.

"These, my fellow patriots, are the warning signs of encroaching collectivism. To save our nation from tyranny, we must exercise our right to vote and participate in the democratic process, ensuring our voices are heard, and our values are reflected in the decisions that shape our society. Let us stand against voter suppression and work tirelessly to protect the integrity of our elections.

"Education and critical thinking are our greatest tools in this battle. We must challenge misinformation and promote an informed citizenry. By staying informed, we can recognize the tactics used to manipulate public opinion and hold those in power accountable for their actions.

"But we cannot stop at awareness alone. We must come together and bridge the gaps that divide us. Let us reject the politics of division and instead embrace the spirit of unity that has always defined America.

"Shouldn't we stand united against our country's progressive slide into socialism—a failed experiment that will never succeed—when we have the diagram, the blueprint, of capitalism at our fingertips? Not to each according to their needs, but to each according to their desires—their own hard work, the fruits of their own labor. Freed from constraints, we can do extraordinary things, and we must once again free ourselves from the constraints that bind us."

Moran paused again to look across the crowd and sip his water. The crowd was surprisingly quiet, staring at him, hungry for the words of their leader. It was time to wake them up. He wasn't running for president. He was there to whip them into a frenzy and prepare them for what lay ahead.

"We must stand vigilant!" Moran cried. "We must

continue to fight! While the enemies outside our borders stand ready to attack, the deadlier threat lurks within. Our government has been infiltrated by subversive agents who seek to yield our constitutional rights to the United Nations and hand our country over to a world government. We see corruption at the highest levels in our society, and we also see that those in power believe they are not subject to the same laws and judicial system as we, the common people, are. They get away with literal murder. They lie, steal, and manipulate us for their power.

"We can see such manipulation in how the news and social media try to divide us by race, religion, and gender. We are doing their bidding if they turn us against each other to fight amongst ourselves. We fought one civil war to hold our union together. If we must fight again, it should not be brother against brother, but as patriots against the injustice of the collectivists who seek to destroy our country!"

The crowd erupted in applause and shouts. Moran had to wait for them to quiet before he could continue.

"It may sound cliché, but when we have God on our side, no one can stand against us. Look at how He moved us all to be here together. Should we allow the one percent of the rich, the gays, or other minorities to sway who we are, how we think, or what we believe? I say *NO!* I say, prepare yourself, stay vigilant, and keep your gun by your side—because soon, we will rise up!

"When tyranny reigns supreme, it is our duty to refresh the tree of liberty with the blood of patriots! We will take back our government and reclaim what is rightfully ours: a government *by* the people, *for* the people!"

Sensing the end of his speech, the crowd erupted again in thunderous applause, clapping and cheering. Moran grinned, happy to have delivered the speech he had labored over for such a long time yet felt was wholly inadequate for the occasion.

The red light on the news camera caught his attention, and he looked directly at the lens, waved, and smiled.

Just wait until the missiles fly.

CHAPTER FORTY

Office of the Director of the FBI
Washington, D.C.

The video stream from Lima, Ohio, to Washington, D.C., was so crisp that if it weren't for the small television screen, Director Keith Scoda would have sworn the men were in the room with him.

He sat at the edge of his desk, listening to his agents report their findings from the all-agency undercover operation at the Militias for a Free America rally. He loosened his tie as SAC Talbot handed the presentation over to Special Agent Rybeck.

Rybeck appeared on the screen, and Scoda tried to remember what he'd read about the man. There wasn't much to the file, but he knew Rybeck was making progress with his investigation.

"Good afternoon, sir. As you know, we ran a joint undercover operation with the DHS, ATF, and U.S. Marshals

Service at the Liberty Brigade rally over the Fourth of July weekend. We identified twenty fugitives and many more with outstanding warrants. We placed trackers on their vehicles and are in the process of hunting them down and bringing them to justice."

"How soon will these stings take place?" Scoda asked. "We don't want to spook Moran or his militia allies."

"We're already executing those arrests as we speak, including that of Fredrick Douglas Pascal, one of the U.S. Marshals' Most Wanted fugitives. Unfortunately, Ohio State Troopers killed Pascal while trying to apprehend him."

Scoda nodded. "I heard about that. Is there any chatter within the militias about it?"

"Just that some of the militia members think Moran set them up to be apprehended," Rybeck replied. "He's seeing some backlash from that, but for the most part, people are glad to see the criminal element eliminated from their programs."

"What about the missiles?" Scoda asked.

A photo of the gun bunker replaced Rybeck's face and he clicked through slides showing the Stinger missiles and Russian engineer as he spoke. "During Moran's welcome speech, ATF Agent Steve Fisher entered the tunnel system beneath the compound. There are several bunkers in the complex. One is used for food storage and the other is stock-piled with arms and ammunition, including a shipment of stolen Army rifles we'd previously installed trackers on. Fisher also uncovered a batch of Stinger missiles. But the most important part is that Fisher spoke to our missing Russian engineer, Kostya Dragomirov, who is being held captive in a bunk room in the tunnel network. He confirmed the Sampson missiles are on-site and operational."

The next slide showed a grain silo. "We think Moran has placed the missiles inside this grain silo. See those hatches at the top? Normally, they're positioned farther down the cone of the roof. They also have hydraulic cylinders attached to them to allow them to swing out of the way for what we believe will be the launch of the missiles. Then, they cut the side of the silo open to allow access to the inside ..."

The field agent trailed off as Scoda held up a hand to stop him. "I spoke to Michael Coppler, and he says he's working with you to outline a raid on Moran's compound."

For several years, Coppler had headed the elite FBI Hostage Rescue Team (HRT). While each field office had a Special Weapons and Tactics unit, Talbot and Rybeck felt the situation at the Liberty Brigade compound warranted the use of the full-time tactical unit. HRT had a history of working high-profile cases involving domestic militant groups and had trained with fellow agencies and elite Special Forces units for situations such as the one they were facing now. Once Talbot had spoken with Coppler, Coppler had issued an immediate recall of all his team members and flown with them to Columbus to prepare for the raid on the compound.

"Yes, sir. We set the raid for the morning of July thirteenth. The plan is to use three Black Hawks: two to transport the HRT team and a third armed with heat-seeking missiles in case Moran fires the Sampsons. We'll assault the compound from the south, setting down in this field here." The screen switched to an image from Google Earth that displayed an aerial view of the Liberty Brigade compound. "We plan to gain access to the underground tunnel system through the barn and move to the bunker."

"Do you have a layout of the tunnel system?" Scoda asked.

"It's not perfect, but we can theorize what the tunnel network looks like based on what Fisher could see and using analytics of our aerial photography that show faint marks on the ground where Moran's people used heavy equipment to dig the tunnels."

The screen flashed again to show an overlay of the tunnel system in white lines against the green and brown of the map.

"Backup plan?" Scoda asked.

"We know there's a tunnel entrance in both barracks. That's how Fisher gained access to the tunnels. If we can't get in through the barn, we'll go via that route. We hope to find Dragomirov as we close in and use him to disarm the missiles."

"Why is he being detained?" Scoda asked.

The picture reverted to Rybeck, and the director saw Rybeck shrug. "Who knows? Moran may be tying up loose ends or just keeping him out of sight during the rally."

Scoda nodded, knowing Moran planned to execute the engineer. "I assume everyone on the team will wear cameras?"

"Yes, sir," Rybeck said. "We'll mic everyone up and have cameras rolling. We have to keep the lawyers happy."

Scoda made a grunting noise, which Rybeck interpreted to be one of disgust, then said, "Keep me posted."

The FBI director turned off the television screen, unlocked the bottom drawer of his desk, and removed a disposable phone he kept buried under a stack of papers. Scoda powered it up and checked the battery—almost a full charge.

He scrolled through the contacts list and stopped at the number for Paul Moran. Scoda began typing a message, informing Moran of the impending raid and that Rybeck's team knew the missiles were at the Liberty Brigade compound.

Scoda's second text message went to his *Washington Post* buddy, Phillip Upton.

Run your story.

CHAPTER FORTY-ONE

Washington, D.C.

Disgusted with the Washington Nationals, Phillip Upton reached for the remote to change the channel. As he did so, his cell phone vibrated and then dinged, announcing that he had a text message.

Upton picked up the device and noticed the message was from an unknown sender. It wasn't unusual for people to text him hot news tips or threaten to kill him because of some exposé he'd written. Out of curiosity, he opened the text.

Suddenly, he sat bolt upright. Upton reread the text message, then jumped up and rushed to his desk. This was exactly what he had been waiting for.

Scoda had finally given Upton the go-ahead to publish the expose he'd handed him at the café in Chesapeake Beach. Upton had already typed out the sensational story, which was languishing on his computer. All he needed was confirmation from his source.

The text message was his confirmation.

The computer seemed to take forever to boot up, and Upton used the time to mentally work through the changes he wanted to make to his piece. Once the computer was online, Upton quickly edited the document and, while he could still scarcely believe the story was true, called his editor at the *Post*.

George Parsons answered the phone with a grunt and an order, "Speak."

Used to his boss' idiosyncrasies, Upton waded right in. "I'm sending you a story. I've vetted the source, and everything in it is correct."

"I'll call you back," Parsons said.

After hitting send on his email, Upton saw Parsons had disconnected the call, and he dropped his phone on the coffee table.

Now, all he had to do was wait.

The story was a bombshell, and Upton knew it. He wasn't sure why Scoda had leaked it to him, but he was glad for the scoop. Breaking stories had been few and far between lately. His lucky streak seemed to end about five years ago—in both his career and personal life. His wife had left him for another man and taken their daughter with her. Upton had moved into this dump of a townhouse with only empty beer bottles and grease-stained pizza boxes for company.

He lit a cigarette as he paced the floor, the baseball game quickly forgotten.

Upton decided to be proactive. He shut off the TV, wrapped a slice of pizza in a napkin, pocketed his keys and cell phone, and then ran to his car.

Walking into the bullpen of reporters' desks, Upton rapped on the window of Parsons' office. The heavyset man waved him off and, momentarily deflated, Upton went over to his desk and sat, barely able to contain the nervous energy coursing through him.

———

A HALF-HOUR LATER, Upton jumped as Parsons rapped on the glass of his office window to get the reporter's attention. Upton rushed into the office and closed the door behind him.

Gesturing to the computer, Parsons asked, "Where did you get this garbage?"

"I have a source."

Parsons grunted his disapproval, and Upton could read the disbelief on his editor's face.

"It's true," Upton stated defensively. "The source handed me this material himself."

Parsons rubbed his forehead as he let out a long sigh. "Fine. But you gotta tell me who this maniac is if you want me to run this story."

"I can't do that, boss. You know sources are confidential."

Parsons pointed to Upton's story that he'd printed out and now lay on the blotter before him. "I can't print this. Do you know how much panic it will cause?"

"But my source wants us to print it," Upton objected.

"Why?" Parsons barked. "What's his agenda?"

"I don't know," Upton admitted. "I didn't press him for a reason. I know he's an *extremely* credible source, highly placed in the government, and I just got a text from him confirming everything I've written."

"You're telling me that your source confirmed a rogue ex-Army colonel has four Russian cruise missiles hidden in the American heartland, and no one knew anything about it until now?"

Upton shrugged. "I didn't ask why he wanted it published,

but it doesn't mean it's true. Even if it is, the people have a right to know."

Parsons swiveled in his chair and pondered his writer for a moment before urging, "Come on, Phillip. You gotta level with me. Who's the source?"

Knowing Parsons would never print the story without him complying, Upton reluctantly told him. "It's the *director* of the FBI, Keith Scoda."

"You've got to be kidding me!" Parsons erupted. "The director of the FBI gave you this story?"

Upton nodded.

Parsons relented, sensing his boss would kill him if he lost the scoop. "If you get him on the phone, and he says he approved this story, I'll print it."

Upton had been afraid of this. Even he had to admit, the story seemed like he had ripped it from the pages of a fictional bestseller, but it was all true.

The reporter pulled his phone from his pocket and texted Scoda. *Editor won't print without speaking to you. Have two hours until print deadline.*

A tense twenty minutes later, Upton's phone rang while he was getting coffee from the machine across the bullpen from the editor's office. He answered the phone as he weaved his way back across the room. In Parsons' office, he handed the phone to the editor. He watched Parsons' expression change from deep speculation to surprise and then resignation.

A minute later, Parsons handed the phone back to his subordinate and leaned back in his old chair. The springs squeaked as the chair strained under his weight. Parsons interlaced his fingers over his stomach and gazed silently at Upton.

Upton couldn't help but smile. He could smell victory.

Parsons groaned. "I'll print it, Phillip—but I still don't like it."

CHAPTER FORTY-TWO

Oval Office
Washington, D.C.

President David Cross slammed the newspaper down on the desk and shouted at his chief of staff, "What happened? Who leaked this information to the *Post!*"

Arnold Gottfried sat in his usual spot on the end of the sofa with his legs crossed. He picked a piece of lint from his immaculately creased pants as he watched his friend pace the room and rant about the hypocrisy of the government and people with top-secret clearances. Gottfried smiled and thought back to a time not so long ago when he and the president had utilized the same tactic, leaking information to the press about a congressman's lascivious behavior to block voter reform legislation.

"What are we going to do?" Cross stopped in front of Keith Scoda, who stood near the door. Upon hearing the news, the president had immediately summoned the FBI director.

"I suggest we move you to a secure location until we can raid the compound," Scoda said.

"When will that be?" Cross huffed in disgust.

"We originally planned to go next week, but with this news being leaked, we've moved up the timetable. HRT will raid on Saturday morning."

"Why wait?" the president demanded.

"We need time to stage everything," Scoda replied. "This is a joint operation with a lot of moving parts."

"Forget that. You tell them to get this done now!" Cross yelled. "We don't need this rogue nut job destroying our country."

"We will, Mr. President," Scoda assured him. "But in the meantime, I want to move you to Mount Weather."

"What for?" Gottfried asked.

"Because we don't know what Moran's targets are. If the White House is one of them, we don't want you anywhere near here."

Cross contemplated Scoda's words for a moment. "Fine, but I'll relocate to Air Force One."

"I don't think that's a good idea, sir," Scoda replied. "These missiles can shoot down your airplane, too."

Gottfried jumped in. "I thought Sampsons were surface-to-surface missiles."

"They are, but Moran has one of the engineers who built the missiles at his compound. He rebuilt the launch controllers Moran purchased from Russia, and if he can do all that, he can program them to act as surface-to-air missiles as well." Scoda glanced at Secret Service Agent Hank Garrity, head of the Presidential detail, and asked, "What's your assessment, Hank?"

"I agree with you, sir," Garrity said. "We're need to take

President Cros to Mount Weather, and we'll put the vice president in Air Force Two. We'll leave tomorrow morning. That should give our people plenty of time to prepare."

"What about the congressmen and senators?" Cross asked.

"We'll get them to Mount Weather unless something else happens," Garrity replied. "No leaks to the press. We don't want to cause more panic than there already is."

Scoda nodded in agreement. He slid his burner phone from his pocket and composed a text on the Signal app to the militia leader, letting him know the plan was coming together exactly as Moran had envisioned.

By this time tomorrow, President David Cross would be dead.

CHAPTER FORTY-THREE

Trapp, Virginia

Two men dressed in jeans and flannel shirts stood with their heads under the raised hood of an old pickup truck along Route 619, just east of Mount Weather. They listened to the drone of the distant helicopter rotors as they stared at an engine that would start at the turn of the key.

The larger man climbed into the bed of the truck and pulled the cover off two plastic cases. He bent, unsnapped the multiple latches, and lifted the lid on the first. The helo was closer now, the beat of its rotors growing louder with each passing second.

As Marine One appeared on the horizon over a distant forest, the man standing by the engine raised a laser rangefinder to his right eye and sighted in on the Sikorsky carrying the President of the United States.

He called out the range as the chopper closed on their position. "Three and a half miles."

The man in the back of the truck hefted the Stinger missile to his shoulder and activated it.

"Two miles."

The man holding the Stinger sighted through the launcher's scope. Immediately, the launcher emitted a low tone, meaning the missile had acquired its target. He steadied the Stinger, centered the aiming reticule, and depressed the trigger. The solid-fuel rocket motor engaged, and the missile streaked out of the launch tube toward the helicopter.

Not waiting to see if his first shot had hit the mark, the man dropped the empty launch tube into the truck bed and opened the second case to retrieve another Stinger. He pulled the missile onto his shoulder as the helicopter above him took evasive action.

The Black Hawk deployed chaff and flares, then dropped precipitously toward the ground before beginning a series of wild maneuvers that slewed the helicopter from right to left.

The first Stinger locked onto a flare and flashed past the helicopter before detonating harmlessly behind it.

"Kill it!" the man by the pickup's hood screamed before slamming it closed. He jumped into the driver's seat and started the engine.

Shouldering the Stinger, the man in the truck bed sighted through the scope again. He went through the launch procedures and fired the second missile.

Just as the Black Hawk's flight path smoothed out and the chopper settled into a more stable flight pattern, the second missile locked on, and the tone sounded in the hunter's ears.

This time, the Stinger missile did not miss its mark. It slammed into the helicopter's cowling just aft and below the jet engine's exhaust pipe. The explosion tore off the rotor head and ripped through the cabin, instantaneously killing everyone inside. The damaged airframe, no longer capable of flight, disintegrated as it fell to the ground.

On Route 619, the truck's passenger placed the missile launchers back in their cases and closed the lids before covering them with the tarp. He climbed into the passenger seat, and the two men drove casually away from the scene of the crime, knowing they'd fired the first shots in the coming revolution.

CHAPTER FORTY-FOUR

Washington, D.C.

Vice President Dennis McGrath climbed into his armored limousine in the underground parking garage below his residence at the Naval Observatory. With the threat of a madman with his own personal cruise missile arsenal aimed at yet-to-be-identified targets, the Secret Service had decided to separate the president and the VP. With a screech of tires, the limo roared out of the garage and onto the street, headed for Joint Base Andrews, where McGrath would board Air Force Two.

The heavily modified Boeing C-32 would climb into the skies and maintain a racetrack pattern from Miami to New York, ready to divert over the Atlantic at a moment's notice. The airplane could stay aloft for days and keep the vice president and his team in comfort for as long as the food held out, and they could complete their scheduled in-flight refueling stops.

Each time the heads of state left their residence, they used multiple motorcades to distract from the actual convoy that contained the POTUS or the VPOTUS. Several Chevrolet Suburbans and Tahoes loaded with heavily armed Secret Service personnel escorted the limousines. At the same time, multiple D.C. police officers raced to block traffic on their motorcycles.

Today, there was no decoy motorcade. The vice president's limo raced through D.C., with motorcycle cops blocking the side streets to prevent the motorcade from getting bogged down in traffic or having to stop for red lights.

"What the hell is taking so long!" McGrath shouted at his driver.

"We're doing the best we can, sir."

McGrath leaned back in his seat, unaware that the president was already dead and soon he would be too.

CHAPTER FORTY-FIVE

Pilot Cory "Shooter" Helm glanced at his co-pilot, Virgil "Red" Crawford, and smiled. They were going hunting for a vice president.

Behind them, Donald "Duck" Fowler and his co-pilot Charlie "Stinky" Torres ran through their checklist and then armed the rockets on their own MD 500 Defender.

"All right, boys," Shooter said over comms, nestling deeper into his harness and preparing for battle. "Let's go make some noise."

Confidently, Red replied, "I have armed the grenades and readied the machine guns."

The two Defenders lifted off from the apron outside their private hangar at Stafford Regional Airport in Fredericksburg, Virginia, some forty miles south of Washington, D.C., as the crow flew.

"Come to one hundred feet and turn east," Shooter ordered his fellow pilot.

Duck didn't need the reminder, but Shooter was in charge, and he felt the need to stick to protocol.

Leaving the airport behind, the two helicopters passed

low over I-95 and turned north above the muddy green waters of the Potomac River. They dropped closer to the water, keeping their helicopters off the radar, but that didn't stop the air traffic controller in the tower at Stafford Regional from hailing the two pilots on the radio and asking what their intentions were. The two military-style helicopters, flying nap-of-the-earth toward D.C., blipped onto the radar as they flew high enough to clear the bridge spans, then descended to water level again, causing a panic at Ronald Reagan Washington National.

"Defender Lead Five Seven Nine Three Victor Yankee, this is Reagan National," an aircraft controller radioed. "Please state your intentions."

As instructed before takeoff, Shooter maintained radio silence.

"Defender Lead Five Seven Nine Three Victor Yankee, this is Reagan National. We have you following the Potomac, traveling north at one hundred knots. Please state your intentions."

"How did they spot us?" Red asked.

"Must have been that last bridge we popped over, but I didn't think we went high enough to be seen on the radar," Shooter replied.

"Defender Lead Five Seven Nine Three Victor Yankee, this is Joint Base Andrews," a new controller said. "We are scrambling fighters for interception. Please state your intentions and move out of restricted airspace."

Shooter mashed the radio button on the cyclic. He said in a dry, calm voice, "Andrews, this is Defender Lead. We have clearance from the FBI for this flight. Reference number Bravo Seven Nine Three Priority."

"Stand by, Defender Lead," the controller at Andrews advised.

Shooter glanced over at his co-pilot and gave him a wink.

Red, so named for the shock of flaming red hair that seemed to grow from every available pore on the man's body, gave him a look that said, "What was that?"

The pilot pressed the intercom button to respond. With a shrug, he said, "I made that up."

"I noticed," Red replied sarcastically as the aircraft crossed the I-495 bridge over the Potomac.

The two pilots fell silent as they checked over their aircraft, ensuring the weapons systems were armed and all the switches were battle-ready.

A call on Shooter's cell phone, which he'd already connected to his helmet via Bluetooth, broke the silence between the two men. He slid the receiver bar to the left and said, "Go."

Their spotter on the ground said, "Devil Two passing Washington Navy Yard. They'll be on the bridge in two minutes."

"Copy that," Shooter replied, his voice straining to remain as smooth, suave as Jack Swigert had been on the Apollo 13 mission when he'd said, "Houston, we've had a problem."

Red reached over, turned the dial on the radio to their second preset, and gave Shooter a thumbs-up when he was done. Shooter clicked the radio button. "Hey, Duck. Hunting season is now open."

Two clicks came back from Duck in the universal sign by pilots that they understood the last transmission.

Shooter banked the Defender to the right, flying up the Anacostia River. Instead of following the river channel, he hopped over the spit of land jutting into the water. To his right was the Navy Yard, the oldest naval shore establishment in the country's history. Seeing it made Shooter miss his days flying SH-60s for Navy Special Warfare.

Recentering himself on the mission at hand, Shooter concentrated on the Eleventh Street Bridge complex, which consisted of three bridges over the river—one of which the vice president's motorcade, was just beginning to cross. In fact, Shooter could see the black limousine as it raced southbound on I-695.

Shooter waited for the vice president's Cadillac to close on the center of the bridge. Without hesitation, he stroked the trigger to fire off his grenades. He saw the telltale streak of rockets from Duck's Defender just seconds before they struck the bridge.

Concrete and steel flew into the air, and the bridge flexed as the explosions compromised its integrity, threatening to dump the entire convoy into the river. Shooter saw a motorcycle cop get blasted off his bike and his body fly over the bridge railing.

The lead Tahoe lifted off its wheels, turned sideways in the air, and landed on its side. The vice president's armored limo hit the nose of the Tahoe and shoved it aside. Ahead, there was a mass of broken concrete and a tangle of wrecked motorcycles clustered around an upside-down police cruiser raging with fire.

Shooter banked his Defender, bringing it to a hover over the bridge to face the oncoming limousine. He let loose another volley of grenades, and the concrete in front of the limo heaved and buckled. The nose of the heavy car disappeared into the smoke, and then, suddenly, the back end of the limo shot straight up in the air as the front wheels dropped into a hole in the bridge. With the Cadillac's nose buried in the hole, the vehicle stood almost vertical.

Red pressed the trigger for the General Electric M134 Miniguns and riddled the limo with bullets.

The back door of the VP's limousine flopped open. Overpowered by gravity, it bounced on its hinges and bent unnaturally toward the ground. Just as Vice President McGrath stuck his head out, Red and Shooter saw a trail of smoke from one of Duck's rockets blaze straight through the limo's open door and exploded inside the vehicle.

The detonation blew off the rear end and twisted steel and glass to make the Cadillac limo look like the end of an exploded cigar.

"Adios, Denny," Duck said over the radio. "You were a lousy senator and an even worse VP."

"Let's make like a fetus and head out," Shooter said to his compatriots.

The two helicopters dropped to the water and scooted south along the Potomac River. Now, they could hear Joint Base Andrews over the radio, screaming at them to set down at Reagan National or anywhere else they had an opening. The Liberty Brigade pilots ignored the radio and poured on the speed, trying to blend into the scenery.

Leaving the snaking path of the river near Quantico, Virginia, the helicopters continued straight overland, following the I-95 corridor south. Several miles north of Fredericksburg, the two helicopters set down in a dirt lot beside the I-95 exit ramp for Centreport Parkway. Two black Chevrolet Tahoes sat idling in the lot, waiting for them.

No sooner had the Defenders' skids touched the ground than Shooter and his men unbuckled their harnesses and flipped switches to shut down the helicopters' engines. Without waiting for the rotors to stop spinning, the men jumped from the Defenders and ran toward the Tahoes.

Shooter glanced over his shoulder at the still-spinning rotor blades of the Defender. In the short time, he'd gotten to fly the little whirlybirds, he'd come to love them, and it broke his heart to leave his machine behind, but it had to be done.

The Tahoe bearing Duck and Stinky turned south onto the freeway ramp. Shooter pulled out his cell phone as the vehicle he was in raced north, back toward the carnage he'd wrought on Washington, D.C.

Shooter made a call that triggered the explosives packed under the rear seat of each helicopter, and the Defenders exploded in twin balls of fire and flame. His Signal app message to Paul Moran told the militia leader that Shooter had completed his assigned mission.

Only one more domino had to fall before a new president could rise from the ashes.

CHAPTER FORTY-SIX

Skyline Towers Apartments
Bailey's Crossroads, Virginia

Speaker of the House of Representatives, Charles Dean Montgomery, ran from the black SUV that had brought him from the Rayburn House Office Building.

He jogged through the lobby of the Potomac Tower and headed for the stairway. Halfway up to the twenty-fourth-floor apartment, he wished he'd taken the elevator. Even though he kept in shape by running on the treadmill and walking with his wife, Montgomery had to stop and walk to the elevator on the twelfth floor. He stood in the elevator car, hands on his knees, sucking giant gulps of air into his sixty-year-old lungs.

The Democrat entered his apartment, feeling foolish for attempting to run up the stairs and still trying to catch his breath. His wife Meredith, a law professor from Georgetown

University, greeted him with a worried look. She knew his health was not the best.

"Are you okay?" the silver-haired woman asked.

Montgomery placed a hand on the counter, leaned over to help expand his lungs, and waved the other hand at her as if to say everything would be all right.

Meredith went back into the bedroom to continue packing her bag. She knew this day might come, and she'd prepared a list many years ago of the items she intended to take with her. She was methodically packing those items when her husband walked into the room, carrying a bottle of water and looking quite flushed. He watched her for a minute, admiring her efficiency, and then opened his own bag to pack.

"We have to make this quick," he said, glancing at his Rolex, a gift from a donor in his home state of Vermont. "We have a half hour to get to the Washington Post Heliport to catch the flight to Mount Weather."

———

LESS THAN A QUARTER mile southeast of Montgomery's apartment, Matt Jennings watched the Montgomerys pack their bags through the scope on his sniper rifle.

Two days ago, Jennings had received a key and an address in an envelope in the mail. He'd driven to Richmond, Virginia, where he'd caught a bus to Alexandria. Once there, Jennings had walked into a post office and retrieved the mail from inside the box using the key he'd received. He'd sorted through the junk, throwing away circulars and flyers, and kept only the manila envelope addressed to Acme Pest Control that contained the photo and address of his target, and the location of his sniper's nest.

Setting up the hide in the condo, Jennings had pulled the

table into the living room, then placed his Barrett MRAD bolt action sniper rifle upon it. Lying on the table, he had a clear view through the open French doors to Congressman Montgomery's apartment. Under him was a thick foam pad to make the oak table more comfortable.

Now snugged up behind the Barrett, Jennings ensured he had chambered a .338 Lapua round, then sighted through the Bushnell scope. He had ten rounds in the magazine, but if he needed more than two, things had gone sideways, and it would be time to run.

The sniper's patience paid off when the speaker rushed into the apartment and leaned against the counter to catch his breath. Jennings waited longer for the shot he wanted, searching for the perfect moment. Montgomery and his wife disappeared into the bedroom. Then the congressman crossed the living room and entered his study, his movements too quick for Jennings to accurately place a shot.

It didn't take long for the congressman and his wife to pack. When they met in the living room with suitcases in tow, Jennings slowed his breathing. He centered the crosshairs of the Bushnell scope on Speaker Montgomery's forehead and stroked the trigger.

The heavy bullet broke through the glass window but deflected off the shattering pane. Jennings snapped the bolt back and seated another round before the gun had settled from the recoil of the first shot. Jennings moved his crosshairs slightly and sent a second bullet down range. This one hit the congressman in the side of the head, killing him instantly while his wife stood in shock, transfixed by the shattered glass of their window.

Jennings's third bullet killed the liberal law professor, snapping her off her feet and flinging her to the ground beside her late husband.

CHAPTER FORTY-SEVEN

Scottsdale, Arizona

"Can't we go any faster?" Secret Service Agent Kelly LeBrock snapped, letting her irritation spill over at the driver. He looked at her from the corner of his eye and took it with a grain of salt. He had never seen Agent LeBrock so agitated. She was usually calm and professional.

Impatient and irritable, LeBrock turned her attention out the passenger side window of the black Chevrolet Tahoe as it edged its way through the heavy Scottsdale traffic.

Six hours ago, she had watched President Cross and his protective detail take off from the White House lawn and had assumed responsibility for securing the residence until the president's return. Since then, they had forced her into the role of lead agent for the president's detail, giving her the responsibility of securing Senator Diane Warrick and returning her to Washington, D.C.

In the wake of the assassinations of the president, the vice president, and the speaker of the House, the Secret Service, the U.S. Marshals Service, the FBI, and virtually every other agency had dispatched security details for senators, representatives, and other highly placed government officials to move them to Mount Weather.

"Remind me again why we didn't fly a helicopter in?" the driver asked.

"Because she's shopping, Rob, and there's no place in downtown Scottsdale to land a helicopter."

Agent Rob nodded. He understood LeBrock was under a lot of pressure to get to Senator Warrick and place her under their protection. Reaching over, LeBrock flipped the switch on the portable siren and light combo installed on the dash. The traffic ahead of them creeped out of the Tahoe's way, clearing a lane for the undercover vehicle.

"We should have gotten a police escort," Rob told LeBrock.

She nodded absently.

A few minutes later, Rob pulled the Tahoe to the curb in front of a boutique dress shop. LeBrock glanced in the side mirror to check that her dark brown hair was still pulled into a neat ponytail. Stepping out of the Tahoe, she smoothed the creases in her pantsuit. LeBrock straightened to her full height of five-six, trying to mentally convince herself that she was up to the task of leading such a prestigious detail. She had always considered herself a plain-looking woman and had tried to blend in with the crowd, but now she regretted not putting on any makeup that morning.

Once the other Secret Service agents had dismounted, LeBrock led them inside, where the sales clerk pointed to a dressing room. LeBrock knocked on the door.

Senator Warrick stepped out, wearing a form-fitting navy-blue sheath dress that clung to her perfectly slim figure. LeBrock flashed her badge and introduced herself.

"You need to come with us right *now*, ma'am," she said urgently.

Warrick flicked her black hair off her shoulder as she turned from side to side, admiring the cut of the dress in a full-length mirror.

LeBrock glanced around at the sales personnel in the store. "Why are these people still here?" she demanded of her team.

Moments later, only the sales clerk who'd been helping the senator and Warrick's personal assistant, Kathy Walsh, remained. LeBrock turned to the clerk and said, "Put it on her charge account. Senator Warrick is leaving."

"Can you take care of it, Kathy?" Warrick asked Walsh, a young woman with light brown hair and glasses, juggling three cell phones. "It seems Agent LeBrock is ready to leave."

LeBrock wanted to explode at the next President of the United States, but instead, she checked that her team had the exits covered as Kathy Walsh paid for the dress.

Warrick wore her new dress out of the store and carried her other clothes in a bag. LeBrock ushered her into the Tahoe, and once the rest of her team was back in the saddle, they headed for Diane Warrick's house.

———

FIFTEEN MINUTES LATER, the trio of SUVs pulled up in front of a glass-and-steel monument to modern architecture set amongst massive brown boulders on the side of a mountain. The house had been Senator Warrick's home for the past thirty years. She lived there alone when she wasn't in D.C. Her husband had passed, and her children had long since moved out.

All Kelly LeBrock saw was a monstrosity she had to secure with too few agents. Someone had orchestrated the deaths of the president, the vice president, and the speaker of the House, meaning Warrick was the next in line to become POTUS. LeBrock had to protect the senator at all costs.

Exiting the Tahoe, LeBrock ordered her agents to take up positions around the house and be ready to move at a moment's notice. They were to shoot first and ask questions later if anything looked remotely suspicious. These were desperate times, and LeBrock feared for her job and her country. Warrick, however, appeared as cool as a cucumber, even though terrorists were probably moments away from making an attempt on her life.

Kathy Walsh was the first to the door, and the personal assistant used the keypad to unlock the wrought-iron front door. LeBrock shoved her aside and drew her service pistol as two other agents stacked up behind her. The three of them hurried through the house, clearing every room.

As she performed her sweep, LeBrock noticed the fixtures and furnishings matched the sleek lines of the home's exterior. She also noted that the place looked more like a model home than one that someone actually lived in. LeBrock guessed it was because Warrick spent so much time in her office suite in the Hart Senate Office Building.

Warrick and Walsh went straight to the senator's home office. LeBrock entered after them and stood by the door.

"Ma'am, we need to leave as soon as possible," she said tersely. "Air Force One is waiting at Luke Air Force Base."

"And you chose to drive across town?" Warrick asked.

"We flew across town on a Pave Hawk to Scottsdale Airport. From there, we had to take the Tahoes, since you weren't in your residence as I'd requested when I called you from D.C." LeBrock couldn't help letting irritation creep into her tone at being ignored.

"I had things to do," Warrick replied evenly, glancing up from gathering papers into her briefcase. "I couldn't appear on television wearing a cheap, off-the-rack suit like my Secret Service detail. How much are we paying you, anyhow?"

LeBrock took no offense to the senator's statement. She'd been wearing her rumpled clothes for almost twenty-four hours. She was just trying to do her job, and if she could only get Warrick onto Air Force One, she could take a deep breath and find the time for a shower and a fresh change of clothes.

———

DIANE WARRICK TURNED to her assistant. "You two are about the same size, Kathy. Lend the agent a change of clothes, would you? We can't have her looking like a ragamuffin."

LeBrock shook her head. "I'm not leaving my post, ma'am."

"As the sitting Pro Tempore of the United States Senate and the future President of the United States, I order you to shower and change your clothes. I'm not riding in any vehicle with a woman who stinks of body odor."

LeBrock subconsciously lifted her arm to smell her pit.

"Don't do that, Agent," Warrick chided. "As I used to tell my children, mind your manners."

Walsh rolled her eyes and then led LeBrock from the room. Turning to Agent Rob, LeBrock told him to keep an eye on Warrick.

As Walsh led LeBrock away, Warrick sank into the chair behind her desk. She'd been expecting the Secret Service to arrive at any moment. The televisions on the wall across from her glass-topped desk showed footage of the burned-out hulk of Dennis McGrath's limousine, of Marine One smoldering in a mountain forest, and aerial shots of Speaker Montgomery's apartment complex. She knew Moran's plan was unfolding as he'd proposed.

She and Kathy had already packed their bags and were ready to leave as soon as the Secret Service had been in contact to advise they were en route to her location. But Warrick hadn't been able to sit in the house and wait. She'd gone shopping instead. Her new dress would be perfect for her first address to the nation.

Going into her bedroom, the future president changed into slacks and a blouse, then packed the new dress into her garment bag.

Kathy and LeBrock were waiting for her when she returned to the office. LeBrock looked much improved in stylish slacks and a blouse with a jacket to match.

"Are you planning to take the SUVs to the airport?" Warrick asked, knowing she was in no danger from Moran's group but still not entirely convinced there wasn't any danger from the crazies who might try to take advantage of the confusion.

"Yes, ma'am," LeBrock replied.

"I'd rather not," Warrick stated. "I went to a lot of trouble to install a helicopter pad in the backyard." She led LeBrock to a sliding glass door that overlooked the rear patio, the glistening blue pool, and the steep, rocky mountain slope beyond. Situated just past the pool was a small landing pad with a white "H" painted in the center. "I'm sure no one told you I had a helicopter pad, so don't feel bad, Agent LeBrock. I only used it a few times when I was governor of Arizona."

LeBrock still felt out of her element and a step behind the game. She dialed a number on her cell phone and requested that the Air Force HH-60G Pave Hawk sitting at Scottsdale Airport fly to Senator Warrick's home and then vector back to Luke Air Force Base.

"The helicopter will be here in ten minutes, ma'am," LeBrock said, ending her call.

Warrick picked up her cell phone and began texting on a

Signal group chat, informing Moran, Gravely, Shipley, and Killian that an Air Force helicopter would pick her up and take her to Air Force One.

"Everything okay, ma'am?" LeBrock asked as Warrick pocketed the phone.

"Just keeping in touch with my staff." She turned to Kathy Walsh. "Let's move the bags to the patio door, so we're ready to go."

After moving two suitcases, two garment bags, and Warrick's briefcase to the door, Warrick asked LeBrock, "What's the plan, Agent?"

"Ma'am, we're going to put you on Air Force One and get you to fifteen thousand feet as quickly as possible. You'll be sworn in as president, and from there, you'll have to execute the duties of the office."

"Are you going to be the head of my protective detail?"

"Yes, ma'am, I will be." LeBrock stifled a sob at the thought of her colleagues who had been killed while accompanying Cross.

"Are you okay?" Warrick asked, a hint of motherly concern in her voice.

LeBrock held a hand over her mouth and bit back another sob, but she couldn't prevent the tears that rolled down her cheeks.

"It's okay, Kelly," the senator said as she wrapped her arms around the shorter woman.

"It's just that so many of my friends and colleagues have died …" LeBrock sobbed.

"I know, I know," Warrick consoled, gently rubbing the woman's back.

The Secret Service agent pulled herself away from Warrick's comforting embrace, straightened her jacket, and wiped her tears away with the back of her hand. Kathy Walsh handed her a tissue, which she used to dry her eyes and blow her nose.

"I'm sorry, ma'am," LeBrock said. "That wasn't very professional of me."

"It's okay, Kelly. We all grieve for the men and women who have lost their lives in these senseless tragedies. I also knew some of those agents who guarded David and Dennis. They were good people."

Warrick removed her hand from LeBrock's shoulder when the agent's cell phone rang. LeBrock answered it, glancing out the patio door at the helicopter descending coming the far rise.

"Carter, Tapia, come in and get these cases," LeBrock radioed to two agents outside the house.

Outside, the Pave Hawk landed on the helipad and disgorged a contingent of heavily armed Air Force Pararescue specialists (PJs) to secure the area. The team fanned out, taking positions around the helicopter, weapons locked to their shoulders and looking for threats on the perimeter.

"Let's go, ma'am," LeBrock yelled over the thunder of the Pave Hawk's spinning rotors.

As they approached the helicopter, an aircrewman motioned the three women and two baggage handlers toward the aircraft, indicating that they should remember to duck their heads. They ran under the rotor arc and jammed themselves into the helicopter, where the crew chief handed headsets to the passengers to allow them to hear and speak and to protect their hearing from the in-flight noise.

Moments later, the crew chief slid the door closed, and the Pave Hawk lifted off, leaving behind the contingent of PJs and most of LeBrock's Secret Service team.

Diane Warrick turned to look out the window as the helicopter gathered altitude to clear the house. Below, she could see the PJs moving out of their defensive positions and meeting with the Secret Service agents.

Out of the corner of her eye, Warrick saw the fire trail of a Stinger missile as it streaked off the mountain above the house and hit the SUV she had ridden in with LeBrock. The rocket hit with such ferocity that it lifted the Tahoe five feet off the ground before flipping it over onto its left side. The gas tank exploded, and hungry flames blew out in all directions.

The explosion startled Warrick so much that it made her jump, and then there was screaming and chattering on the comms network, with everyone talking at once. She buried her face in her hands and shook with fright. Targeting her was not supposed to be part of the plan.

Warrick turned to LeBrock and barked, "Get me on Air Force One, now!"

Knowing the Air Force was doing everything within its power to protect her, Warrick mulled over the question she demanded an answer to.

Why is Moran targeting me?

CHAPTER FORTY-EIGHT

An hour after leaving Warrick's home in Scottsdale, Arizona, Air Force One cruised effortlessly at two hundred fifty miles per hour high above the continental United States. Diane Warrick sat at the same desk where, two days ago, David Cross had written a new gun control bill. She spread her hands across the oiled walnut surface and thought about the work that lay ahead.

While she could not explain the attack on her life, she could rationalize it. Warrick had come up with four plausible explanations. One: whoever had taken a shot at her was not part of Liberty Brigade and was operating on their own. Two: she had enemies she didn't know about who wanted her dead. Three: Moran had taken a shot at her to make it look as if she was a victim of the assault on Washington politicians, and they had waited until she was in the air and out of danger to blow up the SUV.

Or four: her co-conspirators wanted her dead.

LeBrock stepped into the president's office. She explained that the current plan was to stay in the air until they could eliminate the threat on the ground. No one knew how long that would take, but every law enforcement agency in the country was working to bring the terrorists to justice.

Warrick smiled. She wasn't dead—yet. For now, she would carry out the plan.

She picked up her cell phone and checked the Signal app for messages. The text message icon had a small "1" beside it. She pushed the icon with her thumb.

Diane, sorry about the explosion. Had to make it look like you were also a target. Continue as planned. - PM

She put the phone in her pocket as the office door opened again.

"We're ready to swear you in, ma'am," Kathy Walsh informed her boss. "Everyone is waiting for you in the conference room,"

"Thanks, Kathy. Have you phoned Tony yet?" Warrick asked.

"No, ma'am," Walsh said. "I haven't had the chance."

Warrick stood up and came around the desk. "Use the phone there to call your husband."

"Ma'am, I'll do it right after they swear you in," the assistant replied.

"Okay, Kathy. Just see that you do. Tony needs to know you're safe." Warrick gestured toward the door. "Lead the way."

The two women walked into the conference room, with its white wall, blue carpet, and polished oak table surrounded by chairs. The Seal of the United States hung centered on the far wall, flanked on the right by the presidential flag and the Stars and Stripes on the left. Warrick could see the flashing lights on the wingtips reflecting on the windows.

Kelly LeBrock stood at the far end, placing a Bible on a podium in front of the seal. Also in the room was U.S. Marshal Chandler; Arnold Gottfried, Cross's chief of staff; National Security Advisor Amy Perkins; Francine Bostic,

DHS; and Navy Admiral Charles Nelson, head of the Joint Chiefs of Staff; several aides and attendants who had worked for the former president; and select members of the press.

"This way, ma'am." LeBrock motioned her to the front of the room.

An aide came alongside Warrick as she headed for the podium. "Congratulations, ma'am. It's exciting to share this historic moment with you. I mean, you're the first female president." She handed Warrick a sheet of paper. "First, there will be a brief introduction, and then whomever you choose will swear you in. After that, you'll have about a minute to give a speech. We will televise all this live using the cameras at the back of the room."

Warrick turned and saw the lenses protruding from a film room, then said, "I don't have a speech."

"That's what's on the paper, ma'am." The aide pointed to the sheet. "Now, you need to choose someone to swear you in."

They stopped at the head of the table, and Warrick glanced around the room. This was a special moment in history. The United States was under attack, and she was about to be sworn in as the first female president in U.S. history.

"Kathy, I want you to hold the Bible. Admiral, you will administer the oath of office," Warrick ordered.

The forty-year-old man in his spotless white dress uniform stood up from the table. "It would be an honor, Senator." The two had gotten to know one another when Warrick had served on the Senate Armed Services Committee.

Warrick silently read the speech someone had written on the paper as everyone arranged themselves for the ceremony. She was still contemplating the speech when the aide touched her lightly on the elbow. "We're ready, ma'am. Stand over here, please." She pointed to a mark on the floor between

Admiral Nelson and Kathy Walsh in front of the flags flanking the presidential seal.

Five minutes later, Diane Warrick was the forty-seventh President of the United States.

Admiral Nelson turned to the camera and announced, "Ladies and gentlemen, I present to you the President of the United States!" Then he stepped out of the way, followed by a visibly emotional Kathy Walsh, who still clutched the Bible. She would put it away for her boss so Warrick could keep it as a memento of the momentous occasion.

Warrick turned to the camera and spoke off the cuff. "Ladies and gentlemen, we are in unprecedented times. The United States is under attack from terrorists of unknown origin. As I speak, they are striking at the head of this country in an attempt to undermine it. What they don't understand is that the head does not control this country. It is the heart that is in control, and each and every one of you listening today is the beating heart of this great republic. Together, we can throw off the shackles of oppression and tyranny that are closing in on us. We, as individuals, will stand firm and restore this country to its former glory. No individual, despot, or nation can withstand us when we unite in defense of freedom.

"I have taken steps to ensure the safety of our leadership and to stop the launch of those rogue cruise missiles you've all been hearing about. I want to reassure all of you that no matter what happens, we will *not* give in to the will of those seeking to destroy this nation—from the outside or within."

Warrick had to be careful not to suggest that the perpetrators of these attacks would be systematically hunted down and killed in the streets or prosecuted in the courts, as she was one of those animals herself. And the claim wouldn't have been true, anyway. She couldn't say those words and then appear on television with Paul Moran at her side. That would ruin the credibility she needed to be a benevolent dictator.

The people standing around the conference table were aghast at her speech. They had expected her to denounce the terrorists and take a stance closer to that of her liberal predecessor.

Warrick's minute on air was up, and the red light on the camera winked out.

"When this plane touches down, everyone who worked for President Cross is fired," Warrick said casually as she strode from the conference room.

CHAPTER FORTY-NINE

FBI Resident Agency Office
Lima, Ohio

Parker Rybeck felt like a sardine packed in the FBI conference room. Looking around the room, he spotted Ralph Pratt and all the agents who had accompanied him undercover at the militia rally. The sheriff's deputies were back, along with their bosses, and more ATF, Homeland, and FBI higher-ups had joined the party. It was standing room only.

It hadn't taken long for Rybeck's report to make the rounds. Once Phillip Upton's story broke, everyone wanted a piece of the action when it came to assaulting the Liberty Brigade compound. Even the Air Force had sent a representative. General Jordan Green sat at the table conversing with SAC Roger Talbot.

Caroline slid up beside Rybeck and squeezed his hand. He smiled at her, happy to have her there.

"Ladies and gentlemen let's get this started," Talbot said, rising from the table.

Rybeck went to the computer and started his PowerPoint presentation. He detailed their findings from the Fourth of July weekend and presented pictures of the silo, the weapons cache, the Stinger missiles, and of Kostya Dragomirov in his cell.

He took his seat, and Michael Coppler, head of the FBI's HRT team, stood up to speak. Coppler had also prepared a PowerPoint presentation detailing their planned strike. He outlined the logistics and the support his team would need from the other agencies. He spoke for forty-five minutes, and everyone in the room understood the plan when he finished.

Local law enforcement agencies were to set up a perimeter on all crossroads around the Liberty Brigade compound and cordon off all roads leading to and from the site.

The HRT team, including Rybeck, Crane, Fisher, and Hoffman, were to fly in on several helicopters. One of the Black Hawks would carry heat-seeking missiles in case the pilot had the opportunity to shoot down the cruise missiles in flight. In addition, two F-22 Raptors from Wright-Patterson Air Force Base in Dayton, Ohio, would fly combat air patrol above the compound.

Coppler glanced around the room and asked if anyone had questions. When no one said a word, he handed the meeting over to Talbot.

"The last time we were together, I wanted you to keep this under your hats, but we can no longer do that." Talbot swept his hand toward the PowerPoint screen. "This briefing has already been given to Director Keith Scoda and Homeland Director Francine Bostic. All participants will wear body cameras, and the higher-ups will watch the entire operation. They'll also be able to listen to our conversations and give directions if needed. Everyone be vigilant and be safe."

Talbot slapped his hands together, indicating the meeting was over, and everyone made moves to either leave the room or gather in little knots to discuss certain aspects of the raid.

Rybeck saw Burke and Jacobs, the two FBI divers, sitting on the window ledge and went over to speak to them. "Are you guys clear on what's going on?"

The two men nodded. "We'll take our truck up to Kenton and stand by. If you need us, we dive. If not, we're going back to D.C. I have a backlog of work that needs to get done, and it ain't gonna happen sitting around here," Burke replied.

Rybeck looked at Jacobs, who gave him a shrug of indifference.

"You ever work on cruise missiles?" Rybeck asked.

"Not in the field, but I did when I went through EOD school," Jacobs stated. "When I heard we might have to disarm a Sampson, I sat down and read all the technical specs and manufacturer's publications I could get my hands on while you were at the militia country concert."

"Hopefully, you don't have to use any of those skills, and we can capture everything in place. Then we can bring in specialists to disable the missiles," Rybeck replied.

"Amen, brother," Jacobs said.

Caroline motioned for Rybeck to join her, and he was thankful to break away from the conversation with the two divers. "I want to talk to you privately," she said.

"Let's go to my office," Rybeck replied, leading the way.

Once in his office, Caroline complained, "I was hoping to go in with you guys."

"Coppler made the plan. He thinks LEOs should be on picket duty."

"I know," she said disappointedly. "It's my job to protect the people of my county, so I'll do what Coppler asks." She put her hands on his shoulders. "I need to go home and get some sleep. Any chance you can come with me?"

"I wish I could, but I'm needed here."

Caroline leaned in and kissed him softly on the lips, then whispered. "Be safe, okay?"

"I'll see you when this is over," Rybeck said.

Caroline smiled wistfully. "Promise?"

"I promise," he said. "Then we can get that hotel room with the hot tub."

Caroline batted her eyes. "You do know how to tease a girl, Agent Rybeck."

Watching Caroline leave the office, he couldn't help but worry about her. While he was airborne in the helicopter, winging his way toward a confrontation with Liberty Brigade, she would sit in her cruiser, bored out of her mind. He knew that if things went sideways on this op, she would get involved somehow.

When it came down to it, though, Rybeck knew that was one of the reasons he liked her so much.

CHAPTER FIFTY

Bolton Field
Columbus, Ohio

In the early dawn, the FBI HRT team and associated personnel waited to board the three Black Hawk helicopters. The HRT members wore black tactical gear, ballistic vests, helmets, and related combat gear. Each carried an M4 carbine and a handgun of their choice.

Rybeck and his fellow undercover agents had worn jeans, T-shirts, and bulletproof vests, completing the look with windbreakers and ball caps bearing their respective agency logos. Rybeck sported his preferred SIG Sauer P226 and an M4.

Two jet-black UH-60 Black Hawk helicopters sat on the tarmac while a grounds crewman towed a third of a hangar. Air ops had equipped it with two AIM-92 Stinger heat seeking air-to-air missiles per hardpoint and a door-mounted M60 general-purpose machine gun.

The twelve men of the main assault team divided themselves between the two helicopters as their rotors started spinning. Six more backup HRT team members would ride on the third helicopter.

Within minutes, the Black Hawks were in the air, flying north. Rybeck listened in on his headset as the two F-22 Raptors—call signs Whiskey One and Whiskey Two—lifted off from Wright-Patterson, some seventy miles to the south.

Rybeck knew it took just over an hour to drive from Ohio's capital city to Liberty Brigade's headquarters, so it didn't surprise him that the helicopter flight barely lasted twenty minutes.

When the pilot said they were two minutes out, everyone aboard the helicopters double-checked their loadouts and then snapped a round into the chambers of their guns. Rybeck tugged at his gear, ensuring he tucked everything into place. He had done this routine many times before when he was boarding ships as a Coast Guardsman. He tried to tell himself that this was no different, but there was a tightness in his gut and a quickness to his breathing that told him there was no point trying to kid himself. Rybeck tried to breathe deeply, but the uneasiness wouldn't go away.

Rybeck sat on the edge of the seat, ready to be one of the first out the door. Ahead of them, the lead helicopter banked to flare in the wind, and he saw a missile streak out from the top of the compound's rappelling tower and smack the helicopter just behind the exhaust port. The Black Hawk exploded with a deafening crack and slammed into the ground in a blazing heap of metal.

Fighting back a wave of nausea at seeing the wreckage of the helicopter, the pilot of Rybeck's Black Hawk did him no favors by shoving the collective all the way to the deck and dropping the aircraft like a stone toward the ground.

The Black Hawk bounced hard on its wheels. The pilots

cursed as Rybeck tore off his headset and dove out of the bird. Behind him, the HRT team did the same, exiting as quickly as possible before Mad Moran could strike their helicopter with another rocket.

While the plan had been to set down on the open ground in front of the barn, the destruction of the first helicopter forced a deviation in plans. Instead, the surviving UH-60 landed in the field, a short distance from the grain silos.

As soon as everyone was clear of the helicopter, it took off, leaving the team in a blinding cloud of dirt, grass, and billowing dust. Small arms fire echoed off the buildings as the assault force tried to run toward the cover provided by the barn.

No rockets flared out of the rappelling tower but sustained machine-gun fire stitched across the field, sending little geysers of dirt into the air amid the streaks of red tracers. Just ahead of Rybeck, one of the HRT guys took a round to the head and toppled over.

The smell of cordite and the stench of blood filled Rybeck's nostrils, but he kept moving. No one had expected this sort of resistance, but they should have. It seemed Moran would stop at nothing to protect his missiles.

Suddenly, a ripping sound came from overhead as the armored helicopter unloaded its M60 on the rappelling tower. HRT members who had sprawled on the ground to avoid the killing fury of the rappelling tower gunner leaped to their feet and sprinted toward the barn, joining Rybeck behind the safety of the silos.

Except the safety wouldn't last. In a few moments, the enemy would force the assault team to engage once again.

CHAPTER FIFTY-ONE

Paul Moran dropped the empty launch tube after downing the approaching Black Hawk with a Stinger missile. He climbed rapidly down from the tower, jumping off the ladder just seconds before heavy machine-gun fire from one of the other helicopters tore the structure to shreds.

Moran darted for the safety of his tunnels, ready to launch his missiles. While Director Scoda had kept him informed of the raid's timetable, the former colonel had hoped the assassinations of the president, VP, and speaker of the House would draw attention away from him. Scoda had tried to throw the FBI's full weight into finding the perpetrators of one of the most audacious terrorist attacks on U.S. soil. Still, agents like Rybeck, Pratt, and Talbot had lobbied for the raid on the Liberty Brigade compound.

The original plan had been to call in a heavily armed force to counter the FBI raid, but with the accelerated timetable, Moran had been unable to move his chess pieces in time. Instead, he had to rely on what he had at his immediate disposal to repel the invading black helicopters. He wanted to stand in front of one and boast of his supremacy on national television. And with the appearance of a black helicopter, the conspiracy theories would all come true.

Moran entered the tunnel network through the male barracks and jogged along the silent corridor. When he came to the small cell where he kept Dragomirov prisoner, he stopped and peered through the plate glass.

"It's time to test your work," he said coldly.

Dragomirov rose unsteadily to his feet and came to the door. "You are going to launch missiles?"

"That was always the plan," Moran said then started to walk away.

Dragomirov pounded on the door. "You are madman! You can't do this to your own country!"

Moran spun on his heels and came back to the door. "Don't lecture me!" he spat violently. "*You* sold out your country for the promise of riches, and where did it get you? A filthy hole, that's where. You have no concept of what I am doing for my country."

"You are mad," Dragomirov whispered as Moran stalked away. He lay down on the bunk and began to cry. Moran did not need him anymore. He knew he was a dead man just like first mate Oleg Brega.

Moran continued down the tunnel, checking that each guard remained on post. Once in the launch control bunker, he found Steven Jackson sitting in the chair in front of the computer.

"What are you doing here?" Moran asked, concerned for the man's safety.

Jackson smiled. "You didn't think I would let you have all the fun, did you?"

Moran pulled the key from around his neck but found that Jackson had already inserted his key and had turned it to the launch position.

A shout from above echoed down the tunnel, accompanied by the sound of distant gunfire. "They're attacking the building!"

"My guys will hold them," Moran said confidently of his trained militiamen.

CHAPTER FIFTY-TWO

Caroline Thurmond stood beside her patrol car, listening to the action over the radio. She and her Marion County counterpart, Devon Lake, had blocked an intersection just north of the Liberty Brigade compound. From their vantage point, they'd had a spectacular view of the helicopter crash and the destruction of the rappelling tower. Still, the troops on the ground were under serious fire from the militia members.

"We're pinned down by the barn!" HRT team leader Michael Coppler shouted into the radio.

"I can't see you," Dale "Hornet" Castor, the pilot of the armored support helicopter, replied. "There's nothing I can do. I don't want to hit you."

Caroline grabbed the microphone from the dashboard and broke the radio silence that was supposed to exist between the LEOs and the FBI task force. "Rybeck, can you get into the tunnels from the barracks?"

"Negative," Rybeck replied. "We're pinned down and have two wounded."

"I'm coming in," Caroline said. "I'll try to attract some of the fire so you can get to the tunnels."

"Negative. Hold your position," Coppler stated firmly.

"We're pinned down," someone else stated. "We need all the help we can get."

Caroline knew the men were in a precarious situation. Through her Army training, she had learned the best way to break a stalemate was to flank the enemy force. Not waiting for anyone to order her to stop, Caroline jumped into her cruiser and made a K-turn in the middle of the road.

"Hey, we're not supposed to leave!" Lake shouted, but Caroline was already speeding down the road.

She made a hard right into the compound driveway along the quarry and floored the old Ford's accelerator. The back end skidded out behind her as the tires spun on the gravel, but she quickly gathered up the wheel and straightened the vehicle for the next turn. If she overshot it, she would fly straight off a cliff and into the quarry and need to be rescued instead of doing the rescuing.

Slowing slightly to make the next right turn, Caroline kept the cruiser under control as she entered the main compound. She ducked as the windshield exploded and bullets raked the front of the cruiser. Caroline saw the reserve members of the assault team hiding behind several large pieces of farm equipment, but she didn't take the time to slow down. Her vehicle's engine sputtered from absorbing so many rounds. The temperature gauge jumped into the red, and steam billowed from under the hood.

The driveway made a left just past the HQ building. Caroline spun the wheel hard over, fighting for control of the SUV with its slowly deflating tires. Riding on its rims, the patrol car stopped about ten feet from the male barracks.

Grabbing the Mossberg shotgun from the rack, Caroline rolled out of the Explorer and ran for the barracks as bullets tore up the ground at her feet.

CHAPTER FIFTY-THREE

Rybeck watched in heartsick despair as the windshield exploded on Caroline's cruiser. If he'd known that this was what she had in mind when she said she was coming in, he would have tried to do more to convince her to stay at her post.

"Move toward the barn!" Coppler yelled, breaking Rybeck's mental chastising.

Instead of moving with the HRT team, Rybeck rose to go after Caroline's patrol car.

Coppler caught him by the front of the jacket, balling it in his fist and jerking him close. "Where are you going, Rybeck?"

Rybeck pointed to the bullet-ridden patrol car. "To help her."

He shook free of the team leader's grasp and, ignoring the hail of bullets buzzing all around him, sprinted across the road before diving into the trees. Rybeck came up groaning from where the M4 had jammed itself into his side. He rubbed the injury site briefly before getting to his feet and running through the trees that lined the quarry.

Incoming rounds shredded tree bark and snatched at his jacket as Rybeck ran toward the deflated carcass of the patrol car.

A detonation sounded near the barracks. Rybeck went flat to the ground, his face buried in the soft dirt just above the layer of hard limestone. He could smell cordite, burning metal, and moist earth. Listening intently, he could hear the exchange of gunfire between the HRT team and the militia members as he gathered the cool metal of the M4 carbine in his hands, feeling the rough edges of the weapon's Picatinny rail and the smoothness of the plastic handle.

The incoming fire had stopped with the shotgun blast that had sent him to the ground. Rybeck looked up to see Caroline standing by the barracks, shotgun at port arms and staring at the dead guy at her feet. Rybeck jumped up and ran over to her, grabbing her by the arm and dragging her into cover behind the barracks.

"Stay behind me!" Rybeck shouted.

Bullets slammed into the building, and Rybeck shoved Caroline to the ground, covering her while he searched for the source of the fire. More bullets poured in from behind the raised bunker cover nearest to them.

Caroline struggled underneath Rybeck as he shouldered the M4 and sent a return volley of fire at the other gunman.

With the militiamen hiding behind the bunker, Rybeck dragged Caroline backward to a better defensive position. He squatted on his haunches and looked at the woman sitting on the ground before him. Rybeck had knocked the wind out of her, and she was struggling to breathe.

After a moment, she took a deep breath and said, "I'm okay."

Peering around the corner, Rybeck said, "Good, because we need to get into that bunker."

They ducked as bullets slammed into the building.

Caroline grabbed the shotgun and pulled the butt to her shoulder. "Move!" she commanded, swinging up the barrel.

Rybeck rolled left, and the gun bellowed, shooting out flame and buckshot. He turned, bringing up the M4, but saw the buckshot had cut down the man who had been running toward them. Caroline racked the slide and rolled to her feet.

Extending her hand, Caroline said, "Let's roll, sweetie."

He smiled as she helped him to his feet.

Moving to the corner of the barracks, Rybeck peered around it to see if any other militiamen were nearby. Once he saw the coast was clear, he made for the barracks' rear entrance and shoved the door open, ducking back out of the way just in time to avoid taking a shotgun blast to the ribcage.

The buckshot blew out splinters from the doorframe, making Rybeck thankful for his training. *Never run through the door. Open it from the side.* If he hadn't, he'd be dead.

Squatting, he pivoted on his toes, brought the M4 to bear on the gunner on the other side of the doorway, and dispatched the man with two bullets.

He dashed into the hallway and shoved open the bathroom door first. Caroline stepped through with the shotgun, ready to dispatch any hostiles.

Rybeck let the rifle fall on its sling against his chest as he picked up the UTAS UTS-15 shotgun the militiaman had been using before his untimely death. He racked the slide, pumping a new shell into the chamber.

Finding no one in the bathroom, they moved to the office.

Upon entry, Rybeck leveled the shotgun at the space between the cabinets and pulled the trigger. The buckshot blew a twelve-inch hole in the door, and a man screamed in pain behind it.

Grabbing the door and jerking it open, Rybeck saw the man he'd just shot now lay dead on the stairs. He and Caroline stepped over his corpse and continued into the tunnel. With the UTS-15 braced against his shoulder, Rybeck led the way toward the bunkers.

If anyone started shooting at them now, Rybeck and Caroline would be fish in a barrel. There was nowhere to hide in the straight tunnel. Bullets would ricochet off the concrete walls, and even if they didn't score a direct hit, a stray round could still do a lot of damage.

The law enforcement duo ran through the passage and slowed as they approached the first bunker.

Suddenly, the lights cut out, plunging them into an inky darkness so black that Rybeck couldn't tell if his eyes were closed or open. A wail sounded farther down the tunnel, sending shudders down Caroline's spine. She gripped Rybeck's arm, forgetting any combat awareness she had.

Somewhere in the distance, an engine started and hummed momentarily before the lights flickered. In that instant, Rybeck saw a movement in the bunker and fired. A scream erupted in the darkness, and Rybeck, blinded by the blast of his shotgun, saw pinwheels of light flashing before his eyes as he crouched against the floor, pulling Caroline down with him.

A pistol's bark echoed from inside the bunker, and a bullet sang as it ricocheted off the wall above where Rybeck's head had just been. The lead projectile continued to bounce down the tunnel, tracking its movements with a high-pitched whine as it bounced from wall to wall.

This time, Rybeck closed his eyes before firing the shotgun again. He racked in another shell, pivoted, and fired toward where he thought the militiaman guarding the bunker might have moved to.

He was rewarded with a cry of pain when his round struck flesh.

The FBI agent counted in his mind how many shells he

had left. If the dead owner had loaded the UTS-15 to capacity, the magazine tubes would hold fourteen rounds. But if the shotgunner had also loaded one in the chamber, the gun held fifteen. Rybeck had fired four, and the man whose body he'd lifted the weapon from had fired one. Based on simple math, he deduced that ten rounds were still present in the gun—eleven if luck was on his side, but he wasn't holding his breath.

The lights flickered again, but this time, they stayed on. Rybeck led Caroline deeper into the bunker. There was no one else guarding it, and Caroline looked straight ahead to avoid seeing the gore and destruction caused by the shotgun. Acid rose in her throat, and she swallowed hard to keep it from coming out.

They moved unimpeded through the gun bunker, and as they continued farther into the tunnels, they found the cell containing Kostya Dragomirov. Rybeck saw the engineer rise from his bunk and move toward the door.

"Let me out!" Dragomirov shouted.

"Move away from the door!" Rybeck called back after trying the lock. He stepped back two paces, shouldered the shotgun, and sent a load of buckshot into the metal door. Raising his leg, Rybeck slammed it into the door.

It didn't budge.

He blasted another shell into the lock, and the door swung open on its hinges.

"Stay with us," Caroline warned the Russian.

"Give me gun," Dragomirov demanded.

Rybeck had difficulty translating through the Russian's heavy accent. Yet, he wanted Dragomirov to be with them so he could shut down the missile controls.

"Fat chance," Caroline replied for her beau.

"You are cop we saw in store," Dragomirov said in recognition.

"Yes, now stay with us," Caroline said.

"Where are the missiles?" Rybeck demanded.

Dragomirov pointed down the tunnel. "Go straight to control room."

"Can Moran fire them?" Rybeck asked.

The engineer smiled with pride. "They are operational."

Rybeck swore, and Caroline looked at him in surprise. She'd never heard him curse, but Rybeck was operating in a mode he hadn't adopted since the last time he worked on a VBSS team in the Persian Gulf. He'd missed the adrenaline high of combat.

"We've got to stop those missiles," Rybeck said, running toward the control room.

CHAPTER FIFTY-FOUR

Moran stood beside the launch control buttons. Like Rybeck, he was a man who had not seen combat in a long time and relished the rush it gave him. It sharpened his senses and heightened his reflexes. His brain was operating at a level above where it usually resonated.

He turned as he heard the blasts of the shotgun in the tunnel. Motioning to two of his trusted former Rangers, Moran ordered them to secure the tunnel.

When he turned back to the computer control station, Jackson had the screens active and was entering the password. He maneuvered the mouse and clicked the buttons beside the missile coordinates boxes. As the missiles armed themselves, the boxes turned from red to green.

Once Jackson clicked the *Enter* button beside the coordinates boxes, the computer would send an automated message on Signal to Chet Gravely, Ian Shipley, Diane Warrick, General Killian, the men of the Mount Weather assault team, and the militia teams stationed in Washington, D.C.

The text read: *Poseidon's Fury*.

Everyone who received the message had been briefed on its meaning and knew what to do.

"Two for you and two for me," Jackson said as he stood and joined Moran at the row of red buttons on the wall.

The militia leader nodded. He reached out and pressed the button to open the hatches. It took several seconds before all four hatch lights turned green, meaning the hatches had slid open and locked into place.

Outside in the tunnel, a firefight raged. Moran and Jackson watched as the computer system acquired the GPS guidance satellites.

Moran smiled. No one could stop them now.

CHAPTER FIFTY-FIVE

Rybeck ran through the tunnel, passing the door that led to Moran's office in the headquarters building.

A shot echoed from the steps above. Caroline twisted and returned fire with her Mossberg. The shooter tumbled down the stairs, but neither Rybeck nor Caroline waited around to see him come to a stop.

Time was running out, and Rybeck could sense it with his entire being. The sounds of a full-fledged firefight reverberated above him as the HRT team stormed the barn.

"Where are you, Rybeck?" Hoffman called over the radio.

"We're in the tunnels, almost to the control room."

If there was a response, all Rybeck heard was static, not knowing the Faraday cage had cut off their communications.

Rybeck threw himself onto the ground as fire belched from Moran's Marauders up ahead. Caroline landed on his feet, tangling with him as he tried to get his gun up to return fire. He pumped three rounds down range and kicked free of Caroline.

He couldn't wait any longer for the rest of the team to

arrive. In his gut, Rybeck sensed Moran was about to press the launch button.

Jumping to his feet, Rybeck sprinted toward the control bunker. The shotgun thundered as he shot from the hip, racking out empty shell after empty shell until the firing pin smacked home in a near-silent click.

He tossed the shotgun away before pulling up the M4 from where it hung across his chest, still charging down the tunnel and firing at the guards. When he stopped to change magazines, he realized the two men were down, and the way to the missile control room was clear.

Glancing over his shoulder, Rybeck saw Caroline hot on his tail with the Russian not far behind.

Rybeck found the control room door. He let his rifle hang across his chest once again and drew his pistol, ready to breach.

CHAPTER FIFTY-SIX

Once the missiles' internal computers had linked with the GPS guidance system, Moran used his thumbs to press the top two launch buttons, simultaneously firing the first two Sampson missiles.

Above them, in the grain silo, an electrical current shot through the wiring and activated the computer inside each of the dormant missiles. Compressed air blew the missiles from their tubes, shooting them clear of the grain silo until their solid booster rocket engines ignited, propelling the missile on its way. At the same time, several smaller motors fired near the missile's nose cone, forcing the missile over in a ninety-degree course change. The missiles would rocket toward their maximum speed of 447 miles per hour, where a turbofan engine would take over and guide it to the target.

Jackson stepped to where Moran had just stood and raised his hands to press the buttons.

"Don't do it!" Rybeck screamed as he stepped into the room, aiming his SIG pistol at the farmer.

"Drop your weapon!" Moran yelled at Rybeck, aiming his pistol at the FBI agent.

Rybeck glanced over at Moran and then back at Jackson, who grinned as he leaned forward and put his weight on the launch buttons.

Above them, the remaining two missiles shot from their tubes. The blast of the rocket motors kicking in shook the bunker as Moran turned to check the four television screens mounted above the computer monitor. The missiles' nose cameras played across the screens.

Seizing the moment, Rybeck jerked the pistol from Moran's hand, shoved it in his waistband, and then patted the man down. Caroline provided handcuffs and helped Rybeck shackle Moran's and Jackson's hands behind their backs. Neither man seemed to care about being arrested, staring silently at the screens in glee.

Rybeck and Caroline couldn't help but watch in morbid fascination.

"Yo! Rybeck? You down here?" Crane called from farther down the tunnel.

Rybeck stepped out of the control room to see Coppler, Crane, and Hoffman leading a contingent of HRT troops. They all crammed into the bunker to stand transfixed by the drama being played out on the screens.

CHAPTER FIFTY-SEVEN

"Missile launch! Missile launch!" someone screamed over the comms.

Peter "Hawkeye" Goodwin looked down at his screen and saw nothing to indicate a launch. Then, out of the corner of his eye, he saw the first rocket motor engage in a burst of flame, followed immediately by the second. Hawkeye shoved his F-22 Raptor over in a steep dive, gathering airspeed as the missiles turned on their sides and raced away in opposite directions. He tried to lock his radar onto his target, but it wouldn't track because the Sampson cruise missile was so low to the ground.

"Redneck, go for the second missile!" Hawkeye yelled into the radio.

William "Redneck" Gates, pilot of the second F-22, Whiskey Two, was already diving on the second missile, leaving his flight leader to race in the opposite direction.

Redneck saw the missile lie over on its side and start its acceleration phase. The missile shot forward as he swooped in, listening for the lock tone from his heat-seeking missile.

Just as the Sampson flew over the quarry, its motor sparked out, and it nosed over, tumbling harmlessly into the water.

"Splash one," Redneck called over the radio with relief. "And it was a real splash. You're gonna need some divers to get that thing out of the water."

As he spoke, Redneck pulled the stick back to gain altitude. He was in the middle of a loop, looking down on the compound from fifteen thousand feet when his heart sank at the sight of the next two missiles launching from their tubes. Hawkeye knew instinctively that he could not catch both of them, so he picked the one to the right, rippled off two of his AIM-9X heat-seeking Sidewinder missiles, and chased the second Sampson.

The two Sidewinders failed to lock onto a target. They exploded harmlessly over a cornfield, but Redneck didn't watch them, instead diving for the deck to give chase to the second missile. Even though the F-22 could reach Mach 2.25, he had to throttle back to match the speed of the Sampson.

The flight team's orders had laid out the rules of engagement over the United States. Shooting down the missiles was a priority, but they were limited as to where they could engage because of collateral damage. Firing heat-seekers that didn't connect or, worse, locked onto targets other than the Sampsons could kill civilians, and overshooting with their guns could have the same results.

For Redneck, deploying the two heat-seekers without waiting for a guidance lock had been a gamble. There were multiple houses around the launch site that the Sidewinders could have hit or damaged, and there had been much debate about evacuating all the civilians around the Liberty Brigade compound. In the end, the LEOS hadn't evacuated in the belief that doing so would have alerted Moran to an impending raid.

Settling back into his seat, Redneck watched the Sampson cruise at five hundred feet off the ground, using its terrain contour matching (TERCOM) navigation system. The TERCOM system compared the terrain with measurements made during flight by an onboard radar altimeter, allowing the missile to fly closer to obstacles and at lower altitudes, making it harder to detect by ground radar and considerably increasing the accuracy of the missile at the target.

The two F-22s had to stay above three thousand feet, with the Air Force clearing them through local and regional airspace to prevent midair collisions. If the opportunity came, looking down on the missiles would hopefully give the veteran pilots a better chance of shooting them out of the sky.

In the past decade, technology for jet fighters to shoot down a cruise missile had rapidly increased, with Raytheon improving the heat-seeking and infrared performance of their Sidewinders. They'd also developed specialized missiles to combat the cruise missile threat, but Redneck had no special missiles. All he had were the two remaining Sidewinders on board, plus ammunition for the M61A2 20mm Gatling gun. There was nothing he could do but sit back and watch the show as the sun glinted off the Sampson's metal body.

As the Sampson tracked east, the countryside became more populated, and the ability to use the F-22's weapons systems diminished. Redneck wondered about the destination of the missiles. He could hear Hawkeye talking to ground control as he flew west, getting farther away.

He was about to call Hawkeye and wish him good luck when Wright-Patterson Control came over the radio. "Do not engage. Repeat: do not engage. This is an order from the commander-in-chief. Do not engage the Sampson cruise missiles. You are to escort them to their destination only."

Redneck boiled with rage. An enemy had attacked his country from within, and his own government had ordered him to sit on his hands.

CHAPTER FIFTY-EIGHT

An HRT member clamored down the stairs and called out for Rybeck.

The FBI agent pushed through the crowded bunker to where the man stood in the tunnel. "There's a phone call for you."

Rybeck followed the HRT guy up the stairs, and another handed him a cell phone. His cell phone suddenly began to buzz as it received text and voice messages.

"Rybeck here," the FBI agent said, glancing around at the carnage.

With the missiles in flight, the militiamen guarding the compound had given up the fight, literally throwing down their weapons and surrendering, but the damage had already been done. The downed Black Hawk still smoldered, and black smoke from the machine drifted in the clear sky, leaving an acrid stench in the nostrils to accompany the cordite of spent rounds. Machine gun fire had torn holes through the barn's thin metal siding, and dust swirled in the shafts of sunlight stabbing through those holes.

"Do you have any idea where the missiles are headed?" Roger Talbot asked.

"Yes, sir. There are GPS coordinates on the computer. I'll walk down there and read them to you." He started walking toward the tunnel stairs, but the phone cut out on him as he neared the bunker. He looked at the phone screen and tried to dial out, but the phone would not respond. He handed the device back to the HRT team member it belonged to.

After writing the coordinates on paper and looking at the screen displaying the nose camera feeds, Rybeck headed out of the bunker again. Hurrying up the stairs, he found Allen Cohen, an FBI computer technician who had come in right after the firefight had ended, rolling a computer on a cart across the floor of the barn as other team members laid out body bags containing the dead on the barn floor.

Rybeck called Talbot via his cell phone.

"What's going on?" the SAC growled. "I've got you on speaker in the conference room."

"I lost you when I went inside the bunker," Rybeck said.

"I know," Talbot said. "We think it's shielded. When we lost contact with every person who went down there, we figured it out. Got the coordinates?"

Rybeck read them off.

A moment later, voices chimed in to give them the destinations of each missile.

"Rybeck, one of our computer techs will hook us up to the launch computer to see if we can shut off the missiles."

"Cohen's here. I just saw him," Rybeck said, turning to watch the tech running cables from his wheeled cart down the stairs to the tunnel.

"Good," Talbot said. "What else is in the bunker?"

Rybeck wondered what he meant. "We have Moran and Jackson in custody."

"Anything else about the missiles?" a voice that wasn't Talbot's asked.

"A couple of screens show the nose cone cameras, and we found the Russian engineer."

The same male voice asked, "Can you get him to shut down the missiles?"

"I'll try, sir," Rybeck replied, wondering who he was speaking to.

"Call us when you have him in pocket," the voice said.

"Roger that." Rybeck ended the call and ran down into the bunker.

Cohen was busy hooking cables into the back of the electronics rack in the bunker while a dozen onlookers crowded the control room.

"Everybody, clear out," Rybeck shouted, "unless you are an agency head. Assemble in the headquarters building. Pass the word: I want everyone there in five minutes."

The HRT members begrudgingly shuffled toward the stairs.

"What's going on?" Caroline asked. She was just as glued to the screens as everyone else, watching the scenery flash by at 447 miles per hour.

"I need to find Dragomirov," Rybeck said.

Caroline turned to look around, but the Russian wasn't anywhere to be seen. "He was right here a moment ago."

Together, they took off running down the tunnels, searching for the missing Russian. They passed a tunnel that turned to the right that they hadn't taken on the way in.

"Get someone to go down there," he ordered Caroline.

"I'll go," she said, turning down the tunnel.

Rybeck gave her a look that told her to be careful, and they took off running again. He sprinted through the bunkers, checking them for anyone hiding, and then continued all the way to the women's barracks.

He was breathing hard as he burst through the back door and glanced around. Knowing Dragomirov had slipped through his fingers, Rybeck put his hands on his head and interlocked his fingers, then cursed like the sailor he was.

Rybeck's phone rang with the distinct tone he'd give to her.

"Did you find him?" he asked hopefully.

"No, but I found a nice vehicle bunker."

"How in the world did we lose him?" Rybeck demanded.

"We stopped watching him when we got to the bunker," Caroline replied. "Other things were happening, and then everyone crammed in to watch the nose cameras."

"Meet me at the HQ."

Rybeck hung up and ran across the compound. When he'd told everyone to assemble there, the instruction had just been a logistics thing, so the HRT guys were out of the bunker and could get some hot coffee from the kitchen. Now, he realized, it had been an expedient thing to do.

A minute later, he mounted the stairs that led to Moran's office. Partway up, he turned and addressed the men sitting at the tables.

"The Russian engineer is in the wind. Fan out and start a search pattern to find him. I'll leave the logistics to you guys, but we need him found ASAP. He might be able to disable the missiles."

The men grumbled but got up from the tables and moved outside.

Pulling his phone from his pocket, Rybeck reluctantly dialed the number for Roger Talbot.

"Well?" the SAC asked.

"We lost him," Rybeck reported.

"How in the world did you lose him, Parker?" Talbot yelled.

Rybeck shrugged self-consciously. "I don't know. He was

with us when we entered the bunker, but we had to deal with Moran and Jackson, and he must have slipped away in the confusion. I have the HRT guys searching for him as we speak. He can't get past our roadblocks."

"You better pray that he doesn't," Talbot replied. "Find him."

By the time Rybeck got off the phone, Caroline had entered the building. He motioned for her to walk with him to the barn. The computer technician had connected his computer to the one in the control room and was transmitting the nose camera feeds to Washington, D.C., and various field offices across the country.

Rybeck glanced at his watch and saw it was nearly noon. He was suddenly exhausted. The adrenaline was wearing off, and he'd been up since four a.m., coordinating the attack. Caroline also looked dead on her feet.

"Sir?" the technician said to him.

"Yeah. What's up, Cohen?"

"We estimate the first missile will impact in a few minutes."

Rybeck nodded, suddenly wishing he was in bed at home. He needed a vacation. Caroline took his hand, and they walked down into the bunker together. The mood in the room was somber with every eye glued to the screens.

In the bottom right of each screen, a digital readout counted down the time to target. The left computer monitor showed a satellite map with three yellow lines streaking across it, indicating the flight path of the missiles. Every thirty seconds, the dots marking their locations flashed, and the lines grew longer as the program updated. All eyes in the room shifted between the map and the monitors on the wall.

The fourth launched missile was the first to arrive on target as it had the shortest distance to travel to Mount Weather. As it approached the target, it popped up into the air, gaining altitude before arcing over and nosing straight down on its the preset target coordinates.

Centered in the screen was a cluster of five buildings that made up the main offices of the Emergency Operations Center, which, according to conspiracy theorists, contained elevators into the top-secret command bunker of a shadow government.

The nose camera showed the buildings clearly as the Sampson descended straight into the largest of them.

Gasps echoed in the Liberty Brigade bunker as the screen went black.

CHAPTER FIFTY-NINE

Bluemont Farm
Bluemont, Virginia

Kenny Orlando stood in the kitchen of the two-story farmhouse. His cell phone chimed as he poured a cup of coffee. Orlando set the decanter back on the coffeemaker and sipped the hot brew. He fished the cell phone from his pocket and checked the message on Signal: *Poseidon's Fury*.

Orlando dropped the mug of coffee into the sink and ran for the bunk rooms where the men were sleeping.

"Get the men to the trucks, now!" he called over his shoulder to Kyle Nielson, who had been standing in the kitchen with him.

Nielson sprinted out the door to find the group of men on standby duty. Orlando began pounding on the bunk room walls and yelling for the men to muster outside. They stumbled from their racks, hastily pulling on clothes and rushing toward the trucks where their equipment was stacked and ready to go.

The missile would take less than forty-five minutes to cover the roughly 325 miles between the launch point and Mount Weather. The men needed to be rolling, ready for the impact. The Sampson would wipe out much of the facility's defenses and the CORE troops on the base, but they needed to secure the compound quickly and shut down all communications to and from the operations center before the shadow government could start issuing orders.

Forbush, Divert, and Kellogg swung into the driver's seats of the Peterbilts. The men tumbled into their gear and climbed into trailers, pulling out weapons, slamming home magazines, and preparing for the action they had trained for. The massive diesels snorted to life, and as soon as the doors to the trailers had swung closed, they drove out of the yard.

Peeling off in three directions, the drivers knew the routes by heart, having driven them repeatedly in pickup trucks during dry runs. Now, though, they were racing against time in heavily laden semi-trucks.

Divert glanced over at his boss and grinned. They were pumped for action. The training, the waiting, and the secrecy were all finally over.

Orlando nodded in agreement, his smile matching the driver's. There was no need for words between warriors who had trained together and fought side by side.

———

KELLOGG'S TRUCK had the longest route through the back roads, so it took thirty-five minutes for his crew to get into position.

He pulled the semi onto the shoulder of Route 601, and the men went to work, transforming the semi from a mundane-looking daily driver to a combat-ready war machine. They flipped up the M-60 machine gun turret and locked it into place, then attached the ammunition box and charged the weapon. Up front, Kellogg and his passenger, Tim Green, slid the steel plates over the windshield and side windows.

Kellogg knew the men in the other trucks were doing the same.

It was finally time for battle.

———

AT THE BLUEMONT FARM, ex-Army pilot Johnny Collins started the engine of the McDonnell Douglas MD 500 Defender. His co-pilot, fellow Army veteran Kim Greenwood, checked the armament on the stub wings. The Defender carried two M129 40mm grenade launchers and two General Electric M134 miniguns.

Collins would wait for the signal from Orlando and then launch from the farm for the five-minute flight to Mount Weather. Behind him in the twin passenger seats, Karl Kessler and Nathan Drover nestled into their harnesses and checked their gear. Kessler carried an HK PSG1 sniper rifle and an FN SCAR, while Drover preferred a hybrid DPMS rifle as his sole gun for sniping and as a rapid-fire weapon.

If needed, Collins could drop the men off so they could provide sniper overwatch for the militiamen engaged in combat. For now, they would ride along as he patrolled the skies over Mount Weather.

———

THE MASSIVE EXPLOSION caused by the missile slamming into the FEMA compound interrupted Kenny Orlando's thoughts as he stared at his phone, hoping it would ring with another update from Moran. The timer on his phone said the missile was early.

Immediately, he called Collins and gestured to Divert at the same time. Divert picked up the CB mike and gave all truckers the "Go" signal. He dropped the mike, slammed the shifter into first gear, and eased the truck onto the road.

Collins acknowledged the call and was already in the air when it came through. He could clearly see the smoke, secondary explosions, and resultant fires from the missile's impact from his high-altitude perch.

Divert sped the truck up to fifty miles per hour and then turned the wheel hard right at the marked spot on the road, sending the truck into the ditch. It bounced violently on its suspension, almost jarring the men in the trailer from their seats. The cab nosed into the air and slammed into the perimeter fence, the trailer swerving and jerking behind them. If it weren't for the seat belt, the violent gyrations would have thrown the M-60 gunner from his perch atop the trailer.

Gaining the solid asphalt surface of a road inside the compound, Divert straightened the truck and sped toward the west entrance of Mount Weather's tunnel system. Bullets pinged off the front of the truck from CORE troops positioned near the truck's entry point, and the M60 opened up above them. Divert ignored the lead storm coming from the barracks and drove the truck straight to the tunnel entrance. He was grateful for the metal shields over the windshield, but the small slits made it difficult to see where he was headed.

Orlando heard the bark of M4 rifles and suspected that his men had the side doors open on the trailer and were giving as good as they got.

Divert blasted the horn to warn the men that he was coming to a stop and slammed on the brakes. The semi swerved as the tires locked and skidded, the trailer sliding out from behind the cab. All the while, the M60 chattered away above them.

Once the semi finally came to a stop, the men streamed out of the trailer while the M60 gunner continued to provide covering fire. He laid long bursts into the building at the tunnel entrance, taking out the guards and anyone else who got in the way.

Orlando called for a cease-fire and ordered a volley of grenades. The explosions shattered windows and ripped wood frames from their foundations, showering the commandos in debris. Orlando gave another signal, and the men rushed inside, finishing the firefight with the CORE troops.

With their position secure and backs to the tunnel doors, the men from Halberd Security jockeyed the semi-trailer around to provide a base for them to operate from.

Across from the tunnel entrance was a parking lot containing construction equipment, debris, dirt, scrap steel, shipping containers, and aging single-wide trailers used as construction offices. Among the construction equipment was a large forklift that could pick up the shipping containers. Orlando directed two men to move several shipping containers in front of the semi-trailer to shore up their defenses.

"Heads up, boss!" the M60 gunner called down from his perch. "We have company coming."

The Halberd team turned to see a group of about thirty men advancing up the road, keeping to the right, close to the cover of the barracks buildings.

Orlando turned to his men to give orders, but he couldn't find several of them. "Where are Donaldson and Lewis?" he barked.

"Don't know," one of his men replied.

"Fine," Orlando grunted. "You three, get over to the construction equipment and provide some crossfire against these guys. Hostler, take two guys, go around the back of the tunnel entrance, and cover the tree line and the road. And for goodness sakes! Can someone *please* tell me where Donaldson and Lewis are?"

"More company incoming on our six!" the gunner called.

As the men dispersed to follow their orders, the rest of the team watched with weapons ready as a Humvee approached. The M60 gunner swiveled his barrel toward the tan machine until he recognized Bill Lewis standing in the turret behind the Humvee's fifty-caliber machine gun, then traversed his weapon back to cover the CORE troops.

The Humvee stopped beside Orlando, and he asked, "Where in the world did you find that thing?"

In the driver's seat, Donaldson grinned from under a bushy mustache. "You know I've got sticky fingers, sir."

Orlando smiled. "Yeah. I know. That's why I keep you around." Donaldson had always had a reputation for finding the things they needed.

"Cover your ears!" Lewis called out before he depressed the trigger on the fifty cal. A tongue of flame shot out of the end of the barrel as bullets, interspersed with red tracer rounds, chewed up the side of a barracks building, sending the advancing troops ducking for cover.

Lewis eased off the trigger. In the silence, the men could hear the distant gunfire of other combat teams and the smack of the Defender's rotors as Collins provided cover.

Orlando climbed into the Humvee and called two other men to join him. Mounted up, they drove to the barracks and pulled up to where the opposing force had hunkered down. Orlando climbed out and stood on the pavement, holding his M4, covered by Lewis on the fifty cal.

"Listen up, troops!" Orlando called out in his best drill instructor's voice. "You will come out and lay down your weapons. We will house and feed you before shipping you to another duty station. I have no desire to harm you, but if you don't come out and surrender, we will hunt you down, and we will kill you."

No one moved.

Orlando could see several of the men squatting along the barracks wall, weapons trained on him. He waited for another moment, but still, no one stirred.

He gestured with his arm in the opposing force's direction and said, "Light 'em up, Bill."

Bill Lewis squeezed the trigger, and the big gun destroyed the wall of the barracks, killing several men. Orlando waved his hand, and the gun fell silent.

"Come out, men!" he demanded.

Slowly, the CORE troops and other military personnel crept out from their hiding spots and piled their weapons in the back of the Humvee. With the CORE troops stripped of their gear, Orlando's men locked them in an intact barracks building.

―――

ACROSS THE MOUNT WEATHER COMPOUND, Jerry Kellogg, Tim Green, and their men were having problems finding a path through the debris left by the missile strike.

Shattered and toppled trees now blocked the easiest route through the parking lot. Using the Peterbilt's brush guard as a battering ram, Kellogg repeatedly slammed into overturned cars, shoving them out of the way, sometimes having to back up to hit them multiple times.

Green kept checking his watch and scanning for a better route through the debris field. With no alternative, Kellogg continued to plow into every object in their path. Fortunately, they encountered little resistance from CORE troops as they pressed onward.

Approaching the dirt access road to take them up to the east tunnel entrance, Green cursed and pointed at the retaining wall that blocked their way.

"Didn't see that on the recon photos," Kellogg muttered. He twisted the wheel over and pointed the semi at a small tree that blocked the path. The driver gripped the wheel with both hands. "Hold on, Tim."

Green grabbed the CB mike and hollered for the men in the trailer to hold fast.

Kellogg accelerated toward the tree, and Green braced one leg up on the dashboard and closed his eyes.

With a powerful impact, the truck collided with the four-inch diameter sapling just to the left of center, and the semi jolted hard enough that it felt like it had been thrown backward. The tree bent as Kellogg kept the power to the spinning and smoking rear wheels. With a sharp crack, the tree snapped, and the truck bucked as it passed over the stump and then chugged up the hill toward the east entrance.

The M60 opened up and chattered away. Bullets pinged off the Peterbilt's steel-reinforced front end and whined into the distance. Kellogg kept the accelerator down on the floorboard, charging toward the tunnel.

Eventually, he slowed and turned the wheel hard left, bouncing through the grass and onto the helicopter landing pad outside the tunnel doors. The Halberd Security troops streamed out of the trailer, taking up positions behind the cab to return fire.

The incoming fire was intense, and the CORE troops shot the M60 gunner from his seat atop the semi-trailer. A second man crawled up and pulled him free before taking his place.

The new gunner poured hot lead into the building beside the tunnel mouth while a second team member brought his grenade launcher to bear. Four grenades later, the wooden structure beside the tunnel lay in shambles.

With the enemy force subdued, Green set up his own guard post, using the semi as cover, and ordered his men to round up any stray troops in the area.

CHAPTER SIXTY

Watching through the tempered glass, the gate guards at the front entrance to the Mount Weather compound saw the armored Peterbilt 362 with a roof-mounted M60 machine gun turn off the main road and head straight toward them. The M60 began firing, slamming bullets into the guardhouses in an attempt to blow them to pieces. The men watched as the glass cracked into spiderwebs but held.

The phone in the middle booth rang, and the nearest guard picked it up, putting it to his right ear and shoving his left index finger into his left. "Hello? Sergeant Waddell here!"

"Sergeant, this is FEMA Director Kevin Tate. What's going on out there?"

"Sir, we're under attack by a semi with a heavy machine gun mounted on it. I can't contact anyone at Base HQ. There was a gigantic explosion here, followed by multiple small ones. I'm sorry, sir, but I don't have any other information."

"I understand. What's all that noise?" Tate asked.

"Gunfire, sir," Waddell replied.

The guardhouses divided incoming traffic into three lanes,

with the third passing through a giant building where the CORE guards inspected all shipments in minute detail. The roof of the building slanted out to cover the other two guard booths and offer shade to stopped traffic.

Waddell slapped the button at his post to raise the steel barricades to block the traffic lanes and prevent the oncoming semi from entering the top-secret facility. At the same time, another guard reached the peak of the inspection building and threw open the door that hid the fifty-caliber machine gun mounted there. As soon as the guard had it charged, he opened fire on the semi, with the massive bullets striking the steel plates on its windshield and almost punching through them.

Through the spiderweb of bulletproof glass, Waddell stared at the semi. The fifty-cal gunner blew the M60 gunner off the roof of the trailer.

As more guys tried to man the M60, they kept getting mowed down. The semi-truck stopped abruptly and began reversing its course to maneuver out of the line of fire.

Waddell's eyes moved from the truck to a black spot on the horizon. The phone fell from his hand as he realized what he was seeing.

On the other end, Director Tate heard the guard utter an expletive just before the line went dead.

———

Smoke poured off the wing pods of the MD 500 Defender as Kim Greenwood launched a salvo of grenades. The guard shacks and the giant building that housed the fifty-caliber machine gun disintegrated in a series of explosions.

Collins banked the Defender around after passing over the wrecked entrance and made another pass over the crumbling building, shattering the wreckage with gunfire.

The helo circled again and flew toward the impact site of the Sampson cruise missile, looking for targets of opportunity. There were plenty of them as soldiers came out of their barracks and spilled from training sites to shoot at the helicopter or ran toward the wreckage to see what they could do to aid their downed colleagues.

Collins flew along the zigzag of main roads while Greenwood fired grenades into the barracks and laid down gunfire on the men who were shooting at them.

When they had expended their payload of grenades and bullets, Collins radioed Forbush and told him that they were returning to the farm to refuel and rearm. "I'll being back with Griffin guided munitions to take out those antennas."

———

"Copy that. We can handle it," Forbush radioed back to Collins in the Defender as he jockeyed the semi around the bombed-out guard shacks and into the adjacent parking lot.

The Peterbilt crossed onto Old Blue Ridge Road and skirted the edge of the missile crater. Through the open doors of the trailer, the men stared silently out at the destruction.

The Sampson had centered on the main building in the complex, and there was nothing left but an enormous, smoking crater. The impact had obliterated the neighboring buildings, moving outward in a giant circle. Small fires raged where gas lines spewed their contents into the air, and hungry flames feasted on bits of wood.

There was burning lumber, twisted steel, shattered glass, and ruined concrete everywhere. Most of the Halberd men had seen missile strikes during their deployments to Afghanistan, Iraq, or other hot spots around the world. Yet, none of them had seen this kind of destruction on American soil since 9/11.

The truck forcefully plowed through the missile detritus and drove past buildings that the Defender had hit with grenade fire, making its way into the trees farther up the road. Occasional pockets of CORE personnel engaged the semi as it weaved toward the eastern tunnel entrance. Most of the time, the M60 would dispatch these holdouts. Then, the Halberd troops would dismount from the semi-trailer and sweep through the area, making sure they left no resistance before climbing back aboard the slow-moving semi.

Buried amongst the rubble of one building was a Humvee with a turret-mounted M2 Browning machine gun. Forbush barked an order, "Mellark, Richmond, Saylor, Reynolds—dig this rig out, take it back down to the base entrance, and set up a guard post."

The semi continued to snake uphill along the old road to where Jerry Kellogg's Peterbilt sat outside the tunnel entrance. The men dismounted from the truck and supported Kellogg's men as they swept through the area. When the troops returned from their sweep, Forbush stood beside Kellogg's semi.

"We're going to sweep across the base to Orlando's group. You good here?" he asked Tim Green.

"Yeah, we're good. I'm going to send half my force with you. We don't need all these men to guard a closed door. Even if the people inside open the door, we'll have plenty of warning, and we can pin them down with the M60."

Forbush laughed in agreement, then put his arm in the air and circled it above his head, telling his men to mount up. Green divided half his force and dispatched them with Jefferson.

Back inside the cab of Forbush's truck, the radio crackled. "Defender One to Peter Three."

"Peter Three, go ahead," Forbush replied. He could hear the smack of the Defender's rotors as it flew low over the base. He looked out the window to see the helicopter zoom over them and make a long, sweeping turn to the north.

"Just wanted to let you know we're back on station," Collins said.

"Any word from headquarters?" Forbush asked, wanting to know if the pilots had heard from Moran.

"Negative on that, Peter Three," Collins replied.

"Roger that" Forbush said. "We're going to sweep to the west entrance. Leave some of those barracks for us to keep house in."

"Copy that," Collins said as he brought the helicopter in from the north and resumed the hunt for CORE troops or any other armed resistance to the militia invaders.

Now that the Mount Weather facility was secure, the first mission of the Halberd Security force was to round up any survivors and house them in the barracks until it was time to move them to other locations. The new administration would reassign active-duty troops to new bases, and they would send the civilians home.

Their second mission was to sever all communications from the underground city to the outside world. This meant destroying antennas, satellite dishes, communication arrays, cables, fiber optics, and phone lines. To achieve this, the Halberd men used explosives, axes, saws, and machine guns to damage and destroy any communications device they came across. At the bases of the tall antennas, they placed homing devices that the Defender's guided ordnance could lock onto so they could blow down the massive aluminum-and-steel structures.

As they toppled an antenna designed to look like a pine tree, one of the Halberd troopers shouted out victoriously, "Suck it, Deep State! Liberty Brigade is here!"

CHAPTER SIXTY-ONE

Liberty Brigade compound
Kenton, Ohio

In the commotion following Moran and Jackson's arrest and the subsequent launch of the missiles, Kostya Dragomirov finally had his chance to escape.

He'd run through the tunnels, picking up a pistol from a dead guard, and exited through the female barracks.

Dragomirov ran east through the woods that skirted open fields. He stopped to watch, listen, and catch his breath every few minutes, then ran some more. He covered the mile between the compound and the ancient cluster of farm buildings on Fail Road in a little over fifteen minutes. He didn't know if law enforcement had blocked the roads around the compound, but he suspected they had as he had spent hours discussing exfiltration plans with Greg Allende, his friend in the Kenton PD. Allende had said the first thing the Feds would do was put up roadblocks, so Dragomirov asked the officer to buy a small motorcycle and hide it in one of the old barns at a farm on Fail Road. Allende paid the barn's owner to look the other way and not ask questions.

Approaching the barn carefully, Dragomirov scanned the grounds for any police or federal agents who might be searching for him or any other escaping militia members.

Five minutes later, he found the used Yamaha XT350 hidden in a building that had probably once been a chicken coop. He pulled off the tarp that covered the bike's frame and found a black backpack that contained a helmet and a jacket. Also in the pack was a zip seal bag housing a passport in the name of Alexei Gromov, a French-Russian engineer, a driver's license, a credit card in the same name, and a thick wad of cash. It had cost Dragomirov quite a bit of money to organize these documents and to buy Allende's discretion, but it all seemed worth it now.

Dragomirov didn't have a green card or a visa, and his passport hadn't been stamped, but he hoped it wouldn't matter when he exited the country. With the new documents, he could travel without fear of being tracked by the government or Moran's militia. The only drawback would be that facial recognition software could identify him quickly if the U.S. government or Moran had placed him in the system. If Moran had ordered it, the system would flag him as Roger Kozak rather than Gromov. He felt he could deny this, but if he was in the system as Dragomirov, then any number of the alphabet agencies might pick him up and hold him indefinitely.

He would have to chance it for now. If he had to, Dragomirov would just sneak out of the country.

The Russian pulled on his safety gear before rolling the bike outside. After turning the fuel petcock on, he twisted the key and pressed the starter button. The engine on the Yamaha fired right up.

He crossed Fail Road and rode into a field, staying between the heavily wooded creek ravine and the edge of the soybeans planted there.

By the time he made it to the nearest highway, he was hot and tired as he had dropped the bike twice, forcing Dragomirov to pick it up and slowly navigate around the dead limbs on the ground, and weave his way through the high weeds, and under low-hanging branches. Eventually, he quit trying to keep out of the bean field and angled toward the road. He no longer cared if he left a trail or damaged the beans. He just wanted to get as far away from the compound as possible.

Dragomirov's journey took him south on two-lane highways to the Gulf of Mexico, where he turned right and rode to Brownsville, Texas. There, he crossed the border into Mexico.

The next place Alexei Gromov's passport registered was in Belize. He parked his bike in San Pedro on Ambergris Caye, bought a condo, and set about enjoying his hard-earned money.

CHAPTER SIXTY-TWO

Caroline Thurmond felt tired beyond her years, an exhaustion that made her want to lie down and never get up.

The last twenty-four hours had been stressful as she had attended the brief on the militia raid, worked an overnight shift due to chronic understaffing, and then busted into the compound to provide a distraction for Rybeck and the pinned-down HRT team.

Her emotions were strained, and she felt like she would break down. Still, she stood stoically, watching the monitors as the last two missiles raced toward their targets. She couldn't let the men see her break, especially Parker Rybeck.

The top-left screen showed the missile zooming down through the streets of New York City, amid skyscrapers, cars and cabs, and people walking on sidewalks, going about their daily lives. Without warning, the nose camera tilted upward as the Sampson gained altitude to strike. The camera showed nothing but the blue sky of a cloudless July day before the missile rotated over and dropped straight toward the cluster buildings at 1 U.N. Plaza.

Everyone watching could see the line of flags snapping in the breeze in front of United Nations Plaza, the top of the thirty-nine-story Secretariat building, and the General Assembly Building that bordered the muddy East River.

Fortunately, in Caroline's opinion, once the news of the impending missile launch had broken, all U.N. representatives had fled the city.

During the missile's short flight, city officials had worked tirelessly to evacuate the offices and residences around the plaza.

There wasn't a sound in the bunker as everyone stared at the television screen. Rybeck interlocked his fingers with Caroline's, and she squeezed them hard as the missile slammed into the top of the Secretariat Building, and another screen in the bunk turned black.

CHAPTER SIXTY-THREE

Redneck's F-22
New York City, New York

Redneck, in the F-22 Raptor known as Whiskey Two, watched helplessly as he flew over New York City.

The cruise missile nosed over, and the tone sounded in his ears as the Sidewinders on his wings locked onto the Sampson cruise missile. His finger hovered over the trigger of the AIM-9X. The impact of the two missiles would rain fiery debris across the city. Despite his orders not to shoot down the missile, he had decided he would take the shot at the first opportunity.

However, the only shot presented to him was when the Sampson roared straight upward to elevate above its target. Redneck knew he couldn't pull the trigger.

As the missile fell toward its intended target, the Sidewinders lost tone, and Redneck helplessly remained on station, unable to tear himself away. He banked the jet to see more clearly out the side of the F-22's canopy.

Below him, the missile tore through the top of the Secretariat Building, leaving a small hole in the roof. A fraction of a second later, the missile impacted the ground and detonated.

The explosion from the conventional warhead blew out the sides of the high-rise, shooting steel, concrete, and glass into the surrounding buildings. The bottom of the Secretariat Building imploded, and the structure twisted slightly to the right as it collapsed in on itself. The blast blew the flagpoles flat and ripped fabric and rope from the steel, scattering them into the wind or causing them to disintegrate. Buildings across the street shook, windows blew out, and facades crumbled as the shock wave reverberated through the concrete canyons. Trees on Roosevelt Island were torn from their roots. A five-foot tsunami swept across the East River, submerging boats, docks, houses, and buildings from Long Island Sound in the north to the Hudson River in the south.

Redneck let out his breath as the shock wave jostled his fighter jet. He fought with the stick as the turbulent air disrupted his flight controls, and the F-22 bounced until it found calm air.

When he unbuckled his oxygen mask, Redneck found it was wet with sweat and tears. The tears were from the frustration he felt from not being able to shoot down the missile or save the people who had died in the blast. It was senseless to him, and he repeated in his mind the same question he'd asked a hundred times during the last hour.

How could someone do this to their own countrymen?

CHAPTER SIXTY-FOUR

Hawkeye's F-22
Eastern Colorado

Hawkeye chased the last cruise missile along a path that took him across Indiana, Illinois, Iowa, Nebraska, and into Colorado. From the coordinates the FBI had found at the Liberty Brigade compound, he knew the Sampson's target was the NSA Data Center. Based on the distance to the target and speed of the cruise missile, it would take about three and a half hours for the Sampson to reach Saratoga Springs, Utah.

Wiping his brow with the back of his flight glove, Hawkeye noted that he'd been flying for over two and a half hours already, and his plane was running low on fuel.

As he approached the flat plains of eastern Colorado, two sleek, black Lockheed Martin F-35 Lightning IIs appeared on his right wing.

"Whiskey One, this is Block Flight Lead," Colonel Bill "Razor" Gillette called out over the radio.

"Copy, Block Flight," Hawkeye replied. He had been listening to the radio as Block Flight of the 61st Fighter Squadron—the Top Dogs—had launched from Luke Air Force Base in Glendale, Arizona. Block Flight Leader was a personal friend of Hawkeye's. He and the Razor had gone through flight training together and had remained in close contact ever since. Hawkeye was happy to have Razor and his wingman, Steve "Gator" Coughlin escorting the Sampson cruise missile to Utah.

"Hawkeye, vector to Buckley Space Force Base," Razor said. "They'll get you turned around to Wright-Pat."

"Roger that, Razor. Keep your tray table in an upright position, and don't forget to tip your waitress," Hawkeye replied as he punched in the coordinates to Buckley SFB in Denver, Colorado. He banked the F-22 to the left, peeling out of formation.

Razor chuckled as he clicked his radio twice to acknowledge Hawkeye's comment and then settled into his seat to fly slowly behind the missile. The Sampson's R95-300 turbofan engine kept the missile at a constant speed of 447 miles per hour.

Block Lead had a thirty-minute window to shoot down the missile after it flew past Denver, and Razor intended to take it. He'd sworn an oath against all enemies, foreign and domestic, and riding herd on this turd made no sense to him. Razor was going to defy orders and spare at least one of the targets.

Just ahead, Razor could see the flame of the missile's engine as it streaked along, following the terrain toward the very limit of the missile's flight capabilities. With any luck, the Sampson's motor would flame out before it even got to Utah.

The Sampson passed over I-25, startling a semi-truck driver so badly that it caused him to duck in his seat. The swerve of the truck whipped the trailer across two lanes of traffic, barely missing several cars before hitting a guardrail and bouncing back straight.

Razor clicked his mike open and spoke into the radio, "We're going hunting for Russian junk."

"Copy, Block Flight Lead. Happy hunting," General Tom Sherman replied.

He and a large crowd of people watched the radar screen displayed on the wall of Luke Air Force Base's flight control center. They could see the two F-35 Lightnings as green diamonds crossing the screen from right to left. Unable to see the low-flying missile, they relied on a constant stream of chatter from the pilots to act as their eyes. Sherman had asked Razor to take this flight and shoot the missile down, promising whatever help he could give him from the ground.

Razor slid the throttle forward, accelerating away from his wingman, and rolled out in a giant loop to the right, racing around to bring the jet onto the tail of the missile. Gator stayed in position, calling play-by-play for the benefit of those listening.

The F-35's radar display swept across the visor of Razor's helmet, showing him the heat signature of the Sampson as his Sidewinders tried to lock onto it. He steadied his breath, straining against the tight bonds of his harness, to feel the jet beneath him. He felt like a sniper: one shot, one kill. His 'rifle' vibrated underneath him in the buffeting winds coming off the mountains as he flew a thousand feet off the ground. Everything seemed to slow down as the radar lock tone pinged in his ears.

"Missile away," Razor called as his finger caressed the trigger on his joystick. The AIM-9X Sidewinder dropped out of the weapons bay, and the solid-fuel rocket ignited, shoving the missile to Mach 2.7. Razor squeezed the trigger again, sending a second Sidewinder racing after the first.

Inside Flight Control at Luke Air Force Base, the personnel tracked the missiles as two purple dots streaked away from the aircraft. Everyone seemed to hold their collective breath, waiting for impact, and emotions in the room ran high as they awaited the destruction of the Sampson. They had witnessed the obliteration of two facilities on American soil by a ruthless domestic terrorist today. The major news networks were already reporting that Paul Moran, the leader of Liberty Brigade, had been arrested by the FBI.

The Russian-made Sampson hummed along, oblivious to the two Sidewinders racing toward its destruction. Its TERCOM constantly swept ahead, watching the terrain and adjusting its altitude and attitude to rise and fall as the terrain dictated. Just ahead, a mountain rose straight up, and the Sampson jinked to the right to pass through a narrow gap between two cliffs. As it turned, the first Sidewinder crashed into the sheer rock face of the mountain.

Razor slammed his fist into his thigh. A feeling of desperation seeped into the cockpit as the second Sidewinder slid in behind the Sampson.

Just west of Craig, Colorado, the high mountain peaks of Routt National Forest gave way to flatter terrain. Behind the Sampson, the second Sidewinder screamed up its tailpipe and locked onto the Sampson's infrared heat signature.

The closing speed of the Sidewinder was over three times greater than the speed of the Sampson. Its computer failed to properly calculate the speed differential between the two missiles and overshot the Sampson. The Sidewinder attempted to turn back toward its target. As it banked, the infrared scanner locked onto the heat signature of a wildfire raging in the trees below. The Sidewinder nosed over and slammed into the ground, exploding in a massive crater that blew out the fire surrounding the hole.

Gator cursed over the open radio network as he watched the Sampson missile scream away from the crater left by the Sidewinder. His sentiments were echoed all across the country by those watching the scene play out.

Livid, General Sherman grabbed the microphone. "Gator, go to guns."

"Roger that, sir."

Gator nosed the F-35 over, gathering speed as Razor climbed to become overwatch and call the play-by-play. The Sampson crossed into Utah as Gator flipped the red cover up on his stick and armed the F-35's GAU-22A 25mm Gatling guns.

"Negative, Block Flight! You will abort all attempts to stop that missile!" an unknown voice shouted in the ears of the two pilots. "This is President Diane Warrick, your commander-in-chief. I order you to halt all attempts to stop that missile. You've already caused enough damage."

Razor gulped, unsure if he was really hearing an order from the president. "Uh, you copy this, Control?"

"I have shut control down," Warrick replied. "You will take orders from me. Escort that missile to Utah and set your planes down at Salt Lake International."

Chastised, Razor mumbled, "Yes, ma'am."

Razor pulled his aircraft into an altitude-eating climb. Seconds later, he was at ten thousand feet and leveling off to watch the missile do its job. Gator slid into position on his flight leader's right wing as Razor tore off his oxygen mask and screamed into the cockpit, venting his anger.

"Show's about to start, boss," Gator radioed.

Razor no longer cared. He was going to set his plane down and walk away. He couldn't serve a commander-in-chief who had just ordered him not to do everything he possibly could to save lives. It was the exact opposite of why he'd become a fighter pilot.

Ringed out below them, the NSA Data Center comprised eight buildings in a semicircle, curving from due north to the southwest. In the middle of the curve, two large buildings called Data Halls held the data storage servers. Outlying to the north and south of these Data Halls were two smaller buildings known as Power Buildings, connecting the servers to the grid. The final buildings on each end of the arc were Chiller Plants and towers to keep the servers and power generators cool. Beside those last two buildings were small fuel and water storage tanks reserved for if the massive power substation located just outside the facility were ever to go offline.

When Paul Moran had entered the coordinates into the guidance computer in the launch control bunker, he'd used the administration office building as the primary target. It sat squarely between the two Data Halls, and the explosion of the conventional warhead would be adequate to eliminate the Data Center permanently.

The Sampson reached its maximum altitude and nosed over for the final time, racing toward the target. Falling now, faster than its straight-line speed, it slammed into the side of the north Data Hall, missing the administration building by fifteen feet.

Razor forced himself to watch as the missile exploded on impact with the ground, blowing out the sides of the Data Hall, flattening the administration building, and then tearing through the southern hall. The powerful explosion shorted out the electronics of all the computers and blew apart the transformers in the substations and in the power generation buildings, showering sparks like fireworks. These explosions ripped apart the generator fuel lines, ignited the gasoline fumes, and caused the fuel storage tanks to explode in massive fireballs that spread flames and debris across the road to Camp Williams State Military Reservation, home of the Utah Army National Guard. The flames caught on old wooden buildings and raced across the complex, destroying more than Moran could have ever hoped.

Live feeds from civilian news helicopters out of Salt Lake City broadcast the real-time destruction of government facilities to the world. The last building to be destroyed in Paul Moran's bid to reclaim the government for the people of the United States had been a spectacular show.

And one that Razor wished he had never seen.

CHAPTER SIXTY-FIVE

Charlotte, North Carolina

Inside an industrial warehouse owned by one of Chet Gravely's many companies, four hackers sat at their desks, typing away on their powerful computers. Together, their combined computing power outstripped even the latest supercomputer. The hackers had hand-built the servers and hardware and then written their own software to work alongside the standard Windows operating system. Each workstation ran off the main computer, but, if necessary, the hackers could disconnect them to run on a standalone network to protect the integrity of the mainframe or to hide its identity.

All the hackers were highly skilled and capable in their own right, but collectively, they were a formidable weapon. They worked almost in concert, feeding off Red Bull, Mountain Dew, and the occasional cigarette or joint. Once the creative juices were flowing, ideas bounced off each other, and the fingers flew across keyboards, writing code, breaking encryptions, and digitally circumventing countless U.S. laws and regulations.

One of the illegal acts the hackers had performed was to take control of the televised media so that, immediately following the impact of the fourth missile at the NSA facility in Utah, they could stream a video message from Paul Moran to the people of the United States and the rest of the world.

The four hackers watched impassively as the counter wound down and the Sampson missile appeared on the frame of the hovering helicopter's camera above the NSA Data Center. For an instant, the world got a glimpse of sleek finned steel before the Sampson nosed over and slammed into the ground, obliterating the facility.

Teddy, the portly lead hacker with thinning hair and acne scars, reached across the console and pressed a button on his keyboard, sending Moran's message across the airwaves. Cheers rang out from his fellow hackers, accompanied by applause, slaps on the back, and the cracking open of beer cans. Jonelle, a wild girl with multiple piercings and a genius on the keyboard, danced between the black leather couches that ringed their workstations.

The end of the existing government was at hand, and all their hard work had finally paid off.

The hackers found their seats on the couches to watch the short, prerecorded speech on their enormous flat screen, generally reserved for playing Call of Duty or some other first-person shooter video games.

After Teddy had pressed the button, television broadcasts across the country carried nothing but static for thirty seconds before the Liberty Brigade logo—the Stars and Stripes skull with crossed rifles behind it—appeared on-screen. The logo faded away to a recording of Moran standing at a podium in front of an American flag.

"My name is Colonel Paul Moran, head of Liberty

Brigade. My fellow Americans, our country is in turmoil. It was once said that the only way to destroy America was from within, and today, we know that to be true. We have seen the slow destruction of our country through the erosion of our liberties, our religion, and our God-given rights by those we elected to be the representatives of our country. They have subverted their offices and forgotten who they were working for. Their goals became about maintaining their own power, and to do so, they took it away from the people who put them in office.

"Today, we have seen the assassination of this self-serving leadership and the destruction of the United Nations complex in New York City; the shadow government at Mount Weather, Virginia; the NSA Data Center in Utah; and the U.S. Capitol Building in Washington, D.C. Now is the time to rise up and take control of the government, to right the ship, and return our country to the principles of our Founding Fathers.

"Do not fear the militias stepping in to assist in this transition. They are peaceful, law-abiding citizens who love their country and wish to see it restored to order. They are to help law enforcement and local governments keep law and order.

"President Diane Warrick will take charge until new elections can be held to replace all the sitting congressmen and senators. More information will be forthcoming on this.

"As we make these changes, we want you to know that life will continue as you know it. We will reduce and streamline the government so you can keep more of what you earn, have less regulation in your life, and enjoy the freedoms and liberties endowed to us by our Creator."

The screen went blank for fifteen seconds and then returned to the normally scheduled programming, including, as if to underline Moran's point, close-ups of the smoking debris of the NSA Data Center.

CHAPTER SIXTY-SIX

Liberty Brigade compound
Kenton, Ohio

Parker Rybeck's anger flared hot and intense.

If it were not for the arms of Caroline Thurmond wrapped around him, Rybeck would have run up the steps and crossed the compound to the room where Paul Moran sat in handcuffs. He would have pulled his service pistol from its holster, jammed it to the man's temple, and pulled the trigger. Traitors deserved to be executed.

And he was pretty sure he wasn't the only one who felt that way.

Instead of executing the prisoner, Rybeck stood rooted to a spot in front of the bunker's television screen, wondering how deep the conspiracy ran that had enabled Moran to put a handpicked president into the Oval Office.

Am I a pawn in this game, too?

"Hey, Rybeck!" Cohen called to him from the bunker door. "Telephone call for you."

"Yeah, okay," Rybeck replied numbly as he unwound Caroline's arms from around him, his chest wet with her tears.

He dragged himself up the steps from the tunnel. Rybeck walked into what had been Dragomirov's apartment, where Allen Cohen had installed a bank of phones using the existing landline and cell circuits. The technician pointed to a corded phone off the hook beside its base.

"Rybeck here," he snarled into the receiver after picking it up. He was still angry with himself for failing to stop the missile launch and wasn't feeling particularly professional.

"Hi, Parker. It's Talbot. How are you holding up?"

"Not well, sir. I'm actually quite furious at the moment."

"I understand how you're feeling, so what I'm about to tell you isn't going to improve your mood."

Rybeck gripped the phone tighter. "What is it, sir?"

"I need you to put Moran and Jackson on a helicopter and take them to the Allen County Regional Airport in Lima. There will be a plane waiting for you there. You're to escort them to their destination."

"And where would that be, sir?" Rybeck replied, an uneasy feeling suddenly stirring in his gut. "Prison? Leavenworth? Guantanamo Bay?"

Talbot sighed. "I'm sorry, Rybeck, but we've all had the wool pulled over our eyes. Your prisoners are going to the White House."

Rybeck lost what was left of his cool and cursed. "We're putting more traitors in the White House? What are we doing, exchanging one for another? President Cross was as corrupt as they come, and now *Moran* is taking over?"

"I don't like it any more than you do, but these orders come straight from Director Scoda's office."

"Then he's got to be in on it." Rybeck's words burned like acid in the back of his throat.

"I don't know about that, Parker, but I do know that the head of our agency has given us our orders. We are the rule of law, and, by rights, we follow the instructions our superiors give us." Sensing Rybeck was about to protest, Talbot continued. "I'm not saying you have to like them. I'm saying you must *obey* them. Pick someone to go with you. I don't want you executing your charges on the way to Washington."

"Yes, sir," Rybeck replied, intending to follow the oath he'd sworn when joining the FBI. He would support and defend the Constitution of the United States against all enemies, foreign and domestic; that he would bear true faith and allegiance to the same; that he took the obligation freely, without any mental reservation or purpose of evasion; and that he intended to well and faithfully discharge the duties of the office on which he'd entered.

Talbot tried to console his agent further. "You did your best, Parker, and your case was solid. We were just behind the eight ball from the beginning."

"Yeah. Thanks, chief."

After hanging up the phone, Rybeck returned to the bunker, where everyone was still riveted to the televisions. He took Caroline's hand and led her up the stairs, and they started across the compound toward the headquarters building. "We have to take Moran and Jackson to the Allen County Airport. Talbot told me there's a plane waiting to pick them up, and we're to escort them to Washington."

Caroline stopped in her tracks. "What did you just say?"

"I said, we have to take Moran ..."

She cut him off. "I heard what you said. I just don't understand it."

Rybeck looked down at her and rubbed his chin. "Moran and Jackson were orchestrators of this coup, and now President Warrick wants them in Washington. I think they planned this whole thing to the exact detail. Someone leaked the information about the missiles, and I think it was Scoda since he gave the order to take the traitors to Washington. Talbot and I were briefing him personally, so he knew all the details, but I haven't put it all together yet."

"Don't do it," she argued. "Have someone else take them."

"Scoda has ordered me to do it. Besides, I want to keep my eye on these guys. Talbot asked me to pick someone I trust to be my partner. I'd like that to be you."

Caroline mulled it over briefly, then said, "Okay, let's go." Walking toward the door, she pulled out her service weapon and ensured it had a cartridge in the chamber. "We'd better be ready for more surprises."

Rybeck stopped by the room where he had left his M4 carbine and slung it over his body. Caroline retrieved her Mossberg shotgun and threaded more shells into its tubular magazine from a box on a nearby shelf.

The room where Coppler had sequestered Moran and Jackson was on the second floor, with two HRT members outside the door and one inside the room to prevent them from jumping out the window. Rybeck understood now why the two men had been so compliant since being taken into custody. They knew someone would eventually release them and accompany them to Washington. It angered Rybeck to think of their arrogance.

Michael Coppler met Rybeck and Caroline at the door. "I got the message to have my helicopter fly you to the airport. Where are you taking them?"

"To a secure site," Rybeck responded automatically with his practiced answer.

"I'd prefer to send a larger escort team."

Rybeck shrugged. "Me too, Mike, but we've got our orders."

"I've got a team on standby. I can have them escort you," Coppler argued.

"Wish I could," Rybeck replied. "You'll have to take it up with Director Scoda if you want a different answer."

"I don't like it," Coppler stated. "But let's get it done."

The three of them entered the room with the prisoners. Rybeck ordered Moran and Jackson to stand, then checked their handcuffs before explaining what would happen.

"This is Paul's show," Jackson said. "If it's okay with him, I'd like to stay here. I have no business going to Washington."

Moran extended his bound hand, and Jackson shook it. "Thanks for your help, Steven."

"My orders are to take *both* of you," Rybeck replied. "I don't care what happens after we get there, but both of you are getting on that plane."

Jackson shrugged. "Fair enough."

Outside, the high-pitched whine of a starter motor turned into a low roar as the Black Hawk prepared for takeoff.

The HRT team, followed by Rybeck and Caroline, led the two prisoners out of the building and stood by as Caroline and the three men climbed into the helicopter. The crew chief closed the door behind them, and moments later, they were airborne.

———

WAITING for them at Allen County Regional was a Gulfstream V with Secret Service members scattered around the tarmac, anticipating their arrival. Once the Black Hawk touched down, Rybeck and Caroline led the prisoners to the plane. At the base of the steps, Rybeck uncuffed them.

"Thanks for the ride," Jackson said. "I've always wanted to fly in a Black Hawk, but I'm going home. I'll call my wife from the terminal."

Moran hugged his friend and said goodbye, then Jackson walked away as the other three boarded the plane. Rybeck didn't care what Jackson did but jogged over to a nearby Secret Service agent and told him to let the farmer pass. There had been enough bloodshed for one day.

They found their seats inside the plane as the Secret Service personnel stored Rybeck and Caroline's long guns. Rybeck wished he'd had a chance to change out of his dirty clothes and take a hot shower, but he had nothing to change into.

Settling into the plush leather seats with seat belts properly fastened, the Gulfstream surged down the runway and lifted into the sky, vectoring east toward D.C.

"You can relax now," Moran said as he came out of the galley, holding three cans of beer. He passed them around and sat down across from Rybeck. "You did a marvelous job of piecing together that I had cruise missiles at the compound."

"I wanted to stop you from launching them," Rybeck replied bitterly.

"You actually helped us a lot by putting together the reports for Scoda."

"Did he leak the report to the press?" Rybeck asked angrily, feeling betrayed by his boss.

Moran sat back in the chair, sipping his beer. "Yes. He had his orders, just as you have yours."

Rybeck took a long swig of his beer, enjoying the cold beverage despite the circumstances.

"Scoda recommended you and wants you to work for him," Moran added.

"I already work for him."

"I know, Parker. But listen, we need good men to lead this country forward into the new era. We're working to reshape the government, not to make radical changes to the lives of our citizens. There will still be the need for law enforcement—even more so during this transition period. We want you to work with us. You'll still be in the FBI, but we'll reassign you to Washington." The militia leader turned to Caroline. "And you, Miss Thurmond—how about a new job, working with Agent Rybeck?"

"I'm not sure I want a new job working for a bunch of terrorists."

Moran laughed. "Do we consider Washington, Adams, Franklin, or Jefferson terrorists? Those men sparked a radical revolution with words and then actions. The Boston Tea Party was over a three percent tax, and we pay over twice that in sales tax in most states. I see my actions as being no different from theirs. Mine only differs because I destroyed the bastions of socialism on this nation's soil. There was no secret government back then—just a tyrannical king."

"What about all the people trapped in Mount Weather?" Caroline asked.

"They'll be released to go home, and we'll ban all the currently elected politicians from running for government office in any form."

"When will you hold new elections?" Caroline demanded.

"In two years, when the standard cycle comes back around. There will be no presidential election this year, and Warrick will hold office for four years. If she's voted back in, then so be it." Moran shrugged. "In the meantime, there's a lot of work to do, and we … Well, I want you to be a part of it. If you don't want to, we'll send you back to your jobs and lives."

Rybeck finished his beer and went to the galley for a bottle of water. Moran ordered a second beer for himself.

Back in his seat, Rybeck pondered Moran's offer. He liked much of what the man had to say about changing the government and restoring lost liberties, but he'd never really bought into the U.N. and New World Order conspiracy theories.

Rybeck recognized that a few wealthy families controlled a lot of what went on in the world, but he couldn't see how a one-world order would benefit them. There needed to be antagonism, disparity, and conflict for the world to survive. Big business needed cheap labor, people to buy goods, and to establish lines of trade across the continents, competitive markets, and economies of scale. But parity would lead to control, which was the ultimate power and what a one-world government was all about.

Another idea popped into Rybeck's head as he thought about a global government uniting everyone. *How could everyone unite if no one could agree on a religion?*

There were vast disagreements among every religious sect on how to follow the faith and how to act. According to the Bible, only one person could unite the world in peace, and that was the Son of God, not a bunch of power elites at the U.N.—and certainly not Paul Moran.

Rybeck studied Moran. The man was charismatic and had innovative ideas and clever things to say. If Moran was truly set on changing the government and returning it to the people, then maybe working with him wouldn't be so bad.

Out of curiosity, Rybeck asked, "How did you keep the military from getting involved?"

"I know the Chairman of the Joint Chiefs. Plus, I have an 'in' with the new commander-in-chief." Moran winked at Rybeck conspiratorially.

"You think you can really enact the change that you've been talking about?" Caroline asked.

Moran nodded. "With Congress out of the way, we'll make the necessary changes."

"But some of the changes you've been talking about take an act of Congress to enact. You can't just write new laws via executive orders. The president has no power to do that," Caroline argued.

"You are correct, Miss Thurmond. If we have to, we'll place a vote before the people. Let's take term limits for all senators and congressmen, for example. Do you think they'll vote themselves out of a job? They never will, no matter how much bellyaching the American public does about it. So, we make the change for them, set them all out on their ears, and then amend the Constitution through a two-thirds state legislature vote. The president can change the government structure or enforce laws already on the books. If all else fails, we'll simply make the changes." He suddenly leaned forward. "It's called a dictatorship. Nothing can get done with a bunch of old women wringing their hands and making backroom deals. The only way to set things straight is by benevolent dictatorship, returning the power to the people from the corporations, Wall Street, and corrupt politicians."

CHAPTER SIXTY-SEVEN

The White House
Washington, D.C.

Rybeck felt utterly out of place in his dirty and torn clothes and ballistic vest as he and Caroline followed Moran and Secret Service Agent Kelly LeBrock through the halls of the immaculately kept White House.

After the Gulfstream had landed at Joint Base Andrews, a Marine detail had loaded them onto another Black Hawk that had flown the trio directly to the White House.

LeBrock paused outside the Oval Office and motioned to a door marked for the chief of staff. "Agent Rybeck and Deputy Thurmond, I've been instructed to put you in here. Mr. Gottfried no longer works here, so make yourselves comfortable." LeBrock turned to Moran. "You're with me, sir."

Rybeck led the way into the office and closed the door

behind Caroline. They stood alone for the first time all day in the handsomely appointed office. Rybeck shed his FBI jacket and combat gear, then headed for the mini-fridge built into a cabinet. He retrieved two bottles of water, handing one to Caroline before draining his in several long gulps.

Caroline sat down on one of the office couches and wearily propped her feet on the coffee table, not caring she was in the White House and should show some decorum. She wanted nothing more than to take a long, hot shower and fall into bed. Instead, she looked up at Rybeck and asked, "What are we going to do now?"

"Take a vacation," he suggested with a shrug.

"I meant about Moran," she said. "I won't lie. I wouldn't mind working for the FBI if I got to work with you every day."

"Trust me," Rybeck said, "that's not as sexy as it sounds."

"Yeah. I've heard you snore," Caroline joked. "But seriously?"

"Well, we can either go back to our regular jobs, or we can stay here and keep an eye on Moran."

"How do we know we'll work for Moran?"

"I don't know that we would, but it seems logical. I mean, Scoda works for him, so, by default, we would work for him."

Rybeck rifled the cabinets and found a supply of liquor decanters, but what he really wanted was something to eat. He picked up each bottle, removed the cap, and took a whiff before replacing the cap and putting the bottles back in the cabinet. He settled on one, poured a healthy dose of the amber liquid into an old-fashioned glass, and took a long sip.

"You want some?" he asked Caroline. "It's rum."

"With Coke if you've got it. I've got a feeling I might need a little liquid fortification for what lies ahead."

Rybeck found a can of Coke in the fridge, mixed her a

Cuba Libre, and then handed it to her before sitting beside her on the sofa. "We could tell Moran we want to work directly for him."

Caroline took a sip of her drink and sighed. "I still can't believe these people staged a coup and pulled it off. There had to have been a lot of people involved to make it work."

"A lot," Rybeck agreed. "I keep wondering what would've happened if I'd found those missiles sooner. Maybe I could have prevented this from happening."

"You can't blame yourself, Parker. Moran had a plan, and even if we'd stopped them from launching the missiles, they would have done something else."

"Yeah, I guess you're right. Scoda was working against me every step of the way, and I couldn't see it."

Caroline slipped a hand into his. "It doesn't matter what happens, Parker, as long as we do it together."

Rybeck kissed her and snuggled in closer. "I'll agree to that. Let's stick together."

———

Moran walked into the chief of staff's office from the adjoining door to the Oval Office an hour later. He found both civil servants sacked out on the couch. He nudged Rybeck's foot with his and woke the FBI agent.

"Sorry to disturb you. I know you've had a long day, but I think you will want to see this." Moran searched through the desk drawers until he found a television remote. "The president will make a speech in a few minutes."

Rybeck got up from the couch, leaving Caroline to rest. He noticed Moran had taken a shower, shaved, and changed from his combat fatigues into a crisp blue suit with a red power tie.

"Can I ask you something?" the FBI agent said.

"Go ahead," Moran replied.

"If you knew we were coming, why didn't you just launch the missiles? Why did you shoot down a helicopter full of agents and have a shootout with the rest of us?"

"I had to make it look good. If you stopped me, I would be a martyr for the militia cause. I wanted to have maximum exposure to build the drama. I knew the news crews would be called out, and they would track the missiles, but I had no idea you had jets lined up to chase them."

"The Air Force said there was a chance they could shoot them down."

Moran shook his head. "They never had a chance. POTUS ordered them to stand down."

Rybeck's eyebrows rose in surprise, trying to understand everything that had happened.

"Have you made a decision yet?" Moran asked.

"We're going to stay here," Caroline said from the couch. "Someone needs to keep an eye on you."

"Excellent," Moran said. "We need the best people we can get."

Moran mixed himself a drink from the cabinet Rybeck had left open and took a sip as he turned to face the television.

The on-screen image changed from a dog food commercial to that of a news reporter standing on the White House lawn. Underneath the live feed, the news crawler offered updates on current events. Much of the news centered on the missile strikes and the world's reaction, but there were also bites about gun battles in LA, Miami, and Chicago, where gangs and drug dealers battled for positions. At the same time, local law enforcement and militias led the fight to rid them from the streets. Along the southern border, more militias had turned out to supplement the Border Patrol to stop the flow of illegal aliens.

A small countdown clock at the bottom right of the screen indicated the time until the president's address.

Moran sat behind the desk and put his feet up on it. "I could get used to this."

"I think this was what you wanted all along," Caroline replied derisively.

"More or less," Moran replied. "I've been offered the position that goes with this office—chief of staff."

"Congratulations," Rybeck stated dryly.

They turned their attention to the television as the reporter stopped talking, and the countdown ended. The face of de facto President Diane Warrick appeared. Seated at the Resolute desk, Warrick wore a navy-blue sheath dress. Behind her, the American flag and the presidential flag flanked a wide window where the evening light faded into darkness.

The first female president in the history of the United States looped a strand of black hair behind her ear. When she smiled, her entire countenance seemed to light up, and her eyes sparkled. She touched a piece of paper on the desk with her finger and then looked straight at the camera.

"My fellow Americans, the last three days have been very trying for our country, with the loss of our elected representatives and now the destruction caused by these missile strikes. I have declared a state of national emergency and, as such, plan to enact all the powers granted to me as president through the Presidential Emergency Action Documents and presidential executive orders. I have posted those on the White House website for all to review. Until we can regain control of certain areas of the country where resistance and fighting seem to be the heaviest, I am enacting martial law in those locations and dispensing National Guard troops to work with local police and civilian militia organizations.

"For those of you wondering exactly what all these events mean, it's this: The United States is no longer beholden to the world to be its policeman, nor to be a party to instituting a single system of world government sought by outside interests who care little for our sovereignty. Today is a new Independence Day, freeing ourselves from the tyranny and oppression of those who seek to dismantle our republic. Today, we declare ourselves free of the New World Order and the Global Reset.

"With this new freedom comes a lot of hard work. We must take a step back and fix some of the glaring issues we currently face because our past Congress has so frequently kicked the can down the road on pressing issues. It is time that we stopped handing those problems to our children and our grandchildren and fix them ourselves.

"To that end, I am declaring myself a benevolent dictator, with the Supreme Court as my sole check and balance. I am suspending the upcoming presidential election, but in two years, we will hold national elections for both the Congress and the Senate. My goal during these next two years is to streamline our government and reduce its size. We will also focus on bringing businesses back to the United States, paying off our national debt, becoming energy independent, and bringing peace through strength to the world. It is not my plan to become isolationist but to make America the shining light on the hill that all can look to as a model of a representative republic.

"I look forward to working for you, the people, and helping to rectify the crises we face in our country today. I want to assure you that I have your best interests at heart. For now, things will go on just as we know them. The lights will stay on, the gas stations will be full, and the grocery stores will still carry your favorite foods. We're not looking to disrupt your way of life but to enhance it as we make this transition to a smaller, gentler government and a greater, stronger country.

Warrick paused as she finished her speech before adding, "Good night, and may God bless us all."

Evan Graver is the author of Liberty Brigade and the Ryan Weller Thriller Series. Before becoming a writer, he worked in construction, as a security guard, a motorcycle and car technician, a property manager, and in the scuba industry. He served in the U.S. Navy as an aviation electronics technician until they medically retired him following a motorcycle accident that left him paralyzed. He found other avenues of adventure: riding ATVs, downhill skiing, skydiving, and bungee jumping. His passions are scuba diving, fishing, and writing. He lives in Hollywood, Florida, with his wife and son.

To see more of his biography please visit the about section at www.evangraver.com.

Grab you FREE prequel to the Ryan Weller Thriller Series: *Dark Days* while you're there!